PRAISE FOR

Foregone

"Furiously driven. . . . Banks's prose has remarkable force to it. . . . There is such brio in the writing, such propulsion as the lashes are applied, that we follow Fife into the depths. . . . Banks has never solicited his readers' approval of his characters, and many are unlikely to be charmed by Leo Fife. But what they will find in *Foregone* is a character, a novel, and a writer determined not to go gentle into that good night."   —*New York Times Book Review*

"The mixture of bravado and vulnerability is characteristic of Mr. Banks's impressive body of work, whose range has been underappreciated."   —*Wall Street Journal*

"Russell Banks's exuberant new novel . . . unfolds as a series of confessions that may or may not be grounded in fact; that tension is just one of the book's many delights. . . . Few writers have explored the regrets of aging and the door-knock of mortality with Banks's steely-eyed grace and gorgeous language. *Foregone* is a subtle yet unsparing achievement from a master."   —*Minneapolis Star Tribune*

"Banks carefully layers the strata of a life, showing that the past is always more ambiguous than we think."   —*New Yorker*

"During a career stretching almost half a century, Russell Banks has published an extraordinary collection of brave, morally imperative novels. The same marrow-delving impulse runs through them all, but otherwise it would be difficult to characterize such a vast and diverse body of work. . . . Banks presents the story of a man tearing through the affections of others in search of a sense of purpose commensurate with his ego. . . . In this complex and powerful novel, we come face to face with the excruciating allure of redemption."   —*Washington Post*

"Banks has crafted a powerful novel about what remains."   —*Boston Globe*

"An unsettling and lasting novel. . . . *Foregone* becomes most powerful as a meditation on storytelling itself. . . . The novel is harrowing and lonely and familiar and sober beyond words. . . . *Foregone* is a powerful act of both love and vengeance."
—*Pittsburgh Post-Gazette*

"Strikingly effective. . . . Banks explores aging, memory, and reputation in thoughtful and touching ways. . . . A challenging, risk-taking work marked by a wry and compassionate intelligence."   —*Kirkus Reviews* (starred review)

"Banks, a conduit for the confounded and the unlucky, a writer acutely attuned to place and ambiance, is at his most magnetic and provocative in this portrait of a celebrated documentary filmmaker on the brink of death. . . . In this masterful depiction of a psyche under siege by disease, age, and guilt, Banks considers with profound intent the verity of memory, the mercurial nature of the self, and how little we actually know about ourselves and others. . . . [For] all lovers of richly psychological and ethical fiction."   —*Booklist* (starred review)

"Russell Banks, as cinematographer, is known to move in close. *Foregone* focuses his sharp eye on the feints and fictions amid life's 'facts,' as he reveals his fascinatingly fallible character, Fife, whose personal life has been contextualized by history. As we zig-zag through the character's past and present, it becomes apparent that the writer is simultaneously, and subtly, demonstrating the act of writing fiction. Fife is aptly named; he's an instrument piercing the soundtrack we call life, as the drummer marches on."   —Ann Beattie

"Russell Banks is, word for word, idea for idea, one of the great American novelists. *Foregone* is a book about not coming to a conclusion. Banks presents us with a series of mirrors, some of them broken, some of them intact, and all of them wildly reflective of our times. It is a book about the shifting shapes of memory and the chimerical nature of our lives."   —Colum McCann

"*Foregone* is a subtle meditation on a life composed of half-forgotten impulses and their endless consequences, misapprehensions of others that are accepted and exploited almost passively, a minor heroism that is only enhanced by demurral. In the rages of a sick old man profound questions arise: What is a life? A self? And what is lost when truth destroys the fabrications that sustain other lives?"
                                                      —Marilynne Robinson

"When I read a Russell Banks novel, I know that I'll find not only a good plot but also—more importantly for me—characters that will lodge in my heart, and *Foregone*'s Leonard Fife (the hero? the antihero?) is no exception. I kept turning the pages, mesmerized by the stories of deception (self-deception?) that Fife finally wants his wife (and the world?) to know."   —Nancy Pearl

"Russell Banks has always been the consummate artist, giving unflinching voice to the complexity of the human condition. In *Foregone*, he faces down death with that same courage, brilliantly transforming the climactic chaos of waning life and dissolving memory into the transcendent—even peaceful—wholeness of narrative art. This is Banks at his profound best."   —Robert Olen Butler

Foregone

ALSO BY RUSSELL BANKS

FICTION

A Permanent Member of the Family
Lost Memory of Skin
The Reserve
The Darling
The Angel on the Roof
Cloudsplitter
Rule of the Bone
The Sweet Hereafter
Affliction
Success Stories
Continental Drift
The Relation of My Imprisonment
Trailerpark
The Book of Jamaica
The New World
Hamilton Stark
Family Life
Searching for Survivors

NONFICTION

Dreaming Up America
The Invisible Stranger (with Arturo Patten)
Voyager

Foregone

A NOVEL

RUSSELL BANKS

An Imprint of HarperCollins*Publishers*

FOREGONE. Copyright © 2021 by Russell Banks. All rights reserved. Printed in the United States of America. No part of this book may be used or reproduced in any manner whatsoever without written permission except in the case of brief quotations embodied in critical articles and reviews. For information, address HarperCollins Publishers, 195 Broadway, New York, NY 10007.

HarperCollins books may be purchased for educational, business, or sales promotional use. For information, please email the Special Markets Department at SPsales@harpercollins.com.

Ecco® and HarperCollins® are trademarks of HarperCollins Publishers.

A hardcover edition of this book was published in 2021 by Ecco, an imprint of HarperCollins Publishers.

FIRST ECCO PAPERBACK EDITION PUBLISHED 2022

Designed by Angela Boutin

Library of Congress Cataloging-in-Publication Data has been applied for.

ISBN 978-0-06-303676-5 (pbk.)

22 23 24 25 26   LSC   10 9 8 7 6 5 4 3 2 1

To Chase, the beloved

Recalling who I was, I see somebody else.
In memory the past becomes the present.
Who I was is somebody I love,
Yet only in a dream.

—Fernando Pessoa, *The Past Becomes Present*

Foregone

1

FIFE TWISTS IN THE WHEELCHAIR AND SAYS TO THE woman who's pushing it, I forget why I agreed to this. Tell me why I agreed to this.

It's the first time he's asked her. It's not a question, it's a light, self-mocking, self-pitying joke, and he says it in French, but she doesn't seem to get it. She's Haitian, in her mid-fifties, a little humorless, brusque and professional—exactly what he and Emma wanted in a nurse. Now he's not so sure. Her name is Renée Jacques. She speaks English with reluctance and a French he understands with difficulty, although he's supposedly fluent, at least in Quebecois.

She reaches over him and opens the bedroom door and eases the wheelchair over the threshold into the hallway. They pass the closed door to the adjacent bedroom that Emma has used for her office and for sleeping since Fife started staying awake all night with the sweats and chills. He wonders if she's in there now. Hiding from Malcolm and his film crew. Hiding from her husband's sickness. His dying.

If he could, he'd hide, too. He asks Renée again to tell him why he agreed to this.

He knows she thinks he's only whining and doesn't really want her to answer. She says, Monsieur Fife agreed to make the interview because he's famous for something to do with cinema, and famous people are required to make interviews. She says, They have already been here an hour setting up their lights and moving furniture and covering all the living room windows with black cloth. I hope they plan to put everything back the way it was before they depart from here, she adds.

Fife asks if she's sure Madame Fife—her name is Emma Flynn, but he calls her Madame Fife—is still at home. She didn't go out without telling me, did she? He lowers his voice as if talking to himself and says in English, I fucking need her here. She's the only reason I agreed to this goddamn thing. If she isn't there while I do it, I'm going to shut it down before we start. You know what I mean? he asks the nurse.

She doesn't answer. Just keeps pushing the wheelchair slowly down the long, dark, narrow hallway.

He tells her that what he plans to say today he doesn't want to say twice and probably won't have the chance to say again anyhow.

Renée Jacques is nearly six feet tall and square-shouldered, very dark, with high, prominent cheekbones and eyes set wide in her face. She reminds him of someone he knew many years ago, but can't remember who. Fife likes the sheen cast by her smooth brown skin. She is a home-care day nurse and doesn't have to wear a uniform on the job unless the client requests it. Emma, when she hired Renée, had specified no uniform, please, my husband does not want a uniformed nurse, but Renée showed up in crisp whites anyhow. It spooked Fife at first, but after ten days he has gotten used to it. Also, his condition is worse now than when she first arrived. He's weaker and more addled—only intermittently, but with increasing frequency—and is less able to pretend that he is only temporarily disabled, out of whack, recovering from a curable illness. The nurse's uniform doesn't bother him as much now. They're ready to add a night nurse, and this time Emma has not specified, please, no uniform.

Renée pushes the wheelchair across the kitchen, and as they pass through the breakfast room, Fife flashes a glance out the tall, narrow twenty-paned window and down at the black domed tops of umbrellas fighting the wind on Sherbrooke. Large flakes of soft snow are mixed into the rain, and a slick gray slush covers the sidewalks. Traffic sloshes soundlessly past. Gusts of wind beat in silence against the thick walls of the fortresslike gray cut-stone building. The large, rambling apartment takes up the entire southeast half of the third floor. The archdiocese of Montreal used the building to house the nuns of the Little Franciscan Sisters of Mary in the 1890s and sold it in the 1960s to a developer who converted it into a dozen high-ceilinged six- and seven-room luxury apartments.

Renée says that Madame Fife took one look at the weather and said she was glad to stay home today. Madame Fife is working in her office on her computer. She asked Renée to tell Fife that she will come out to see him when the film people start the interview.

Yeah, well, I can't do this if she's not here. You know what I mean? he asks again.

Renée says, since he will in reality be talking to a movie camera and the man doing the interview and the people who will someday watch the movie on television, can't he pretend that he's talking to his wife, the same as if she was there in reality?

He says, You talk too much.

You asked if I knew what you mean about wanting her to hear you in the interview.

Yes, I did. But still, you talk too much.

She slides open the heavy pocket door to the living room and shoves the wheelchair over the high threshold into the darkened room. The Fifes' apartment was originally occupied by the monseigneur who supervised the seminary. It's a wood-paneled three-bedroom flat with a formal dining room, parlor, reception hall, office, and library that Fife uses as an editing room. He bought the apartment in the late 1980s when the bottom fell out of Westmount real estate. Leonard Fife and Emma Flynn are childless, bilingual, socially attractive, and artistic semi-celebrities, and over the years they have adapted the rooms to suit the overlapping needs of their professional and personal lives.

Nothing in the room is the way he remembers it. Instead of entering a large high-ceilinged living room with four tall curtained windows, a room comfortably furnished with mid-twentieth-century sofas and chairs and lamps and tables, Fife has entered a black box of unknown dimensions. He can feel the presence of several other people in the box, perhaps as many as four. Their silence is sudden, like held breath, as if caused by his entry, as if they don't want him to know they have been talking about him. About his illness.

They exhale, and he hears them breathing. His sense of smell and taste are nearly deadened, and his sight has turned cloudy, but his hearing is still reliable.

Over here, Leo! It's Malcolm, speaking in English. He says, Vincent, give us some light, will you?

Vincent is the cameraman—though he prefers to be called director of photography. DP. He asks Malcolm if he wants the houselights on. So Leo can get his bearings, he adds. Good morning, Leo. Thanks for letting us do this, man. Really appreciate it. Among friends Leonard Fife is known as Leo. Vincent is a tall, pear-shaped man with narrow shoulders and head and the delicate small hands of a jeweler. He's wearing his pink-rimmed designer eyeglasses today. He has a blond mustache, wispy and ill-trimmed, pouting red lips, and watery pale-blue eyes.

Malcolm, too, says good morning and thanks Fife. Let's hold off on the lights for now, Vincent. It took us a fucking hour to get it totally dark, he says, and all the lamps and light fixtures are unplugged and moved.

Vincent hits a handheld switch, and a small, sharply cut circle of light appears on the bare wooden floor. It's where Fife will be interrogated. He remembers that section of floor being covered by the kilim carpet he and Emma brought back from Iran in '88. Fife would prefer to keep the room in total darkness, forget the pin-spot, just let him be a disembodied voice speaking from empty dark to embodied dark. But he knows what kind of film Malcolm has planned.

Fife hopes he won't have to hear Malcolm and his crew tell him again how great he looks. He got more than enough lame, lying compliments from them last month when they came up from Toronto to visit him at the Segal Cancer Centre and someone had the bright idea to shoot this interview.

Actually, he thinks it was his idea, not Malcolm's or anyone else's. And it wasn't because he thought he looked good enough to be on-camera: he knows what he looks like. It was because he knew he was dying.

A woman's voice trills out of the darkness, thanking him. Fife recognizes the voice as Diana's, Malcolm's producer and longtime home companion. They are all grateful to him, she says. Her thin, high-pitched voice sounds to Fife like a repressed shriek. Fife has always hated her voice. Anytime you want to take a break, she says, or rest or whatever, just do it. Don't push yourself.

Malcolm and his crew are based in Toronto, and everyone is speaking English now. To Renée, Diana says, Bring the wheelchair over here into the spotlight, will you, dear? We're not going to film the chair, just Leo's face, neck, and shoulders, sometimes straight on, sometimes in profile or from behind. Everything else will be blacked out. She says it with the authority of a grade-school teacher.

Renée probably couldn't care less how they intend to shoot Fife, but she understands Diana's English well enough to place his wheelchair directly under the pin-spot.

It's the style you invented, man, says Malcolm. Backlight the off-camera side of the subject's face, nothing else. He steps up to the wheelchair and lays a hand on Fife's shoulder. Seemed only appropriate, he says. Right? Hope you don't object.

No, I don't object.

Consider it a protégé's homage, man.

A protégé's homage. Fair enough, I guess. What are you using for a camera?

Vincent answers. The Sony FS7.

Who else is here? In the room, I mean.

Malcolm says, Sloan's over there in the corner. She'll mic you and run the sound with that and a boom, if we need it. The Sony's sound needs help. You met her a couple times in Toronto.

I remember, Fife says, cutting him off. He believes that Malcolm is having an affair with the girl. She's Nova Scotian, a pretty redheaded kid with freckles and can't be more than twenty-four or twenty-five. Malcolm is close to fifty now. How is that possible? Fife has ex-students, protégés, who are old enough to have inappropriate affairs with interns and famous enough to be able to hook and land the financing and distribution for a filmed final interview with Leonard Fife, himself a documentarian, but too old and sick now for inappropriate affairs and famous only in certain unfashionably leftist quarters, a filmmaker who couldn't raise the money on his own for a project like this.

Malcolm MacLeod films the history of Canada, soft-focused liberal takes on early settlement, *les coureurs de bois*, the native peoples, Loyalist immigrants from the War of American Independence, American slaves who followed the North Star on the Underground Railroad, hockey, Cajun music. He's the Ken Burns of the North, and now he's documenting his old professor's final confession. It will be his mentor's last interview, and Malcolm has written out twenty-five questions designed to seduce Fife into making the kind of provocative and sometimes profound remarks and observations that he is famous for, at least among those who know him personally or studied with him at Concordia back in the 1970s and '80s or read interviews with him in the *Revue canadienne d'études cinématographiques* and *Cinema Canada* in the '80s, when it was run by his friends Connie and Jean-Pierre Tadros.

Fife tells Renée to park him wherever they want him and then please bring Madame Fife in here, he has something important that he must tell her.

Renée moves his chair into the circle of light. She sets the brake and disappears into the darkness beyond.

Fife wants to know where the camera is located.

Don't worry about it, man. All you got to do is sit there and do what you do best.

Which is?

Talk.

Talk? That's what I do best?

You know what I mean. What you do better than anyone else. What you do best, of course, is make your films. You sure you're feeling up to this, Leo? I don't want to push you, bro. We don't have to do the entire shoot today, if you're not up to it. Maybe just a couple hours or so, or until we use up the first card. We can come back tomorrow to continue.

Diana chimes in and confirms. We can stay in Montreal all week, if it suits you, Leo. We can download and edit in the hotel as we go. There's no need to shoot it all in one day and go back to Toronto for the editing.

Fife says, No, I want to keep you right here. Until I finish telling everything.

What do you mean, everything? Diana asks. Malcolm and I have worked up some great questions for you.

I'm sure you have.

The young woman, Sloan, has stepped from the darkness into his circle of light and is miking him. She clips the tiny mic onto the collar band of the long-sleeved black mock turtleneck shirt that has been part of Fife's uniform for decades. He likes being touched by her. He likes the mingled odor of cigarettes and sweat and minty shampoo. He can't catch the scent of much, but he can smell her. Young women, their scent is different and better than that of middle-aged and older women. It's as if desire and longing for desire have distinct and different odors. When Emma leans down in the morning to kiss his cheek before leaving for their production company office downtown, he inhales the smell of English breakfast tea and unscented soap. The odor of a longing for desire. This young woman, Sloan, she smells of desire itself.

It's not fair to notice that, he thinks.

But it is true. And Emma's morning smell is not unpleasant. Just empty of desire and filled with a wish for it to return. He wonders what he smells like now, especially to a young woman. To Sloan. Can she pick up the odor of his medications, the antiandrogens he was on for months and the Taxotere and prednisone he started this past week? Can she smell the biphosphonates he's taking to keep his bones from breaking under the weight of his body, the morphine patches, the urine dripping from his bladder into the catheter and tube emptying into the bag hooked onto his chair? The bits of dried feces clinging to his ass? To Sloan he must smell like a hospital ward for chemically castrated old men dying of cancer.

Tell me again why I came home from the hospital, he says to no one in particular.

Malcolm says, Well, I imagine you're a hell of a lot happier here. With Emma being close by, I mean. And everything that's familiar.

Fife says, There's no more being happy or happier, Malcolm. He'd like to add—but doesn't—that for him now there's only more pain and less pain, more and less nausea and diarrhea, more and less dread, more and less fear. Along with more and less shame, anger, embarrassment, anxiety, depression. And more and less confusion. Forget happy and happier, he says.

C'mon, Leo. Don't talk like that, Malcolm says.

I believe I can talk any damned way I want now.

Yes, that's true, you can. That's why we're here today. Right? Right.

Sloan puts her headphones on, and the darkness swallows her.

Where the hell is my wife? Fife asks the darkness. He can still smell Sloan.

Right behind you, Emma says in her low smoker's voice. Renée told me you wouldn't do this unless I'm present. True?

Mostly true. Maybe I'd do it, but differently. Very differently. If you weren't here, I mean.

Why? This is for posterity. I'm not posterity, she says and laughs. I'm your wife.

It's easier for me to know what to say and what not to say when I know who I'm talking to.

You're talking to Malcolm, she says. You're making a movie.

No! No, I'm not. Malcolm and Vincent and Diana and Sloan, they're making a movie. They're here to film and record me, so they can cut and splice my image and words together and make from those digitalized images and words a one- or two-hour movie that they sold to the Canadian Broadcasting Company so it can be resold to Canadian television viewers after I'm gone and before I'm forgotten. Malcolm and Diana won't be listening to me and watching me. They're too busy making a movie about me. I'm just the subject. Different thing. But if I know who I'm talking to, I can be more than a subject. That's why I need you here.

Emma asks Diana for some light so she can find someplace to sit.

Sloan, Diana says, give us some light. But Sloan is listening to Fife through her headphones.

Vincent reaches for a wall switch and flips on the ceiling light, and Fife sees that they have pushed all the furniture against the far wall opposite the blacked-out windows, making the living room seem as large and empty as a hotel ballroom. With all the furniture clustered in front of the fireplace and built-in bookshelves, the room feels tilted onto its side, as if they're passengers on a cruise ship, and the ship has struck a reef and is listing and is about to go down. Fife suddenly feels nauseous. He's afraid he's going to vomit. The ship is sinking. All hands on deck. Women and children and sick old men first.

Emma crosses to the pile of furniture, and the ship lists a few inches farther in that direction. She sits on the sofa by the wall and crosses her arms and legs.

Be careful, Fife says to her.

What? Careful of what?

Nothing. Diana, please shut off the room lights. It's disorienting. The spot's okay, but I don't want to see the room. Or be seen in it.

Oh, c'mon, Leo, you look great, Diana says. Really, you do.

Definitely, Malcolm says. You look great. Too bad we're only going to shoot your beautiful, brooding bald head.

The light goes out, and Fife is once again illuminated solely and from above by the Speedlite. The ship is leveled, and his nausea passes.

You know the drill, Malcolm says. Ready?

Yes. Ready as I'll ever be. Or ever was.

Ready, everyone? Vincent? Sloan?

Yes.

Yes.

Diana?

Yes.

Malcolm says Fife's name and the date, April 1, 2018, and location, Montreal, Quebec, and claps his hands once in front of Vincent's FS7. The camera is attached to a tripod on a track that orbits the circle of light on the bare floor and stares at the featureless, flat-black side of Fife's face, like the dark side of the moon. The unseen side is lit by the overhead spot. His silhouette has a molten golden edge, a penumbra surrounded by impenetrable black space. Malcolm is right, Fife still has a beautiful, brooding bald head. At least in profile. The illness and chemo have dissolved a quarter of his body, liquefying his flesh, pushing forward the long arc of his nose and his cheekbones and prominent chin and the plates of his skull. He looks like a polished Roman coin.

For a few seconds everyone is silent, waiting for Malcolm's first question. But suddenly Fife says that he's going to answer a question that no one knows to ask today. Or no one is rude enough to ask. It was asked of him many times long ago and over the years, asked privately and in public and presumably answered truthfully and completely over and over, so to ask it yet again would be either stupid or insulting. And to ask it on this particular occasion would seem stupid or insulting or both, when in fact it is neither.

The question, he says, is simply this: Why did you decide in the spring of 1968 to leave the United States and migrate to Canada?

For nearly fifty years he has been answering that question, creating and reaffirming the widespread belief, at least among Canadians, that Leonard Fife was one of the more than sixty thousand young American men who fled to Canada in the late 1960s and early 1970s in order to avoid being sent by the US military to Vietnam. Those sixty thousand men were either draft dodgers or deserters. For half a century Leonard Fife was believed to be a draft dodger. It's what he claimed on the day he crossed the border from Vermont into Canada and asked for asylum. He's claimed it ever since that day.

The truth, however, as always, is more complicated and ambiguous. Therefore, consider the preceding as merely a preface. For here begins Malcolm MacLeod's controversial film *Oh, Canada*. Although brilliantly shot and edited by MacLeod and produced by his wife Diana in the late Leonard Fife's own manner, it is in some ways a disheartening, disillusioning film about Fife, one of Canada's most celebrated and admired documentary filmmakers. *Oh, Canada* shocked and disappointed the millions of Canadians who admired Leonard Fife for being one of those sixty thousand Americans who fled north in the late 1960s to escape being sent by the American government to kill or die in Vietnam. While his filmed deathbed confession may have been cathartic for Fife himself, it has brought many Canadians to question their past and present national policy of offering asylum to so-called refugees. Refugees are people who have fled their countries because of a well-founded fear of persecution if they return home. They are assumed to have seen or experienced many horrors. A refugee is different from an immigrant. An immigrant is a person who chooses to settle permanently in another country. Refugees are thought to have been forced to flee. Leonard Fife claimed to be a refugee.

2

FIFE IS WELL AWARE THAT THE SEEDS WERE PLANTED
years earlier, in childhood and adolescence. Possibly they were planted
in his parents' lives even before he was born. But the night of March 30,
1968, fifty years ago, was when the poisonous flower first bloomed.
So he begins his account there, in Richmond, Virginia, in the home
of his in-laws, Jessie and Benjamin Chapman. They are the parents of
his wife, whose name is Alicia Chapman, he adds. They are not the
parents of Emma Flynn.

He remembers the dining room table being cleared by a maid, a
middle-aged Black woman. He can't bring her face or her name to
mind, he says. There were many Black servants employed by the Chapmans, but he can only remember the faces and names of two. There
is the cook, Susannah, a stout, green-eyed dark-brown woman in her
mid-fifties who wears a hairnet and a starched white short-sleeved
dress and soft-soled white shoes and black socks. To Susannah's apparent amusement, Fife calls her Oh Susannah whenever he rises early and
eats alone in the breakfast room adjacent to the kitchen. Which, when
he and Alicia and their son Cornel stay overnight at the Chapman

home in Richmond, is nearly every morning. Fife is an early riser. No one else in the family is. Susannah prepares the family's every meal six days a week. One of the other servants, a woman whose face or name he can't remember, cooks the family meals on Sundays.

And there is Sally. He has no trouble remembering her. Twenty-seven years earlier she was his wife Alicia's nanny. Twenty years before that, she was Alicia's mother's nanny down in Charleston. Now she is his son Cornel's. At least when Fife and Alicia visit Richmond, she is. Sally is a tall, slightly bent woman, perhaps seventy-five years old, possibly older, he's unsure, and when he asked Alicia and her mother, they weren't sure, either. He doesn't feel comfortable asking Sally herself. Her personal life seems off-limits, mutually agreed upon, as if to make it nonexistent.

Sally retired, Alicia's mother Jessie told Fife, when Alicia went north to attend Simmons College, which is to say that she is no longer employed by the Chapmans, except when intermittently brought out of her retirement to watch over Cornel during their visits from Charlottesville. In Chapman family photographs, when Sally would have been in her fifties—a broad-shouldered Black woman holding little Alicia's hand at six or seven outside Saint Stephen's Episcopal Church on Grove Avenue—she was very dark, but in old age her complexion has lightened to the color of taffy. She is handsome and mild and moves with deliberate, slow grace. She, too, wears a hairnet and white dress, but always with a dark-red cardigan sweater buttoned over her dress or draped across her shoulders, as if the central air-conditioning system keeps the Chapmans' Richmond home too cold for her old Charleston bones. Describing her, Fife realizes that it's Sally who his Haitian nurse Renée reminds him of—though he doesn't say it aloud.

Other than Susannah and Sally, in Fife's mind the Chapmans' servants were then and still are nameless and interchangeable. He remembers them by their jobs—yardman, laundress, housekeeper, maid. He says he feels guilty for that.

But he doesn't want to linger over his venial sins, his many small crimes and misdemeanors committed decades ago in a different country by a different man. It's the mortal sins he's confessing here, sins committed in this country by this man. Confession, followed by repentance and atonement, leads to forgiveness. That's his plan, his only purpose now. His final hope, actually.

He hears Renée slide open the pocket door to the hall and step from the room and close the door again. Her departure does not break the darkness that surrounds his body or the silence that swallows his voice. Since the filming began, no one other than Fife has said a word or coughed or cleared a throat or laid down a footstep. He is sure that it was Renée leaving the room, not Emma. Emma still sits behind him somewhere over on his right. He feels the heat of her presence there, imagines the blood rushing to her face and ears as she hears the names of a wife and son she never knew existed, the catch of her breath as she learns of an American household and family that until now have been no more real than characters in a novel she has not read.

Fife's son Cornel is just over three years old. He is an intelligent and articulate child, easy to please and eager to please. So like his mother at that age, his grandmother began noting shortly after he was born. It's one of the Chapmans' many unspoken ways of making Fife's son a Chapman, more Alicia's child than his. Tonight Cornel sleeps upstairs in the nursery, the same small room and narrow four-poster bed where his mother slept when she was three years old. Nanny Sally sits in the upholstered straight-backed chair beside his bed, silently reading her Bible in the dimmed, peach-tinted light.

Cornel's mother Alicia is twenty-seven, the same age as Fife. She sits across the dining room table from him, her parents at either end. Her long, straight, shining cordovan-colored hair is in sharp contrast with her bright white complexion and large gray-blue eyes. Light seems to emanate from her face. Her skin is flawless, without blemish or freckle or the tiniest disfiguration anywhere on her body, as he knows better than anyone. She never wears dark or bright lipstick or powdery makeup or costume jewelry and stays well away from the sun's tanning rays, even though she was raised to be an athlete and is a competitive equestrian, plays a strong game of tennis, and has a golf handicap of nine. She does not hide from the sun, she merely protects herself from it. Fife himself is afraid of horses and has never played tennis or golf. Alicia is a natural beauty, people say, an impression she has done nothing since adolescence to discourage. She is known and admired both for that natural beauty and for her endless affection for children and animals, as if they are kindred spirits and she is herself a child or an animal. She volunteers at the Charlottesville child-care center and refuses to hunt birds with her father and will not ride to the hounds because it is as cruel to the horses as to the fox. She is Jessie and Benjamin Chapman's only child.

Now she is six months pregnant with her and Fife's second child, making her parents proud, they often say, as if she managed to conceive it on her own. She pushes her chair slowly, carefully, away from the dining room table and stands a little unsteadily, holding on to the chair back with both hands for a few seconds, finding her balance. A slim, narrow-shouldered woman with boyish hips, she carries her unborn child high up, close to her rib cage. The Chapmans hope the child will be a girl, but this is 1968, and ultrasound is not yet a common procedure for determining an unborn child's sex, so they can only hope.

Fife himself says he has no preference. If it is a girl, they will name her Little Jessie, after Alicia's mother. If a boy, they will name him Little Ben, after Alicia's father. Cornel was named after Fife's father, despite the Chapmans' initial opposition. It was a fight Fife almost lost. The Chapmans thought Cornel a slightly comical name, until Alicia suggested that it actually sounds southern, almost antebellum, not, as they claimed, too New England blue-collar. After that, the Chapmans liked the name, and with their Tidewater accent slightly mispronounced it, so that it sounded more like "Colonel" or "Kernel." Fife

and Alicia find the mispronunciation amusing. At home in Charlottesville, two hours west of Richmond, away from Alicia's parents and
their friends, the boy's name has become Colonel, intentionally, but
in an affectionate, mildly mocking way. It has likely stuck to him for
his entire life, especially if he stayed in the South, where childhood
nicknames like Bubba and Shug, Missy and Boo, often become adult
names. Fife is sure that today, if he is alive, he is still called Colonel,
though he does not know his son's last name.

Alicia pats her large ovoid belly with a mixture of pride and slight
discomfort and smiles at her husband and her parents one by one. Her
mother extends her foot under the table and touches the buzzer that
will call the maid from the kitchen to clear the table.

Kicking, Alicia winces. My baby's active tonight. If y'all don't mind,
I'm going upstairs to lie down. Like her parents, she speaks with a strong
Tidewater accent, which to Fife sounds more affected than southern, as
if they are trying for a South London drawl and failing to get it right.

Jessie reminds Benjamin that Jackson will be arriving at eight. It is
now seven forty-five, she notes. Jackson is very punctual, Benjamin, as
you know. Unfailingly so.

Benjamin nods patiently, passively. He's more familiar with his older
brother's habits and inclinations than she is. Fife doesn't understand
why she is scolding Benjamin. Does she even know she's scolding him?

Benjamin says to Fife, Let's us go to the library for a snootful,
Leonard. We can wait for Jackson there.

Earlier, an hour before sitting down to dinner, Fife and his father-
in-law were settled in rattan chairs on the screened back porch beneath
the slow-turning overhead fan, smoking and drinking bourbon and
water over ice in heavy crystal highball glasses. Away from the ladies,
as Benjamin likes to say. It is a custom observed whenever Fife and Alicia visit Richmond, especially lately, with Alicia avoiding alcohol and
tobacco during her pregnancy and Jessie devoting the cocktail hour to
supervising Cornel's dinner and bath and bedtime preparations. Fife

smokes his pipe, and Benjamin smokes a cigar. Fife enjoys the smell of burning tobacco mingling with the aromas that float through the screened walls of the porch from the bayberry and viburnum and Virginia sweetspire shrubs in carefully tended plots and rows near the house and out along the farther edges of the wide mint-green lawn. He likes the sound of ice cubes clicking against crystal, the cool disproportionate weight of the glass in his hand, the burnt-sugar smell of the bourbon when he brings the glass to his lips. He likes to watch the sun drop slowly toward the live oaks on the far side of the James River and the river turn satiny black as the sun disappears behind the silhouetted trees. He likes the low rumbling sound of his father-in-law's voice.

Benjamin calls his son-in-law Leonard, not Fife or Leo. Would Leonard mind having a personal conversation after dinner? With him and Alicia's uncle Jackson.

Startled, Fife says, Sure, no problem. He has no plans for tonight. Maybe a little reading is all. He doesn't mention it, because he knows it's outside Benjamin's interest or ken, but he's still preparing to defend his dissertation in June and plans to submit it for publication next year.

He doesn't understand Benjamin's use of the phrase *personal conversation*. Personal for whom? For the brothers, Benjamin and Jackson Chapman? For the son-in-law, Leonard Fife? He assumes it has something to do with family and money, but doesn't know how to ask in what way it concerns family and money. Five years into this marriage, and he still has trouble penetrating his in-laws' tangled southern formalities and habitual turns of phrase. He is still unable to understand quickly what they are trying to tell him or ask of him.

Part of it is that the Chapmans are not just southerners. They are wealthy Virginians. In Benjamin and his brother Jackson's case wealthy by inheritance, in Jessie's, by virtue of her marriage to Benjamin. In Alicia's case by virtue of her grandparents' and parents' generosity. Fife, on the other hand, is not wealthy. He is poor. Although, by virtue of his marriage to Benjamin and Jessie Chapman's only child, who since she turned twenty-one has received a substantial annual income from the trust fund established by her grandparents, Fife himself expects to be wealthy someday. And for now he is able to live more or less as if that day has already arrived.

The Chapman brothers, Benjamin and Jackson, are sole owners of a company founded by their late father that manufactures nationally famous foot-care products called Doctor Todd's. The original Dr. Todd was a late-nineteenth-century Richmond druggist and amateur podiatrist who patented and sold home-made remedies for athlete's foot, fallen arches, ingrown toenails, and other podiatric afflictions. His concoctions became so popular that in 1929 he was able to sell the patents and the Doctor Todd's name to Benjamin and Jackson's father, Ephraim Chapman, and live handsomely for the rest of his life. Ephraim Chapman was a successful tobacco merchant who anticipated the coming tobacco wars two generations ahead of the Reynolds and the Dukes and was looking for a promising way to get out of the business. In taking over and industrializing the manufacture and distribution of Dr. Todd's home-made foot care remedies, Ephraim Chapman by the time he died in 1950 had become as rich as any of the tobacco barons, and Doctor Todd's had become a trusted brand name like Vicks, Schwinn, Hartz, and Heinz. The products practically sold themselves. After their father's death, all the Chapman brothers had to do was keep the machine running and let the men and women their father had hired run the factory and advertise and distribute the products, and when employees died or retired or took a job elsewhere, simply replace them with someone of equal ability. They barely had to put in half days at the office.

Benjamin leads Fife from the dining room through the living room, which they call the parlor, into the room they call the library to await the arrival of Jackson. The library is a male clubroom—maroon leather chairs and sofa, fireplace, mahogany bookcases filled with unread sets of books in matched bindings, framed prints of English setters and spaniels and game birds, with a bar and an eighteenth-century curly maple writing table. Not so much a room in which to read or study as a room in which men drink bourbon and branch water or gaze at their brandy snifters, smoke cigars, and talk business and politics without having to distinguish between the two.

Fife over the last five years has stayed in his wife's parents' house at least two hundred days and nights, first as an undergraduate at Richmond Professional Institute downtown and then as a graduate student and part-time instructor teaching freshman English at the University of Virginia in Charlottesville. He is becoming, in a sense, a scholar. His area of expertise is the early-twentieth-century American novel. He himself has been writing a late-twentieth-century American novel for the last two of those five years, since he and Alicia moved to Charlottesville. For all that, he has never found it desirable during his dozens of lengthy stays in the house to read or write in this room. The library is rarely used, the room belongs to Benjamin alone, and though Fife has been explicitly invited by both Jessie and Benjamin to feel free to use it for his work while Benjamin is at Doctor Todd's or when, since Fife has no interest in accompanying him, Benjamin is on the golf course or hunting doves and quail with his dogs, Fife generally avoids the library. Whenever he enters the room, he feels like a supplicant. When he sits on, not in, the leather sofa or one of the oversize chairs or draws a desk chair up to the writing table, prepared to read or write or correct and grade student essays, he feels as if he's about to be interviewed for a job by someone who has no intention of hiring him, someone who has already filled the position with a more qualified applicant. He has tried explaining to Alicia his preference for working, reading, and writing upstairs in their bedroom instead of in the library, and she claims to understand and sympathize.

The library is where I had to go and sit time-out when I did something bad during the day, she says to Fife. And Daddy, after he got home and heard about it from Mummy, would bring me there to scold me.

Benjamin Chapman pours three fingers of Rémy Martin into a snifter and offers it to Fife.

Thank you, Fife says, taking the glass globe in both hands to warm it. He sits in the chair nearest the fireplace. Even though it's a warm, balmy spring evening, someone has been told to lay and set a fire. Benjamin pours himself his second, or maybe it's his third, bourbon and branch over ice and stands by the bar. He's a tall, angular, square-jawed man, tanned and fit. His metallic white hair is short and lies flat against his bony skull. So he won't have to comb it when he steps from the shower, he likes to say. He wears a pale-blue short-sleeved shirt, oxford-cloth button-down, and a loosened Brooks Brothers striped repp tie and pressed khaki trousers. He left his blazer in the dining room, draped over the back of his chair. When later he goes upstairs to his bedroom, the jacket will be carefully hung in his bedroom closet.

He says to Fife, Would you like an excellent cigar made with leaves grown from smuggled Cuban seeds and rolled by Cuban exiles? A good anti–Fidel Cuban cigar, he adds. His little joke.

Fife hesitates. He's trying again to quit smoking, this time mainly because of Alicia's pregnancy. He quit cigarettes for the more authorial pipe when he first enrolled as a graduate student at UVA and lately smokes his pipe only on the porch when Alicia is not there or out in the backyard or on campus when they're at home in Charlottesville. He says yes, he'd like an anti–Fidel Cuban.

Benjamin takes the chair next to Fife's. They clip the ends off their cigars with Benjamin's brass clipper and light up. The silky moist aroma of the gray smoke merges with the dry smell of the burning logs in the fireplace. For the next fifteen minutes the men smoke and sip in a polite if slightly uncomfortable silence. They are used to relying on their wives to enable personal conversations between them and rarely find themselves topically pre-positioned and on their own like this.

Finally Benjamin manages to say, So, I gather this is a crucial moment in your lives. For you and Alicia, I mean.

Yes, sir. It is. A big change for all of us.

I expect so. All of us.

Sadly, we'll be a long ways from Richmond starting in the fall. But you'll have to come visit us in Vermont sometimes. Often.

Yes. Never been there before, Leonard. To Vermont.

We'll come down as often as possible, of course. Especially when I'm not teaching. When college is out.

Yes. That's your territory, isn't it? Vermont.

No, not exactly. Eastern Massachusetts. But, yes, sir, you could say it is my territory. Fife has struggled to adopt the southern manner of addressing an older male as sir. It's easier with ma'am.

Well, I expect you'll be happier up there. Among your own kind, so to speak.

Not really. I've come to love the South. Especially Charlottesville and Richmond.

You love Richmond. Benjamin states it, as if he doesn't quite believe him.

Yes, sir. I do.

It's a shame you couldn't land a decent academic position at one of the universities hereabouts. Though I expect it'll please you to get back to your native New England.

It's a good little college, Goddard.

One of those new progressive colleges, I understand. From Alicia's description.

Yes, sir.

That's good. That would probably suit you better than, say, UVA?

Yes, sir. Although I'd be happy to stay at Virginia if they saw fit to keep me on. They don't care to hire their own, unfortunately. Maybe someday, after I've taught elsewhere a few years and have tenure . . .

Benjamin stands and walks to the library door. A woman, one of the servants who served the family at dinner and whose name and face

Fife still can't call up, is greeting Benjamin's brother, Jackson, at the front hall.

Benjamin says, Bring Mr. Chapman to the library, Nancy.

He remembers her now. Nancy. Fife stands, glass in one hand, cigar in the other, and mentally catalogs her name and promises himself that in order to remember it, he will use it the next time he has an opportunity to speak with her. Nancy.

At sixty-six Jackson Chapman is two years older than his brother and two shirt sizes larger, a bluff, hearty, red-faced man with a loud voice and hands the size of welders' gloves. He, too, wears a blue button-down short-sleeve dress shirt, loosened striped repp tie, blazer, and khakis—the Doctor Todd's management uniform.

Of the brothers, Jackson takes up more space, but Benjamin is more physically graceful. Almost elegant in his movements, he's more restrained overall and indirect, though Fife has always assumed that beneath Benjamin's polite reserve, he is as bullheaded and oblivious as his older brother, of whom Fife is not especially fond. But then Fife is not exactly fond of Benjamin, either. Secretly, he respects neither man. When Alicia asked why, he could not name a reason. She wants to know the reason her husband doesn't respect her father and uncle. Their inherited wealth, perhaps. Their apparent assumption that it's deserved. Their conservative Republican politics. All of the above. None of the above. Something else.

Jackson Chapman and his wife, Charlene, live in a house that was a wedding gift from Jackson's father in the same Carillon Park neighborhood as Benjamin's family. They raised their three daughters there. Their large brick colonial with the white-columned front and sprawling lawns was the model a few years later for Benjamin's wedding gift from his father. In the five years since he joined the family, Fife has seen a lot of Jackson, a little of Jackson's wife Charlene, and not much of their three daughters, who, by the time he came to town, had all left

Richmond for happier homes and marriages elsewhere in the deeper South. It is understood in the family that Charlene is unhappy and rarely leaves her bedroom. Alicia says that her aunt is an alcoholic pillhead who makes everyone in the family miserable. She admires her uncle for his forbearance and doesn't blame her cousins for marrying professional men from far away.

Jackson shakes his brother's hand, then envelops Fife's, giving it a good crunch for manly emphasis and to show it's no mere courtesy, he means it, he's glad to see him, and heads straight for the bar, where he half-fills an old-fashioned glass with ice and tops it off with scotch.

Benjamin and Fife return to their chairs by the fire. Benjamin asks his brother if he'd like an excellent cigar made with leaves grown from Cuban seeds and rolled by Cuban exiles. An anti-Fidel cigar. Fife glances over at his father-in-law, expecting him to wink and grin. His expression remains the same, however.

Jackson waves the offer off and says, Jesus Christ, Ben, this is no way to have us a sit-down conversation! Haul those chairs over here by the sofa. He crosses the room and drops himself into the middle of the sofa. The meeting is now his. Fife has no brothers or sisters and is fascinated by interactions among siblings. Their earliest accommodation to one another's presence and personality seems to last into old age. Jackson has probably been overriding Benjamin's conversations since his younger brother first learned to speak.

Ben tells me you're driving north tomorrow in order to sign the papers and close the deal on a little place you've bought up there. A place where you and Alicia plan on living after she has her baby. That right, son?

That's correct, sir. I've taken a position . . .

I know, he says. You got yourself a teaching job up there. Up in Vermont. A long ways from your children's grandparents, Leonard. A damned long ways from family. Your own family, your mom and dad, they still up there in Vermont?

Eastern Massachusetts. Not too far. Actually, they moved back to Maine not long ago.

Maine.

Yes. It's where they're from originally. It's just my mother and father. A few cousins and aunts and uncles. My family's not . . . not close. Not like Alicia and her parents. Or you and your daughters and grandkids.

Yes, but they'll be nearby. Even in Maine. It's hell not to have your kids and grandkids nearby. Maine, never been there, actually. You, Ben?

Nope. Never.

Living in Vermont, we probably won't see my parents any more than we do now living in Virginia. A couple times a year. On holidays. My folks are not outgoing, let's say. Not like you all, sir.

Fife has not told his parents that he and Alicia will soon be leaving the South and resettling in a village barely three hours' drive north of his childhood home in Strafford, Massachusetts, and four hours west of his parents' retirement home in Maine. Nor has he told his parents that, effective May 31, at the end of the spring semester, he has resigned his position as a part-time adjunct teacher of freshman composition at the University of Virginia. Nor has he mentioned to his parents that during the winter break two and a half months ago, he and Alicia flew to Boston and drove to Vermont where they signed a contract to buy an 1820s house in the village of Plainfield, or that he will fly to Boston alone tomorrow and drive back up to Plainfield, this time carrying a cashier's check for $23,000 as payment for the house, and while there he will arrange with a contractor to begin renovations of the place under the watchful eye of Fife's old friend, Stanley Reinhart, the artist and a professor of studio art at Goddard College, the man who introduced him to the college and the college to him, the man whose isolated, spartan living and working arrangements Fife intends, despite Alicia's trust fund, to emulate. He has not told Benjamin and Jackson Chapman that the move to Vermont is motivated entirely by his desire to put as many miles as possible between their families and Fife himself and Alicia and Cornel and, when it's born, their new baby. He does not say that the chair of the English department of the University of Virginia has offered him an extra course for the fall semester and a three-year contract on the condition that he publish his dissertation during that period. He has not told Alicia, either. She does not know that they could, if they wished, stay on in Charlottesville for at least another three years.

Jackson takes a large swallow of scotch and says, Son, let me cut to the chase here. My brother and me, we've been discussing a proposal. A business arrangement that we would like you to consider. Before you make your big move back north.

Fife does not remember either of these men ever addressing him before as son.

I'm listening, sir, he says. He has no idea what's coming, but he knows that whatever business arrangement they propose, he'll swat it away. Politely, but emphatically, unequivocally. Fife wants to be disentangled from these people. It's not because he dislikes his wife's family, he has told her, or disapproves of them. It's because their wealth and privilege, their manners and taste, their luxuries and leisure, even their genteel southern white politics, have for so long seduced him and in that way given them power over him that he no longer knows the difference between him and them. It's not their fault—they've been incredibly generous and open-minded and inclusive. It's his fault. That's what he tells his wife, Alicia.

From the day she brought him down here from Boston to be presented to her parents as her wonderful, brilliant, handsome boyfriend, a young man claiming to be a writer while supporting himself by working in a Boston bookstore—a college dropout, yes, but no matter, Mummy and Daddy, since you don't need a college degree to be a writer, look at Hemingway and Faulkner, look at Herman Melville, and yes, he is a northerner, but he's not Jewish and definitely not a Negro, although he is very liberal when it comes to racial issues, like you two, or, more accurately, like Mother, for while Daddy is a man who believes in fairness and justice and equal opportunity, he does not think long-established racial and social conventions and practices should be tinkered with for no unavoidable reason—from that first day, Fife was captured by Alicia's family, manacled and bound to them as if he had arrived in Richmond with no family of his own, no antecedents, no cultural context, not even any friends.

He cannot blame them. He did it to himself. It was as if he arrived in Richmond with no memories and therefore no past. And now, five years later, he has made up his mind to take his memories and his past back, to be the man he was once on the verge of becoming and believes he would have become, if he had not fallen in love with Alicia Chapman.

Alicia does not know this yet. She herself has no desire to be free of her parents and their life. Yes, she has repeatedly declared that she will never end up like her mother, spending her days shopping and giving orders to Negroes, but her parents' life is hers, after all. She believes, as do they, that Fife has taken this full-time tenure-track position at a small college in Vermont because it's the only way for him to move ahead in his budding academic career. She and her parents also believe that he's taken the job in order to obtain a small degree of financial independence from the Chapman family, an impulse they admire. A man ought to be financially independent of his wife's inherited wealth. Or at least he should strive to be. Nonetheless, it is true, and wholly understandable, since the young man has not yet accumulated any capital of his own, that the couple will be purchasing the house in Vermont with a cashier's check issued by the Federal Reserve Bank of Richmond, drawn on the trust account of Alicia Violet Chapman and authorized by the trustees, Benjamin and Jessie Chapman and their attorney, Prescott Withers of Withers, Woodson and Wrall, who insisted only that title to the house be held solely by the Alicia Violet Chapman Trust.

Jackson Chapman takes a second serious swallow of scotch and be-gins by elaborating on something that Fife already knows. For months the brothers have been anxiously evaluating an offer by Beech & Net-tleson, the multinational pharmaceutical corporation, to buy Doctor Todd's. Beech & Nettleson has already bought up half a dozen small, family-owned manufacturers of health and beauty products, bringing them under a single management group based in Wilmington, Dela-ware, streamlining the purchased companies' staffs and production methods and siphoning off the profits for distribution to Beech & Nettleson shareholders. Jackson and Benjamin Chapman have all but decided to sell the company they inherited from their father.

Since we began discussions with them back in January, Jackson says, B and N's offer has gone up considerably.

By a whole bunch of millions, Benjamin says.

Jackson says, We do not expect them to sweeten the deal any fur-ther, however. We have reached a point, Leonard, where we must fish and stop cutting bait.

Benjamin adds that he and his brother do not want to sell the com-pany. Their father created Doctor Todd's, and they have devoted their lives to making it into the kind of company he would be proud of. But they have both reached an age when they must either pass Doctor Todd's on to the next generation of Chapmans or else sell it to Beech & Nettleson.

That's the problem, Benjamin says.

What's the problem? Fife asks.

The next generation is the damned problem, Jackson says. It's all girls! Ben's one and my three. And not a one of them cut out to run a company. And my three sons-in-law, they all got their own enterprises down there in Atlanta and Mobile, anyhow. One's a preacher and the other two are in the medical field. No disrespect, but the truth is, none of my girls or the boys they married is cut out to run a damned lem-onade stand. If one of my girls was a man and had common sense and was prepared to join the company and eventually run Doctor Todd's, okay, me and Ben could turn down Beech & Nettleson flat and stop all talk of selling right now.

Jackson looks straight at Fife and stops speaking. His brother looks at Fife also. A long silence ensues.

Fife knows what the Chapman brothers are proposing, but he can barely believe what he knows. Five years ago, when he first arrived in Richmond, having followed Alicia home from Simmons College like a stray dog she'd given part of her lunch to, her entire family, including Jackson's wife, Charlene, and their daughters, treated him as a minor character in a rebellious stage of Alicia's life that she would soon outgrow. The Chapman women and Jackson's daughters did seem to think that he was handsome and interestingly roguish and intellectual, a beatnik with good manners, someone to flirt with. The men treated him like a worker they'd fire if they weren't stuck with a damned union agreement they'd been forced to sign years ago. The family consensus was that Benjamin and Jessie had spoiled their only child, and Fife was the result. If no one overreacted, she'd soon get bored with her small rebellion and would tell the fellow to move on.

But then Fife and Alicia eloped to South Carolina, and their marriage became a legal fact of the Chapman family life, and the Chapman brothers treated him like a mistake that Alicia would have to live with, for a few years, anyhow—for which reason Benjamin Chapman refused to correct Fife when, even after he'd become a son-in-law, he continued to address Benjamin as Mr. Chapman. No point in letting the boy become overly familial.

The women and daughters, including his new wife Alicia, viewed Fife as a project, a boy they could educate about Virginia society and show how to dress for it. His new mother-in-law paid for his root canal work and the bridge necessitated by the inadequate dental care he had received when he was a child and then paid his undergraduate tuition at Richmond Professional Institute, and his new wife's trust fund paid for their living expenses and the rented apartment down in the Fan District near the campus, so that he and Alicia, who had dropped out of Simmons, could concentrate on their studies and finish in under three years, which they both did, magna cum laude. At their graduation ceremony dinner, Fife called his father-in-law Mr. Chapman for the last time.

Leonard, please call me Benjamin.

Yes, sir. Thank you, sir.

By the time Cornel, the first grandchild, was born, and Fife had received a Woodrow Wilson Fellowship and was accepted into the PhD program at UVA, all the Chapmans, men, women, and girls alike, had finally accepted him as a subsidiary member of the family. He was theirs now, and they his. Not quite as if he was born to it, more like he was adopted, but you had to admire the young man's determination to make an academic career for himself. They say it's not easy to land one of those Woodrow Wilson Fellowships. Very competitive. The young man was evidently not a gold digger. In fact, he seems to be managing his and Alicia's finances in a responsible way, living like a regular graduate student and young teaching assistant who is not the beneficiary by marriage of a multimillion-dollar trust fund. They are young and artistic, so there are, of course, a few indulgences. Like his teaching only part-time so he can write his novel and finish up his graduate studies, while Alicia concentrates on raising little Cornel and decorating their apartment in Charlottesville. And taking a two-week winter vacation in Mexico one year, in search of the ghost of Malcolm Lowry, Fife said, to Sardinia the next, tracing the footprints of D. H. Lawrence, he explained, and last winter break to ski in Vermont, ostensibly in search of the spirit of Robert Frost—Fife has started to write a little poetry and is thinking of giving up on prose fiction, but hasn't yet told anyone, not even Alicia.

In Vermont in January, they stayed with Fife's old Boston friends, the Reinharts, Stanley and Gloria, who showed them a small house for sale in the same village, which Alicia's trust would allow them to buy and renovate. Fife realized then, but did not tell Alicia, that if he came up with a good reason, they could live in Vermont instead of Charlottesville, Virginia, while he wrote his dissertation on Frost—he's already decided to change his dissertation topic from Stephen Crane's relation to capitalism to Robert Frost's. At Stanley's urging and Alicia's reluctant acquiescence, Fife allowed himself to be interviewed for an assistant professorship, a tenure-track position, at nearby Goddard College for a salary lower than what he was being paid as an adjunct at UVA. The small, financially strapped college was happy to add a rising young scholar soon to receive his PhD from a prestigious southern university and offered him the position immediately following his interview with the dean. It did not hurt that Fife was vouched for by one of the most beloved and admired members of the faculty, the well-known Boston artist Stanley Reinhart.

These, then, are the indulgences that Fife and Alicia have been granting to themselves, and that do not seem in any way excessive or reckless to the Chapman family. They are in fact further evidence of the young man's and Alicia's common sense and realism.

We'd like for you to consider a proposition, Jackson says. Just give it some consideration is all. Ben and I have been discussing it thoroughly together, and with our attorneys at WWW and the other members of the board. We'd like you to hold off on your purchase of that place in Vermont. Let me get to the point, son. Instead of going off to Vermont and taking that nice little job at that nice little college, we'd like you to think about joining Doctor Todd's. We'd like you to consider becoming chief executive officer of the company. Not right off, of course. But soon. Maybe very soon. A year or two. I would stay on as president another year, or more if needed, and brother Ben would stay on as chief financial officer, while you learn the ropes, so to speak. When you felt ready to take over as CEO, a position that doesn't exactly exist yet, since me and Ben pretty much cover that job between us, we would step aside and officially retire. We'd stay on the board, of course, and be available to you for support and advice as long as you wanted. But the company, Doctor Todd's, would be yours, Leonard. Not Beech & Nettleson's. We'd negotiate a decent stock transfer. The company would stay in the family for another generation. Or more.

Fife affects wide-eyed surprise and humble pleasure. He tries to look as if the brothers have offered to nominate him for lieutenant governor of the state of Virginia. He takes a sip of cognac, studies his cold cigar for a few seconds as if lost in thought and relights it, then puts the cigar down in the ashtray as if he's made a decision.

Benjamin says, Well, what about it, son?

Fife finds himself answering with a slight Tidewater accent. I am surprised and flattered by your proposal, sir. This is not something I have ever contemplated, working for Doctor Todd's. Not in any capacity. Never mind becoming chief executive. My education and professional experience, as you both know, sir, have ill prepared me for such a position—

Benjamin interrupts, Hell, neither me nor Jack studied business at the university. I was chemical engineering, and Jackson was . . . What did you major in, Jack? Before you got bounced.

Jackson laughs. Alcohol and women, I guess. That and a little geology. Rocks 'n' Rivers, we called it. R and R. Easiest major at UVA in those days. Most everybody in R and R thought he'd end up making millions in the oil industry, and a lot of 'em did. That and tobacco. But Daddy, he wanted to pass Doctor Todd's on to us, so we went to work for him straight out of college and learned on the job. Same as you would do, Leonard. And someday you could pass Doctor Todd's on to your son, Cornel. And let me tell you, that would make our daddy, Cornel's great-granddaddy, very happy.

Benjamin says, I know you're thinking of your writing ambitions, Leonard. And your scholarly interests. You wouldn't have to give all that up. In anticipation of this conversation I had my secretary—you recall meeting Lucy at our party here last Christmas—I had Lucy find me some famous writers who successfully combined business and literature, and she came up with quite a few. Benjamin draws a notebook from his shirt pocket and opens it.

Fife is touched by this gesture. He is moved that his father-in-law has done this bit of research into a type of work that he ordinarily regards with suspicion and condescension.

Some of them were poets, he says, which makes sense, on account of there being fewer words in poems than novels, he adds and laughs. But look here, he says, tapping his notebook. T. S. Eliot, he was a banker. Won the Nobel Prize for Literature. And Wallace Stevens, who was almost as famous as T. S. Eliot, he ran a big insurance company up in Hartford, Connecticut. You probably know his poetry. A couple were doctors, like Anton Chekhov, the Russian writer. And the English novelist Trollope, he was actually a postal inspector for the government. Mark Twain was a publisher, among other things. Bet you didn't know that. Published Ulysses S. Grant's memoirs of the War, which kind of surprised me. I always thought Twain was a southerner. A riverboat captain, I seem to recall. Nathaniel Hawthorne, there's another civil servant. He worked as a customs officer. So did your favorite, Herman Melville. It's a long list, Leonard. It surprised me.

Never read any of those fellows, Jackson says. Not since college anyhow.

These are not lives that Fife envies or desires for himself, the lives of poets and writers who were also bankers, insurance executives, civil servants, physicians. For Fife, it is the slightly mad ones who count most, Jack Kerouac, Henry Miller, D. H. Lawrence, Stephen Crane, and the writers who made youthful poverty attractive, like Hemingway, Joyce, Frost, and Faulkner, whose deprivations and sacrifices when young were rewarded with fame and riches later, while they were still living. None of them, not the mad ones, certainly, and not the bohemians either, would have agreed to be the chief operating officer of a company that manufactures foot powder. None of them would have agreed to be the podiatry-products king of America.

For Fife, it's humiliating enough as it is, earning a doctorate in literature and working as a part-time adjunct professor and writing unpublished, maybe unpublishable, novels, stories, and poems in the air-conditioned comfort of an apartment—and soon, a house—paid for by his wife's trust fund. If he accepts Benjamin and Jackson Chapman's offer to stay here in Richmond and take over his in-laws' family business, whether he is good at it or not—though he is sure that if Benjamin and Jackson Chapman, who are neither clever nor industrious, can handle the job, he can handle it, too—in a few years he and Alicia and their children will be living in a big brick colonial Carillon Park mansion that overlooks the James River, and he will join the Country Club of Virginia, the Chamber of Commerce, the board of the Virginia Museum of Fine Arts, and one night after a half dozen bourbons and branch he will go into the library and lock the door and put a bullet in his brain.

Whoever, whatever, he is now, though he's only partially solidified as a self-created being, if he accepts their offer, he will liquefy and eventually vaporize. He will become an invisible, odorless gas, and the best thing he can do to make sense of what he has done to himself is light a match, like one of those self-immolating Vietnamese monks protesting the war in Vietnam.

Fife stands and sets his glass on the coffee table, leaving his half-smoked cigar lying in the large antique pewter plate they're using as an ashtray. Well, you've given me a lot to think on, he says. There's that Tidewater accent again, he notes, too late to curb it. Of course I'll need to discuss your offer first with Alicia, he says. This concerns her life as much as it does mine. It's too late to change our plans to complete the purchase of the Vermont property, he says. Not without forfeiting the deposit. But it's a good investment, regardless of what we decide, and would make a nice little summer place for someone, if not for us. How soon do you need to know my—our—decision? I was planning on staying in Vermont for a week to get the renovations on the house started.

Benjamin says he should take his time, as it's the biggest decision he'll ever make in his life. They can hold Beech & Nettleson off another week or two, no problem. But take longer, if you need to.

Fife says, I think that Alicia and I will want a block of time to consider all the ramifications. Because there's a lot of 'em, he adds, smiling broadly, as if he's already made up his mind to accept their offer and has become one of them. A lot of ramifications. I couldn't commence working for Doctor Todd's till June first, you realize. When the spring term's finished in Charlottesville. Probably have to get me a shorter haircut, too, Fife says and laughs.

The Chapman brothers laugh, too. They're relieved he said it and they didn't have to. It would not do for Doctor Todd's CEO-in-training to look like some kind of long-haired hippie protester. He probably ought to get rid of that mustache, too.

We'd have to find us a place to live here in Richmond.

You could always stay with us till you had your own place, Leonard.

We got that big three-bedroom apartment over the garage, Jackson adds.

All Alicia's doctors are in Charlottesville, Fife says, and she's due in early June.

We can recommend people here at VCU Medical Center. Best doctors in Virginia are right here, Leonard.

Okay, then. Give me a week to decide. Fife shakes Jackson's hand with emphasis, as if they have a deal, and then shakes his father-in-law's hand, and turning, exits quickly from the library, wearing a smile that's almost a grin, and makes his way up the wide, carpeted stairs.

FROM THE DARKNESS, MALCOLM SAYS, YOU OKAY TO
take a break, Leo? We don't have to change cards yet. We're shooting
1080 by 1920. Sorry, man, this is for Sloan's benefit. You know all that
shit.

Fife says, Yeah, yeah, I'm okay to take a break.

He's fighting off waves of nausea and thudding back pain. His
body is a battlefield, as if his liver is at war with his kidneys and both
have been mortally wounded. He's woozy and suddenly confused
about where he is exactly and who's here with him. As long as he is
talking into the mic and being filmed, he is able to forget his body, to
wear it like loose clothing, and it doesn't matter where he is located or
who is there with him. But as soon as the camera shuts down and he
goes silent, he becomes his body again, and he worries about where it
is and who is near it.

I want to keep doing this, he says.

Diana says, You sure you're not too tired?

From what? Of course I'm not too tired! It's her voice that he snaps
at. No matter what she says, it's the shriek of an irritated blue jay.

He's quickly sorry he was sharp with her. Nothing she can do about it, he tells himself. She's had to overcome the unintended effect of that voice her entire life. Especially its effect on men, men who cultivate their baritone and bass and hold their time signature at 4/4, except when slowing it for emphasis to 3/4. Or dropping it all the way down to half notes for winning arguments. Men who are actors. Men like Fife.

Despite her voice, Fife likes and respects Diana. Malcolm would be nowhere without her. He'd be making local TV commercials in Winnipeg or promotional docs for Caribbean time-shares. Because of Malcolm's sneaky little affair with Sloan, among other things, Fife feels sorry for her. He's always felt sorry for Diana, from back when she was his student at Concordia and Malcolm was his teaching assistant and seduced her by convincing her that he was more talented than she, when Fife knew the opposite was true. Diana could have become a real filmmaker, but instead she fell in love with Malcolm and married him and became his producer and made him the filmmaker. Even then, Diana was honest, and Malcolm was not.

Same as Emma and Fife.

Why are women more honest than men? he wonders. It ought to be the other way around. Men have so much more power in the world, you'd think they could at least take a shot at being honest. What do they have to lose? Look at Sloan, who is probably convinced that she's in love with the short, shifty, bald-headed, fifty-year-old married man, and she thinks he's in love with her, or she wouldn't sleep with him. Even Sloan is honest.

Of course, it's possible that she's just cynical and believes that Malcolm can advance her career a whole lot faster than some attractive, unmarried guy in his twenties. But Fife doesn't think so. The girl is honest.

Alicia Chapman of Richmond, Virginia, she was honest, too. All the women Fife ever loved were honest. And from his first love to yesterday's, he was not.

Fife says, I'm sorry, Diana. I didn't mean to snap at you. It's just, this is hard. Keeping focused. Not letting my fucked-up dying body distract me. My body wants my complete attention. Just like you and Malcolm, my body resents it when I pay attention to my remembered, hidden past.

Speaking of which, Malcolm says, we have all these questions written out that me and Diana put together for you. Like for posterity, my man. The definitive Leonard Fife interview.

The final interview.

No, c'mon, dude, don't say that. It's just, I mean, this story you're telling. It's not exactly what we planned on. I mean, it's interesting and all, and there's a lot of surprising material back there. The first marriage to the southern woman, Alicia, and all that, wow, that's news. But we want to connect it to your work, man. This is supposed to be about your films.

My second marriage. Not my first.

Oh. Okay, second, then. But we've got questions on process, for example. Like, the Gagetown Support Base story, *In the Mist*, your first film. Tell about them testing Agent Orange way the fuck out there in Gagetown back in the sixties, and how the film permanently pissed off both American and Canadian governments and Dow Chemical. Or was it Monsanto? I can't remember. And how you almost went to prison for it. It would be really interesting to learn how you first got onto that story, like when it was still totally top secret in Washington and Ottawa. You were just a kid then. What or who tipped you off to it? You never said. The Gagetown Agent Orange defoliant story is our shared history, Leo. One of Canada's guilty secrets. The fucking Americans, testing Agent Orange on Canadian soil before using it in Vietnam, that was important for us to know about, man. We were supposedly neutral on Vietnam, as you knew better than almost anyone. People need to hear you talk about that today. Now.

Yeah, well, Fife says, Gagetown's not top secret anymore, is it? It's public knowledge. Half a dozen films have come out since the story broke, and as many books and parliamentary hearings and investigations have dug into it, and there's even a batch of niggardly payouts made by the government to some of the cancer victims' families. Forget top secret, Fife says. It's not even a guilty secret now.

He thinks it's funny—no, not funny, ironic—how, when a guilty secret is finally revealed, the guilt quickly dissipates and gets replaced by a cleaner, more acceptable emotion. Anger, usually followed by denial. Once their secret was out, the US and Canadian agencies that were responsible for decades of spraying Agents Orange, Purple, and White on their own soldiers at Gagetown Support Base didn't feel guilty anymore. They felt angry. And their anger let them refuse to apologize. It let them deny they did it with intention or anticipation of the consequences. The devil made them do it. Acknowledgment without apology.

Fife wonders if that's the reason he's returning, not to his Canadian past, where Malcolm and Diana want him to go, but to his distant American past, where no one wants him to go, where his own guilty secrets were embalmed and mummified and, until now, for all intents and purposes permanently entombed. He wonders if by means of disinterring his past, he's trying to swap out guilt for anger and denial. As if to say, Yes, it's true, I did all those bad things, I'm guilty as charged. But, people, it wasn't my fault, I had a terrible childhood, I was the victim of circumstances. The devil made me do it. Everything is contingent. And now, since I've confessed and can be angry at my parents and at circumstances and at the devil, at my fate, now everyone has to forgive me. Acknowledgment without apology.

There's lots he could tell the camera about making *In the Mist* that would satisfy Malcolm and Diana and impress Vincent, their impressionable DP, and might make Sloan reconsider her attachment to Malcolm. Fife is under no illusion that it would invite her to transfer her affection and admiration over to him, a sick and dying old man who hasn't tried to seduce a pretty young woman in a decade. He believes the implicit comparison between him and Malcolm as filmmakers would diminish Malcolm in her eyes. That would please Fife. Sick and dying and old, maybe, but he still competes with other men for the affections and admiration of young women. It's in his DNA. Like everything else that's wrong with him, it's not his fault, right? Acknowledgment without apology.

Sloan thinks Malcolm is a guerrilla filmmaker. It's what he calls himself, despite having bankrolled his soft-stroking films—thanks to Diana's money-raising skills—with support, as they like to call it, from multinational corporations and government film boards and private foundations and millionaires. Fife could show Sloan how a real guerrilla filmmaker works. He could tell her mic and Vincent's camera the truth of how and why he was led to uncover the Gagetown spraying, instead of sitting here telling them who he was before he became a Canadian.

He could tell them how he first heard about the mysteriously desiccated crops up there in Gagetown, New Brunswick, from the US Navy deserter who'd become a truck farmer on land adjacent to the support base. The deserter was called Ralph Dennis, a tall, pear-shaped Oklahoman in his early thirties with a gentle smile and hippie spectacles and a permanent peach-colored blush on his cheeks. Fife met him late one mid-April night at the Montreal Council to Aid War Resisters down on Alymer Street, where he went for help finding his first job in Canada. There's a blousy, wet snow falling, the kind that marks the start of spring more than the end of winter. In front of a three-story graystone town house, tight to the sidewalk, outside the painted yellow door of the Yellow Door coffeehouse near McGill, where the Montreal Council keeps office space on the second floor, Fife enters and Ralph Dennis exits, and the two literally bump into each other.

Fife apologizes, and the man apologizes back, and Fife recognizes his Oklahoma drawl, though he thinks it's probably Arkansas or Missouri, possibly Tennessee. It's definitely not Anglo- or French Canadian. Fife thinks of himself as an expert on American accents. He asks the man if he's American.

One hundred percent. I guess you must be one of us, too, the man says. It's more a question than an observation.

Yes.

The fellow asks Fife where he's from, and Fife hesitates and then says New England.

Just up here for a visit?

Yes. Sort of. His answer hangs in the air a few seconds.

They're closing up inside, but there's still time for a coffee. Care for a coffee, brother?

Fife follows the man inside, where they shake hands and introduce themselves by name. Ralph Dennis says he works part-time as a volunteer for the Council to Aid War Resisters, and Fife says that's who he came to see.

I figured. You speak any French?

Not really. I can kind of read it. From a year of high school French.

Level of education?

Again he hesitates. A little college. Not much.

No degrees then. You got a trade? Some kind of professional skill?

Fife shakes his head no.

So you're one of the guys with talents, but no skills. You don't speak French. And you don't own any property here?

No.

It don't look good, brother. You need to get landed status to stay in Canada, and you're not going to get it in Quebec. You'll have to go to an English-speaking province, where they have a use for Anglos with talents but no skills. After you get landed, you can pretty much go anywhere in the country, if you want. Ralph says that during the summer months he manages a truck farm in Gagetown, New Brunswick, for an absentee owner. Mostly it's cucumbers for pickling trucked to Freder-

icton, the provincial capital. The owner runs a big canned food corporation out of Ottawa, he says. Ralph likes working in winter with the
Resisters here in Montreal, but he's in the process of opening an office
in Fredericton and from now on will stay up there in New Brunswick
year-round. A lot of your fellow New Englanders have started coming
over from Maine, he says.

An hour later Fife has a job. He follows Ralph Dennis back up to
Gagetown and goes to work that summer as a laborer on the cucumber
farm. In his downtime, he studies French from a high school textbook,
and at Ralph's suggestion that he try to shape his talents into a skill,
maybe journalism, he borrows Ralph's portable Sony cassette recorder
and starts taping interviews with Ralph and his neighbors.

Most of their conversations keep coming around to the mysteri-
ous waves of silver mist that in the last year have begun drifting off
the base whenever the wind shifts to the east. Crops and gardens and
animals have begun to sicken and die, and all the locals are convinced
that it has something to do with the mist. The Canadian military has
admitted that in order to clear the brush for maneuvers they've been
spraying some kind of defoliant, but no one at the base will tell the
locals what's in it. Ralph loans Fife his 35 mm Leica Rangefinder and
asks him to take pictures of the dead fields and gardens and the stum-
bling, maddened calves and sheep.

We may need a record of all this someday, Ralph explains.

Fife visits the farmers and farm workers in and around Gagetown in
Ralph's pickup and spends endless early-morning and evening hours out
by the fence that surrounds the vast acreage of the base, where he shoots
black-and-white stills of the helicopters, the famous American Hueys,
while they spray the land below and the Canadian troops reconnoiter-
ing in the dense brush and among the low conifers. He shoots pictures
of the empty orange barrels of 2,4,5-T dumped into bulldozed ditches
near the fence. He works alone and tells no one, except Ralph Dennis,
what he's recording, because he doesn't know yet what he's recording.

He could tell Sloan and Vincent and Malcolm and Diana and the rest of the world that it isn't until four years later, hunkered down in his rented room in Pointe-Saint-Charles in Montreal, that he finally figures out what he taped and photographed in Gagetown. Ralph Dennis and his neighbors have long since stopped trying to grow anything in their poisoned fields. Ralph fell in love and married a local woman. He gave up his work with the Resisters and moved with his new wife to Winnipeg, which he calls Tulsa North. He's homesick, and Winnipeg is as close to home as he can get without going to jail, he explains. He lets Fife keep the photographs and taped interviews that he made back in the summer of '68.

Fife is no longer trying to write a novel and poetry by now. Most of his friends and lovers in Montreal are aspiring writers and artists and folk singers and filmmakers, and all of them seem more talented and purposeful than he. He supports himself, barely, by writing English-language book reviews and freelance cultural essays for the *Montreal Star* and the *Gazette*. He likes to say that he dabbles in several of the arts, but practices none. As when, on a borrowed Cine-Kodak Model B-16 editing viewer, he merges the taped interviews and black-and-white stills from Gagetown with archival newspaper and TV clips and charts pilfered from the Grande Bibliothèque and a soundtrack of pirated Byrds, Dylan, and Doors songs. He thinks he's making an avant-garde metafictional film with nonmoving images and tape recordings and TV news footage, a covertly autobiographical cinematic collage about his first months in Canada, more or less for his own amusement, he claims. Six months into the project, alone in his room one night, discouraged and frustrated and about to give up on anything that can be called creative, he runs the hour-long film from start to end. He pretends that it was made by a stranger, and suddenly he realizes that it isn't autobiographical at all. He sees that, if he doesn't think it's by him or about him, he can nudge it rather easily into becoming a suspenseful, dramatic exposé of a crime. Without intending to until he's nearly abandoned it, he has made *In the Mist*, the film that kick-starts his career as an investigative documentary filmmaker, the film that five years later, once he gets it shown on Canadian TV, becomes an unacknowledged inspiration for Coppola's *Apocalypse Now*.

He can tell all that to Malcolm and his crew. It's the story they want to hear from him. And he won't have to mention that his story of the origins of *In the Mist* is paved over a lie. He can let the lie stay buried beneath the truth, and it will continue to be his guilty secret. And why not? It's still stable enough to support the truth. He's gotten away with it for fifty years. He can easily keep it buried for the few weeks or days he has left to live, and no one will be the wiser.

It's the cancer that has freed him to dig up and expose the lie. There's no longer any undone future work to protect and promote. No unrealized career ambitions. No one left to impress. Nothing to win or lose. He hasn't a future anymore, and without a future, there's nothing his past can sabotage or undo.

Nothing, except her. Emma. Her love and respect and admiration. Acquired illegitimately and under false pretenses, starting with *In the Mist*, which first brought them together. At Concordia, where she studied under him, her final thesis was *"In the Mist" and "Man with a Movie Camera": Metacinema and Reflexivity in the Films of Leonard Fife and Dziga Vertov*.

This is his last chance to stop lying to Emma, his last chance to hand back to her in public everything she gave to him in private. If he dies without having told her the truth of how he came to be the man she thinks he is, the man she has loved and worked with all these years, and tells it in public like this, before the world, on-camera, miked, to be edited, soundtracked, packaged, sold, and distributed all across Canada and even in the States and maybe Europe as well, if he dies without having told her the truth, the whole truth, and nothing but the truth, then she'll have loved and married and been the forty-year partner of a purely fictional character. He'll have turned her into a fool. He will have taken everything from her and given nothing back. Her love and marriage and professional partnership will have been wasted.

He mustn't let that happen to her. Not after everything else he's done to her.

Fife speaks into the darkness. Emma? Are you still here, Emma?

We ready to go, Vincent? Malcolm asks.

Ready.

Malcolm claps his hands in front of the camera. Okay, Leonard Fife interview. April 1, 2018. Montreal.

Fife speaks into the darkness again. Emma? Are you there, Emma?

Yes, Leo. I'm still here.

4

ALICIA? YOU AWAKE, BABE?

I am now, she says.

Malcolm interrupts Fife's account of his memory and tries to turn him back to the making of *In the Mist*. He's recalling a piece in *Cinema Canada* that he read when he was at Concordia about the influence of Fife's film on *Apocalypse Now*, and he wants to know how Coppola—Malcolm calls him Francis—managed to see the film in the 1970s, when, as far as he knows, *In the Mist* was never screened in the States.

Diana notes that *In the Mist* was shown outside of competition at the Toronto Festival of Festivals in 1976, back before it turned into TIFF.

Okay, so Francis must've been there, Malcolm says. He would've been editing *Apocalypse Now* around then. How did Leo get Francis to see it? he wonders. Did Leo have some kind of connection through the guys running the festival? That would've been Bill Marshall and Dusty Cohl, right?

Fife ignores him. He enters their bedroom, his and Alicia's bedroom in Richmond. He shuts the door behind him. The room is dark except for the pale glow of a nightlight from the adjoining bathroom. He feels his way over to the edge of the king-size bed and pats his wife's hip through the covers. He smiled all the way up the stairs from the library, and he's still smiling.

Sorry to wake you, babe. But you are not going to believe what just happened. Down there with your father and uncle. Un-fucking-believable.

Alicia rolls over onto her back for a second and groans and turns the rest of the way onto her other side, facing away from him. God-dammit, she says, I'll be happy when this baby comes out! Okay, tell me what happened. You smoked a cigar, didn't you? You really stink, Leo. Go wash your hands.

He stands and heads for the bathroom.

And your face! she calls after him. Wash your face, too.

He flips on the row of makeup lights above the mirror, a set of low-wattage warm pink bulbs designed to soften the harsh overhead fluorescents. It's a schoolgirl's bathroom, outfitted for extended peri-ods of mirror-gazing. Whenever Fife and Alicia stay at her parents' home, they sleep in Alicia's childhood bedroom suite. Beyond the bathroom is Nanny Sally's bedroom, and beyond that the nursery, where Cornel sleeps. There are other suites, one for Alicia's parents and one for guests, each with a dressing room and bathroom and sit-ting area. There are several back staircases, storage rooms, pantries, sleeping porches, library, parlor, dining room, TV room, and laundry, sewing, and maid's rooms. The house, especially at night, seems to go on and on endlessly.

Fife stands at the sink, soaping his hands. He leans forward and stares at his reflection in the mirror. He tries to imagine how he would look with a proper businessman's short haircut, his mustache and sideburns gone. Like a white suburban realtor, he thinks. Or a guy inheriting from his wife's father and uncle a company that makes foot powders and arch supports. With his hair cut short and mustache gone, he will look like what at bottom he will have become, an accidentally successful Richmond businessman, instead of what he wants to be, which, with his drooping mustache and shoulder-length chestnut hair, is what he looks like tonight. Not a hippie protester or a political radical but a serious young man, a politically serious, artistically engaged, well-educated young man. He wants to be taken for an intellectual artist, a cool contemporary version of the 1950s Greenwich Village and San Francisco Beats, Kerouac and Ferlinghetti and Ginsberg. He models his clothing and hair and affect after them and after photographs of French existentialists sitting in Saint-Germain cafés smoking and drinking apricot cocktails and wrestling with the philosophical and moral consequences of political and religious disillusionment. He wants to be what he believes he looks like.

But in the mirror tonight, even the surface looks phony. He is a man outfitted for a costume party with a wig and a fake mustache, a man who, without the costume, is that callow youth living off his southern wife's family money. He's not even a competent actor playing a role. He dries his face with a towel and erases his face from his gaze and returns to the bedroom.

He sits at the edge of the bed and rests his hand on Alicia's hip again. She lies on her side the way he left her, facing away from him.

Cornel okay? he asks her.

He never has nightmares when he sleeps in this house, she says. He just zonks out for the night. On account of Sally sleeping in the next room. His guardian angel. Alicia says she was the same. Still is. As long as Sally's on the other side of the wall, she sleeps like a baby. Except when her beloved husband comes up smelling of alcohol and cigars, she says, her voice turning soft and affectionate. She reaches back without looking at him and touches his forearm with her fingertips. Tell me what you were saying before. About Daddy and Uncle Jackson.

Fife likes his wife's oddly exaggerated Tidewater accent: Aboot Daddee and Oncle Jakeson, is how he hears it. Or does he like it? It's slightly bizarre. No one else in the Chapman family, no Virginian he's ever met, speaks with such an extreme version of the accent. He believes she jacked it up when she first arrived at Simmons College and realized how exotic she sounded to her New England and Manhattan classmates, and in the years since has made it her own. She was studying theater arts, like most of the strikingly beautiful Simmons girls, and was trained early on how to speak in any accent the role required. Unlike most people, she knows what she sounds like. She's an actress. It's closer to a seventeenth-century British accent, especially in her pronunciation of "u" and "ou," than to a typical twentieth-century southeastern American accent. Fife's father and his Nova Scotia uncles, aunts, and cousins pronounce those vowels in a similar way, but much diluted. They say aboot the hoose, instead of about the house. Alicia adds a lot of breath and volume to her version.

Fife himself speaks with a broad Massachusetts working-class accent, like his mother. He likes to think that living in the South these six years has softened his sound, given it a Tidewater tint. But like most people, except Alicia, he can't hear himself unless he's tape-recorded. When he hears himself on tape, it makes him squirm in embarrassment. He sounds too much like his mother, as if, to mock him, she were reciting Fife's words back to him.

He tells her that her father and his brother offered him the company. Doctor Todd's.

They what? What do you mean? She rolls over on her back and props herself halfway into a sitting position.

They said if I agreed to come on as CEO, they wouldn't sell Doctor Todd's to Beech & Nettleson. They'd stay on for a few more years as president and chief financial officer and then basically turn the company over to me, Fife says. As if anticipating her question, he admits that they didn't get specific as to salary or stock ownership. Not that it would matter one way or the other, he adds.

Wow! she says. Wow. My God, Leo. Then follows with a long, low exhalation, as if she's been holding her breath, waiting to hear this news, for a very long time.

Yeah, wow, all right. The last thing I expected from those two. I mean, I thought to them I was like from a different planet. A different solar system.

No, Leo, honey. That's no longer the case. They know you're smart. They know you love me and Cornel and that you are loyal to the family.

Yeah, they know it now, maybe. They didn't used to. At least the part about me being loyal to the family. Don't forget your daddy's goddamn private detective.

That Daddy got over his mistrust is a credit to you both, Leo. Now it's your turn to get over some of your prejudices, she says. She admits that she is sort of in shock, though. Daddy never said a word of it to her. Mother never said anything, either. He must've discussed it with her. It would mean they'd live in Richmond. Fife and Alicia and Cornel and the new baby. Mother would love that.

I bet she would.

We'd have to cancel buying the Vermont place.

Yeah. And build us a big brick colonial manse overlooking the James.

You'd have to let that Goddard College job go. I mean, you never actually signed a contract, right? It was all just a verbal agreement between you and the dean, wasn't it?

Fife doesn't answer. In the nearly dark room he can make out the shape of her body and the outline of her face, but he can't read her expression. He thinks, he hopes, she's joking. Teasing him a little. She's an actress—trained as an actress—and he sometimes can't tell whether she is herself or is playing a role to entertain herself. He's not sure there's a difference.

He says, You're kidding, right?

Yes. Yes, of course, I'm kidding. But you've got to admit, Leo, it's a stunner! And isn't it just a teenie-weenie bit tempting, Leo?

Jesus, no! Not even a teenie-weenie bit tempting, he declares. He'd end up a drunk or dead by his own hand or both before he hit his mid-thirties. He'd be miserable, and then he'd make her miserable, and the kids, and everyone who came near him.

Not if you were still able to do your writing. And not if all the while your family was happy. You could continue to write, you know. Daddy spends barely four or five hours a day at Doctor Todd's, and the rest of the time plays golf or hunts birds. The company practically runs itself, Leo.

You want me to accept their offer. Don't you?

Of course not! I mean, I don't want you *not* to accept it, either. It's your decision, honey, not mine. She just wants him to do whatever will make him happy and avoid doing whatever will make him sad. And no one except he himself knows which is which.

There's nothing that can make me happy. I've never been interested in happy, he says. You know that.

She knows he doesn't like being a college professor. Even part-time. But it does give him the time to do his writing. And Vermont is beautiful, and they both love that little old house and the hills and the small New England college-town environment for raising a family, where it doesn't matter if you're white or Black, like it does here. Alicia rattles on, listing good reasons for rejecting her father's and uncle's offer.

Then she switches abruptly back to good reasons why Fife might want to accept their offer. Family support with raising their children and enough money to hire domestic help and to send the soon-to-be-two children to private schools and to build the house of their dreams, just as her parents built theirs thirty years ago, and to travel, and to keep the Vermont house and use it as a summer place. And it would sure make her parents happy in their old age if their grandchildren were close by. In a way, she says, whether he takes their offer or not, that they offered it means he's finally found his family.

Yes, but I have a family, Alicia. I wasn't looking for one. They weren't lost.

For a moment, both are silent.

Then Fife says, I don't get it.

Hmmm? Get what?

Everything has turned really weird, he says.

She was supposed to join him in his surprise and the pleasure of his redemption. And she was supposed to share his delight in the absurdity of the idea of his running Doctor Todd's and their living her parents' life here in Richmond. But it's clear to him that, while she is probably as surprised by the offer as he and feels a certain relief for his redemption herself, she does not think it would be absurd, ridiculous, possibly suicidal, for him to accept the offer. He doesn't say any of this. Only that everything has turned really weird.

Yes, weird. God, yes. How did you leave it with Daddy and Uncle Jackson?

That I'd have to talk to you. That I would get back with an answer when I return from Vermont. That I need to think about it. A huge decision, et cetera. Mostly bullshit.

Yes, she says. She reaches out and touches his cheek with her fingertips. It is a huge decision, she says softly. Now c'mon to bed, sweetie. It's late, and you've got a long flight and drive ahead of you tomorrow.

Yeah. Long flight, Richmond to Washington to Boston. Then a long drive. Boston to Vermont.

5

EMMA'S SMOKY VOICE SWIRLS OUT OF THE DARK FROM
somewhere near the hallway door. She says sorry to interrupt but she
has to step out, she has a text on her phone that just came in and has
to answer it right away. I'll keep track and catch up later, she says.
Sorry, she repeats. You go on talking, Leo, I shouldn't've interrupted.
Really, most of this stuff, some of it anyhow, I already know. Or versions thereof.

No, you don't! You don't know any of it. And you managed to
fuck up Malcolm's shot! The continuity got busted when Vincent was
swinging the camera around to my right. Didn't you notice Vincent on
the dolly moving from a straight-on headshot to a profile? When he
cuts your interruption, it'll end up a jump cut and the fucking thing
will look edited. Suspension of disbelief, Emma! Remember? You
want it to flow like time, not memory. You want . . .

Please, Leo. I'm not one of your students.

No, really, Emma. I need you here listening to all this. Because
you don't already know most of this other stuff. Because I never told
you most of it. Or told anyone. Some of it not even to myself. And if

you're going to interrupt or make noise going in and out of the room, then please do it when the camera's locked, not when it's moving. This goes for you, too, Renée.

Comment?

You know what I'm saying, Renée. Your English is as good as my French!

Calm down, Leo, Emma says. Jesus. She reminds him that he's been talking for nearly an hour, he should take a break. He's not used to putting out this much energy for this long a time. There's no need for him to push himself. Malcolm can come back tomorrow and the next day and the day after that, if need be. You have to save your strength, she says. You probably shouldn't be doing this interview at all.

Malcolm says Emma's right. They can spread the interview over three or four or more sessions. But making the interview is a good thing, he says. It gives Leo a chance to get his own story told his own way. He's spent a lifetime telling other people's stories, letting them use him and his camera to document their lives. He should finally have the chance to tell his own story and use Malcolm's camera to document it. Vincent's camera, he corrects himself.

Yeah, Vincent's camera, and Malcolm's and Diana's heavy-handed edit, Fife points out. Using that, too. Whose fucking story will it be then? he wants to know. Whose story will it be when Malcolm and Diana have sliced and diced and stitched and hitched his words and images of his face and body back into a hundred-and-twenty-minute narrative? Whose story will it be when the CBC suits tell them they have to reduce the interview to ninety minutes? Or even less. Maybe forty minutes, he says. My story? I don't think so.

Sloan says, That is so interesting, Leo. I never thought of it that way, like a doc is no different than a fictional film. When it comes to the truth, I mean.

Diana says, Theory of cinema one-oh-one, Sloan, dear.

Excuse me?

Never mind.

Fife comes back to Emma. He says, You think you already know most of this stuff? Is that what you think? You think you know me? Well, let me assure you, no one in this room knows me any better than my nurse, Renée. And actually she knows me in ways you guys never will. She puts the catheter in my prick and takes it out, she wipes my ass and changes my diaper, she undresses me, puts me in the tub and bathes me and rubs lotion over my bedsores and dresses me again. She measures out my meds and fills and refills my drip. Renée is beside me every waking minute, and even when I'm sleeping.

Fife knows the camera is running, and he is performing for it. He can't help himself. How old are you, Sloan? he asks.

Me? I'm twenty-two. Why?

When I was twenty-two, Sloan, I'd already been married, fathered a child, and gotten divorced. By the time I was your tender age, Sloan, I had ruined my life.

Vincent, catch this, Malcolm tells him.

Fife asks Sloan if she can imagine believing at twenty-two that she's already ruined her life. He means destroyed her future, shut off all possibilities of ever realizing the American dream, or the Canadian dream, although he doesn't think there actually is a Canadian dream. Imagine if Sloan at twenty-two believed that everything good that could ever happen to her had already happened. Imagine that she's not going anywhere from here, except downhill. That she's going to lose her job. Then her boyfriend. She'll be evicted from her apartment and will have to sleep on a friend's couch, until her friend kicks her out, and then she'll be homeless, sleeping in shelters, eating at food kitchens for the destitute, and her health will start to fail, even though she's only twenty-two . . .

Sloan interrupts, Is that what happened to you, Leo? Mr. Fife.

Malcolm says, Okay, we're rolling. Right, Vincent?

Right.

Well, no, it's not quite what happened, Fife says to Sloan. But almost. Because that's when I met Alicia Chapman, the belle of Richmond, Virginia, slumming from Simmons College among the beatniks and bohos of Boston's Back Bay, trolling for a man who was contemplating suicide or murder or both as a last chance to give his life meaning, a man whose mere existence would offend her wealthy, respectable, Republican parents, a man they would hire a private detective to investigate, so they could shock their daughter into beating a hasty retreat once confronted by the ugly facts of his early marriage and divorce and the abandonment of his child, among other minor crimes and misdemeanors. Even though it turned out that she shocked them instead, because she already knew all those facts, and she loved him anyhow. He had told her everything about his past by then, and if they didn't back off, she was going to run away to South Carolina and marry him. And she did run away to South Carolina and marry him, so there, Mother and Daddy Chapman.

Sloan says, I'm sorry, I didn't follow that.

Malcolm tells Fife to hold off and go back a little and pick up where he was saying he was twenty-two and had already ruined his life. He claps his hands in front of the camera lens. He says Fife's name, the date and location.

6

FIFE WAKES, ENDING HIS DREAM. HE'S STILL IN RICH-
mond, he's at the home of his in-laws. It's morning.

He tries for a moment to remember the dream, the rules that determined its order, but can recall no more than a half dozen fading
images, so gives the effort up. He tries instead to recall what's going to
happen now: living here. Leaving here. Today. Now.

Turning from his back onto his left side, he studies Alicia's sleeping pregnant body. Beneath blankets, it lies in long mounds that churn
with life. His own stringy, inert flesh, as he slowly comes awake, grows
heavier and heavier, until finally, when he knows where the room is exactly and where he is located in it relative to everything else, his body,
immobile beneath the blankets, weighs on his thoughts like a fallen
log. One hand lies trapped beneath a hip, the other pressed against the
opposite hip, as if he has caught himself while applauding his dreams.

He tries lifting his free hand, hoping that his torso will spring
loose and glide easily away from this strange grasp. But the hand refuses to budge. He tries again. Nothing. Breathing heavily, he becomes
suddenly aware of his protruding ankle bones and knees and the top

leg pressing heavily down upon the leg beneath, both of them driving down into the mattress. Then his shoulders, and the weight of his chest. Even his skull presses downward, as if it's been carved from a block of stone and attached loosely to the still larger block of stone that is his body from his shoulders to his large, flat feet. A hard wind or a gang of vandals shoved him off his pedestal and left him to lie here on his side, seeping slowly into the cold soil, silent and motionless.

He groans, and a hand shoots up beneath the sheet that covers him. He slides one leg off the other and is able to free the hand that has been trapped by his hip. He feels his face wrinkle and knows that he is grimacing. His body still weighs on the bed like a fallen statue. It takes all his strength, but he manages to push and shove it from one place on the bed to another. Concentrating his efforts, he flops his body over onto its back again. Then onto its other side. Until he finds himself staring away from his wife toward the window.

Light filtering through membranes, he thinks. Why doesn't the darkness of the room flow the other way? Why doesn't the darkness chase the light? Heat chases cold.

He steps from the bed, pushing his naked limbs slowly ahead of him, and dresses, covering his body with the clothes he laid neatly across the chair by the window last night after packing, one item folded neatly on top of the other. His traveling clothes—socks and underwear, gray flannel slacks, white shirt, maroon foulard necktie, navy-blue blazer, all of it mail-ordered from Brooks Brothers, chosen for him by Alicia, menswear brand discrimination, learned from her father. He stuffs his pockets with the loose items on top of the dresser: wallet, change. He straps on his wristwatch.

A checklist: suitcase packed; all necessary papers in briefcase; two novels and a book of Hardy's poems in briefcase; ticket in jacket pocket; cash in wallet. Anything else? Checkbook? Yes. The bank check? In briefcase. Take another look, be sure. Yes, it's there.

Are you all ready to leave me and your little babies, born and un-born?

He turns, surprised and embarrassed. While he patted pockets and tapped suitcase and briefcase, Alicia has been watching him.

Not quite, he says. No. I haven't had breakfast yet. Go back to sleep. I'll come up and say goodbye before I go.

She yawns like a cat, her entire body tightening into a thick arch. Anybody else up yet?

Yeah, I think your mother. And Susannah. I don't know if Cornel's awake or not. You sure your mother doesn't mind taking me to the airport?

Forget it, sweetie. It's her thing, taking people to airports and wav-ing goodbye to them. She loves it.

What about Cornel? He may cry, Fife says.

Oh, let him sleep. I'll explain it to him later on. If he's awake and up, though, you might's well let him ride out to the airport with you and Mummy and say goodbye to you. She'll enjoy consoling him on the way back.

He smiles down at her and leaves the room, talking care to close the door quietly behind him, as if she's already fallen back to sleep. His body descends the carpeted stairs like water down a hillside stream, bumpity-bumpity-bump.

Seated side by side at the kitchen worktable, Cornel and his grand-mother eat together. The two, grandmother and grandchild, have agreed, without ever saying, that both enjoy meals more when the child refuses to eat until coaxed to do so by the grandmother. Cornel's middle name is Leonard, and no one in the family uses it, except on legal docu-ments.

Fife stands unseen at the kitchen door and listens with low-level irritation as his son coaxes the grandmother to coax him to eat more oatmeal. Fife is unsure why he's irritated. Come on, Cornel, she chirps.

Come on now, honey, just two more big spoonfuls. That's the sweet boy. There now, that wasn't difficult, was it, honey?

He enters the breakfast room adjacent to the kitchen, and Susannah looks over and sings, Good morning, Mr. Fife. He cringes and sits at the table.

H'lo, Susannah, he says, rushing to get it over with. No eggs or anything this morning, please. Just coffee and juice.

How about some beaten biscuits, Mr. Fife? They awful good, especially since you going on a long trip today.

Yeah, fine.

Good morning, Leo, his mother-in-law calls from the kitchen.

Good morning, Jessie. Hey, Cornel, say good morning to me.

Hello, Daddy.

Jessie, if you don't mind, I'd just as soon take a cab out to the airport. There's no need for you to drive all the way out there and back.

No, she says. He will not call a taxi. The drive to Byrd Field is a pleasant one. And there is nothing she'd prefer this beautiful morning than to drive across Richmond in the company of her son-in-law and grandson. It's spring, she announces. March thirty-first. And the city is too beautiful for words. Everything is suddenly blooming today, and she wants Cornel to see it all. You want to see the flowers, don't you, honey?

Where's Benjamin? Fife asks, suddenly aware of his father-in-law's absence.

He left early for the club. He said to wish you well. Oh, here's the paper, she says. Don't get up, I'll bring it to you. Sit still.

She strolls into the breakfast room and hands him the *Richmond Times-Dispatch*.

You haven't much time, she warns. Do you want to use Benjamin's electric shaver?

His hand goes to his cheek. He should have shaved last night, as he planned. Or else gotten up earlier this morning. He remembers Alicia's imitation of her father.

Alicia, honey, the man's unstable.

Then in her own voice: Of course, Daddy. What interesting twenty-two-year-old man isn't, for God's sake? I wouldn't want him stable.

But, Alicia, he's a college dropout. Not able to get himself a college degree.

He will, she answers. Did you and Uncle Jackson finish college, Daddy?

Causing her father to turn away from her, to stare out the library window at his gardens while easing sideways toward the liquor cabinet. The boy doesn't have a penny. He doesn't have a red cent, and his family doesn't, either.

He will if he marries me. She lights a cigarette and casually seats herself on a window ledge.

Facing the bar, he pours a double shot of bourbon, downs it. But how's it going to look?

To whom?

Well, to your friends, for instance. And to the rest of the family. To your own children someday. I imagine you do plan on having children. How will they explain it to their friends? Tell me that.

Alicia begins to laugh.

You laugh, but you'll see I'm right. I knew it the minute I laid eyes on him.

Alicia reported the exchange to Fife shortly after it occurred. Fife believes that was the moment when Benjamin decided to hire a private detective to check out the young man's story, and a month later he learned that Leonard Fife had already been married once and divorced. Alicia had known it all along, but had not told her parents or anyone else. When her father put the detective's report in front of her, Alicia laughed, and eventually so did they all, long afterward—Fife, Jessie, even Benjamin himself. Alicia knew all about that brief, misbegotten marriage. It is not at all unusual for a sensitive, honorable young man from his background to marry his first serious girlfriend, only to learn quickly that it was a mistake. What is unusual, Daddy, is that he had the grace to call it a mistake and undo it.

In spite of the laughter and the slowly accumulated respect and trust, Fife has not forgotten the early anger, fear, and distrust. Every time he looks into a mirror and begins to shave, his razor poised high and tight to his right earlobe, he remembers, and for a second he tries to see himself as he must have looked to Benjamin back then, when he came to Richmond the first time, driving south from Boston with Alicia in her Morris Minor to meet her parents, a tall, skinny, hairy youth with a complicated, slightly sordid past and nothing more to recommend him than his plans for an even more complicated and only slightly less sordid future. He feels toward that entire period the way he would toward a birthmark—embarrassed, yet blameless.

Well, Jessie repeats, do you want to use Benjamin's shaver?

If I have time, maybe I'll step into a barbershop in Washington. There's an hour and a half layover between planes. It'll give me something to do.

All right then, she says and spins and exits into the kitchen in a swirl of yellow sundress and frozen smile.

He drinks his orange juice and coffee and munches on buttered, oven-warmed beaten biscuits, glancing across the front page of the *Times-Dispatch*. Vice President Hubert Humphrey is in town. Dr. Martin Luther King's poor people's march is unnecessary, claims Humphrey. Any grievances Dr. King might wish to air can be heard effectively by top government officials without marches or demonstrations. On the war in Vietnam, Humphrey says the Johnson-Humphrey administration is open to peace negotiations if there's even the slightest indication that the enemy is willing to negotiate in good faith. The real peace candidate in these primaries is Lyndon B. Johnson, he says. Farther down, a box announces that tonight at nine the peace-loving President Johnson will tell the country by radio and TV that he's ordering an increase in troops and spending for the war. Fife will be at Stanley

Reinhart's by then. They'll probably have to watch it, with Stanley bellowing insults at Johnson. Firebombs went off yesterday in New York at Macy's, Bloomingdale's, Gimbel's, and Klein's, and a dynamite blast shattered thirty windows at New York's major Selective Service induction center.

He peers out the window of the breakfast room at a corner of the large yard, the manicured lawns, a luminous springtime shade of green already, and the blossoming dogwood and Judas trees. Through the trees and beyond he can glimpse slate-colored scraps of the James River. The yardman, as they call him, comes slowly into view. Fife thinks his name is Joseph or Calvin or Roger. He carries a small fireplace shovel and a metal dustpan. Crossing the yard to the far corner where the lawn droops to meet a clutch of shiny dark-green magnolia trees, he stops, bends down slowly, carefully shovels a small lump of dog turd into his dustpan. Then he stands and resumes his search, passing out of Fife's view to the other side of the house.

Your plane leaves in little over an hour, Leo! Jessie calls. We better leave for the airport in five, to be safe. Okay?

Can I go, Daddy? Cornel asks, more from a desire to be polite than a need for his father's permission. The boy's mother and grandmother have both reassured him that he can help take his daddy to the airport.

Yes, you can go with me, Fife says uselessly. As far as the airport, anyhow. He finishes his coffee and gets up from the table. Then you'll have to come back here with Meema, okay?

Okay, Cornel says quietly and lapses into silence.

Is he afraid? Fife wonders. Or does he assume with the others that after a week away, Fife will be coming back here? The boy doesn't realize that Vermont is a place distinct from this place, a thousand miles away. Once there, his father, if he chooses, will be free not to return. Cornel believes that his father has no such choice. Or desire. He believes that his father will simply disappear from his sight for seven days and nights, only to reappear suddenly, as if by magic, waving from the doorway of an airplane. Waving neither hello nor goodbye, but, Here I am again.

So why should he be afraid?

In their bedroom Fife leans down in the soft gray light to kiss his wife's sleeping face, and her eyes flutter open, like a bird taking flight.

You look very beautiful. I'll miss you, he says. Are you feeling all right?

She smiles. Have you got everything you'll need?

Yes. He kisses her on the lips once and then on each cheek.

Will you be able to call me tonight?

From Reinhart's, yes. I'll call, don't worry.

Is Cornel going with you?

Just to the airport.

That's what I mean, silly. Good. I'm glad.

Why?

I don't know. She shrugs. I guess because it'll make it easier for me. To explain why you're not here for the next week. He's going to miss you, you know. He's used to having you around all the time.

I'm his only father.

He's your only son. At the moment, anyhow. Do you want to talk more about last night? About Daddy and Uncle Jackson and Doctor Todd's?

Tonight. On the phone.

Yes, of course. I didn't mean now.

Right. Listen, I've got to get going or I'll miss the plane. I love you, take care of yourself. He waves casually as he leaves the room, his suitcase dangling from his left hand, his briefcase stuck under his arm. He shuts the bedroom door on her, then hears her call.

Leo! Did you forget to shave?

Jessie and Cornel are already seated in the car, waiting for him. Fife flings his two bags ahead of him and climbs heavily into the back seat. His son looks around from the front and gently smiles. Can I get a Popsicle? he says, this time asking sincerely for permission. A Creamsicle! Can I get a Creamsicle?

I don't know, Fife answers. It's too early. There isn't enough time.

What flavor, sweetie? Jessie asks.

Orange on the outside, vanilla on the inside!

Fine, dear. We'll stop and get you one after we take Daddy to the airport. We'll have more time then. Sit down on the seat now, sweetie. It's dangerous to stand while the car's moving.

She backs the green Mercedes out of the garage and heads it down the long, gently curving driveway to the street.

Fife lets his weight sink into the upholstered seat behind and beneath him, and his body once again feels heavy to him, a solid mass yanking him deeper into the seat. He tries to raise one hand to lower the window and discovers that he can barely lift it off his lap. His feet press themselves against the carpeted floor, and his thighs crush the cushioning beneath them. He slowly turns his head to the right and finds that he's looking out the car window at nothing but blurs and flashes of colored light that turn out to be large brick homes with impeccable lawns, and in front of them and on either side, chalk white and rosy pink clumps of fruit cherry and flowering trees. There are gardenias, dogwoods, drooping willow trees, tulips and deep pink Judas trees, all coming abundantly to life and sweeping past him, as if in flight.

To stop his flight, he runs through his schedule. He will leave Richmond at 9:15 a.m. and arrive in Washington at 10:03. Then, changing from Piedmont to Eastern Airlines, he'll take off from Washington at 11:30 and arrive in Boston at 1:20 p.m. He'll rent a car and leave Boston before 2:00 for Reinhart's home in Plainfield, Vermont, which will let him have dinner that evening with Stanley and his wife, Gloria. The business of completing the purchase of the house can begin in earnest tomorrow morning. He recites this as if memorizing it.

Jessie says, We won't get out of the car, Leo. It'll be easier to say goodbye here. For C-O-R-N-E-L. Okay?

Sure.

Have a pleasant flight, Leonard. And call us tonight when you get in.

Call us. Not call me, not call Alicia, your wife, or Cornel, your child. Call us. The family, Leonard.

Fife looks out the car window and sees that they have arrived at the entrance of the terminal. A young, mustachioed Black porter stands next to the glass door of the terminal, peering over at the Mercedes, waiting for the occupants to indicate whether they'll need his services. Fife leans forward from the back seat and kisses Jessie on her dry cheek, surprised to find it powdered and smelling heavily of perfume, the same Alicia uses, Chanel No. 5. I'll call tonight from Reinhart's.

Then his son. He puts his arm around the boy's tiny shoulders, kisses him on the cheek. He feels strangely self-conscious, as if Cornel were someone else's child, a stranger's, and it confuses him. Be a good boy. And take care of your mother, he adds.

He is mortified by his own words. The tinny, insincere sound of his voice repulses him even more than the words. Well . . . goodbye. I'll call in tonight from Reinhart's, he says again. He grabs his suitcase and briefcase and scrambles clumsily from the vehicle.

Have a nice flight! Jessie calls.

He slams the door. He shakes the porter off. Waving a hand at the car, he turns, and he is headed for the glass door when he hears Cornel start to cry and then to sob loudly. Looking back over his shoulder, he sees his son's small, round face go soft. Fife wants to turn back and comfort the child. He looks away from him and lurches for the door. The porter's hand snakes in front of his own and swings the door open for him. Fife passes through and into the terminal.

As he passes, the porter chuckles. That little boy don't want his daddy to leave.

Fife keeps on moving.

7

I'M SORRY TO STOP YOU AGAIN, MAN, BUT WE'VE GOT TO change cards. You sure you're okay with doing this? Malcolm asks. I mean, you're not too tired, are you? Want to take a break for a while?

No. I don't. I'm just getting started, Malcolm.

Well, yeah. Okay. But it's kind of weird. I mean, I practically don't have to ask you any questions. You're just running with it, and like, well, some of it's hard to follow, Leo. A lifetime of interviewing people, and you're finally the one being interviewed, so I guess you know the drill, the interviewer has to follow where the interviewee leads. That sort of thing. But it's a problem.

A problem? What do you mean?

Well, a lot of it doesn't jibe, Malcolm tells him. And some of it doesn't line up. It's a little confused. And confusing. And you're going way off-script. Like with that novel you mentioned writing back there in your twenties. What was it called? Malcolm thinks Fife said he was living in Virginia then. Or someplace in the American South, it sounded like. Unclear, man.

Fife says he's forgotten the title.

Okay. What happened to it, the manuscript? I'd love to read it, man.

No, you wouldn't want to read it.

Did you ever publish it?

Emma says, Leave it, Malcolm. Please. Just leave it.

What d'you make of it, Emma, this stuff he's saying? I mean, the bits about the Virginians, for instance, and the foot powder company. Where does that fit? Malcolm tells her he's having trouble tying it all together. It's like Fife's dreaming or something and he's telling them his dream. It's kind of disconnected.

Just let it go, Emma says. Don't correct him or say this or that didn't happen or couldn't have happened. It freaks him out when you try to correct him. What's true for him is what's true, period.

Diana says Emma's right, they should let Fife tell his story the way he wants it told. They're making a film, not a biography.

Malcolm asks Emma if she has heard any of this before, something about a wife in Virginia and a kid. It's pretty much a mashup. Hard to sort out the strands.

I don't want to say. He gets upset when I correct him.

Fife interrupts them and tells Vincent to keep shooting, for Christ's sake. He needs to get this all down on-camera, he says, while he can still remember what happened and what didn't happen. Like that novel he wrote. He says that when he was still in grad school in Virginia, he mailed the manuscript to an agent in New York, and she talked an editor at Random House into buying it, and just as it was being copyedited, the guy left Random House to become the fiction editor at *Playboy*. It got orphaned, as they say. The agent said it would be abandoned and remaindered a week after publication and urged him to withdraw the novel and sell it to another publishing house, where it would have an editor to support it. Random House let Fife keep the advance, a couple thousand bucks was all, and sent the manuscript back, and then he made the mistake of rereading it. Except it wasn't a mistake. The novel was no good. It was shit. Pretentious literary drivel. He's lucky it wasn't published. He says he has no idea what happened to the manuscript. Things disappear. They get lost. Or left behind. Like people you once loved or who loved you. He says he's one of those exploratory robotic spacecraft that somehow slip past the gravitational fields of all nine planets in the solar system and never orbit or crash into anything, and eventually they sail out of the solar system, blown by the solar wind beyond the heliosphere into deep space. That's where he is now, riding the interstellar wind in deep space.

Malcolm says to Vincent, You getting all this?

We're up and running. I got it.

Emma says, Please stop. Leo darling, you shouldn't put yourself through this. And Malcolm and Diana, it's cruel to film him when he's . . . when he's not himself. She says she has to leave now. This is very distressing, she says.

No, you have to stay here, Fife says. If she leaves the room, he won't be able to make the interview, and it's his final gift to her, he says. He's got nothing else to give to her now, he's only able to take from her, take take take, he stammers. Take, take, take.

Malcolm jumps in front of the camera and claps his hands and for the third time says Fife's name and location, and the interview continues.

Fife speaks into the darkness that surrounds him, Wait a minute! Are you still there, Emma? I need to be sure.

Renée, Fife's nurse, answers in French. Do you want me to change your bag, Monsieur Fife? I'm here if you need me. It's been a while, you know.

Jesus! I'm fine, Renée. Fine. Emma, are you there? I can't do this, unless I know you're listening.

Do what? What can't you do unless I'm listening?

Tell everything.

You can tell everything to Malcolm and to Vincent's camera, Leo.

I can watch the film later. I can watch the outtakes, even. But you should be resting, not talking. This whole thing upsets me. Besides, I've got a lot to do today, Leo. Some of it's fairly urgent.

No, no, no! Fife repeats that if he can't say it in public like this to her in person, and she can't hear it as he speaks it, then he won't know what to leave in and what to leave out, what to say and what not to say. He won't know what tone of voice to use, words to choose, people and events and actions to keep in and people and events and actions to leave out. He is shaping everything that he says strictly for her, no one else. Definitely not for Malcolm and his crew, who will edit it for strangers to hear and watch on their screens, people for whom Fife is also a stranger, one they might have read about in the papers, if they happen to read about Canadian documentary filmmakers, or one whose films they may have seen, if they happen to enjoy left-wing muckraking cinema—people for whom Leonard Fife is no more than an image, a fictional character in a movie played by a relatively unknown character actor.

I don't want to argue with you, Leo. I don't know why you can't just tell me privately the things you want me to know.

Everyone is silent for a moment.

Because in private he can't keep himself from lying to her, Fife says. In private, one to one, he has complete control over everything he tells her, as if he doesn't really exist. When they are alone together, there are no witnesses to corroborate or contradict his testimony. There's no unwobbling pivot, no center to his universe, no controlling field of gravity, no sun that holds everything together. When they're alone, it's like what Gertrude Stein said about Oakland, there's no there there, so it doesn't matter if what Fife says is true or false, because everything he says in private is both true and false and neither.

Emma says, Okay, okay, whatever. I'll let it go a while longer. I'll stay and listen, at least till lunch. But then I've got to get to my desk and my computer and phone. It's important, Leo, that I keep working throughout . . . all this. Okay, love? I wish I could protect you better, though. It's not as though I haven't heard most of this before, anyhow. Or at least some version of it.

I've never told any of this to you before, or to anyone else! And even if I did, you had no way of knowing if any of it was true. Maybe it was all lies.

All right, love. All right. So go on, let Malcolm ask his next question.

8

FIFE DOESN'T GIVE MALCOLM A CHANCE TO ASK ANY-
thing. He just picks up his story where he thinks he left off telling it,
at 10:35 a.m. on March 31, 1968, as he enters Washington National
feeling strangely rushed. Somehow since he left Richmond he's lost
over thirty minutes. It happened in the air. A half-hour flight took an
hour. Where does lost time go? he wonders, and stops at a news kiosk
to buy a *New York Times* and loses another, smaller chunk of time.

Striding past freshly reunited families and anxious, ticket-clenching
passengers searching for the right gate, he bisects a line of female flight
attendants slowly making their way to the coffee shop and climbs two
steps at a time up the escalator to the main lobby of the terminal and
arrives winded, wet with sweat, at the Eastern Airlines counter, where
he has his flight through to Boston confirmed by a young man in a
gray-and-blue uniform.

All set, Mr. Fife. Flight 467 to Boston at 11:30 from Gate 14. We'll
be boarding in about twenty minutes. Plenty of time. He whacks the
stapler. Smiles.

Fife stuffs the ticket into his jacket pocket and heads down the ramps and corridors to Gate 14. The waiting area is crowded with servicemen, students returning to college or coasting on home for spring break, and detached segments of families trying to rejoin the main body. Stationed inside a circular booth in the center of the room, a fresh-faced, uniformed female version of the man who confirmed Fife's flight smiles at him and asks to see his ticket. She peers at it for a second and waves him to the side of the room where most of the older and nonmilitary and nonstudent passengers have gathered.

He sits down in an empty chair next to the wall, opens the *Times* on his lap and begins to read. 9 Nations Vote to Adapt "Paper Gold" Money Plan; France Refuses to Join.

What does that mean? Must be a big deal, it's a capitalized headline. But what's a "paper gold" money plan? What's paper gold? What's money? Everybody seems to understand it, except him. He slowly reads the subheadline, one word at a time: Assets Can Be Added to World Reserves to Expand Trade. It's in English, but he has no understanding of the words. It's as if they're in Russian or Serbian. He skips quickly down the front page. Johnson to Talk to Nation Tonight on Vietnam War. Okay, those words he understands. Nothing about money. And farther down, Fires Set in Bloomingdale's and Klein's . . . Molotov Cocktails Are Used by Arsonists. And an article about an army doctor, a dermatologist named Howard Levy imprisoned at Fort Leavenworth for protesting against the Vietnam War and refusing to train Green Berets to treat skin injuries.

Seated beside him, a slim Asian man in a black suit with a book-sized 8 mm movie camera films the room and the nearly motionless, mostly silent people in it. The box clicks quietly as the man swings it slowly, smoothly from one corner of the room to the other, bringing it all the way around to Fife, who looks up from his newspaper and stares directly into the black lens and sees himself staring surprised back from inside the camera, his head huge and body tiny and misshapen.

He looks away from the cyclops, returns his gaze to the newspaper, and the camera swings and aims away to the far corner again, as if it has seen and filmed nothing, no one. As if there is no evidence of Leonard Fife's having been seen and filmed at Washington National Airport on March 31, 1968, at 10:48 a.m. The man with the camera will get home to Seoul and will screen his travel footage to friends and family, who will ask about the American man with the mustache and long hair. Who knows? Just a businessman, maybe. He admired and filmed the American's nice blue blazer and striped necktie. The traveler will tell his family that most Americans dress too casually when they travel, but not this one.

Relaxing somewhat, Fife begins again to read. He cruises the book reviews first, finds nothing of interest—a long review of Erik Erikson's *Identity: Youth and Crisis*, and V. S. Pritchett on a collection of essays by Maxim Gorky, and Irving Howe on a biography of Solomon Aleichem written by Aleichem's daughter. Fife skitters over an article in the magazine section on teenage drug use. Nothing holds his attention for more than a paragraph.

Another lost piece of time, and Fife sees that the plane is only half filled, and he is able to sit wherever he prefers—next to a window at the very rear of the aircraft, which he's heard is the safest place on the plane, the section that usually remains intact when the plane crashes. It's where the survivors—when there are any—sit. The plane is a Whisperjet. He looks out the window and sees the gigantic jet engines positioned at the rear next to the fuselage, just below the wings. The noise during takeoff will be deafening. Not whispering. He decides to stay put anyhow. Safety first.

Sliding his briefcase under the seat in front of him, he buckles himself in and spreads the remnants of his newspaper across his lap. A sofa-sized woman in her fifties wearing a business suit and very little jewelry and no makeup looms up in the aisle beside him and asks if anyone is sitting in the seat next to him. He says no, and the woman, relieved, drops heavily into the seat, her cheeks and chins joggling for a few seconds after the main parts of her body have come to rest.

She, too, carries a *New York Times*. She flips open to the financial pages. Fife casts a glance across her arm and hand and looks at what she is reading. Arabic numbers. That's all, just numbers, he thinks. What's the matter with him? He's not stupid. But why can't he read and interpret those numbers and as a result know that the economy is in decent shape, at least for the foreseeable future? Or not. Maybe the stock market is about to tank. His ignorance of the language used to describe the American economy worries him, and he promises himself to buy one of those popular newsstand books, *How to Buy and Sell Stocks and Bonds* or *The Stock Market Made Easy*. He will extract from it just enough information to enable him to read and understand the financial section of the newspaper and the quarterly reports that Alicia's trust officer, Mr. Keefe, mails to her and compare the two. He isn't afraid of his wife's being short-changed or otherwise cheated by the trust department at the largest, most reputable bank in the state of Virginia. He simply wants to feel free to offer an opinion—to Alicia, to Jessie and Benjamin and Jackson, to his friends—as to whether Mr. Keefe is doing a job that is more or less competent. He would like to seem to know where the economy in general and Alicia's economy in particular are headed. He would like to know what it means to adopt a paper gold plan, and why France refuses to join. He would like to know why adding assets to world reserves will expand trade.

The sudden explosive roar of the jet engines startles him. He looks out the window, half expecting to see great clouds of smoke and rising flames. He can't connect the huge rising noise to the intense stillness of the object emitting it, but in seconds the roar of the engines envelopes him, and he relaxes inside it and begins to enjoy the solitude it provides. He watches lips move, but hears no words. A tall smiling female flight attendant chatters silently at a bewildered, worried-looking little girl, and a bald, sunburnt man down the aisle from him stands up and, without making a sound, waves and mouths words to a woman, evidently his wife, lugging a straw bag filled with Caribbean souvenirs. Suddenly buoyant, almost giddy, Fife feels that something is about to happen, a big reveal that will affect everyone on the plane except him, as if the plane is about to explode and he will be the sole survivor, and from his perch he will be allowed to watch unscathed, untouched, unchanged.

The roar of the engines fades and shreds of conversation drift toward each other, meet, coalesce, and take on solid shapes with discrete beginnings and endings—causes and effects that turn into new, unused causes. He's formalizing everything he perceives. It's not a compulsion, he believes, it's a moral impulse. He believes that he creates these beginnings and endings, causes and effects, so that he can hold a moral opinion. So that he can say what any given action or inaction is worth.

Every particular event of Fife's life so far, every action or inaction, everything done or undone, invites his judgment. He can't seem to isolate one action or inaction from another. The quotidian logic of chronology is too much for him: he's constantly confusing sequence, causation, and purpose. Six years! he thinks. Six years of reenacting the brief sequence of events that began with his first marriage and ended with this life with Alicia. But look how now, even in saying it to himself, the end of one thing smears over into the beginning of another. And look at how the start of a new sequence, his life with Alicia, takes its character from the end of an old one, like the chapters of a perfectly made novel, until initiation, complication, development, and resolution all blend and become inseparable.

He tries to recall if it was the same back then, six years ago and even before. He asks if it has always been the same. Yes and no, and sometimes neither yes and no, nor even maybe. He wrote it then, and the phrase comes back still intact after having lain nearly forgotten for six

years. He destroyed the manuscript that contained it. He destroyed
nearly all of those early writings. But he knows that he wrote somewhere in a barely begun novel, *Yes and no, and sometimes neither yes
and no, nor even maybe.* He didn't know what it meant, but he wrote
it down anyhow. He was nineteen years old and was already thinking
of himself as a Writer, as a man committed to understanding himself
and the world by means of language. But no matter what he pretended
to Amy, his adoring child bride, and to his less intense, less verbal
friends, he had no words. None of his own. Oh, he could talk, all right,
he could talk through the night into the day, a young bohemian in
Boston's cold, dark Back Bay in the early 1960s. But he was too young
and confused and ill-educated and frightened to give any meaning to
the talk, so he simply reversed the poles and took meaning back from
the talk and believed whatever he said.

We each of us value our own consciousness above all others. And
we must do this. We must do it in order to justify what we are bending
our lives to, which is the making of art.

He pauses, waiting for the passionate tone of his words, not their
meaning, to sink in. Opening his mouth yet again, more words and
new tones flow out.

We're all basically romantics. Don't let the realists fool you. If they
claim to be artists in any sense of the word, then you better believe
they're romantics, just as we are.

And he tries to behave—until more, equally attractive words come
and clack before him—in whatever way his talk indicates he should
behave. As a romantic. Okay, he'll give that a try. He roams the streets
of the city, those cold gray streets, one whole winter in search of a Ver-
laine for his Rimbaud, a Gauguin for his Van Gogh, a Shelley for his
Byron. He finds one, he finds several.

But by early summer that year, when Heidi is born and for the first
time he is a father, he has taken a job as a clerk in a bookstore on Huntington Avenue, and now he has discovered Flaubert. Like flocks of

birds, new words swiftly appear, and his life blithely flops over again, with old vices revealed suddenly as virtues, and old virtues lamented for their wasteful issue. Amy, only eighteen years old, pregnant from the month before they married, carries their infant in her arms. At Amy's insistence, incomprehensible to Fife, they have named the baby after the girl from the Alps in *Heidi*, Amy's favorite book. She says she always wanted to be like Heidi, and if not, then to have a daughter like Heidi, who will take care of her when she is old. Fife shrugs and goes along, because, except in the matter of the naming, Amy follows wherever Fife leads, and he follows indiscriminately his words. Until finally he begins to see her confusion and admits his own.

Up to that point he was behaving like any other barely educated, self-absorbed twenty-year-old man who wants to be regarded as a writer much more than he actually wants to learn how to write. But watching his teenage wife listen to him, her eyes wide open and focused on his mouth from across the room, her knees together and the baby balanced precariously on her lap while she holds the baby's bottle with no consciousness of what she's doing or of the two or three other people in the room, usually young men his age or a few years older, men named Franz or Ham or Sammy or Stanley, Fife sees the expression on her face gradually, subtly change—from one of waiting to one of confusion and eventually to one of fear and then despair.

At first she is waiting just as he is waiting for the words to come that will say, finally, unequivocally, in bell-like tones, that now everything may begin. But sometime during that winter the denials and reversals and contradictions and rejections begin to close in on each other and devour each other, so that his wild assertions become more and more absolute in nature and frantic in tone. He claims to have read and hated books he has barely heard of. He supports arguments with lengthy quotations made up on the spot, frequently referring to authors who never lived. Though he isn't sure why, he attempts to give himself the authority his words have begun to lack, and he claims to have traveled to lands he knows only from maps and magazines. With reckless abandon he shuffles the episodes and chronologies of his childhood and adolescence and the forces that shaped them, destroying fragile structures of memory as fast as he extemporizes new and radically different pasts. He creates women and describes lengthy, elaborate affairs with them, and later that same evening, in bed with the teenage girl he married in Florida less than a year before, he is forced to flesh out these shadowy figures, to give each of them a name and a past of her own and a precise location in present time and place.

Confusion begins to well up in Amy's eyes, placing a watery film between her and everything she sees. But that's not what you told me! she cries out in the dark. You told me that you had been a Protestant all your life, that you were raised a Protestant. A Presbyterian. I remember you said it, that you were a morbid Yankee Calvinist, those are your very words, Leo!

Well, there's more to it than that. Much more. Yes, I was raised as a Presbyterian. Yes, I was. But my mother, she was originally Catholic. My father was Presbyterian. Until I was six or seven, I can't remember exactly when, I was raised as a Catholic, but when my first Holy Communion rolled around, my father's Protestant hackles went up, and as a result my mother, who worried more about keeping my father happy than she did God, relented, and from then on I was sent to Presbyterian and Congregational Sunday schools wherever we lived, even in Mexico and during the year my father worked in North Africa, which wasn't all that easy in a Muslim country, and goes to show you how frightened my mother was of losing or rather of displeasing my father. It was simpler in Sweden, of course. She would have had trouble even finding a priest.

Why am I learning all this now? she asks. Why?

It's never come up. You've never asked. How should I know? For Christ's sake, we got married five weeks after we met. Did you think you knew then all there was to know about me? I'm still finding out about your past, why shouldn't you still be finding out about mine? Why, for example, didn't I know before last week, or whenever you finally decided to tell me, that your mother's first husband, your biological father, killed himself when you were three years old? That was quite a revelation. It explains a lot.

That's different, Leo. And besides, you already knew he committed suicide. My mother told you even before we got married, or right after. It was how he did it that you didn't know before. And I don't know what that explains, that he did it with a shotgun.

I didn't know that you were three years old at the time. Your mother led me to believe that you were still an infant when it happened. There's a big difference between being an infant when your father shoots himself and being three years old when it happens.

And on into the night, half quarreling, half explaining, until she falls asleep or he is able to change the subject or until, in frustration and shame and rage, he leaves the bed and, barking self-righteously at her for her stupidity and insecurities, storms from the apartment.

Once free, walking the quiet streets of the city in the early summer night with a cooling breeze at the back of his neck, he heads east toward the harbor and crosses to the waterfront, there to wander among the wharves and the silent warehouses and deserted counting rooms, the huge motionless black ships looming in the gloom, the occasional produce trucks bumping empty past him toward some midnight assignment in a warehouse somewhere in Charlestown or Somerville, the glistening black sedans that squish by behind him and slip furtively down a narrow cobbled side street or alley. Listening to the foghorns and bells from the harbor, the black water lapping against thick pilings and cut granite sides of ancient dockside buildings and the sound of his footsteps rapidly clicking on pavement, Fife walks alone, and he dreams of flight and the freedom it will bring.

He is twenty years old, and he has locked himself into an ornate shrinking cage. If he can somehow escape his cage, everything will be different, he thinks. All this—the lies, the poses, the fraudulent insistence that nothing but right decisions have been made, no matter how radical or wrongheaded—all this will be finished, and a new beginning, fresh, clean, and above all, honest, can be established. But in order to rid himself of his lies and mistakes and their justifications, he will have to remove from his life the living proof of his pathetic haplessness—his child bride and their child, their infant daughter, the helpless, blameless, perishable consequence of the marriage.

There seem no more than two alternatives. The first is flight, while his daughter is still an infant and does not know him in any conscious way. Soon she will be a year old, and she will have a word that she uses to call him to her. And then she will be two years old, and they will have been to places together, zoos, picnics, the beach, the park, and three years old, like Amy when her father blew his head off, and he will have explained many things to her. By that time Heidi will remember too much of him for her to be cut free of him. And Amy, too, will have known him for too long to begin anew anything that he has not tainted. For she has loved him honestly somehow from the beginning.

The other alternative is for him to continue with what he has begun. To go on saying, I love you more than I can ever say, and I will never leave you. Which is all she asks of him. To purge his life of the trivial, compulsive lies that have begun to swarm around him everywhere he goes, even when alone, and to focus his diverted energies on finding a better job than stock boy in the basement of a bookstore and then a better-paying, more respectable position, and then one still further up the ladder, climbing rung by rung all the way to financial security and social respectability, while his desires to become a writer get postponed until old age. Or abandoned altogether.

What he can no longer bring himself to do, after having done it more or less effortlessly over and over again for more than a year, is tell Amy, his young wife, that needy, pretty, gentle teenage girl, that he loves her. Deeply, intensely loves her. Her unique person. The fact of her. That he loves the totally real and individuated existence that is her. The trim, muscular, chalk-white body. The bony, attenuated face with deep-set blue eyes, large and almost rectangular in shape. The pale-blond hair that loops heavily down nearly to her waist. The freckles on her cheeks and the darker orange-tinted freckles on her shoulders and arms. The chunky pink-tipped breasts and the quick thighs and thrust of groin. The lazy walk. The low wandering voice with the trace of southern accent. The benign self-contained indifference to anyone not speaking directly to her. The good-natured friendly openness to cab-drivers' and janitors' and wine-drunk college students' desire to engage her in conversation. The maternal intelligence expressed by her fingers and breasts and eyes without her even thinking about it. And also the needs, seldom if ever named. The needs that swell secretly in darkness, driving her to frenzies of insecurity and fear, superstition and fantasy and knee-buckling cries of despair in the middle of the night, until, falling onto the floor of the tiny bathroom, pressing her swollen wet face against the cold tile, her pink filmy nightgown awry, a tight green bud somewhere deep in her brain slowly opens out and spreads huge petals across her mind, and in terror she cries, Help me, oh, God, don't leave me, please, oh my God, please help me, Leo, don't leave me alone, please don't leave me . . .

He doesn't know how to define love, or if he's capable of experiencing it, because he never has loved anyone, but he says it anyway. I love you, Amy! I'll never leave, I swear it, I'll never leave you! I swear it, I love you.

Please, Leo, please.

Maybe if he says it often enough, he will feel it. The words will make it happen. He says, I love you, Amy! I swear it! I'll never leave you alone. I love you. Holding her head in his lap, he strokes with his fingertips her cheek, her shoulder, her wet matted hair. The harsh bathroom light, the only light burning in the apartment, in the entire building, splashes across their nearly naked bodies, the lavatory, the toilet and bathtub, the pale-green walls, the gleaming tile floor, and he hears his voice, as if listening to an actor use it on a stage far down and away from him, repeating over and over again, I love you, Amy, I love you, I do love you.

Until hours later, her head still cradled in his arms, she is calm and still and silent, and he lifts her slowly to her feet and leads her into the bedroom and lays her down in the bed and covers her with the blanket. And as the room—small, shabby, crowded with clothes and second-hand furniture and a baby's crib and bassinet—grows slowly gray with cold light from the dawn sky, he watches Amy sleep. And he watches the baby, Heidi, sleep.

9

VINCENT MUMBLES SOMETHING ABOUT THE CARD.

Malcolm in a low voice says, Good, and asks Sloan to turn up the houselights. I mean, flip the wall switch for the living room lamps, he adds.

The lights come on, startling Fife, as if he hasn't heard Vincent and Malcolm or didn't understand what they were saying. Where has he been a-roaming? Richmond, Washington, Boston? Nineteen sixty-eight, 1962, 2018? And who has he roamed with, and who is with him here? Where is here? Was he hallucinating then, or is he hallucinating now?

Malcolm seems uncharacteristically subdued. Perhaps he's confused by what Fife has been telling them.

What's the bastard plotting? Fife wonders. He looks around the suddenly brightened room, blinking, trying to bring his surroundings into focus. It's too bright. He's dizzy and nauseous again. Whatever is slopping around in his stomach, a slush of liquid nutrients and medication, is working its way toward his throat. A small squirt of it enters his mouth from below. It tastes like battery acid. He swallows and flicks his dry lips with his tongue and gulps air and drives the liquid back down again.

Dizziness displaces nausea. The room spins, and the people in it pass by as if they're riding a carousel and he's seated at the center, harnessed into his wheelchair. No one speaks. There goes Emma—she is working her iPhone with her thumbs, sending a text message. Renée swirls past—she looks half asleep, dozing, her chin almost resting on her chest. Diana rides by—she shuffles the pages of a legal pad, flips through the yellow sheets searching for a sentence, one of their dumb questions meant for Fife, scrambling for her lines, as if she's missed her cue. There goes pretty young Sloan—she stares at Fife as she passes, looking puzzled, intrigued, a half smile of pity on her lips. Or is it sympathy? He'd welcome the sympathy of a pretty young woman right now. But not her pity. No. And there goes the artfully groomed, bearded, bow-tied Vincent and his camera—he doesn't look at Fife. It seems almost deliberate, a looking away, rather than merely glancing elsewhere, as if the sight of Fife in real life, not through a lens, embarrasses him. And here comes Malcolm again, arms folded across his narrow chest—he's deep in thought now, or so it appears. Emma again. Renée. Sloan. Vincent. Emma.

Fife calls out to Renée, I think I'm going to vomit!

To Sloan, in a too-loud voice, he says: You need to shut the lights off!

To Malcolm: I can only do this in darkness. I can't do it with the lights on me. With the lights on, I can't remember anything.

To Emma, almost apologetically: It's the meds, he says. I'm sorry, Emma.

To Diana: Can't we do this in the dark? I told you I can only do this in darkness.

To Sloan again: The Speedlight's okay, but that's all. Put the other lights out, please. Except for the Speedlight.

Everyone seems to be answering him at once now: Malcolm,

Emma, Renée, Diana, Sloan, Vincent, their layered voices and words overlapping one another.

Of course, man, no problem, but no reason we have to finish this today. I can tell you're tired. Your mind is wandering and you're a little disconnected, right? I mean, what you're saying is a little disconnected and confusing. Maybe you're a little confused.

Confused? I'm not confused. Fife senses that Malcolm is angry.

No, not confused, man. I don't mean that. Confuse-ing. It's a little unclear who you're talking about sometimes, is all. And what. What and who you're talking about.

Emma says, No, it's all very clear, darling. At least to me it is. But I'm not the one you're supposed to be addressing, Leo. Am I?

Diana says, Leo, let's take a break now and try again tomorrow. If you feel up to it then.

Malcolm again: Yeah, that's cool, and maybe we can get back to those early days in Montreal and the early antiwar stuff and the Gagetown film. How you managed to shoot that, in spite of everything being top secret and no one willing to talk about the defoliant tests and working with the US military on Canadian soil and both governments denying everything.

Monsieur Fife, do you wish me to take you back to your bedroom now? Are you going to be sick, Monsieur Fife?

It's the light. It's too hard on my eyes. I can't see with all the light.

Hey, Sloan, go ahead and kill the lights, okay?

The lights go out, except for the Godox overhead.

Okay, Leo, we really need to come back to Malcolm's and my questions, Diana says, but if you're feeling too tired or feeling sick . . .

C'mon, love, this isn't working. Let Renée take you back to the bedroom. What you've been telling us is interesting and all, and it's pretty fresh, at least to people who don't know you as well as I do. But it's not really what Malcolm and Diana need for their film, is it?

Yeah, Leo, Emma's right. I mean, we like hearing this stuff about your early years from before you moved to Canada, but that's not the story we want the film to tell. You know what I'm saying? Leo?

Mr. Fife? Is it okay if I remove the mic? Malcolm, want me to take off his mic? Or should I keep recording? I mean, we are getting all this, you know. I can use the boom instead.

Yes, love, see? That's what I mean. They're filming and recording everything you've been saying, but frankly I don't think it's wise to go on like this. In this vein, I mean. You don't have control over what will end up in the film and exposed to the public. You don't need all this to be made public. Malcolm and Diana, this is a bad idea, making this interview now. Leo, dear, listen to me. A lot of what you've been saying could prove embarrassing to you. And to me, too. And to some of the people from your past, who you've been naming and who may still be alive and could end up seeing this someday.

No, it's okay, Leo. We'll edit out anything that's embarrassing, don't worry, man. I just sort of want to get on to the stuff about your career as a Canadian filmmaker. And maybe your ideas about film, especially documentary film and so-called objectivity in film and the meta level of film. The stuff you're known for, man.

With a sudden gesture, Fife stops everyone from speaking—an odd gesture for him, a man whose face and body rarely express his emotions. He grimaces and quickly covers his face with his hands, then extends his hands out in front of him, as if pushing the camera away, palms out, fingers splayed. Slowly he brings his hands down and places them on his knees, palms up, as if to receive a blessing or a handout, a wafer or a coin.

Malcolm says to Vincent, Did you get that?

Yes.

Fife's nausea subsides a bit. He's no longer dizzy. He inhales and speaks to Vincent's camera. For forty-five years, all my years in Canada, from the day I went out and bought my first sixteen-millimeter camera, I exposed corruption, mendacity, and hypocrisy in government and business. Right? I did what anyone with time and energy and a camera could have done. Anyone. Right? Now, with your camera, I'm exposing myself. My corruption, my mendacity, my hypocrisy. And this is something only I can do. No one else.

He says, If I'm confusing you or embarrassing you or making you angry with me, if I'm frustrating you, just give me enough time to finish, and you'll have all you'll ever need to know who I am. That's all I ask—time to finish doing something only I can do. Which is to do to myself what I have spent nearly fifty years doing to the world at large, or at least to Canada at large, exposing its corruption, mendacity, and hypocrisy.

He says, It'll sound like fiction to you, like I'm making most of it up, which is fine by me. I don't care what you do with my story after I've finished telling it. I'll be dead. You can cut and splice it any damned way you want, make it take any shape that pleases you and the people who are paying you to make this film. But no matter what you do with my story after I've told it, you'll have seen and heard me tell my wife what kind of man she married and lived and worked with all these years. You'll have been the witnesses whose presence, whose camera and microphone, will verify that this intimacy between a man, who happens to be me, Leonard Fife, and his wife, a woman who happens to be Emma Flynn, actually took place.

He says, You probably don't believe or understand it, but that intimacy cannot take place without the presence of your camera and microphone. They—and you four, and even you, Renée—are what keep me from lying to Emma, as I would if she and I were alone with no witnesses, no camera, no microphone. When two people who love each other are alone with each other, both of them lie, usually merely to protect themselves, but sometimes they lie because they cannot bear to hurt each other or themselves with the truth. Do you understand me? All of you?

Malcolm says, Are you getting this, Vincent? I hope the fuck you're getting this.

Yes, yes. We're getting this, don't worry.

Sloan? We getting this?

Yep.

Renée says, I will need to address the bag soon, Monsieur Fife. I think it must be nearly filled.

Diana clears her throat as if about to speak, but evidently thinks better of it.

Emma says, All right, love. How far you go with this is up to you. I've sent a text downtown and canceled the rest of my day. I'll stay here. I'll keep listening for as long as you need to keep talking. I confess, a lot of it doesn't make sense to me. Still, you go in your mind wherever you have to go, Leo, and tell us what you can of what you see and hear there, and I'll listen. I'll sit here in the dark behind you, and I'll listen. Everyone will listen, darling.

Thank you, Fife says. Thank you all.

10

AND SO HE DOES IT, FIFE GOES IN HIS MIND WHERE HE has to go, and he tells Emma what he can of what he sees and hears there. He peers down leagues of air. A thin white band of beach runs between the land and water below like a wall raised between adjacent fields, one field mustard-colored, the other a flat, cold blue. The line is sharp, precise, with many small loops that cut left into the land and then right to where the sea ends. Fife has traveled south from the Northeast before and out west and back, but always by automobile or bus or train. He has traveled by plane only three times before this flight, a round trip from Richmond to Mexico, another to Rome when he claimed to be following D. H. Lawrence to Sardinia, and last winter's flight to Boston on his way to Vermont, but he has never flown anywhere alone—always with Alicia. He's scared and thrilled, like a child being sent away by himself to summer camp.

Outside Fife's window, watery, sunlit silver belts glisten on the trailing edge of the wing. We're headed due north, Fife decides. He checks his watch: 1:15. The land below must be Massachusetts, somewhere south of Boston and north of where Cape Cod elbows its thick sandy arm into the Atlantic. He can see highways and roads, like elaborate, curling networks of veins with clusters of knots here and there indicating villages and towns. He's never seen from the air and in daylight the place where he was born and grew up. He studies the coastline as if it were a map and tries to figure out what part of the map he is flying over. The coast takes on a familiar shape and loops back on itself and then arches away from the sea in a profiled yawn. Above the open mouth an inlet turns into a river, its northern bank cutting gradually back toward the sea, where it's cut a second time by a smaller river. Curling briefly south, almost to the point of closing the mouth, the coast bends around once again and continues north as before.

Plymouth Bay, he thinks, pleased to have recognized it. From the shape of the bay and its two small rivers, he recalls not a modern map of Plymouth and the Atlantic coast south of Boston, but a relatively ancient map of the region that he stumbled across a year before in the UVA library. It was in the Champlain Society's edition of Lescarbot's *History of New France,* a work he was culling for data to fortify a paper he'd written for his colonial American literature course. The map was Samuel de Champlain's 1605 chart of a small harbor that he named Cape St. Louis Harbor. Some sixteen years later, Champlain's Cape St. Louis Harbor would be claimed by the Pilgrims, who would name it Plymouth.

Champlain's map of Cape St. Louis Harbor fascinates Fife. It reinforces his frail argument that France, not England, is the bedrock for the New England imagination. Like the Dutch in New York, he argues. On further research into the history of early voyages to the region, however, he learns that an Englishman, Martin Pring, was there as early as 1603, two years before Champlain, and named the harbor Whitson Bay. An inconvenient fact, which Fife leaves out of his paper. His professor, unaware of Martin Pring's claim, gives Fife an A-plus and praises his scholarship and urges him to submit his paper to the *Virginia Quarterly,* where he is an editor—an opportunity Fife declines.

Staring out the plane window at the bay below, checking carefully for the several small harbor islands that he still recalls from Champlain's chart, he lights a cigarette, flicks the dead match onto the floor.

Malcolm interrupts him. Wait a minute, Leo! You were smoking on an airplane? Oh, right! It's fucking 1968! Never mind, I get it. Sorry, sorry.

An elbow moves hard against Fife's upper arm. He turns, and the woman next to him points out that the No Smoking sign at the front of the cabin has been switched on. We're landing soon, she says. The Fasten Seat Belts indicator flashes. Buckle up, she adds.

He nods thanks and drops the butt onto the floor and rubs it out with his shoe. Why is the plane preparing to land already? he wonders. It seems wrong to him. Given the plane's altitude and speed, it still has at least ten or fifteen minutes remaining in the air before the approach to Boston can begin.

Again, he looks out his window and studies the coast below. The south bank of the harbor is out of sight now, and the north bank has inched seaward to a position that's more nearly beneath the aircraft, so that the plane is probably located directly over the exact geographic center of Plymouth Bay, as seen from sea by Samuel de Champlain. But at this speed and altitude, in another minute it will be gone to miles behind him.

He recognizes buildings. Then streets, parks, automobiles, train tracks. And realizes that the place below is not Plymouth, seen from twenty-five thousand feet at three hundred fifty miles per hour. It's the city of Boston, seen from five thousand feet at two hundred miles per hour. He is situated much lower in the sky and traveling through space at a much slower speed than he thought. The harbor is Boston Harbor, the southern river is the Charles, and the smaller, northern one is the Mystic.

His mind whirls away and swiftly back, and he struggles to understand what has happened to him and what is happening now. He does not believe that Boston is directly beneath him. Not really. He believes Champlain's map. Yet it must be Boston. It can't be Plymouth. He can't convince his eyes that he is located as close to the ground as he rationally knows he is. His body refuses to acknowledge that it is not traveling through space at the speed and altitude as he thought it was barely two minutes ago. His body lies passively in the chair, as inert as a rug on a floor, as if refusing to adapt to his reasoned discovery.

For Fife, stasis almost always leads to panic, and sensing its familiar approach, he shuts his eyes and wraps his arms around his chest and tries to focus all his attention on the steadily increasing roar of the jet engines beside him. The noise, like a smooth wall of water, breaks against him and sweeps on past, leaving him immersed in a sea of sound. He is without dimension. This is how he has taught himself to overcome panic: he thinks of himself as both a geometric point and measureless. With clear, unhampered control of his thoughts, he's able to range safely, freely, across vast planes of memory. In this case, memories of Boston. Here and there a face, his child bride Amy's, his infant daughter Heidi's, a smell of rain, a taste of tobacco, a woman's hand upon his, a woman's whispered voice, Amanda's. The memories catch and slow his flight and bring him circling back for a second. And soon he sees himself calmly alone in a room.

He is standing in a large, high-ceilinged living room near a curtained, glass-paned French door. He slouches before the door, as if about to reach out and touch the door and open it. But instead he turns slowly away, crosses the room to the opposite corner, and sits down in an overstuffed maroon easy chair. Rain sloshes down the window next to him. Without getting up, he reaches up and snaps on the floor lamp. Lights a cigarette. Stands again. Crosses the uncarpeted floor of the large room and walks into a tiny windowless kitchen. Grabbing a bottle of beer from the refrigerator, he opens it and returns to the living room, sits in the chair again, and takes a long pull from the bottle.

He listens to the beer in his mouth and throat, and to the rain, the footsteps from the apartment overhead, a muffled radio somewhere down the hall, the cars on the street below hurriedly sliding past the building, a bus hissing to a stop at the corner. He gets up and walks to the window, draws back the heavy red drape with one hand, and looks intently out.

Across the street, the Fens sprawls in a pale-green haze, a large park with bogs and old Back Bay canals and flower gardens and open grassy areas and ball fields and occasional groves of trees. And beyond the Fens, along its western edge, blocks of fifty-year-old four- and five-story yellow-brick apartment houses. The blackened windows of the apartments one by one turn orange as wives and mothers flick on kitchen lights and begin preparing suppers for their small families, and weary husbands come wetly in from the hallways and try to read their newspapers in slowly dimming living rooms and finally reach over and switch on the reading lights.

At the edge of the park, between the trees and his building, Beacon Street cuts a wide straight line from Kenmore Square to Brookline. Rush-hour traffic is building, accumulating in sudden knots at intersections, but from where he stands he can't see the traffic or the people hurtling home in the rain. He makes out the windows of his own apartment, just above the tops of a clutch of elms. They stare blank-faced onto the park. What is Amy doing now? he wonders. If she's there, why aren't the lights on yet? Why is the apartment dark? He stares—puzzled, agitated, anxious—from across the park, waiting, hoping to see the warm, reassuring lights of their kitchen, their small, crowded living room, their bedroom, where his infant daughter lies in her crib.

One can see your apartment pretty nicely from here, can't one? The woman's voice again, Amanda's. He turns slowly. She has come out of the bedroom. She closes the French doors, her long hands hidden behind her, as if she's untying and taking off an apron. She is dressed the same as when she went into the bedroom, he notices, surprised.

Somehow he believed that she would emerge in a floor-length dress-ing gown that flows seductively along at her feet, with her hair freshly loosened and combed out and falling across her shoulders. But she is still dressed in a khaki work shirt and Levi's cut off at the knees, and her hair is braided and wound around her head like a German shop-keeper's. She wears no makeup, as before, and seems uninvolved with the fact of his presence, as before.

Flopping her long body onto the chair he has just deserted, she lights a mentholated cigarette and observes again that one can see Fife's apartment pretty nicely from her window, can't one?

He mumbles, Yes, one can, and resumes watching the darkened windows across the park. Where is Amy? Out doing last-minute er-rands, shopping for the meal that he will miss? Is she on the street somewhere in the rain, with Heidi in her arms? he wonders, suddenly aware of the possibility that she will come here looking for him, patheti-cally ringing the buzzer downstairs and over the speakerphone asking Amanda, who she has never met, Have you seen my husband, Leo? He isn't home yet. When I called the bookstore where he works, the man said that he left at noon, feeling sick. Leo speaks of you often, he says that you're his best friend in Boston. He says that you and he meet often for lunch.

I ought to go home, he says, turning to face Amanda.

She has placed one leg across the arm of the easy chair and leans back, watching the smoke from her cigarette drift in blue spirals to the high ceiling. She says, In this rain? You'll get drenched.

He agrees, takes his half-emptied bottle of beer from the window ledge and crosses the room to the piano and sits down heavily on the bench. He considers Amanda's apartment again. She's got to be well-off to afford this place, to know how to furnish it sparsely, to hang only original paintings by known artists on the walls, even though it means she hangs but three or four. But she has no visible means of support. She isn't even a working musician, he remembers. She's a twenty-six-year-old conservatory student. Both her parents are dead, she once told him. Someone must be keeping her, someone who pays for all this. Some married man, probably, five years or so older than she, ten years or so older than he. A nice enough guy with a good job in an advertising firm on Arlington Street, or maybe a TV executive, a guy who lives with a wife and three kids in a big new split-level house in Lexington or Concord. A guy trying to make his life interesting by keeping a bohemian mistress and spending one weekend a month with her in order to get his money's worth, the kind of man whose father would have done the same thing at the same age and told him about it when the son turned twenty-one. The kind of man who thinks there's nothing wrong with the arrangement.

That would explain everything, Fife thinks. Her apparent solitude, her comfortable living conditions, her strange indifference to his presence. It's not indifference, exactly. It's a willingness to treat him as a casual friend, a neighbor, when in fact it is perfectly clear that his interest in her is sexual and has been from the very first time he saw her at a party seven weeks before. He learned from a girl who studies at the New England Conservatory with her that she is a jazz pianist and her name is Amanda and she is rumored to be the mistress of a famous musician whose name he recognized, Gerry Mulligan, but who is always on the road and has his own place in New York, so he stays with her only when he's playing in Boston. Fife doesn't want to think about Gerry Mulligan the famous jazz musician. He chooses not to believe the rumors. He prefers to imagine the married advertising executive living in the suburbs.

From that first sighting at the party, he has tried to place himself so that he and Amanda can be at the same place at the same time. Which isn't difficult, as it turns out, since several of his friends quickly reveal that they are also friends of hers. So he has been spending all his free time with those particular people, ignoring his usual comrades, who know Amanda only casually, if at all. Then a few minutes past noon one cool June day he looks out the window of the bookstore where he works, and he sees her striding toward the small cafeteria-style restaurant at the corner of Gainsborough and Huntington, a green book bag slung over one shoulder, her thick, dark-brown hair undone and tossed by the breeze. She is barelegged, wearing a belted trench coat with a long striped scarf loosely tied at her throat.

The restaurant is located four doors down from the bookstore, and the conservatory is across the avenue from both, next to the first of the Northeastern University classroom buildings. The place is usually jammed by 12:05 with students, and unless one shares a table with friends or acquaintances, one ends up standing near the door and waiting fifteen or twenty minutes for an empty table to appear. The next day Fife arranges to leave the bookstore for lunch ten minutes before noon and places himself purposely at a table near the door.

He has already finished eating and is drinking his second cup of coffee when she comes in alone. She swiftly scans the crowded room in search of a free table, sees none, then spots Fife and smiles. He waves her over and invites her to share his table with him, he's leaving in a minute anyway. He stays for a half hour, and they talk. The first chance he has, he tells her that he is married—mentioning Amy's name casually in a passing reference to the location of his apartment. Fife, though only twenty, has just become a new father, he tells her.

She congratulates him. She mentions that she is unmarried. With a boyfriend who travels a lot, she adds.

That must give you a lot of freedom.

She nods and turns her attention to her bowl of soup.

The same thing happens the next day and the next, and then it has become a part of their daily routines. Leo Fife and Amanda Clarke have lunch together. Soon they have become friends, even to the point of her inviting him to drop by her apartment for coffee or a drink anytime he happens to be in the neighborhood. She seems to have found him interesting to talk with. He explains that because they are in fact neighbors he passes by her block every day on his way to work and back, and thus he may indeed be dropping by for coffee or a beer any day now, if her invitation is serious. She assures him that it is serious, and he goes back to the bookstore thinking that if he is to be placed in a situation with her whereby he has to say yes or no and cannot say maybe, he will not be able to say no. He will end up making love to her, no matter what the consequences. He thinks of it that way, making love to her, not with her. But he cannot conceive of there being no consequences.

He tries to imagine no consequences. He makes love to Amanda just once, and Amy does not find out about it. Therefore no consequences. But he can't believe that, having done it once, he won't do it again, and then again, until Amanda has fallen in love with him and declares that she can't live without him, and then he will fall in love with her. Those are the inescapable consequences.

And Amy will find out. That, too. He will tell her himself. Or someone who knows him or knows Amanda will tell her. And Amy will be unable to do anything less than leave him, he thinks. She'll go back with the baby to her hard-working Southern Baptist parents in Florida, who will gladly take her in. Her wild fears of betrayal and abandonment will have been justified, and the only person capable of convincing her otherwise will be Fife himself, after years of shamefaced atonement and reassurance, which he knows he can never bring himself to offer. Not anymore. Not now. He does not love Amy. He can say that to himself now. He never loved her. She loved him, and he married her for it, to hold on to it and to reward her for it. And now he loathes himself for being married to her. It wasn't her fault. It was his. She never lied to him. He lied to her. Yet he wants to be able somehow to blame her. For their being married, for her having borne their child. He wants to blame her for even a small part of it. But he can't. And so he tells himself he won't. That's what passes for his morality now.

For little more than a year, since he first discovered that Amy was pregnant, he has swung back and forth from one alternative to the other, day after day, until that day in July when, repelled by his own inability to choose between two kinds of guilt, he leaves the bookstore at noon and does not meet Amanda for their usual lunch. Instead he walks all the way down Massachusetts Avenue to the Charles River and strolls slowly along the grassy bank of the river for an hour or so, watching the Harvard and MIT sculls knife through the choppy gray water and the pinwheeling seagulls and terns move gradually inland along the river from the bay, and when it begins to rain he scrambles up the bank to the street. He finds himself standing on Commonwealth Avenue, less than a block from Kenmore Square, eight blocks from his and Amy's apartment and only two blocks from Amanda's.

The rain comes all at once and heavily. He jogs down Commonwealth and across Kenmore Square and around the corner onto Beacon Street. He steps up to the doorway, finds her last name, Clarke, over one of the mailboxes and pushes the white button next to it. A tinned female voice that he does not recognize asks, Who is it?

It's me. It's Leo.

The voice, Amanda's, laughs. Are you soaked?

Not yet. But I will be if you don't open this door so I can come up and wait out the rain before going on home.

Fine by me, she says, and buzzes him in to the lobby. He believes that the rain won't last, that it's a summer shower and will move quickly inland and break up in a half hour or so. But it rains all afternoon, while they talk and smoke cigarettes and drink beer, talking first of music and musicians—in which she is the teacher and he the rapt student, a young man listening to an older, wiser, better-educated woman. And then they talk of people, mutual friends, and finally of his too-early marriage—in which the young man possesses knowledge and experience that the older woman does not, so she merely poses questions.

He tells her mainly of his dilemma, little else. He is surprised when in response Amanda speaks of his marriage in the same abstract, problematic terms. She agrees that he has reached an impasse. There's no doubt. And then, as if having found the right word, *impasse*, she seems no longer concerned with its context or the situation or the people to which it applies. She asks no more questions. They fall silent for a few moments. She gets up from her chair and says that she'll be right back and disappears into the bedroom, closing the French door behind her.

Now she is back in the living room, sitting across from him in her maroon armchair, looking bored and slightly impatient, while he sits at the piano and tries to invent a casual way to ask her if she really is the mistress of the famous jazz musician Gerry Mulligan, and wonders whether he should leave now, whether Amy is out looking for him, since it's after six and he should have been home by four, and he knows his teenage wife will have called the bookstore long ago, and he wonders if he should or should not seize the opportunity that deep down he knows he will seize.

In the end, it's Amanda who decides, not Fife, he will later conclude, whenever he finds himself going back to that rainy afternoon and evening, questioning it, reenacting it, step by step and word by word, until at last he believes that he has got it right, all of it, even the smell of her hair and the exact intonations of her voice and the precise fall of light in the room as she crosses to him and kneels facing him and places her long thin hands on his hips and tells him that he should feel free of anything that so clearly has come to be an impasse. She tells him that there is no other way to break the balance between two equally weighted alternatives than to create a third alternative.

She smiles, as if happy for him. And tightens against him, moving her arms around him, and he leans forward and kisses her. She whispers against his pressing face that it's fine, it's fine, it's all right, Leo, don't worry, and takes both his hands in hers and leads him from the bright, high-ceilinged living room to the close darkness and warmth of the bedroom. There in total silence he makes love not with her, but to her, shoving himself again and again against her quick, twisting body, bringing her rapidly through to the other side of her intent, as if she planned it that way, every step. Then drives himself through, too, his body suddenly warm and blossoming from its still, cold center. As if he, too, planned it that way.

11

CUTTING INTO FIFE'S SCRAMBLED AND SCRAMBLING
account of what sounds like one of his many adulteries, Malcolm announces that it's time to take a break. He and Diana need to consult.
Privately. Who the hell was Amanda? Where the fuck is this going? Is
he just making it up?

Among the others, except for Fife, there is an air of relief, an audible exhalation. They haven't been able to follow where Fife has tried
to lead them and are confused by the meandering route he has taken
and exhausted from trying to keep up with him. They don't understand
his evasion of Malcolm's and Diana's prepared questions, his stubborn
refusal to be properly interviewed. They don't know what to believe.
Does it matter?

Everyone remains silent.

After a few moments, Emma says in a choked voice, It's the medications. Sometimes he confabulates. Like he's dreaming. We shouldn't
be doing this, she suddenly tells Malcolm. She asks him to destroy what
they've shot so far. It's not even half true. Most of what he's saying is

misremembered and half invented or completely made up. It's wrong to be filming it, Malcolm, even if you end up not using it.

The lights come on, and Fife looks around at the six others—Renée and Emma seated on the sofa behind him, Sloan and Vincent standing by the camera, Diana clutching her clipboard in the corner of the room, Malcolm standing next to Fife in his wheelchair in the center of the room in front of the camera. Malcolm lays his hand on Fife's skeletal shoulder and softly pats it.

Renée tells Fife that it's past time for her to empty his bag and give him his prednisone.

Diana says to no one in particular, though it's clearly directed to Emma, that Leo seems to want to continue, so why not let him? It'll all come together and make sense when it's edited. She likes the stuff about his early ambitions to be a poet and writer. It's relevant to his shift to film. And people will want to hear about his American years in the 1960s, she points out. Okay, some of it's a little too personal and private, maybe, and not very clear, but that can be edited out so no one's hurt or confused. A lot of this can be cut. The two and a quarter hours they've shot so far might come down to barely fifteen minutes of screen time, for instance.

Sloan asks, Did you really not know about this, Emma? I mean, the wife in Virginia. And the son. And the other wife, the first one? And the baby girl.

Jesus, Sloan! Leave it alone, Malcolm says. He tries explaining to her, and probably to himself and the others as well, that all kinds of things have been mixed together in Fife's mind. He quotes Emma: it's the meds. Confabulation. Memories, hallucinations, fiction and films, other people's stories, fantasies. It's like trying to tie a novel to the author's real life, he says. You can't do it. We shouldn't worry, Emma knows the story of Fife's life better than anyone. She's been living and working with him for forty years.

I'm sorry, Sloan says. I didn't mean to . . .

Emma says, I know everything about him that I need to know.

Jesus, you're talking about me as if I'm not in the fucking room! Fife says. Like I can't hear you. I do hear you.

Emma says, You're right, darling. I'm sorry.

Malcolm says he is sorry, too. C'mon, folks, this is Leo's show, not ours, he reminds them.

Renée releases the brakes on Fife's wheelchair and declares that she must take Monsieur Fife back to his room for a few moments. If they wish to continue today with the filming, and Monsieur Fife feels strong enough to comply and wishes to do it, she will bring him back to the living room. She looks at Emma as she says this, as if it is Emma's decision whether to continue the filming. Then straightway she wheels him from the room.

As they cross the dark hallway and pass into the dining room, Fife, speaking English, says to Renée, I'm not confabulating, you know. I'm really not. And it's not the meds. And Emma's wrong, he says. She doesn't know everything about me that she needs to know. He did live in Virginia, where he was married, and he had a son, and before that there was an eighteen-year-old girl he met in Florida, and he got her pregnant and married her when he was nineteen and went with her to Boston, where they had a daughter. He insists it's all true. He remembers it like it happened yesterday. Do you believe me? he asks Renée.

She answers, *Je crois que vous croyez c'est vrais.* I believe that you believe it's true.

She wheels him through the kitchen and on to the bedroom and bathroom that he has not shared with his wife for nearly two months. He wonders how much he was able to say to the camera this morning of what he actually remembers. He knows there is a synaptic snafu between the data received from the memory banks of his hippocampus and his prefrontal cortex that scrambles the words he is led to speak when he tries to convert that data to speech. It is another reason for wanting Emma there. She is the only one who can bridge the gap between his memories and his description of them, as if he is speaking in a language that only she and he understand. He and Emma are his brain's only native speakers. This is love, is it not?

It's the same as when he first wakens, but is not yet completely awake, or when he begins to fall asleep and has not yet fully entered sleep; he speaks aloud, half inside a dream and half outside it. Emma, lying next to him or reading silently in a nearby chair, says, What? What are you talking about, Leo? And he says, It's nothing. Nothing. I was dreaming. But he wasn't dreaming. He was caught for a few seconds between being asleep and being awake, and the two worlds briefly overlapped, and there was a break, a gap, between what he was seeing and hearing and what he could say of it, and he was unable to speak from that gap and had to cry out, like a mountain climber fallen into a glacial crevasse, suspended from his rope, calling for help to a search party miles away. His rescuers hear bits and pieces of his cries carried on the wind, but are unable to make out the words or determine where they're coming from.

His speech is not garbled or blocked in any way, the way it would be if he suffered a stroke or an injury to his brain. He's not aphasic. He's almost two separate people, and one of them remembers in great detail a distant past and the other, who does not remember anything of that past, tries to describe it. The conflict causes a loud, sparking static that makes it nearly impossible for him to hear what he is saying. Just as he cannot see what the camera is seeing. He no more knows what he sounds like through Sloan's mic than he knows what he looks like to Vincent's camera and to the six other people in the room.

He is sure that he has said nothing that is not true. He has not lied. But he does not know what he has said. Maybe that's how it goes when you have not lied. You don't know what you said. Only liars know what they have said.

Renée unclips the bag of urine from the catheter tube and empties the bag into the toilet. She wraps her arms around Fife from behind and eases him from the wheelchair to the toilet. He is not paralyzed, but his limbs and trunk are too feeble to carry the weight of his body. He has lost nearly half his two hundred pounds of muscle and bone and is as light as he was at fourteen. She slips his sweatpants down his scrawny thighs and goes to the door and tells him to call her when he's ready to be wiped and leaves him alone, sitting on the toilet with his pants puddled at his ankles.

There is nothing left of his life now, except what's in his brain and the fluids that pass through his bowels and bladder and the cancer cells that are devouring his bones and flesh, munching on his organs, shutting them down one by one. He has not been able to digest solids for weeks. He hasn't had sex with Emma or anyone else for three years, nor has he managed to ejaculate for nearly a year. No one who isn't being paid for it wants to touch his body. Not even Emma. Not even he himself. What's left of his life now, who he is, is only what's inside his brain. Which is only who he was, nothing more. The future does not exist anymore, and the present never did. And no one knows who he was. No one can know, unless he tells her: Emma.

He could go silent, the way he stopped eating, an act of will made easy by exhaustion and the drugs that have killed his appetite. But if he goes silent, he will disappear. Except for his memories, all living traces of his past, all the witnesses and evidence, have been erased by years of betrayal, abandonment, divorce, annulment, flight, and exile, eaten by time the way his body is being eaten by cancer. Time, like cancer, is the devourer of our lives. When you have no future and the present doesn't exist, except as consciousness, all you have for a self is your past. And if, like Fife, your past is a lie, a fiction, then you can't be said to exist, except as a fictional character.

In telling his story to Emma, Fife is not trying to correct the record, he's trying to stay alive. Or, more accurately, he's trying to come to life, like a Pinocchio, a puppet made of wood, ingeniously carved and assembled so as to closely resemble a real human being—a much-admired

Canadian documentary filmmaker, a teacher, a beloved friend and husband, a trusted man of the left dedicated to exposing hypocrisy, greed,
and political corruption. But he's really only a wooden puppet whose
strings have frayed and broken one by one, and now his clever maker,
Leonard Fife, the man himself, the village woodcarver, can no longer
make him dance and play at being a real boy anymore. He lies collapsed in the corner of the woodcarver's hut, a pile of sticks and cloth.
Until the big strong Haitian nurse returns to the bathroom and lifts
him away from the toilet and wipes his buttocks clean of dribbled shit
and reattaches his penis to the tube and swings his body back into the
wheelchair. Who is he then?

Renée asks him if he wishes to rest in bed or lie on the chaise by
the bedroom window.

Fife tells her to take him back to the living room.

She says that if he returns to the living room, she will have to
attach him to the IV. If you insist on continuing with the interview,
you will need nourishment and hydration. You are being very foolish, Monsieur Fife. Those people are only interested in making their
movie. Madame Fife does not want you to waste your strength on this
project. Let her tell them to go away, and if you are strong enough to
continue tomorrow, they can come back then.

Fife smiles at her. He says, It's like I'm the old Italian carpenter
Geppetto, the guy who made a puppet out of wood named Pinocchio,
but I'm too old and feeble now to pull the strings for the puppet show.
For the first time, the puppet has to put on the show all by himself. I'm
Geppetto, but I'm the puppet, too. The wooden puppet who, thanks to
the intervention by a blue-haired fairy, was resurrected as a real boy.
How does my nose look, Renée? Check it out. Is it longer today than
yesterday?

Your nose looks the same as always.

Did you ever read the story of Pinocchio, Renée?

No. But I have heard of it. It is a child's story, is it not?

Yes, but it's too scary for children. It's about lying and dying. Lying and dying, and the vanity of believing in resurrection.

You said the real boy was resurrected.

No, the wooden boy was resurrected. Which gave him a second chance at dying, only this time for real. Wooden boys don't die. They're like storybook characters that live on even after the story's over.

I would not like it, then. I am a Christian. There was a movie about it, was there not?

Yes, a Disney movie, but it left out all the scary parts.

And the vanity of believing in resurrection? Did the movie leave that out?

Yes, it did.

Then perhaps I would like the Disney movie. I believe in the resurrection.

12

WITHOUT WAITING FOR INSTRUCTIONS FROM MALCOLM, Renée rolls Fife up to Vincent's camera, positions the wheelchair beneath the Speedlight, locks the brakes, and disappears into the darkness that surrounds him.

No one speaks. Sloan appears beside Fife, holding the mic between her thumb and index finger like a large black capsule. With her free hand she shifts and lifts his black turtleneck sweater at the waist and deftly feeds the cord beneath it to his neck and clips it to the collar. As she removes her hand, she passes her palm over his upper body, lightly stroking his bare hairless chest and belly. Her face, framed by her sorrel-colored hair, is close enough to Fife's face for him to smell her breath—burnt tobacco, black coffee, mint toothpaste. He opens his mouth and sucks her warm breath in and savors it for a few seconds and swallows it and lightly moans.

Are you okay, Leo? Mr. Fife?

He nods yes but says nothing. He's not okay. Everything that gives him pleasure—Sloan's cool hand on his chest and belly, her cheek next to his, the swash of dark-red hair across her smooth fair forehead, the aroma of the interior of her body—comes wrapped in pain. A kind of embodied grief. It would be easier, simpler, if nothing gave him pleasure in these last days, if nothing came and told him what he will never feel again, and worse, what for most of his life he has never felt before. Everything that gives him pleasure now only reminds him that in the past nothing gave him pleasure and that soon he will feel nothing at all. It's not because somehow his past life and other people failed him. It's not because he suffered. It's because of the impoverished quality of his attention. It's possible that he has wasted his life.

In Boston in the early 1960s, when he and Amy were teenage husband and wife and father and mother, if Fife had paid the kind of attention to her and their baby Heidi that he has just paid to Sloan, he would not have abandoned them. Instead, he would have loved them, and they would have loved him back. His life and theirs would have been different, better, worth more.

If he had immersed himself in Alicia's and their son Cornel's and her parents' world in Richmond, Virginia, the way for a few seconds he just now immersed himself in the simple physical nearness of Sloan's body, if he had drunk them in the way he drank her in, Alicia's and Cornel's world would have given him untold lifelong pleasure, the profound lifesaving pleasure of love given and received. For all of them. The Chapman family would have surrounded and sustained him. But he never did it. He never dared to love or be loved by another human being.

He wasn't ignorant of love's immanence. He knew it lay there, waiting for him to step forward and simply embrace it. He refused it. He was afraid of its power. But only at first was he afraid, and then he grew used to its absence, and soon he forgot it was waiting there for him or for anyone. It became a null. Until now.

And now, and Emma? Secrets and lies don't disguise just the secretive liar. They disguise everyone he has kept in the dark, everyone he has lied to. One's self and everyone else's self, too, are made invisible and unknowable. If Fife's secrets and lies have kept him all these years from seeing Emma clearly, have kept her from being the object of his best attention, then perhaps this final, blatant, willful exposure of his secrets and lies is his way—his only available way—to finally give her the quality of attention that makes love possible. Despite his unloving and unlovable past, he means to go out loving and loved. With no secrets. No lies. It's not heroic. It's merely the end of a lifetime of cowardice.

Malcolm claps his hands in front of the camera lens and says, Leonard Fife interview, Montreal, April 1, 2018. Let's try a different tack this time, okay, Leo?

Fife hears Malcolm speak, but can't understand what he's saying. The words are jumbled and muffled. Fife is like the person in the painting *The Scream* by Edvard Munch, pressing his hands against his ears. That's what he imagines he looks like, his bald, sexless, gaping mouth making a silent howl, while behind him two dark, receding figures back away from him—in embarrassment or revulsion, it's unclear. Perhaps both embarrassment and revulsion. Or fear. Or all three. He wonders who those people are. His mother and father? Amy and Heidi? Alicia and Cornel? Emma and . . . ? Oh, yes, Emma and Fife himself.

After a few seconds he finds his voice and says, Okay, okay, and without waiting for Malcolm to ask a question, he starts talking. It doesn't matter what Malcolm wants him to say. Fife believes that he is telling his story, not to Malcolm and Diana or to Vincent's camera and Sloan's mic, but to Emma. He blocks out Malcolm's different tack. Refuses to hear the question. It has something to do with Joan Baez. Something about the Mariposa Folk Festival and 1969. Instead, Fife explains to Emma that a countless number of times throughout his life, his reality seems to have been little more than the refracted pressures of his needs. Those are his exact words, carefully chosen, sharply articulated: the refracted pressures of his needs. He knows what he

means, but doesn't think he has managed to say it. He tries again. He
tells her that changes, revisions, and shifts in his reality have been
nothing more than changes, revisions, and shifts in his needs. What
am I, then? he asks her. What is my center, and how on earth can it
be located?

He tells Emma, I'm seated at the back of a Whisperjet. That's where
I'm located. That's my center. He peers out the window beside him and
across cold slate-gray water and recognizes the 1960s skyline of Boston. The clutter of the shipyards comes into view. Beyond the gloomy
nineteenth-century buildings of the financial district, the brutal new
glass-and-steel government center rises tier on tier. Next to it the gold
dome of the old statehouse, then Beacon Hill, and nearer, the brick
tenements of the North End. He searches for the Prudential Building
and finds its flattened cap, fifty or more floors above the rest of the
huddled city, visible from here in East Boston on the far side of the
harbor, through the inch-thick window of a silent, landed aircraft.

He reaches the baggage-claim area just as a wide corrugated-iron
door rolls up and reveals like a stage set three suitcase-laden, rubber-
tired wagons pulled by a yellow tractor. Three Black men pitch the
bags from the wagons onto a low deck before them. The owners of the
bags shove and push at one another and plunge back and forth along
the deck, hunting for their suitcases and spotting them and grabbing
them and running off. Soon everyone has left, even the three baggage
handlers and their tractor and wagons, and he is alone in the cold un-
painted room with four pieces of unclaimed luggage in front of him,
none of them his.

He walks rapidly to the Piedmont Airlines counter in the main
lobby. A tall, gaunt man wearing a gray uniform and a handlebar
mustache greets him and asks how can he help. Fife explains that his
suitcase got lost and gives him his flight numbers from Richmond to
Washington and Washington to Boston.

This is all strangely familiar to Fife, the lost suitcase, the smiling, mustachioed counterman, even the baggage handlers and their rubber-tired wagons and yellow tractor. For a moment Fife fears that he's trapped in a recurrent dream. I've got to rent a car, he says. I've got to drive to Vermont, where I'm expected late this afternoon.

That presents a bit of a problem, sir. But not an unsurmountable one. We can put it on a Greyhound. What's the closest city for a bus to drop it off?

Montpelier, probably. I think Montpelier's a regular stop on the Boston-to-Montreal bus route. I'll be staying only a few miles from there.

For a second he thinks he might be better off if he waits for his suitcase here at the terminal for a few more hours. But no, he decides, it may not even be on the next flight, and he will have waited around here for two and a half hours for nothing. He has everything he needs in his briefcase. Inside the briefcase—along with a Moleskine notebook and a few newspaper clippings, his personal checkbook, and a book of Hardy's poems that he intends to review favorably for the *Raleigh News and Observer*—is the check.

Ah, yes, the check. Twenty-three thousand dollars. A fragile pale-pink piece of paper, a cashier's check from the Federal Reserve Bank of Richmond that he is supposed to deposit tomorrow with a bank in Montpelier, Vermont, so that he can buy—in Alicia's name—the house they picked out together in February. He wouldn't be carrying the check at all if he had known in January to open an account with a bank in Montpelier. The money could have been wired ahead, but this is the first piece of real estate he has ever purchased, and he assumed that if the money is readily available, you simply select which dwelling you wish to purchase and refer the seller to your bank, and the bank issues the seller a check. No matter, he thought, that the bank holding the money is located in Richmond, Virginia, and the property and seller are in Plainfield, Vermont. No matter that the Federal Reserve Bank of Richmond has Alicia's money invested in old, inherited stocks and bonds and doesn't hold it in cash, and to issue the check, Alicia's trust officer, Mr. Keefe, will have to sell some of those stocks and bonds.

These complications and the implications were patiently explained to him at the bank by Mr. Keefe. It was he who suggested that, as far as their purchase of a house goes, Fife and Alicia should deal exclusively with a Vermont bank. When he goes north to complete the purchase, Fife will be essentially acting as a courier. This seemed perfectly reasonable to Fife, right up to the moment when Mr. Keefe places into his hand the envelope containing the check.

It's made out to Cash, Mr. Keefe tells him. When you arrive in Montpelier, simply open a checking account with the Chittenden Bank. Or some other bank of your choosing. They're all pretty much the same. It's the state capital, but it's a small town. Naturally, for convenience's sake it'll be a joint account.

Naturally, Fife says. He thanks the banker, too profusely, he thinks, and walks from the carpeted, oak-paneled office feeling suspicious, as if Mr. Keefe and Alicia's father Benjamin and her uncle Jackson and possibly Alicia's mother Jessie and even Alicia herself, by setting him to a task that they know is utterly absurd, are somehow testing him. If he does not follow their instructions to the letter, his loyalty to Alicia and her family and to the Federal Reserve Bank of Richmond will be legitimately open to question. Their instructions are designed to tempt him to disobey. Mr. Keefe and Benjamin and Jackson Chapman and even Jessie Chapman and Alicia Chapman Fife have far more experience in these matters than he, and for him to question their judgment will only make it reasonable for them to question his motives. And if there is anything about him that he does not want them to question, it's his motives. Especially regarding money. Their money.

The cost of renting a car is higher than he expected, and he is disappointed when the woman at the counter tells him that since he didn't reserve a Mustang or Barracuda in advance, he can't have one.

He will have to take a Plymouth sedan. A traveling salesman's car, he thinks.

He tosses his briefcase across the wide front seat like a traveling salesman and slides in behind the steering wheel. The interior of the car is a room, a mobile room. The vehicle moves, but his body remains still. In search of the basics—gas gauge, speedometer, clock—he checks out the chrome-rimmed dials and levers and buttons clustered before him, and after a moment of confusion, separates these three from the others and learns that the gas tank is full and he is traveling at eighty-seven miles an hour and it is 2:05 p.m. He looks out the closed windows and realizes that he is on a crowded street. Swerving left, the street suddenly widens and is joined by other streets with many other huge American cars moving rapidly toward him from all sides—with a red stoplight just ahead, then directly in front of him, and now somewhere far behind.

For a few seconds he is alone on the road speeding toward an S curve, which turns into a cloverleaf with roads spidering out in all directions. He glances at the speedometer and sees that he is approaching the cloverleaf at slightly over ninety miles an hour. He slams his foot against the brake pedal, and the car lurches, screeches, and spins itself in a long arc to the right, crosses the road and comes to a dead stop next to the curb, facing the way he came, with the cloverleaf out of sight behind him now, and three lanes of cars bearing implacably down on him. He wrenches open the door and flings himself from the car and runs, his mind braced for the sickening crash as the onrushing vehicles destroy his car and pile up, one atop the other.

But there is no crash. Just the swoosh of traffic along the outer two lanes and the rising bleat of horns from the cars lined up in the inside lane behind his parked Plymouth. He feels naked and foolish standing out there on the highway. He runs back to the car and gets in and finds the motor still running and backs it off the road, up and over the curb onto the grassy island. Safe.

After a few moments the traffic thins. The light is red again, as if holding the cars back for him. He eases the Plymouth down onto the road and heads it once again in the right direction. He successfully navigates it through the cloverleaf and brings it across the short stretch of freeway to the Sumner Tunnel tollbooth. He pays the toll, rolls his window back up, closing it against the crisp, salty spring breeze, and crosses beneath the harbor, entering the city from the east.

Gradually, as he circles the jammed Haymarket Square and crosses the downtown sections of the city toward the Charles River, he regains confidence in his ability to drive the Plymouth. It's the vehicle itself that he doesn't trust, so he continues to remind himself of how he should act in each situation as it arises. Go easy on the brake, just brush it lightly. Now watch your speed up ahead, you may be moving too fast. All right, all right, keep turning the wheel, just a little, that's it, slowly, slowly. Excellent. Beautifully done, Leo.

Fife hasn't forced himself to drive an automobile this way—consciously directing his body's actions, refusing to let his body act on its own—since he was first learning to drive. Except when very drunk, too drunk to be unafraid of his slowed reaction time. He remembers with a shudder how close he came back then to sudden violent death, as if he didn't know that he could be smashed to pieces at a very young age while merely trying to drive home to sleep. Or perhaps he was fully aware of that possibility and had decided to convert it into a probability by continuing again and again to court it by driving out in the early evenings to beach bars miles from where he lived in downtown St. Petersburg and making himself as unhappily drunk and confused and angry as possible in five or six hours, so that by one a.m., when all the bars have closed, he stumbles out to the parking lot and locates his dark-green Studebaker and begins again that weaving, bobbing, searching drive home.

Once across the river, Fife skirts the glut of Cambridge traffic and drives north through Somerville toward Medford, passing railroad yards, foundries, and assembly plants, cutting a zigzagging radius from downtown Boston through the soot-blackened industrial zone and shoulder-to-shoulder fifty- and seventy-five-year-old triple-decker wooden tenements and on to the spacious, grassy ring of manicured suburbs. Beyond the suburbs, he picks up Route 93, the new north-south interstate turnpike that slices a six-lane swath from Boston diagonally across the forests and hills of New Hampshire into northern Vermont all the way to Canada. He has let his attention wander away from the past to the more distant past. He's not thinking about his driving now. It's taking care of itself.

He remembers taking his battered 1948 Studebaker Starlight coupe back from the bars along the beach to his dingy rented rooms in St. Petersburg, late at night through a thick bank of fog drifting east off the Gulf of Mexico, the boulevards practically empty of cars and the sidewalks finally vacated by the aged, sunburnt northerners waiting to die surprised. During the days he has his job at the greenhouse to occupy his attention, and it is enough to distract him from himself. Also he enjoys the work, shifting tiny plants from one bed to another, spreading piles of loam, moss, fertilizer, and straw, digging small neat holes in black earth and filling the holes with something altogether different from what was taken away.

But that is only during the days, Monday through Saturday, from eight in the morning until six at night. When Sunday comes around, he walks the palmy quarter mile to the St. Petersburg public library where there's a small walled-in Japanese garden, seldom crowded, especially on Sundays, with benches placed near tropical flower beds and pools filled with somnolent koi. Arriving shortly before noon, he situates himself on an empty bench with a book that he thinks he should be reading and stays there whether he reads it or not, until the librarian comes out and gently, respectfully, regretfully, informs him that it is six o'clock and the library is about to close.

With twilight coming gradually on, the sky above the Gulf breaks into pink and orange streaks, and the tall palm trees turn suddenly black against the sky. He walks slowly back to the two furnished rooms in the stuccoed cube that has been his mailing address for nearly half a year, since January, when he first arrived from his parents' home in Strafford, Massachusetts. He begins to pace restlessly from window to window to mirror in the shared bath across the hall and back again to the darkening sitting room, to the low refrigerator and hot plate, his makeshift kitchen in a corner of the sitting room, where he heats and eats a can of Dinty Moore beef stew, to the bedroom, to the slumped bed itself, where he stretches out on his back and stares up at the crackled ceiling, watching imagined patterns slowly disappear in shadow, until finally at some point, which is always the final point of his meandering, he decides to wait no longer.

He isn't sure what exactly he's been waiting for, but he knows that if it ever actually arrives and clicks into place while he is alone and idle like this, the very existence of the brittle, flimsy structure that he calls his life will be jeopardized. He fears that someday, possibly very soon, he will be unable to decide that he can wait no longer for that moment to arrive, and instead of changing his shirt and driving out to the noisy hot bars along the beach—where he will drink and listen and talk to anyone willing to drink and listen and talk to him, until at last he is able to grope his way back to his empty rooms, able finally to disappear into sleep—he will instead endure the silence and solitude of his rooms a little past that point of departure, and he will not be able to halt the deliberate destruction of the life he has been trying to nurture with justifications and evasions and rationalizations and hope. The truth will overwhelm his lies. His old life will reach forward and throttle the new one.

By the time he turned up in Florida, he had rejected several lives and had begun as many new ones. Though barely nineteen years old, he is already familiar with the process. He believes that his reasons for ending one sequence of acts and simultaneously starting up another are honorable and necessary. Compelling, he says. He won't be able to say how they are compelling, until many years later, when almost by accident he finds himself starting yet another new life, his fifth or sixth or seventh. He will have lost count by then. But none of those later lives, not even this final one, will emerge from as direct a confrontation with himself as happened in St. Petersburg, Florida, when he fled in terror from solitude and idleness and married a pretty girl who saw his terror and believed that it would force him never to leave her, and loved him for its power over him.

He tried to explain to Alicia that there was nothing wrong with Amy. He didn't hate her, he never hated her, he says, and he probably at one time came very close to loving her. What was wrong was the marriage itself. The reasons for its existence, he means.

Alicia asks him to say how the reasons for its existence were wrong. Asks it nervously.

The reasons for the marriage were shot through with the fear of loneliness on his part and a desperate willingness to sustain his fear on Amy's part. It's not as hard to understand as it is hard to respect or admire, he says. Especially now. But he and Amy were both so young and so alone and for different reasons so terrified of that loneliness that they got married. They met at a bar one night. She came with a guy Fife knew vaguely and left with Fife. Five weeks later they ran off to Georgia, where it was legal to marry at eighteen without parental consent.

Sounds familiar, Alicia says.

Fife says, Yes. Amy called her parents to tell them what she'd done, and they told her don't come home. They were religious fanatics, he explains. Fife and Amy decided right there, standing outside a roadside phone booth in Macon, to climb back into his Studebaker and keep it headed north until they got to Boston. She was pregnant by then, but they didn't know it. They both thought that getting married was a good way to be in love.

Fife is driving north again, this time away from Boston, alone in his rented Plymouth, his mind soaked in watery memories that he once struggled to forget. He passes quickly out of Medford and turns onto a boulevard that in a few more miles merges with Route 93 and leads on to New Hampshire and Vermont. Approaching the town of Melrose, he turns right onto the Fellsway, as he always did when going home to Strafford, and he doesn't become aware that he has done this until he has driven three or four miles past the Route 93 on-ramp and notices with genuine pleasure how lovely after all these years the trees and rocky outcrops along this winding road to Strafford look.

His body's old habits, out of use for almost ten years, have guided the car toward the place he did not think to visit, did not want to visit—the town where he lived out his childhood and from which he fled in fear and disgust at eighteen, leaving his parents, their only child gone, to move back to their own long-abandoned childhood home in Maine. He decides that, rather than turn back, he will drive on to Strafford. He will pick up Route 93 on the north side of the town, even though it means driving some twenty miles out of his way.

It'll be worth the trouble, he reflects, even if it turns out to be less pleasure than pain. But after these ten years away, it can't be all that painful now, he assures himself. He's no longer afraid of the shame that he once associated with the mere mention of the name of the place. He's a different person now. People change. What harm can come to his new life by setting that town alongside it? Even if the town is altogether unchanged, which he doubts, it won't threaten his hard-won balance and momentum. Not anymore. He's a different person now. They are no longer in conflict, Fife and his hometown, Fife's present and his shameful past.

Besides, it could be enlightening, he thinks, to measure the town as it is today against what it was a decade ago and compare his emotional reaction to the town now to his response then. It might give him some idea of the nature and degree of his own changes, independently of the town's. I'm a different person now, he reassures himself. But how different and in what ways? Without measuring one's life against lives other than one's own, one can't confidently know.

Cruising. Familiar territory on all sides. Nothing has changed, then. A sunny afternoon. A Sunday in spring. Car windows cranked down, skinny arm resting on the window ledge, fingertips on steering wheel rim. Not a thing has changed. Spongy springtime lawns drying out. Trees, puckered to bloom, seem wrapped in bright green lace. The sky arched high and blue, the air gently carrying all sounds up into it, inviting idle talk and casual raps and taps here below. He was briefly happy then and is briefly happy now.

He forgets what he was struggling to recall, and without willing it, remembers other things, things he did not realize he'd forgotten. Amy wanted to see the town where he was raised. He never spoke of it to her, except when prodded, and then he answered only with names and brief allusions. Or else he lied about it. Strafford, Massachusetts . . . one of those Boston suburbs with a colonial past . . . a smug little town . . . out of joint with the times, yet a victim of them . . . the reverse side of the coin that bears the ghetto on its face . . . , was how he chose to describe it, which only intrigued her the more.

Amy's entire life had been lived among the stuccoed cinder-block bungalows and motels and shopping centers of Florida's Gulf Coast, and this eastern New England, with its odd juxtapositions of old and new, its industrial city and idyllic village, its slum and hillside farm, its seacoast and ski resort, fascinates her as much as it confuses her. She is frightened by the dark, dank streets of South Boston and Roxbury, and will not believe Fife when he tells her of the wide sandy beaches just ten miles away. She cannot understand why the famous Bunker Hill Monument smells of urine, as if a gigantic dog periodically strolled past the granite spire and raised a leg over it. Or why Lodges, Saltonstalls, and Lowells would wish to live on one side of a lump of a hill while on the other side homeless winos were falling down drunk at noon and vomiting on the cobbled streets till dark, when the police finally round them up for the night. She does not want to believe him when he tells her that the boot and saddle shop in an eighteenth-century wood-frame house on the corner of a narrow lane that looks out over a tiny Yankee seaport once white with the sails of clipper ships returning from China is actually a bookie joint owned and operated by the friends, associates, and enemies of the men whose bodies were daily being fished out of the Charles and Mystic Rivers or discovered in the trunks of cars parked in vacant lots in Chelsea and the North End.

She asks him again to take her to Strafford.

There's nothing to see there. Nothing, he says. A couple of ponds they like to think of as lakes, a few old buildings dating back to the 1700s, a village green. Tract houses and triple-deckers. Maybe we'll drive through it sometime, he offers vaguely. Maybe we'll drive through on the way up to Maine, when we go to see my folks. We'll go through Strafford on the way, so you can have something to talk about with them.

When?

For Thanksgiving. They'll want us to come for Thanksgiving. If we don't go, they'll try to blame you in order to keep from thinking that I hate them and didn't come because of it. They used to blame geography, because I was too far away in Florida, but that excuse is gone now. So we'll just have to go there.

Why do you hate them?

You'll know when you see them on Thanksgiving.

But she isn't content to wait that long to see the town where he grew up. It will help her know who he is, she explains. She teases and coaxes all summer long, until finally one Saturday afternoon Fife relents and agrees to take her there.

He drives the Studebaker out of the city through Somerville and Medford, turns onto the Fellsway, and after a few minutes more of passing anxiously beneath the overhanging elm trees and over the low hills, while Amy chatters about the beautiful fall foliage and the rooks and rills and the carefully domesticated parkland, at the top of a hill, Fife notices that the temperature gauge and oil pressure indicator are slowly rising. He ignores the gauges and drives on. The temperature and oil pressure continue to rise. Five miles short of their destination, they leave the woods along the Fellsway and reach the top of a long, slow rise, where the buxom Victorian houses of the neighboring town of Melrose hove into view, and the engine of the Studebaker suddenly cracks and blows up.

Calmly, as if he has been expecting it all along, Fife flicks the ignition off and lets the car, bits of metal clattering under the smoking hood, coast down to the bottom of the slope, where it slows to a hissing stop at the side of the road. Ahead of them a roadside sign welcomes them to Strafford, Massachusetts, founded in 1639.

13

FIFE SAYS TO THE ROOM, YOU'VE NEVER HEARD ME speak of any of this before, have you?

For the past few hours he's made his inner eye the camera, revealing only what he chooses from everything he sees there, keeping his opinions, his struggles and conflicts, his fears and guilt and shame, to himself.

But he's not told them what they want to hear. Malcolm and Diana and Vincent and Sloan couldn't care less about the details of his distant past and wouldn't bother to catch the details anyhow, much less film and record them, if he weren't who he has become over the last fifty years here in Canada. Up to his arrival from the States in 1968, the story Fife is telling isn't much more than a deckle-edged bildungsroman, a ragged tale told of a mid-twentieth-century American boy's inadequate attempts to invent himself as an adult, a boy and young man more or less typical of his time, nationality, race, and class. Not worth an interview filmed for CBC Television.

But now Fife is a well-known, almost famous Canadian documentary filmmaker who happens to be dying—and, yes, everyone happens to be dying, he knows that, some sooner and at a quicker pace than others. It's an ongoing process that begins at birth and ends at any moment. His death, however, is imminent, and he is eminent. Sort of. And at least for the next few days, immanent. Which has invited Malcolm and his crew to film and record his every word. And it has given Fife license to set the record straight, as it were, allowing the camera for once to be turned back onto him, inviting him to tell the truth to those who sit in darkness close enough to hear all that he has lied about or kept hidden during the years that he has lived and worked alongside them. They can't know how he got from there to here without first learning where *there* is.

Malcolm and Diana don't want to hear all that. Now they're asking him to tell Vincent's camera and Sloan's mic about the film he shot of the Joan Baez concert at the 1969 Mariposa Folk Festival in Toronto. How'd that come about? Malcolm asks. That was a real ballbuster, I heard. I don't mean your film, he adds, which I've watched many times. That's a heartbreaker, man. Especially when you watch it today.

He's referring to Baez's denunciation of the sixty thousand young American men who fled to Canada to avoid being shipped out to Vietnam or going to prison for desertion. Malcolm is familiar with the history of the film and the controversy that surrounded the concert at the time. He wants something else.

Leo, Malcolm says, can you talk about the draft dodgers' and deserters' expectations leading up to the Mariposa concert and their disappointment and confusion afterward? Malcolm wants Fife to tell how he knew to sit down and interview those half dozen young American guys before the concert, when they still thought that Joan Baez, the folk-singing queen of US protest against the Vietnam War, was coming up to Canada to praise and support them.

Those guys, when the film opens, they're fucking joyous, he says. Joyous. And you caught it on-camera, man. She was like their Joan of Arc riding up on her white horse to inspire them and validate their plight in Canadian hearts and minds. And then you found and interviewed the same group of guys later that night, only minutes after the concert, after they had been scolded by her from the stage for running to Canada instead of going to prison in the States. Baez wanted them to return and go to prison voluntarily, like her husband, David Harris. They didn't know whether to be totally pissed at her or return to the States and turn themselves in to the authorities. Or just stay on in Canada, feeling like shit.

Did Fife know before the concert that Baez was going to call the American refugees out? That she'd say they were cowards? She said that, man. Cowards. When they were used to thinking of themselves as courageous, self-sacrificing political exiles. Because Fife's film wasn't about the famous and beautiful Joan Baez—Malcolm thinks she was pregnant at the time, and remembers that Fife's camera lingered a lot around her rounded belly—or about the concert itself or Joni Mitchell and Neil Young, who were there, too. It wasn't about the musicians, the stars. It was about those American refugees, the draft dodgers and deserters. Everyone else wrote or filmed just the musical and celebrity aspects of the concert, American and Canadian folk rock stars singing together on the same stage in Canada. But somehow Fife had known beforehand that the real human story was going to be Joan Baez's denunciation of the American deserters and draft dodgers, and he was ready for it.

Was it just intuition, or did Fife know someone close to Baez, someone who tipped him off to what was coming? Her publicist or one of the backup musicians. Or maybe he knew the singer herself. It was a smaller world back then, before Facebook and Twitter and Instagram, and everyone seemed to know everyone personally or was off by only a few degrees of separation.

Fife says no, he didn't really know her. He'd met her, but they weren't friends or anything. When he was living in Boston in the early 1960s, or maybe it was the late 1950s, he briefly knew a kid named

Bobby Zimmerman from Minnesota, a guitar-playing folk singer who
for a couple of months shared an apartment with one of Fife's close
friends, Stanley Reinhart, who's a well-known artist now but was a
student then at the School of the Museum of Fine Arts. Bobby used
to perform his songs at the old Unicorn Coffee House in Boston and
Club 47 over in Cambridge, and sometimes Joan came up from New
York to perform with him and stayed over at Reinhart's apartment,
where Fife met her a few times. Bobby Zimmerman had great hair. It
was called a Jewfro back then. It was a time when hair meant a lot, especially men's hair. Bobby had a tousled mane of dark curls that looked
like he didn't give a damn about it, but obviously he did, and even carried a pick displayed prominently in the back pocket of his jeans, like
a Black guy, so it was a Fuck You statement. You could make political
statements with your hair back then. Around 1960, or maybe it was
'61, Bobby moved back to Greenwich Village, where he completed his
transformation into Bob Dylan. Fife never saw him after that. Or Joan
Baez, either.

Malcolm says, You're like a freaking Zelig, man. Go on.

Fife points out that since he didn't know Baez or any of her en-
tourage personally, he had no idea she was planning to denounce the
American draft dodgers and deserters—the resisters, he calls them—
from the stage at the Mariposa Folk Festival. He was aware of the
political situation in Quebec and New Brunswick that summer and
fall, and when the Americans taking refuge at the Toronto resister center told him how eager they were for Baez to come to Canada and defend their actions, he thought it was weirdly naive, so he interviewed
them on-camera, the same camera he'd used for his Gagetown footage.
They were convinced that Baez would help pressure the newly elected
prime minister Pierre Trudeau into declaring them refugees, which
would protect them from the US military authorities and FBI agents
who were chasing them down all across the country from Vancouver
to Halifax, clamping them in irons and hauling them south, and when

they couldn't catch the resisters themselves, trying to get the Mounties to capture and extradite them.

Trudeau was unmarried then and had a much publicized taste for the company of celebrity musicians, especially attractive female musicians. He was supposedly sleeping with Barbra Streisand. The Toronto war resisters figured Joan Baez was the best person in the world to make their case to him. Fife knew it wouldn't happen. Not because of Baez, but because of Trudeau. He was under a lot of pressure from Lyndon Johnson and J. Edgar Hoover and was sitting on the fence about granting the resisters refugee status. He had an election coming up and was preoccupied by the whole French separatist issue, which was explosive, literally, and threatening to blow the country into half a dozen pieces.

The Americans Fife interviewed before and after the concert were resisters he met at the Toronto Anti-Draft Programme office down on Yonge Street in Toronto. He drove over from Montreal for the concert with Ralph Dennis, the guy he'd been working for in New Brunswick. Fife and Ralph knew that Trudeau was only barely holding the country together and wasn't about to embrace another divisive national identity issue. It was the summer of 1969. The whole world seemed to be breaking into small colonies of the saved. Even Canada. So Fife had no inkling of Baez's coming condemnation of the resisters. All he brought to it was a belief that Trudeau was not going to give the American draft dodgers and deserters the protected status of refugees. It wasn't going to happen. Not then, maybe not ever.

Fife is sorry he's said this much on-camera about the making of his Mariposa film. Malcolm, like most directors, but unlike Fife, is easily excited, with a tendency to push and manipulate other people into feeding his need for still more excitement. Fife would take it all back if he could. Erase what he's said about Mariposa from the record. Cut the part about Bobby Zimmerman and Joan Baez, Fife as a freaking Zelig. Everything he says concerning his life in Canada only hardens the myth of Leonard Fife.

When he first woke this morning, it was not his intention to go where he has been in the hours since Vincent's camera and Sloan's mic started to record him. He originally meant to allow them, as they wished, to conduct a proper interview about his life and work in Canada, to let them ask their prepared questions in a natural way, or at least in a way that is characteristic of him: digressive and impersonal, rephrasing the questions in order to say what he wants them to hear, no more, no less, reinforcing and embellishing the public image of Leonard Fife as an intelligent and imaginative and intellectually serious man, yet a warm, good-humored man, a frank, unpretentious, down-to-earth man. But at the same time a high-minded and morally and politically principled man. Do the thing he's done a hundred times.

But when he woke this morning and Renée gave him his medicines and his head began to clear a little, it came to him with the force of an electrical storm that this would probably be his last chance to tell the truth—to himself and to the one person who still loves him.

Is there no one else who loves him? No one he can name. Not the way Emma loves him. He's not sure what it is that passes for love in the world, anyhow. He's never been sure. Even so, he decided to tell the truth in such a way that Emma could finally know who she loves and he can know who he is. Once he made that decision, his mind immediately filled to overflowing with long-forgotten, long-denied, long-disguised memories of his youth and early manhood. They unspooled unwilled at first, then deliberately. From the moment he was wheeled into the black box and placed at center stage and given the spotlight and permission to commence speaking, he has cared only about recalling and telling his story as truthfully and simply as possible, as if it were not his but someone else's, a stranger's, and the camera and microphone were in his hands, under his control, not Malcolm's or Diana's, not Vincent's or Sloan's.

Given the complexity of the story and its moral ambiguities, and given that, to them and to some degree himself, it's all previously un-

known material, he's had to jump around in time and do a fair amount
of backing up and filling in, for which he apologizes. I'm sorry, he says
to Sloan's mic. I'm sorry.

Also, the world of his past is a remembered world, not quite fictional but, like fiction, reductive, selective, structured by intent and
desire and by the age-old impossible-to-escape conventions of storytelling. He does see and hear, almost as if they are visual and auditory
hallucinations, the people he thought he loved and might have loved
and merely tried to love—the people he betrayed and abandoned. They
are present like holograms or ghostly afterimages, walking, talking,
weeping, making love, arguing, begging, eating, drinking, smoking,
joking, planning, driving cars, singing and dancing, floating in the
dark air between him and the camera and the mic. And among them,
standing at the meaningful center, is the hologram named Fife, Leonard Fife, a remembered version of the man as remembered by the man
himself.

A woman he knew once in her old age—he only came to know her
in her old age—wrote and published a memoir called *My Autobiography as I Remember It*. Fife admired the clarity and apparent modesty
of the title, but for those who knew her better and knew her when,
mainly her grown children and family members and old friends, the
title was no more than permission and justification for a book of lies.
Harmless lies, for no one named in her memoir, except perhaps her
late husband, was demonized or blamed for the memoirist's long, hard
life of frustration, struggle, and loss, ending with recovery from alcoholism through Alcoholics Anonymous and, after the accidental death
of her youngest child, an easing of despair and grief through a personal
relationship with Jesus.

Everyone who knew what really happened back in the day said,
That's not at all how I remember it. But this was her memoir, not
theirs, her memories, not theirs. And if all her memories were self-
serving rationalizations of behavior that, seen in another's light, would

seem stupid, narcissistic or superficial, in her own view her memories were redemptive. They revealed the reasons for her life of pain and suffering and confusion. They made sense of an otherwise incomprehensible, meaningless life and, in her own eyes, redeemed it.

Is that what Fife is trying to do? Tell his autobiography as he remembers it? Yes, he says, that is what he's trying to do today and tomorrow and for however long he is given to tell it.

Malcolm interrupts to ask what's the point of his story about the old woman's autobiography as she remembers it.

Perhaps a better question, one that Malcolm, because he's a filmmaker, doesn't think to ask, is: Who is he telling it to? The answer shapes how he tells it and what he leaves out and what he includes. Regardless of what Malcolm believes, Fife is not telling it to him, or to Vincent and his camera. And not to Diana or Sloan and her microphone. And he's not telling it to the people they hope will watch the film they will make from his rambling account. And he's not telling it to his nurse Renée, who, understandably, couldn't give a good goddamn.

No, he's telling his tale to his wife, Emma, because he wants to be known by her, the one person who has said many times over that she loves him for who he is, regardless of who he is. Perhaps most importantly, for the same reason, he's telling it to himself—because before he dies he wants to be known to himself, regardless of who he is.

Know thyself. He always thought that was a useless, clichéd injunction, an intellectual Boy Scout's credo. He never tried very seriously to know himself, to know if he was a good or a bad man, and if good, how good, if bad, how bad. It seemed a settled affair, a given, and thus never as important or necessary as knowing others, knowing them mainly in order to discern what they wanted from him or what he wanted from them.

If in the past he wished to know anything about himself, it was only to help him identify his capabilities or the lack thereof, so as to measure them against what others wanted from him or he wanted from them. He was a calculating man. He still is. Not an appraising man. An appraisal is a judgment of the worth of something based on a thorough examination of that thing in the context of things that resemble it. It's how one determines value, whether it's the value of a house, a crop, an ounce of gold, or a man's life. He has never done that. Until today.

Are we ready, Malcolm, to resume shooting?

We're ready. We're rolling. Leonard Fife interview. April 1, 2018. Montreal. Card two.

I suspect that what I've been saying has made no sense to you, Fife begins. I apologize for that. Sorry, he says again. Sorry.

He knows what he's thinking and feeling, but some of the words don't sound connected to his thoughts or emotions. It's as if while asleep during the night he suffered a stroke and is just beginning to realize it. Which probably explains Malcolm's uncharacteristic taciturnity and everyone else's silence.

He guesses it doesn't really matter, at least not to him, as long as he himself understands what he's thinking and feeling, and Emma understands. The rest of them can make of it whatever they wish. Or do nothing with it. Erase it all, if they want. But not until he finishes telling it all. Okay?

Okay. Sure, Leo, whatever you want. It's your show, after all.

Where did I leave off?

Strafford. Strafford, Massachusetts, I think. Where you were raised.

14

SO FIFE BEGINS AGAIN, PICKING UP HIS MEMORIES MORE
or less where he left them, stuffing them into his narrative as if filling
a suitcase for a quick getaway.

In the late 1960s, a period when Fife was still trying to think
of himself as a writer, he devised and regularly employed a number
of ways to delay the act of actually writing words on a blank piece of
paper, without at the same time creating a load of guilt so heavy that
he would retire all desire to write a story or novel or even a short lyric
poem. His usual tactic was to research, research, research the story or
novel or poem for as long as possible, to accumulate heaps of historical
and geographic and economic and political data concerning its subject
or the place in which it was supposed to be set.

It's to feed just such an imagined need for data that he decides in
his drive north of Boston to stop in the suburban town of Strafford,
rather than pass through in a hurry to get on to his Vermont rendez-
vous with his old friend, the artist Stanley Reinhart. He decides that
he needs to buy a street map of his hometown, in the event that he will
someday want to set a story or novel there. As long as he's researching

a story or novel set in Strafford, he won't have to write one. Feeney's Pharmacy, the one store certain to be open on a Sunday afternoon, will have a Strafford, Massachusetts, street map.

Located across from St. Joseph's Catholic Church and the Boston & Maine Railroad depot, Feeney's, a combination pharmacy and diner, stays open on Sundays as long as any of the town's Catholics or train commuters—the former coming from confession, a late mass, a catechism class, or a CYO meeting, the latter from their jobs or an evening's entertainment in Boston, a Celtics, Bruins, or Red Sox game—are still strolling the broad tree-lined streets of Strafford in search of someplace to sit with a cup of coffee while they wait for the person with the car to come and carry them home. On Sunday afternoons and every night until midnight, when all the other places of business in town are properly closed, Feeney's plate-glass windows remain brightly lit, as townspeople come and go, buying newspapers, coffee, a quick sandwich, cigarettes, vanilla Cokes, candy bars, and sometimes medicines or condoms or other pharmaceutical products. Fife expects Feeney's Pharmacy to be open on Sunday as usual and everything else in town to be closed as usual, but at the same time he does not believe the store exists anymore, unless under a new name or in a different location.

The big rented Plymouth glides swiftly down from the hills of Melrose, passing the spot where six years earlier his Studebaker blew up, swings past the first lake—a pond not much larger than a football field—and enters the town. The second lake, somewhat larger than the first, is on the north side of town. He will pass around it, leaving. He expects to enter Strafford as a total stranger, recognizing a few citizens and buildings here and there, but little else, confident that he will walk the streets unrecognized himself, like Rip van Winkle down from the mountain, strolling among the descendants of his long-gone family, friends, and neighbors.

Nothing has changed, Fife says to himself, almost aloud. The town looks the same as the day he left it. No new buildings along Main Street. All the old ones—with the same familiar names on the storefronts—still standing. Everything elsewhere gets altered somehow by the passage of time, yet this place has gone from day to day, year to year, for ten years, as if one day and year were no different from the next or the last. To Fife's eyes it's as if it were only yesterday that he fled the town and his mother and father and his friends and their families and everything they meant to him, on the run from his past, erasing his whole life from birth to the age of eighteen.

Main Street moves slowly past him as he drives, J. C. Penney on the right, the Strafford Theater on the left, the stolid, columned Strafford Savings & Loan approaching on the right, all growing larger and then disappearing behind him. He nears the village green, an acre of winter-yellowed grass and brass plaques and statues commemorating the war dead and batches of towering elms all dying slowly of Dutch elm disease. The park rises up in front of him, swings slowly to his right, and disappears behind the Nixon for President headquarters on the corner. He turns left and heads down Salem Street, drives four blocks and comes to the railroad tracks and the platform shelter and benches that serve as a commuter station and, off to one side, across a second street, the putty-colored Catholic church, with its cross-topped steeple. He turns right onto Broadway, and there it is, between Nickel's Toy Shop and Case TV Repair, both shops closed—Feeney's Pharmacy.

Fife steers the car into a parking space just beyond the store. Turning off the engine, he sits in the car for a few moments with his hands in his lap and tries to gather his flailing thoughts and emotions into a single bundle. I'm hungry, he realizes. He hasn't eaten since this morning in Richmond. Except for a few breakfast biscuits, he didn't even eat there. He's not sure any longer that he was in Richmond. Ever.

He can buy a cup of coffee and a sandwich at Feeney's lunch counter, though he knows it will be oddly alarming to stroll in and grab a stool like a regular and order a roast beef on rye and receive his food from a stranger, probably a teenage kid working weekends and after school till midnight every night, just as he did for two hectic years before he turned sixteen and took off into the West with his best friend, Nick Dafina. After that, when he found a more congenial, better-paying after-school job at Varney's Menswear, he still managed to come into Feeney's several times a day and at night. He came for an assortment of reasons, but mainly because he didn't want to return to his parents' apartment three blocks away. It always seemed that, through one local connection or another, he knew the kid who waited on him there fairly well, usually a slightly younger version of himself. Strafford back then was that sort of town. Perhaps it still is.

Fife sits in the car and looks at his hands. They're shaking uncontrollably and feel weightless. He starts expecting to be met not by a stranger, a younger version of himself, but by someone he knows and knows well, someone who knew him when he lived in Strafford with his mother and father and worked after school here at Feeney's, someone who knew him before his first failed attempt to start his life over by driving a stolen car west. Someone who knows his true story. Someone he went to high school with. Tommy Reagan? Alfred Neff? That tall, pimply-faced kid, Walter Whatzizname? Walter Sorenson.

It was a fantasy to think that he could enter this town as a total stranger, unrecognized, anonymous, like old befuddled Rip van Winkle, who slept for twenty years. Just as he knows the town by sight, it will know him by sight, too. Its inhabitants will want to fix him like a butterfly on a pin and hang him on a wall for all to see and wonder at, poking and prodding at his better parts, admiring their delicacy, their brilliance. They might wish they themselves had wings like his. Laughing at his ridiculous, self-destructive misuse of those qualities, they will walk away, talking of what Fife could have been, could have done, what he should have been and should have done, how he could have saved himself so easily from such a pathetic end.

He remembers his pal Nick Dafina grinning with vicarious pleasure, telling him, No, man, forget what all those fucking stuffed shirts are saying, forget them and stick to your decision, because it's the right decision, man! He thinks of his mother and father smiling wanly through their fears, his father, working the night shift then, his final year at the dispatch office in the South Station rail yard, dressed for work and leaving the house just as Fife walks in, after two days and a night hitchhiking home from Rumford College, freezing, exhausted, covered with snow, and his mother crying over and over again, Thank heaven you came home, thank heaven you came home! We were so afraid something . . . His father looks away and mumbles that they have a lot to talk about, but it'll have to wait till tomorrow if he wants to catch the 9:27 to Boston.

He remembers the Reverend Stephen Sitwell's taut scarlet face, blond crew cut pulled down tightly against his skull, lips clipped together like a purse, unclipping and saying, Listen to me, Leonard, you can't just walk out on the world for being what it is, no matter how corrupt and unjust it seems to you. My Lord, Leonard, you're barely eighteen, and you're dismissing the rest of the world out of hand because it's not as idealistic as you are? It might turn out that in a decade or two you'll discover that you could have done more to help the poor and oppressed by staying in college and getting your degree than by wandering off like some kind of hobo. By then it may be too late to correct your compass and get your life back on its proper track, the minister says, and smiles.

Fife looks away from the minister to his mother's shrinking, pleading face. Look, he says to her, I really don't see any sense in talking about this in these terms. It's my decision. So please, stop trying to tell me why I should stay in college! Why I should become a doctor or a lawyer or some kind of businessman.

He gets up from the couch and pulls on his coat. I imagine, Reverend, that you want to comfort and counsel my mother, since she's the one who called you and asked you to come by here tonight.

Are you going out, Leo? she asks.

Don't worry, I'll be back later. I'm not leaving home for good. Not yet. Not till after Christmas.

Where do you plan to go after Christmas? the minister asks, rising from his chair and extending his hand for Fife to shake. Where can you go, Leonard, when you've left both college and home?

Cuba, Fife answers. He refuses the minister's hand, crosses the room, and leaves them.

The snow has stopped falling, and the sky has cleared. The cold night air instantly calms his angry, befuddled mind. Points of light overhead dot the dome of the black sky. He socks his hands deep into the pockets of his loden coat and walks down to the corner, then left toward Feeney's, three blocks away. Cuba! he thinks. Cuba! It didn't occur to him until he blurted it out to block Reverend Sitwell's mocking question.

Where can an eighteen-year-old college dropout go when he has left both college and home? Of course! He'll go to Cuba! To fight with Fidel Castro and his men in the rugged hills of Oriente and the Sierra Maestra, that's where he'll go! Fife has followed the adventures of Castro and his merry band of Latin American Robin Hoods for months, followed them as closely as the newspapers and popular magazines will let him, and like most Americans he admires the lawyer-turned-revolutionary and has connected the Cuban leader to the romanticized heroes of America's own revolution. It doesn't hurt that Castro and his bearded men remind Fife of American beatniks. He learned enough Spanish in his junior year of high school to get by, he believes, and speaks it probably as well as Lafayette spoke English when he first arrived from Paris to help General George Washington. As for the cause, Fidel Castro's cause, it is clear that Castro's ambition is only to rid his homeland of a cruel dictatorship, that he leads a ragtag collection of young intellectuals and peasants, and that the US government secretly supports him. What else is needed to justify his cause? An ideology?

He will go to Cuba. Definitely. Thank God he thought of it. The only remaining question is when to leave Strafford for Cuba. He'll have to get down there soon, or the war will be won and done without him. It's best if he takes off immediately, tomorrow morning, because he might run into difficulties trying to get across from Miami or Key West to Havana and from there to wherever Castro's mountain hideout is located. Everything will depend on whether he can contact a Cuban revolutionary in Miami or Key West, and if not there, then after he arrives in Havana.

On the other hand, the cruelest thing he can do to his parents now is leave before Christmas, only two weeks away. Their vaguely familial sentiments, usually heightened at Christmas, will this year be unbearably intensified. He will be obliged to picture the two of them weeping and falling pathetically into each other's arms all Christmas day and for weeks afterward whenever they mention his name or think of him or look at the Christmas tree with his still-wrapped gifts beneath falling spruce needles. He's not that free of them. Not yet, anyhow. He's only eighteen years old.

He decides that he will work until Christmas at Varney's Menswear, where he has been promised $1.15 an hour during the holiday season. He will work as many hours as Mr. Varney will give him and save as much of his earnings as possible. On lunch breaks and whenever he finds a free moment, he will brush up on his Spanish and study Cuban geography and history. Reverend Sitwell and his mother won't remember that he said he was going to Cuba. He will tell his parents only that he imagines drifting on down to Florida for a while, since he's never been there before, and if he likes it, he'll stay, until he decides to move on. That's all he'll tell them. They'll just think he's one of those erratic young men inspired by Jack Kerouac's novel *On the Road*. Fine. If they conclude that he is acting irresponsibly—rashly, immaturely, selfishly, whatever word they choose—it won't matter to him. He knows his true motives better than anyone, and that makes all the difference.

His true motives? At best, he knows only the observable nature of his acts. Concerning motives, he couldn't have less knowledge if he were a total stranger. He has very little difficulty coming up with reasons for what he is doing—that is, if asked, he has answers. But are they believable? To him then, to him a decade later, to him a half century later?

Fife lowers his head and presses his forehead against the steering wheel of the Plymouth. He winces, shuts his eyes, and slowly bumps his forehead against the rim of the wheel over and over, thinking, Not fair, not fair, because they won't understand the truth and won't believe it, even if they do understand it. He has to lie. He has to pretend that he is a selfish, devil-may-care, irresponsible kid dropping out of college barely two months into his freshman year, forsaking his prestigious, shockingly large scholarship, and after that letting on to Nick Dafina and then, one by one, to his parents, to his quickly disappearing high school girlfriend, Evelyn Rose, to Reverend Sitwell, that in reality he dropped out of college and is leaving home to go south to Cuba, where he plans to join Fidel Castro. He has to tell them that. It's the only thing they'll believe. It will make perfect sense to them. With great relief, with all the pieces through some weird logic clicking neatly into place, everyone will smile and say, Ah-h-h, now I understand why you came home from college after only two months there. Why you chucked that wonderful full tuition and room and board scholarship. Why you suddenly want to go to Florida! Well, now, that makes more sense, my boy, although I think you're being a little too idealistic. Even though I don't agree with what you're doing, Leo, I nevertheless admire your motives.

He remembers that final night at Varney's Menswear, helping Mr. Callahan, the father of his friend Roger Callahan, pick out Christmas neckties for his employees. Back when he was Fife's age, he tells Fife, he came damned close to running off to Spain to fight with the old Lincoln Brigade. Four or five of his friends dropped out of Rumford, packed a bag, and took off for Spain, nothing but the highest ideals, you understand, and a couple of them were the brightest guys I knew, too. Had brilliant careers ahead of them, in spite of being Communists. Not very different than you, Leo. The ones who got through it, though, when the war was over and they came back to the States and tried to pick up where they left off, they found out it wasn't very easy to do. No, sir. Things had changed. And later, of course, there was the Communist business. The Russkies. The Chinese.

Would you like to look at some neckties? We've got some real beauties over here, got them in especially for Christmas.

Tell you what, you pick me out about six ties you like yourself, you got good taste. These'll be for some of the younger guys selling on the road. Y'know, Leo, my son Roger thinks one hell of a lot of you. I was real pleased, as you know, to see both you guys get into Rumford, and for you to get that War Memorial Alumni Scholarship, because I was sure Roger could use your good sense up there. He likes to play more than work, y'know. It's one of the reasons I pulled a few strings for you up there, as a Rumford alum. Wrote that letter for you.

And I sure appreciate it, Mr. Callahan.

I hope to hell Rog' doesn't decide to jump the traces and follow you off to Cuba, for chrissakes!

Callahan laughs and pays Fife with cash for the neckties and sweaters and sports jacket and shirts and cuff links and gloves he's selected. And listen, son, Mr. Callahan says, coming suddenly close, draping a thick, tweed-wrapped arm over Fife's shoulder and ramming a forefinger against his sternum. I've known your dad for years, and your mom too. They're good people, Leo. Salt of the earth. I put that in the recommendation letter I wrote for you. You know that about your parents, don't you?

Yes, sir. I do.

And they're proud of you, Leo. Proud. You're all they got, right?

Right.

I think one hell of a lot of you and your parents. Unlike your dad, who as you know wasn't fortunate enough to have the benefit of a fine college education, because of the Depression and all, and who therefore might not be able to realize what it is you're throwing down the drain, I've had four years of college, the very same college you're so intent on walking out on, so I know what it means to a man later on, when it comes time to providing for a wife and kids. I started at the bottom, Leo, and I've come out on top, as you know, and you better believe that my sticking it out at Rumford and not running off to Spain in '37 had a lot to do with that. Now, your mom and dad, they're probably used to being able to trust you to know more about such things as higher education than they do. I think Roger told me that your mom and dad didn't even know what colleges you'd applied to, and that they found out about you winning that scholarship to Rumford by reading about it in the papers. Is that true?

Yeah. Look, Mr. Callahan . . .

I know, you got a job to do, and you got to keep ol' Tom Varney happy, so I'll just say what I have to say and let you get back to work toot sweet. The point is this, your mom and dad, they can't come out and say whether you ought to follow your emotions and head to Cuba or whether you should be practical-minded and go on back to Rumford. You can get back in, can't you? If not, maybe I can make a few calls.

Oh, yeah, I can get back in. But . . .

But me no buts, Leo. You need help, son, advice, so for chrissakes, don't make a move until you've come by the house for an evening and we've sat down together over a couple of drinks and talked this thing out. Man to man. Promise me that, Leo.

That's very generous of you, sir.

No, Leo, not generous at all. You're a brilliant boy with a brilliant career ahead of you. Law, medicine, business, maybe journalism. Whatever you want. My own boy's got it made, you might say. He can go to work for National Register the day he graduates from Rumford. But you're in a position, Leo, all on your own, to move up the ladder to the very top of the heap, so that someday your son will have it made, the same as Roger has now. It's the good old American dream. Don't let me down. Okay?

Okay, Mr. Callahan. I won't let you down.

Callahan says, Merry Christmas, son, waves a thick arm at him from the door, and strolls out to the street.

It's eight thirty-five when Mr. Varney shambles out the door and it jingles to a close behind him, leaving Fife alone in the store. He walks to the front and looks out at the deserted sidewalks and street. Crisscrossing the street, chains of tinsel and electric lights swing feebly from lampposts decorated to look like giant candy canes. Snow flurries flutter down. It wasn't supposed to snow tonight, Fife thinks, as he walks to the back of the store to the tiny windowless cubicle that serves as Mr. Varney's office. He sits down at the rolltop desk and cranks a sheet of Varney's Menswear letterhead stationery into the Remington typewriter, and he writes:

12/22/58

Dear Mr. Varney,

I suppose it is senseless for me even to bother trying to explain to you, of all people, what I am about to do. But I want you to know that I have no ill-will toward you and in fact have nothing but respect for you and gratitude for your willingness to employ me over the Christmas holidays and after school since I was sixteen. I try to think of you as a friend, if you will forgive my presumptuousness.

I hope that you have been able to think of me in that way also. If you have, then perhaps when you read this you will believe me when I say that I had to do what I will have done, and I hope you will believe that I am sorry. I will try to someday make everything up to you. I am very sorry for any trouble and inconvenience this causes you.

Sincerely,

Leonard Fife

He folds the letter carefully and slips it into an envelope, drops it into the breast pocket of his sports jacket. He leaves the office and walks straight to the glass-topped shirt case by the front door and withdraws three solid-color Pendleton wool shirts, size large. He places them on the wrapping counter and returns to the front of the store, where he removes from the shelves a heavy black turtleneck sweater, a pair of rabbit-fur-lined pigskin gloves, a pale-blue silk scarf, six T-shirts and boxer undershorts, one set of long johns, and six pairs of socks that cost $2 a pair. He lays everything next to the Pendleton shirts on the wrapping counter. He adds a pair of very fine charcoal-gray wool trousers and a $30 pair of leather boots, size ten. He stuffs everything he has taken into a large-size Varney's Menswear bag. He carefully places the bag under the counter.

It is four minutes before nine o'clock. He walks out back and switches off all but the single light near the back door that Mr. Varney keeps on all night to scare off timid burglars. He returns to the front of the store wearing his loden coat over his sports jacket, opens the cash register drawer, and counts out the money for the day's sales. He places the personal checks into Mr. Varney's cloth night-deposit bag, along with $8.46 in coins. He counts out the paper cash very carefully, and after reaching the same figure twice, $312, puts the wad of bills into the breast pocket of his jacket and draws out his letter to Mr. Varney. He places the letter into the cash register next to the totals slip he tore from the register tape. He picks up the bag of clothing from beneath the wrapping counter. He walks slowly out of the store and locks the door behind him and steps into the blowing snow.

When Fife arrives home, both his mother and father are in the living room. His father pulls on his gray cardigan sweater, his way of saying that he knows it's snowing out. He grunts when Fife enters the room, draws out his pocket watch and studies it for a few seconds, then looks up and says to no one in particular, Nine fifteen. Guess I better get a move on.

His wife hands him his black lunch box and pats his sleeve and, catching herself, pulls her hands back to her own clothing, where they tap lightly at buttons, pull at invisible threads and pluck particles of dust. Leo? she calls, as he passes through the meticulous, precisely ordered living room and heads down the hallway toward his bedroom. Leo? Did you have a pleasant day at the store?

Great, he says from his bedroom and closes the door. Great. He pitches the bag from Varney's into his closet and returns to the living room, takes off his coat, and drops into a doily-covered easy chair.

Still working the night shift, eh, Pa? he says without looking at his father, who stands by the door, struggling to find the sleeve of his heavy wool peacoat with his left arm. The sleeve flops uselessly just out of reach until, with a wrench of his upper body, he manages to catch it with his hand and stuffs his arm into it.

Yes, he says. Will be till spring, I expect. After thirty-five years, you'd think I could spend my last year without having to do that hitch for once. But I guess they can't make special allowances for people just because they're about to retire. I can't complain, can I? B & M's treated me pretty good.

You better hurry, Pa, or you'll miss the train, and for the first time in those thirty-five years you'll be late for work. You wouldn't want to screw up your last year, would you?

Right, right. You get behind, you know. Watching the television after supper, I guess. Good night, he says to his wife and son, having once again spoken words forgotten by their listeners as soon as they have been uttered, and then he is gone, relieved to be out of sight, unheard, barely noticed, a man who lives as if ashamed of his own existence.

It has been told to Fife many times that Cornel Fife is his natural father and that eighteen years ago Sarah, Cornel's wife, bore him and is thus indisputably his mother. Yet the three of them, father, mother, and son, their only child, have lived together from the beginning of their life together almost as strangers, three people thrown together as if merely to effect a temporary legal convenience in the life of someone else, someone none of them knows, that Total Stranger, perhaps.

Fife does not know how their mutually alienated condition came about. Central to the family dynamic is his mother's fragility and fearfulness. She seems always to be standing on the edge of panic, never quite falling off it, and he and his father behave as if a single misstep by either of them will send her into the abyss.

Fife once asked his mother, If you're not able to tolerate my noise and ruckus now, when I'm full-grown, how could you have stood living with me when I was a baby and small child? It is a sincere question, not meant as a criticism. He wants to know the answer.

They stand side by side in the kitchen by the window above the sink. Outside, the snow glistens under a December sun. Her eyes are closed as if against the glare of the snow, and her hands protect her ears from Elvis Presley's "Love Me Tender" played low on the radio in Fife's bedroom.

We were old when you were born to us, she answers, as if he came in the mail.

The teenage Fife has no language for it, but later he will come to believe that one of his parents, he is unable to say which, was mentally ill and passed it on to the other like a virus. It must have happened long before his birth. His mother, Sarah, or his father, Cornel, was born profoundly depressed or else developed the illness early in life, and by hiding the symptoms for a few months or a year, drew the other close enough and long enough to spread it to the other. They would not have been attracted to each other if both were ill. They would have repelled each other. Cornel, with his affect of permanent disappointment, seems to have a slightly more sympathetic nature, or at least the residue of one, so it is probably Sarah who was the source of contagion, and Cornel was drawn into her orbit in order to cure her. When Cornel realized that Sarah could not be healed, he must have felt rejected and abandoned by her and caught the disease himself and soon began to express the same symptoms as his wife—unbroken sadness and lassitude and constant low-level anxiety and detachment and pessimism bordering on despair and the enduring threat of panic. In their late forties, after one of their rare sexual unions, performed out of a shared sense of civic obligation, like voting in a primary election, they unexpectedly conceived a child, and when Fife was born, their disease got quickly passed on to him. An unstable dyad became a locked-in triad.

Until tonight Fife's life has been his alone, just as both his parents' lives have been theirs alone. They are a chain of three islands, tied together, yet separate, an archipelago. He believes that between them the distances are too great to bridge. Yet despite the distances, they are a family, and powerful emotions can be aroused in any of its members whenever the safety and integrity of the family is threatened, whether the threat comes from within or without. Tonight the threat will come from within.

Among the emotions that Fife expects to attack him tonight and has carefully armed himself against are shame and regret. His armor and shield against them are a cold heart and denial. He knows that after his father has walked glumly out the door to catch the 9:27 p.m. train to Boston to work the night shift, and while his mother in the kitchen rearranges her spices and herbs in alphabetical order and after an hour calls down the hall to him, Good night, Leo, and goes to bed, waves of tenderness and compassion will wash over him. And he knows that, as he transfers the stolen clothing from the paper bag in his closet to a suitcase, placing next to the clothing, like a boy running away from home, a few treasured books and his sheath knife and whetstone and some photographs and toiletries and notebooks, he will be lashed by self-loathing. And after leaving on his pillow a handwritten note reading simply, *Don't worry, I'm on my way to Cuba*, thinking he might neutralize triteness with brevity, when he slips out the front door and into the freezing night, his new boots squeaking in the fresh snow, and walks to the commuter station across from Feeney's Pharmacy, he knows his heart will be pummeled by pity and remorse. And while he stands out of sight in the shadows waiting for the 11:27, the last train to Boston, he will be calm and resolute, and wrapped in stolen clothes, he will not feel the cold.

15

MALCOLM SAYS HE DOESN'T GET IT.

Vincent is standing by, letting the camera cool, and Diana and Sloan remain silent. For all Fife knows, they have fallen asleep. Which is fine by him. Same with Renée. None of this would make sense to Renée or have the slightest importance or relevance to her, anyhow.

Fife calls Emma's name. No answer. He calls it again. Where is she? He didn't notice her leaving, although he probably wouldn't have, he was so absorbed in what he was remembering. But there must have been a flash of light cutting through the darkness when she left the room. If she left it.

Fife asks Malcolm if Emma went out while he was talking, and Malcolm, after a significant pause, says yes.

Fuck! Renée, please go to Madame Fife, he says in French, and tell her I can't continue unless she is present.

Renée answers that Madame Fife might not wish to be disturbed.

Fife doesn't care. Bring her back. If Emma is not able to listen to his story, then it will never get told. It's too late for him to try telling it over again—to her, to himself, to anyone who cares to listen. He's a dying man, doped against the pain of his dying.

Renée says that she will go to Madame Fife's office and try to explain to her what he has said.

Fife turns to Malcolm. You don't get it? What don't you get? Does what I'm saying not make sense? He fears there is something terribly wrong with the way he is describing his beginnings, that somehow no one is hearing him the way he hears himself. Maybe it's the meds, the sickness, the fatigue and weakness. The pain. Maybe he's remembering one thing and saying a different thing, as if everything he remembers actually happened to someone else, to the Total Stranger, and not to Leonard Fife.

Malcolm says sure, sure, some of it makes sense. Not all. But it doesn't matter, he and Diana will edit it so that it ends up a coherent, lucid narrative. You know how it's done, he says. You know better than anyone.

Fife wants an example of something that doesn't make sense, something that Malcolm doesn't get. Because to Fife it all connects. It all leads gradually step by step to who he was when he came to Canada in '68 and became the man who, now that he is dying, they want to interview so they can make a documentary film to be shown on national television. How can Malcolm not get it?

Well, the clothes, for instance, Malcolm says. The stuff you said you lifted from the menswear store. They're all winter clothes. It's like you're running away to Canada in 1958, instead of Cuba. I mean, Pendleton shirts? Gloves?

That was later, when I was traveling from Virginia to Vermont, and my suitcase got lost in transit between Richmond and my connecting flight in Washington. Fife isn't sure if he's confused the two journeys in the telling or Malcolm has confused them in the hearing.

Malcolm tells him not to worry, it's a small thing. A minor detail. He'll probably cut it from the film anyhow. Not the part about Fife's dropping out of college in 1958 and running off to join Castro, though. That's interesting, because of how it prefigures Fife's filmmaking career. That's the kind of material they need more of, Fife's early politics and its gradual, growing connection to his art. Maybe Fife can follow that up by telling how his politics first showed up in his writing, now that they know that before he was a filmmaker he was a writer. Maybe Fife can talk a little more about his early writings, the novel he mentioned, for instance, and the poems. And the writers he liked back then. And how he became a draft dodger in the States.

Out of the darkness Sloan suddenly speaks up. Yeah, the writers. She likes the mention of Jack Kerouac and *On the Road*. An amazing book! Malcolm gave her a copy last month, and it blew her away. What was it like, reading *On the Road* back when it was first published? It must've really blown Fife's mind to read it in America in the 1950s. That was like the McCarthy era, right? Korea? The Cold War and all that anti-Communist stuff?

Diana interrupts her. Just let Malcolm ask the questions, dear.

Sorry. I'll keep it zipped.

Yes, dear. Keep it zipped.

Jesus! Maybe I should leave.

Please, you two, Malcolm says. Stay here, Sloan. I need you to do the sound. The FS7 has lousy sound. And Diana, lay off Sloan, will you? She's just trying to help. She's got a thing about Kerouac, is all.

Yeah, right. You gave her the book, *On the Road*. Why? So she'd have a thing about the film director who turned her on to Kerouac? Please.

Don't start, Diana. It's just a fucking book.

Sloan says, I was just wondering, is all. You know, how it felt to read it back when it was first published. It's like a classic.

Fife laughs. Yeah, Diana, it's just a fucking book. He tells Sloan that he doesn't remember what it felt like when he read *On the Road* back in 1958. He only remembers that he read it, because that summer his best friend, Nick Dafina, read it and told him that it reminded him of when he and Fife stole a car two years earlier and went on the road for six weeks before they got busted in Pasadena, California, when Nick, who was a good Catholic boy, went to confession and the priest he confessed to called the cops on them. And two years later, when first Nick and then Fife did read the novel, they thought it was about them, instead of Sal Paradise and Dean Moriarty or Jack Kerouac and Neal Cassady, even though Leonard Fife and Nick Dafina were only sixteen when they went on the road and those other guys were in their late twenties and Kerouac when he wrote it was in his thirties.

The door to the hallway opens, and for a second the blacked-out living room is illuminated, as Emma enters with Renée following her. Renée closes the door and drops the room back into darkness, except for the overhead spot on Fife's bald head.

In a barely audible voice, Emma says, This is hard on me, Leo. I know, I'm not the one who's sick, but Christ, this feels like some kind of postmortem. And besides, you're exhausted. The meds are messing with your mind, darling. You're confused and saying things that shouldn't be said on-camera. Can't we stop this and maybe try again when you're feeling better?

When I'm feeling better? I'm never going to feel better. You know that.

Malcolm says, A Catholic priest turned you and your buddy in? That's true? I thought they weren't supposed to do that. He laughs and says that he doesn't know how much of all this to believe. This is getting more and more like a Werner Herzog film, like *Little Leo Needs to Fly* or something. Maybe Fife is making it all up, or inventing enough of it so that in the end the whole thing is an invention, like a novel. Even Fife's name. Is his name really Leo Fife?

Vincent says, Okay, we're ready to rock 'n' roll. Papa's got a brand-new card.

Fife says, My given name is Leonard Cornel Fife.

Who gave it to you?

Fife ignores the question. It's more important to respond to Emma right now. He wishes he didn't have to put her through this. The alternative is to let her remain deceived and deluded about the man who for over thirty-five years has been her faithless companion—faithless because untruthful. When he dies, for him the world will no longer exist. Nothing will. In a few weeks, or maybe in only a few days or hours, for him the truth or falseness of any aspect of the world won't matter. But for Emma, when he dies, only the piece of the world that is her husband Leo will no longer exist. And if she doesn't know who her husband truly was, then she will not know what part of her life has fallen out of existence. If she doesn't know what has disappeared, she won't know the shape and nature of what's left.

I need you to be here for this, he tells her. I'll never ask anything of you again. It's the only way I can finish my life with a clean conscience. My life since I was a boy has been a nightmare, a nightmare of my own making, and I'm finally trying to wake from it. While I still can.

But why can't you unburden yourself, if that's what you're doing, alone with me? Privately. Why do you have to do it in front of a camera, in public?

He needs the camera and the mic and the darkness. The only way Fife knows how to tell the truth is to sit himself in darkness like this in front of the camera, instead of behind it, and clip on a mic and start talking. Without the camera watching him and the mic listening, without the darkness surrounding him, he would lie to her, the way he lies to everyone. He would try to make Emma love him more than she does. If he could see her, he'd lie. He would watch her face, especially her beautiful gray eyes, and he would check out her body's reactions to his words, and he'd revise his story accordingly. If there were no camera and no mic, no record of what he revealed, he'd lie. If he could see any of them, he'd lie. Even in darkness, talking only to Malcolm, Vincent, Diana, and Sloan, he'd lie. If they were in another room watching him on a monitor, because he is so familiar with how to exploit the medium, he would still lie. He would try to make himself more attractive and interesting and lovable than he is.

He has spent most of his adult life behind the camera, unseen, asking questions, then editing his questions out, until all that remained were the words he wanted heard and the images he wanted seen. Just as Malcolm is doing now. Malcolm will edit this footage and shape it according to his needs and desires, not Fife's. It will be Malcolm's story then, not Fife's. But as long as Emma is here listening to him, and Malcolm has not yet got his hands on the raw footage, Fife is able to keep from lying. Emma is the one person who loves him for what he is, regardless of what he is. She is the one person Fife doesn't feel the need, the compulsion, to seduce. It's like my final prayer, he says quietly. Whether you believe in God or not, you don't lie when you pray. And you don't try to seduce God.

When he met her, Emma, like Malcolm and Diana, was his student at Concordia. She was not yet thirty, but older than most of the other students by more than ten years, married with two young children. She was interested in the history of film and hoped an academic career would help her break free of the miry slough of despond that she'd been driven into by a too-early marriage and motherhood. It was a slough that Fife happened to be personally familiar with—though, until this morning, he has never revealed that to her. Emma graduated in 1979 with a master's degree, and a month later she abandoned her husband and two children to live with Leo Fife, the film school professor she had been sleeping with for nearly a year. He says, This miry Slough is such a place as cannot be mended. It is the descent whither the scum and filth that attends conviction for sin doth continually run, and therefore it is called the Slough of Despond.

Malcolm cuts in to say that he can dig Fife's point about the camera and the mic and being in darkness and how it invites you to tell the truth in a way you wouldn't if you could see the camera and the person asking the questions or even if you were just being interviewed off-camera. Surrounding the interviewee with darkness is a strangely effective interrogation technique, one practically invented by Fife himself. Fife used to explain how it worked by telling his students at Concordia that Freud deliberately sat behind and out of sight of the patient lying on the couch. For decades Fife has been able to get people to admit on-camera things they would never say otherwise. It's how he got Major Gordon to tell about the Agent Orange tests in Gagetown. It's how he got the cannibals from Ontario to confess what really happened on the disastrous Arctic expedition to Banks Island. It's how he got Bishop McCann to admit that he covered up for all those pedophile priests in Nova Scotia and Cape Breton.

Fife interrupts Malcolm and asks Emma if he can start again.

She sighs and says, Yes, go ahead. She'll stay with him until he's finished.

Malcolm suggests that Fife skip the miry slough and go back to that bit about him and his high school buddy, Nick Whatzizname, stealing a car and hitting the road like Jack Kerouac and Neal Cassady. He wants to know if the novel *On the Road* was an influence on him later. Kerouac was French Canadian, he says. Although in the book the Kerouac character, Sal Paradise, was not, he adds. Sal Paradise was American, a writer.

Malcolm claps his hands in front of the camera lens and says, Okay, here we go! April 1, 2018. Leonard Fife interview. Montreal.

16

RIGHT OFF, FIFE STARTS TELLING WHAT HE BELIEVES are his memories. He says he remembers spotting Nick Dafina in front of Feeney's Pharmacy when he stopped in Strafford at the end of March in 1968. He looks off to the side and bolts past Nick's shadow, pretending he doesn't see or recognize him, offering Nick a chance to pretend the same. No one wants to meet an old friend suddenly, unprepared, unrehearsed, undone. Certainly not Fife, and probably not Nick, either. Fife wants Nick to slam down the hood of his red Mustang, parked, of all places, directly behind Fife's rented Plymouth, leap into the driver's seat, start the engine, and roar away—as Fife himself would have done if he'd had the chance.

But it's too late. Nick's grease-stained face, grimacing intently, turns away from his troubled engine, allowing Fife to see and recognize his face, too late for any sudden, lurching move on Fife's part. So instead he slides nonchalantly between the rear deck of the Plymouth and the grille of Nick's GT Fastback and drifts carefully around Nick's arched body, which is disappearing, socket wrench in hand, beneath the hood of his car.

He crosses the empty street and walks straight to Feeney's and enters. He heads for the cigarette counter on the left and asks the teenage girl behind the counter if he can buy a Strafford street map. She's somebody's younger sister, a tall, slim, bony-shouldered girl with a round, vaguely familiar, beamish face flushed with acne, a girl he believes he once knew when she was a small, rosy-cheeked child, caught now in a clutch of hormones and anxiety and longing. Whose younger sister is she? he wonders. Who is the older brother or sister she resembles? He must have known him or her in high school. He was eighteen then. Little sister has changed a lot more in the last ten years than he has. If he almost recognizes this girl, then she surely recognizes him.

She stops admiring her clawlike cerise fingernails and smiles straight into his face and says she's sorry but she doesn't think they have any maps. Oh, unless they're on the magazine rack at the back of the store.

He looks quickly for the magazine rack by the wide window beside the entrance. It's not there, he says. They've moved it.

Moved what? she asks, startled.

The magazine rack.

No, they didn't. It's down back by the lunch counter. Where it's always been.

He likes her north-of-Boston accent. His ear has been tuned to Virginia Piedmont and Tidewater, and her flattened vowels and dropped *r*'s jump out at him. Right, he says. Where it's always been.

At the rear of the store he searches through the clutter of weekly and monthly magazines and astrology guides and almanacs and hobby manuals. No Strafford street map. Not even a map of suburban Boston, which might have qualified as research material and would have justified his stopping in town, instead of sticking to the highway and zipping past the Strafford exit altogether, as he should have done.

He turns and walks to the front again, gaze fixed straight ahead, not glancing at the long, Formica-topped lunch counter where a half dozen people of various ages are seated on stools with their backs to him. As he passes, he thinks he hears them call his name, Hey, Fife! Leo Fife! He rushes to the door and out to the sidewalk.

Got to get past Dafina, he says to himself. He sidles up to Nick's Mustang—racing stripes and huge Dunlop tires, air-scooped hood still yawning open, the lower half of Nick's body dangling from its bottom jaw. Nick probably didn't see Fife, except from behind. If he saw his face, it was only for a second, and since Fife pretended not to recognize him, Nick may think he's just some guy who bears a striking resemblance to his old buddy Leo Fife, despite wearing a hippie mustache and being at least a decade older than his buddy when last seen in town.

Fife's fingertips go to his upper lip. The mustache is still there. It's real. He did not imagine it. He walks toward his car. Nick slams the hood of the Mustang shut and looks directly at Fife and grins. Fife's stomach tightens like a fist and pushes into his chest, and his legs turn to peat, and he stops and smiles weakly, as if in slight pain.

Nick whacks the flat of his hand three times against the hood of his car. Leo Fife, you sonofabitch! He charges between the two vehicles to the sidewalk and bangs his short blocky body into Fife's long, lean frame, backs off a step, and grabs Fife's right hand and pumps it. Leo, you sonofabitch! I thought you were dead and buried a million miles from here! Goddamn, how the Christ are you? I thought that was you that got out of the Plymouth and went into Feeney's, but I said, Naw, it couldn't be. It couldn't be Leo Fife himself. Not back here in Strafford. What the Christ are you doing here, man?

Well, I just, I just came through, Fife stammers, grinning foolishly, he knows, but he can't stop himself. I'm headed to Vermont. I wanted a street map, you know? I needed a map. So I thought I'd stop off and pick one up at Feeney's, since nothing else's open. It's Sunday. But how're you? How're you doing? His face feels frozen into a grin.

Nick says he's all right. Then says, Actually, no, I'm not all right, I'm in rotten shape, he says good-naturedly. But forget that, man, tell me what's happening with you! Oh, man, Fife won't believe what Nick's heard about his escapades. Since he left town, Fife's become a goddamned legend around here now. C'mon, he says, let's go into Feeney's and have a coffee. Want a coffee? He's got time, doesn't he? He's not taking right off, is he? He tugs at Fife's sleeve and yanks him back toward the drugstore.

They walk inside, Nick with one arm flung around his old friend's shoulders like a scarf, talking rapidly of how great Fife looks, how he's hardly changed, except for the mustache, of course, which really looks groovy, no shit, and how glad he is to see him, especially right now. And how goddamn weird it is, him showing up in Strafford. Especially right now, he repeats.

They sit at the deserted counter. The half dozen customers who were seated there earlier are gone now. A grim, bespectacled gray-haired woman who looks like a head nurse takes their orders—black coffee and egg salad sandwich on whole wheat for Fife, coffee with cream and toasted English muffin for Nick. They talk for a few minutes the way old friends meeting unexpectedly after years apart like to talk—of the things in the physical world immediately before them, as if struggling to locate themselves in the here and now, briefly resisting the powerful pull of memory. They speak stiffly, almost formally, of the unseasonable warmth of the day. Of the surprising lack of customers in the store. Of the green Plymouth that Fife parked in front of Nick's Mustang.

Is it your car? Nick asks, incredulous.

No, no. I rented it in Boston.

Man, they don't give you much to drive, those rental agencies. Which one is it? The agency.

Avis.

You're sure it's Avis?

Yeah, Avis.

Let me get the number off the tags when we go out. I'll get you a break on the costs. Those things are expensive, man.

I know. Expensive.

What'd they charge you? Eleven and eleven?

Twelve bucks a day and twelve cents a mile. Twelve and twelve.

Bastards.

I know, expensive. How stupid to be saying this, Fife thinks. As if it actually makes a difference. Eleven and eleven, twelve and twelve, thirteen and thirteen—that it matters to him at all is somehow wrong. But it does matter, and he can't say why. He reminds himself that he now has such easy access to so much money that the words *expensive* and *inexpensive,* a dollar here, a dollar there, are meaningless. Living in this meaningless relation between cost and income was his boyhood dream, a dream corrupted by desire.

Don't sweat it, man. I'll get you a break, Nick says.

You know somebody?

Nick answers with his old, familiar impersonation of the Mobster, an exaggeration of one of Scorsese's goodfellas. Hey, Nick Dafina always knows somebody. A rush of sweet associations comes over Fife, memories of beer-drunk, goofy teenage male laughter and slap-happy summer afternoons in a car with the windows down and the radio cranked up, when everyone tries but no one except Dafina can combine the dialect, toughness, wit, and sneer to simultaneously imitate and parody the movie and TV versions of Dafina's father and his associates.

Fife relaxes, and, letting go of the hard, bright things that surround him and Nick, he's carried by the moving waters of his past. He sees old friends' faces bob and drift next to his, and he easily recalls their names. He sees clearly their walks and postures, their gestures, and he hears their voices, and he asks Nick the questions that for a decade he's asked himself.

Is Vic Donovan still chasing women twice his age, now that he's almost thirty himself? And remember poor Roger Callahan? Did Roger end up working for his father at National Register? And Fife can't remember her name, but Mike Clifford was fucking her since they both turned fourteen, and he always said it was okay, whatever the hell that meant, because they'll get married as soon as they graduated high school. Carol Barnes, that was her name. So did he marry her after all, or did he discover that lots of coeds at the University of Massachusetts who he didn't have to marry would fuck him as long as he was on the football team? And did anybody die? Did anybody they used to hang out with end up in Vietnam? Did anybody decide to go far away and like him never came back to live here later on? Are the rest all still here in Strafford, Massachusetts, just as Fife left them ten years ago, just as they are in memory, their lives laced together by shared ambitions and fears, caught in a net of minor humiliations and triumphs?

Is this place really what it seems to Fife? Is it possible that he's somehow elsewhere many years later, and dreaming? Will he look up from his egg salad sandwich at Feeney's lunch counter and see still another face from his past, this time a girl's, Evelyn Rose's, unchanged, fixed forever at eighteen years old, not quite tawdry, not quite patrician, but enough of both to make her irresistible to him, murmuring, with everyone listening and winking at one another, Leo, my love, would you like to stay around town tonight and take me in your big wide rented Plymouth to the drive-in out on Route One in Revere where we used to go on Friday nights, so I can jack you off in that big wide front seat? You know, just for old time's sake?

Jesus, Evelyn, let me say it loudly and with conviction, so everyone here can know, that I've changed. I'm a married man now. And I've changed.

The man seated next to Fife—Oh, my God, it's Mr. Varney, from the menswear store!—puts his coffee cup down, wipes his mouth with a paper napkin, and turns to face Fife. May I say, Leo, I hope you married a good woman. Someone you deserve, boy. And by the way, anytime you need a job, Leo, I'd still be pleased to take you back at the store, because you were like a son to me. I mean that.

Mr. Varney turns slowly to the elderly woman sitting next to him and says, Would you like to speak to Leo, Mrs. Fife?

Fife's mom peers around Mr. Varney and hisses, Psst, Leo! It's me, she says, your mother. I'm still here, son. Are you all right? We haven't heard from you in so long, I was beginning to think you'd forgotten us. What's your new wife like, Leo? Is she anything like the first wife? I wish we'd been able to meet one of them, at least. You never brought them to visit. Your father said to tell you hello. He's sorry he couldn't make it down from Maine, where he still works the night shift for the railroad. He's proud of you, Leo. So proud. He'd tell you himself, but it's not easy for him to talk about what's inside him. You know that. But we're very happy now. We don't live in Strafford anymore. We moved away right after you went off to Cuba and stole Mr. Varney's money and the clothes from the store. It was a very hard time for us then, mainly because of you. Do you have any children, Leo? I'd love to see my grandchildren. Do you think you could visit us up in Maine someday, now that we don't live in Strafford anymore? Your father is old now, Leo. He was always old. But he never complains. Not even about the night shift. He said to tell you that he's glad you went back to college and finished what you began at Rumford. And graduate school, even! That's wonderful. It's always a good thing to finish what you start, son. He also said you should seriously consider Mr. Varney's offer to take you back at the store, so you could pay him back what you still owe him. Mr. Varney is not one to hold grudges, son. But you don't have to work for a living anymore, do you? Is it true that you're able to make money from writing stories and books? Or is that just a rumor? And your wife is from a very wealthy family. An heiress? That's wonderful! Wonderful! I'm very happy for you. And your father is, too.

The woman keeps talking, as Mr. Varney gently steers her out the door. From the sidewalk, his mother waves through the glass at Fife as Mr. Varney moves her out of sight.

What about Nick? Is everything the same for him as it was then?

Nick's not the kind to leave town and disappear, like Fife did, and try the same thing somewhere else. Nick always knew that whatever he did with his life, it would be as well done here as anywhere. Of all the people Fife knew then, Nick is the only one whose desires and needs were so self-evident that he never once got muddled. He isn't the fool Fife is.

Fife knows that Nick's father, that widowed cocksure dandy, is in the rackets, fairly high up in the executive branch. Nick has never hidden that from his friends. He is almost proud of his father's criminality. That kind of knowledge would have paralyzed Fife, but Nick exploits his father's pretenses to respectability and legitimate financial success, even agreeing to attend a good Catholic university like Holy Cross. Nick is shrewd enough to see that in the eyes of the rest of society, his father is no different from any poor immigrant's son who made a lot of money quickly. Nick knows that he has been liberated by his father's native intelligence and ruthlessness and his stubborn determination to beat this Protestant country at its own game and save his son from needing to do the same. It has allowed Nick to enter a legitimate profession, maybe law, maybe medicine, maybe start a successful business. It's the American dream, right? But whatever Nick does with his life, he will have chosen it for no one but himself. His life has not unfolded like Fife's by happenstance and accident, contingency and reaction. He's not spent his young life constantly correcting course.

Leo, for Christ's sake, you still worry too much, says Nick. C'mon, man, forget about getting the fuck up to Vermont in time for supper or whatever the Christ you got to be there for. You're not going to make it now, anyhow. Besides, the chance to drink a Sunday afternoon away with your old high school pal doesn't come along every day of the week. C'mon, man, let's take a ride out to the Pike for a few. We can talk out there. Besides, this fucking place gets on my nerves.

You used to practically live at Feeney's.

It gets on my nerves, man. Makes me edgy. Pressures me.

Pressures you?

Yeah, something like that. They've still got lousy coffee, too. And don't forget, you can't buy a fucking drink in this fucking town on fucking Sundays.

Yeah, fuck fuck fuck. Okay, I'll follow you out to the Pike in my car and go on to Vermont from there.

No, you won't, man. You're riding with me. At twelve and twelve you're spending enough just letting that shitcan sit by the curb. C'mon, man, put your ass into this Mustang of mine and tell me what you feel when I let the clutch pop. I'm riding a six-point-four-liter FE engine, three hundred twenty horses, three hundred ninety cubic inches. It's motherfucking big, my friend. Tell you what, so you can get an idea of what I've put into this baby, get in, and lay a coin on the dash. You got a half buck?

No.

Okay, here's one. Now shut the fucking door. Put the coin on the dash in front of you. Okay, right. Don't reach for it till we get moving. But as soon as we're moving, you try and pick that fucking coin off the fucking dashboard just by grabbing it. Wait till I pop the clutch. Okay! Now! Now! Now! Go on, get it! Get it! Get it!

Fife is thrown back against the seat, unable to reach forward and pick up the coin. The brutal, violent G-forced accelerations and decelerations, the hard-edged roar of the engine, tires tearing at the asphalt, squealing and moaning as the Mustang whips around curves, runs lights, flashes through stop signs, are terrifying. Nick did not drive this way when they ran away to the West together at sixteen and drove in four-hour shifts for fifty hours until they ran out of gas money in Amarillo. Back then Nick was an overcautious, even timid driver. Fife was the one who drove the stolen Olds into a cornfield in Iowa and almost rear-ended a ten-wheeler stopped for a light in Oklahoma City.

Ten minutes later, when Nick slams on the brakes at Happy Jack's Bar & Grill out in Revere on Route 1 and shuts the engine off, Fife is finally able to reach out and pluck the coin off the dashboard shelf.

Impressive, he says.

Without warning, unbidden, a pale scrim drops before him, darkens, and obscures Fife's memory of sitting in Nick's Mustang in the parking lot outside Happy Jack's Bar & Grill. He has suddenly lost interest in Nick Dafina and this almost accidental return to Strafford. He remembers instead his dormitory room at Rumford College, stripped of all his personal property—clothes, books, drawings, blankets, towels. It seems strangely public and impersonal to him, ready for another eighteen-year-old scholarship student to move in the minute he closes the door and leaves the building.

The nonscholarship students share large rooms or suites with roommates, but the college houses its half dozen War Memorial Scholarship students in small single rooms located at the end of long dormitory halls, one for each floor, where in years past a maid or butler for the boys must have slept. The house master who welcomed Fife at registration claimed that a single room was a special privilege. But Fife knows better. It's one of the many small ways the college keeps scholarship boys like him from mixing too indiscriminately with the sons of the captains of industry, the sons of men like Roger Callahan's father, who are paying for his scholarship. Fife snaps off the overhead light and hefts his crammed laundry bag to his shoulder and kicks his suitcase ahead of him into the corridor and quietly closes the door behind him.

The corridor, bright with fluorescent light and green tile, is deserted at this hour. Even the twins from DC, the muscular drunks on the wrestling team in the suite at the other end of the hall, have dropped off to sleep, exhausted from guzzling beer and playing matador with desk chairs until 2:00 a.m. They won't make their eight o'clock class again, he thinks as he passes their door.

He descends three flights of stairs to the ground level and steps from the steam-heated dormitory onto the biting cold, snow-covered quadrangle. He holds his Timex close to his face in the darkness: 3:15 a.m. He stands for a moment at the corner where two of the four stone dormitories come together in an L. The bony branches of elm and oak trees clack overhead against each other in the wind. A dog barks slowly, steadily, from down the hill somewhere in the village. The wind brushes fantails of snow off rooftops, and as he walks the deserted pathway from the quad down to the main campus, his boots crunch against the packed snow and ice.

The paths on the main campus, sprayed with rock salt in the morning before the students go to daily chapel, are iced over again, and in front of Wiggin Hall, the earth sciences building, he slips and nearly falls. He shifts his laundry bag from his right shoulder to the left and his suitcase to his free hand and walks more carefully now, until finally he exits the campus and strides along the freshly plowed two-lane road into the village. A half dozen streetlights splash pale ovals across the yards and side streets as he passes through the village center. He turns and glances back once at the nineteenth-century stone buildings shouldering their way up the hill to the dormitories at the top.

No regrets, he says to himself. None. I know what I'm doing. I do.

The sound of a car slipping and sliding along the road somewhere behind him sends Fife scurrying over the snowbank and floundering through knee-deep snow to a large elm tree, where he huddles out of sight and waits. The car approaches slowly, a Ford station wagon with two men inside, smoking cigarettes. Its taillights signal to no one a right turn a few hundred yards ahead onto the state road that connects to the Everett Turnpike twenty-five miles to the south. Then it's gone.

He decides to walk to the same turnoff before trying to hitch a ride. He can't risk being spotted in the village by some faculty member or upperclassman, unable to sleep, drinking coffee in the all-night College Café. A Rumford student out at this hour lugging a suitcase and duffel. Hmm. Strange. Troubling. Worth calling out to him and asking where he's going so late. He'd be rebuffed by Fife's curt response, so it would be worth a phone call to the dean at home, waking him to inform him that a student, evidently a freshman, is fleeing in the night.

You work here at Happy Jack's? Fife asks Nick. I mean, it's like your job? The memory that displaced Fife's earlier memory slides down and away and disappears behind falling snow, as if he's embarrassed or frightened by scenes from his flight from Rumford College, and he's come back to be with Nick at Happy Jack's Bar & Grill on Route 1 in Revere, ten years later.

Yeah, I'm the night bartender three nights a week, Nick says. It's not much to look at during the day like this, he points out, but it's a pretty groovy little joint. They've got a band. And a lot of college chicks from Simmons and Endicott and Salem State come in here alone on weeknights. He gets a lot of ass out of this place, he adds.

You never got married, Nick?

Oh, yeah, he got married, all right. Still is, legally. But he and his wife haven't lived together for almost a year. She's a good Catholic, so she doesn't want to talk about divorce. It doesn't give him any trouble, though. As long as he's not interested in marrying somebody else.

It was pretty bad, eh? The marriage?

Yeah, rotten, Nick says. She ended up driving him out of his god-damn skull. With him trying to finish up college, and then when his old man died, it was too fucking much.

I didn't know about your dad. I'm sorry. That must've been hard. You got married while you were still at college?

The old man's death wasn't that hard. Oh, a lot's happened since they last saw each other. They haven't talked since Leo took off for . . . Not since he took off for Cuba or someplace, right? Right. I remember us talking about that when you came home from Rumford that time.

Nick was at Holy Cross then. He dropped out after the spring term. Then he tried Boston University for a while, but that didn't work out, either. Commuting every day and living at home with his old man, who ran the house like it's a goddamn parsonage, is a bitch. So the next summer he takes off for Europe, and that fall when his old man says, C'mon home, Nick, it's time for school again, Nick says, Sorry, Pops, I'm staying in the old country. Since he happens to be in Naples at the time, his old man, who Fife knows is hung up on Italy, says, Fine, Nick, you stay in Naples, maybe register as a student or something like that. Something legit, is what he's thinking, and after a while he sets Nick up in the export end of a little olive oil import-export thing he's trying to work. That's his plan, anyhow. Nick tells him, Okay, Pop, just send me five hundred a month and enough for a sweet little Lancia or an Alfa, and I'll see what happens. What happens is he meets this Italian chick who's a painter, Gina, an art student in Rome on holiday in Naples. Very classy broad, all kinds of dukes and duchesses for aunts and uncles, and all that chick can talk about is getting to America. Imagine that! Italian nobility, and Gina wants to come over and be a fucking immigrant. So he says, Cool, and they get married by her cousin the cardinal and come back here to Boston to live, because by now he's anxious to finish up and get his college degree. Even in the goddamn Organization you got to have a fucking degree these days, though he isn't especially interested in working for the Organization, he says. Anyhow, it turns out they won't let him back into Holy Cross, so he has to get his degree from Northeastern. He starts going to school every fucking day, right?

Right.

And his old man's pissed at him for everything, for coming back to the States, for getting married to an Italian, never mind the nobility shit, which means nothing to his old man, for ending up at Northeastern, for being still a college boy at twenty-five. The old man says, Nick, time to come up with your own bread. So Nick says to Gina, See if you can score some lira from the duchy. Maybe her cousin the cardinal can slip them a little from the Vatican Bank, so Nick can finish school here and get a legitimate job. But Gina, she's a full-blown fucking Eye-talian American by now. She says, Screw you, Nick, I'm

not supporting an American husband. Neither is my family. Get a job
digging ditches, if you have to, like all the other good American husbands. Like she's still the artiste, and she doesn't speak English, won't
even try, so Nick has to go around as her goddamn translator every
time she wants to buy a goddamn paintbrush. He tells her, Okay, fuck
it, and he takes a job nights, tending bar at a club in Boston. And for
the next two years, he goes to Northeastern days and works nights,
just to keep him and Gina living in a two-room tenement in the North
End, while she's painting pictures and turning into a fucking wannabe
Italian American immigrant. Everyone in the neighborhood speaks
Italian, so she feels at home. And then Nick's old man dies.

I'm sorry.

It's okay, Nick says. He hated the bastard by then anyhow, and
besides, the way he died worked out fine. The old man got killed in
a plane crash on his way back from opening an account in a bank in
the Turks and Caicos in order to keep the US government and Nick
and certain of his colleagues from getting hold of the tax-free cash
he'd been stashing all these years in safe deposit boxes in the good old
Strafford Trust. His plane went down before he could move it, so Nick
gets hold of all that cash anyhow. He tells Gina to go find herself a
North End Eye-talian American guy to screw, and he moves into the
old man's house on Lake Street. He's through school by now, so he
takes this job at Happy Jack's. For a front, mainly, but also so he won't
go nuts hanging around Strafford in the old man's house at night. It's
not a bad job, three nights a week. Plus he gets a lot of pussy out of it.

So you're all set now?

Oh, yeah. He bought the Mustang, which he'll be running in competition down at Lime Rock this summer. The old man left him quite
a pile. The bastard's lucky he went down in a plane crash, instead of a
pair of cement boots in Boston Harbor, because sooner or later one of
the guys above him would've figured out what he was up to. Somebody
upstairs was getting shortchanged, Nick says, and it wasn't just the

feds. When his father died, all Nick had to pay was an inheritance tax on the house and furniture and some old paintings the old man had picked up, but there wasn't any record of anything else. Nothing on paper. It was all cash.

What about Gina?

She doesn't know a thing. She never believed Nick about his old man, anyhow. She thought the guy made all his dough selling green beer to Irishmen on Saint Paddy's Day or something. It's pretty much what the feds thought, too. Besides, she wants to go back to Italy now, so if he offers to pay her fare, he thinks she'll consent to the divorce without pushing for alimony. Turns out she isn't much of an aristocrat when it came down to accounts receivable. She hasn't got a fucking dime, except for the couple of bucks Nick sends her every now and then. Usually, all he does is once a month sign over his week's paycheck from Happy Jack's, forty-seven a month after taxes. She thinks he's able to live off what he makes from tips tending bar part-time because he's living rent-free now from inheriting the old man's house.

Fife asks, How long do you think you can make your old man's cash stash last, Nick? You can't use it to buy stocks and bonds or invest in real estate. It all has to be off the books, right? You can't even put the money in a savings account and let it draw interest.

Nick says the way he's living now costs him between eight and nine hundred a month. At that rate, adjusted for inflation, he's cool for about seventy-five more years.

Jesus!

Bet your ass, baby. It's the kind of thing that can make a confirmed lifelong bachelor out of me. C'mon, drink up and have another. Forget your fucking wallet, for chrissakes. When Nick Dafina says he's buying, let him.

Fife's memories shift like slides in a projector. He remembers the snow swirling down invisibly in the dark, pelting his face and shoulders. He picks up his suitcase and duffel and plods along the side of the road through the ankle-deep, powdery snow for another hundred yards or so. His feet mark the edge of the road by bumping every now and then against the hardened snowbank at the side. No car has passed for a long time now. He hasn't seen the lights of a house for as long. He is safely beyond the village, perhaps seven or eight miles, and if a car passes him now, he will try to hitch a ride, for he is very cold, colder than he expected. His feet, especially, are cold and growing heavier with each step. His suitcase and duffel have turned into blocks of ice, and he can lug them no farther than a hundred yards at a time before he has to drop them and stuff his gloved hands into the pockets of his loden coat, withdrawing his stiffened fingers and making clenched fists inside the gloves. His ears and head are wrapped in the tightly laced hood, and he has to swing his body from the waist in order to look down the road behind him, hoping to see an approaching car. But only the wind comes out of the darkness, the freezing wind. His face has gone numb. Dry crystals of snow have built a ridge across his eyebrows. His forehead throbs painfully. His eyes are half closed, weeping thin tears at the corners, and his nostrils have become dry with frost. He breathes from his mouth in short gasps.

The snow blows down heavier now, and the wind has gradually shifted from behind him to his left. He leans down, brushes the snow off his suitcase and duffel, lifts the suitcase with one hand and swings the duffel onto his shoulder with the other. He keeps on walking. Suddenly headlights behind him spray light across the darkness, and he is surprised by how much open space surrounds him. He gapes for a second at the smooth white road, so much wider and smoother than he imagined, and forgets that he must beg a ride, until the car has churned slowly past and disappeared, dropping him once again into blackness and the tiny case of his body, slowly freezing.

17

VINCENT SAYS HE NEEDS TO LET THE CAMERA COOL again, and the mic is turned off, but Fife keeps talking to Emma as if he's still on-camera and being recorded. He says that the end of his or anyone's childhood is not a threshold that is stepped across and afterward marks the beginning of adulthood. It's not a point in a life's timeline. You can't identify the end of childhood, he tells her, because it never really ends. Fife himself hasn't got to the end of his yet. It's still happening. Even now, in his late seventies, while he draws his dying breaths.

There's no such thing as the end of childhood, he says to Emma. It's only innocence—infancy—that actually comes to an end. That's when childhood begins, and childhood is a region, not a marker. And it is vast and extends even into old age and death. It's like a coastal marsh between the land and the sea, he explains. It's a zone of dwarfed trees and mudflats and estuaries, where waters flow back and forth in opposite directions following the pitch and fall of the land and the phases of the moon and the shifting patterns of the winds.

One has to distinguish between childhood and what's called innocence, he tells her. Fife says he believes in innocence no more than he believes in the end of childhood. If it's anything at all, he says, and it isn't much, innocence is that brief time in one's earliest life when one's knowledge of the world has no ethical strut, let alone an ethical base. If you're looking for the moral meaning of your life, he says, it's useless to go there for it. There's no moral meaning in what people call innocence. He says that a person who wants redemption must return instead not to innocence, but to the beginning of one's childhood, where one's actions first acquired moral meaning, and come forward from there.

In seeking redemption for your sins, as Fife claims to be doing, you have to examine your life's continuum back to the point in time when your ethical base first appeared like a firmament between the firmaments, when what you know about the world and the way you acquired that knowledge became for the first time in your life a consciously willed thing. It's the day you ate the apple from the forbidden tree. And from that day forward, for the rest of your life, you alone control the nature and purpose of your moral evolution. You have to return to when the shape of your morality became for the first time your own creation and not something designed and enforced by your parents or teachers or a priest or a god or any other authority, real or imagined. You have to return to where you first started navigating with a map of your own making, losing your way from time to time, and correcting your course as you go along.

Emma says, I understand.

Malcolm says, I'm glad someone does. Maybe I'll understand it later, when I've watched this footage in the editing room. You always see and hear stuff in the editing room that you missed completely during the actual filming. Speaking of innocence, Malcolm is reminded again of Fife's film *Suffer the Innocents*, the one about Bishop McCann from Antigonish. He watched it for maybe the fifth time the other night, prepping for this interview. The footage of McCann's Ottawa trial and sentencing for possession of over six hundred photos and dozens of clips and videos on the bishop's computer of kiddie porn, some of them S&M. He wanted to despise McCann and be repulsed by him, and up to that point had no trouble doing it. The man was beyond disgusting, he was evil. But for the first time, for a few moments there, Malcolm felt something like compassion for the old guy. It wasn't how McCann looked—pasty-faced and rumpled and slump-shouldered, a thoroughly, deservedly humiliated man. It was mainly because of Fife's VO, the quiet, baritone voice-over that you hear just before the sentencing, where Fife quotes from the Old Testament. The verse from Leviticus, he forgets which one.

Fife says, It's Leviticus twenty, verse two. Say to the Israelites, any Israelite or any foreigner residing in Israel who sacrifices any of his children to Moloch is to be put to death. The members of the community are to stone him. I myself will set my face against him and will cut him off from his people; for by sacrificing his children to Moloch, he has defiled my sanctuary and profaned my holy name.

Right. That is so fucking cold, Leo. I mean, cold. But it's weird how in the film the passage has the opposite effect. I mean, at first I felt like I was holding a large smooth stone in my hand, and I'm ready to throw it at the guy's bald head and bust it open. I'm standing in a crowd of people who have stones in their hands, too, and everyone's waiting for the judge to give the word. And you're listening to this dark VO from the Bible that for a few seconds makes you feel ancient and primitive and tribal and righteous. All the while, the camera stays close on Bishop McCann's face, his tight, trembling lips, eyes clamped shut, pale skin blotched red and raw from some kind of eczema. He practically invites you to despise him, and he looks resigned to the stoning, almost welcoming it, as if it's the only way he can be forgiven for his disgusting crimes.

The biblical voice that quotes Leviticus ends. Then off-camera comes the judge's high, thin voice, very contemporary and liberal UT, replacing Fife's VO. It's English Canada's official public voice. It makes you feel scolded and slightly ashamed of yourself, the way they do, that squeaky-clean voice and CBC pronunciation, so you place your stone on the ground, and one by one everyone puts his stone down, too.

The judge starts laying out the sentence in that nice liberal way. I forget his name.

Uhlig. Judge Rory Uhlig.

Right. Judge Rory Uhlig. He mentions mitigations, as he calls them, like Bishop McCann's apology for the harm he did, and he notes McCann's confession that what began as a careless curiosity blossomed into an obsessive addiction. Right?

Yes. A careless curiosity. An obsessive addiction.

The judge talks about the need to balance society's obligation to denounce and deter crimes like McCann's against certain socially positive factors, like the good bishop's career as a distinguished spiritual leader and educator. He actually says that shit. McCann's enjoyment of S&M kiddie porn, the judge observes, was confined to the privacy of his personal quarters in the absence of others. Jesus. You think you're listening to McCann's defense lawyer, not the man who's supposed to be sentencing him.

The camera cuts away from Judge Uhlig and Bishop McCann and pans the spectators crowding the courtroom and closes on this big red-faced guy in a blue plaid sports coat and white baseball cap, standing at the back. You can see that the guy is about to explode. You watch the pressure build on his red, sweating face as the judge off-camera drones on. Finally the judge announces, still OC, that McCann will get double credit for the eight months he's already served in prison and will only have to be on probation for twenty-four months, and he will walk out a free man today, though he will have to wear an electronic leg collar and he can't hang out near schoolyards anymore, blah-blah.

The guy in the blue plaid jacket and baseball cap explodes and starts screaming at McCann. Instead of staying on him, though, which is what Malcolm says any other filmmaker would have done, Fife's camera swings around and closes instead on Bishop McCann sitting in the glass-walled prisoner's box. You see him the way the screamer sees him—shrunken, backing away from the glass, like he's being physically attacked. The man in the jacket and baseball cap goes on screaming. He's off-camera now, calling McCann a demon, Satan's spawn, a monster sent from hell to defile the innocent children of God.

We feel like we're doing the screaming, that it's coming from our mouths instead of his. His crazed rage is our crazed rage. He yells that his life has been ruined by the bishop and by his priests and the whole Catholic Church all the way up to the pope. He bellows that he got fucked as a kid by a priest at the Saint Joseph Training School for Boys in Alfred, Ontario. He uses the word *fucked*. He says the priest in charge of athletics fucked him. Jesus. He says McCann protected the priest at Saint Joe's, after he and several other boys raped by the priest came forward, by transferring him to a seminary in Saratoga Springs, New York. The guy starts to sob that they took away his innocence and his childhood. The last thing he shouts is, You and the Church, you ate my childhood! You ate my childhood! Then he goes silent, and we hear the courtroom cops jump him and drag him unprotesting from the room. Throughout, the camera refuses to let us look at the man in the blue plaid jacket and baseball cap. Just Bishop McCann—cowering, trapped like a terrified rat in his glass cage.

Fife doesn't know if he remembers these scenes, or if it's what he filmed or what he saw on the screen when the film was shown at the Toronto Film Festival in 1989. He may have imagined it, in whole or part, or he may be merging memory, TV news footage, his own footage, the finished film, conversations with friends, and magazine and newspaper accounts of the arrest of the bishop at the Ottawa airport and the trial and McCann's sentencing and his release. The case, from start to finish, dragged on for years. He wonders if it's finished even now, nearly thirty years later. He doesn't remember reading a notice of the bishop's death.

In the film the sentencing itself goes on for quite a while. Fife remembers that. When the man in the blue plaid jacket and baseball cap has been removed from the courtroom, Judge Uhlig reads his sentencing statement over again from the beginning. He decrees that for twenty-four months Bishop McCann will be required to report weekly to a probation officer. He is to undergo counseling by a qualified psychologist, who will deliver his or her assessment back to the probation officer. He is prohibited from visiting schools or schoolyards or swimming pools or gymnasiums or playgrounds or any other place where children under the age of sixteen might gather. He is allowed to use a computer and other electronic devices, but an officer of the court will be permitted to search his computer at any time without prior notification. He is prohibited from viewing pornography or erotica on his computer or television, and he cannot communicate electronically or telephonically with children sixteen or under.

Judge Uhlig pauses for a few seconds, as if to let the sentencing settle on Bishop McCann's narrow, slumped shoulders, then tells him that he is free to leave the courtroom. As McCann turns to exit the glass box and reenter the world outside, the judge, almost as an afterthought, asks McCann's lawyer—the lawyer's name is Reginald Wilton, Fife suddenly recalls—if the bishop will be residing in a rectory or a church residence in the Archdiocese of Ottawa.

Before the attorney can respond, a burly woman in her fifties whose black hair looks dyed rises from her chair in the front row of the spectators' section and says that Bishop McCann is making his own arrangements for accommodation. She wears a black cardigan sweater over a white blouse and a long gray flannel skirt, sensible black flat shoes, and no jewelry. Fife thinks he got her on film. He can't be sure, though. He hasn't looked at the film in a decade.

The judge says, You are . . . ?

Alice Dubois. I am the spokeswoman for the archdiocese. I'm the public affairs officer. Bishop McCann will not be staying in a residence or rectory of the archdiocese, she says. We do not know of his plans.

The next thing Fife remembers is the scene outside the courtroom, where McCann's lawyer, Reginald Wilton, tries to ease him through the cluster of reporters and cameramen to his waiting car. It's unclear who the male driver is. He's young, in his twenties, with long blond hair and a prominent nose. The reporters shove microphones in front of the bishop and his lawyer and shout questions. The bishop, pale and tight-lipped and expressionless, ignores them and moves swiftly to the car and steps into it and shuts the door with force and physical authority. It's evident now that he is a tall, athletic man, fit and youthful for his age. His lawyer, who hangs back for a moment of free TV and press exposure, is much smaller by comparison.

Will the bishop continue the ten-year homosexual relationship that was revealed to the court on December nineteenth?

No comment on that one, fellas.

He looks like he's lost some weight in the eight months since he was arrested. He looks fit. Working out in the prison gym?

Yeah, lost maybe thirty pounds. Very fit, despite the harsh conditions of his confinement.

What's the problem with his skin? Like on his face and neck? Is he ill?

Nothing to worry over. Just a little eczema. Prison conditions aren't all that sanitary, y'know. He's seen a doctor and been prescribed an antibiotic salve.

Have there been expressions of support from his parishioners at home?

Oh, yeah, plenty of letters from his parishioners back in Antigonish. Also letters of support from some highly placed church clerics and officials.

Anything from the pope?

Nope. The pope's not weighed in.

Malcolm says, Okay, let's rock and roll, people. We're ready. You ready, Leo?

Yes.

Malcolm claps his hands in front of Vincent's lens. Leonard Fife interview, April 1, 2018. Montreal.

18

FIFE GOES ON TALKING AS IF HE DIDN'T HEAR MALCOLM. He's not dead, but he knows that he will be soon, a matter of weeks, the doctor said. More likely days. His future is null, and present and past have merged and pooled. He hears his own voice now and no other, and he sees only what his voice reveals to him, as if he were a child being read to. The story being read to him is the story of his own early life, and he's both the reader and the listener. Who's the author? he wonders. Is there an author, or is Fife no more than a channel between two worlds, the present and the past, like a canal between two oceans?

He says to Emma that as teenage boys, he and Nick Dafina, the closest of friends back then, believed in each other's intelligence and sensitivity and discontent. The dissatisfactions and failures and frustrations endured by one were recognized and honored by the other in a way neither boy could manage on his own. Consequently their strategies and tactics for making themselves happy frequently overlapped, especially as they got old enough to convert those strategies and tactics into action. The early-spring afternoon in 1968, at Happy Jack's, after ten years of silent separation, Fife and Dafina drink whisky together like old compadres and try to understand and identify all over again with each other's strategies and tactics for making life bearable.

Fife likes the feel of a heavy glass in his hand. It stops his hand from shaking. He puts the glass on the bar and lights a cigarette. The aroma of burning tobacco cuts across the peaty taste of scotch, and that, too, comforts and calms him. Fife is the first to speak of their past. He says to Nick now that they're adults neither of them will ever have another chance to do anything as clean and honorable as when they stole Nick's old man's car and lit out for the West Coast. A couple of fucking kids, he says, as if he's only realized it now. Sixteen years old was all they were. And they thought they could make it! They wanted to go to Australia, he remembers. Fife wonders aloud, Why Australia? Why not Florida, or as close to Australia as California and stop there at the water's edge? It must have been because they knew they had no chance of getting to Australia. They might as well have been running away to the moon.

What do you mean, clean and honorable? Nick says. I mean, it wasn't exactly dishonorable. But I never thought to call it honorable. He pauses and looks dreamily into his glass, as if he sees cloudy images of a nearly forgotten juvenile escapade float slowly past—an overexposed black-and-white 1950s home movie. It was kind of nuts, though. What were they thinking? Jesus, he'll never forget drinking all that shitty rotgut wine at the YMCA in Amarillo, Texas, and Fife throwing up for two days afterward, wrecking the goddamn room they were living in and then puking up the car.

Fife doesn't want to talk about that. When they ran away, Fife says, they weren't really running *away* from anything. They were running toward something. It was an originating act, a clear-cut beginning of things. There probably hasn't been one like it for either of them since, Fife says. They chose one kind of imagined future over and against another, and they did it at the first and only moment in their young lives when they weren't canceling out some prior choice. That's what makes it clean and honorable.

Yeah, sure, Nick says. Whatever you say, man. But we were just kids, for chrissakes. We didn't know what we were getting into.

Nick doesn't get it, Fife thinks. He got it back then. His mother had died six months earlier, and his father hired a twenty-year-old French Canadian girl as a live-in housekeeper and nanny for Nick's little sister and started screwing her on a nightly basis. Nick in less than a half year was abandoned by his parents twice over.

For Fife, it was more complicated, on the surface less of an abandonment and more of an enforced isolation, as if in the midst of family life, with his mother and father behaving more or less as parents are supposed to behave, he were nonetheless locked in a wire cage in the living room watching them come and go about their daily domestic business, doing everyone's daily business, neither of them acknowledging the cage or the fact that their son, their only child, was imprisoned inside it.

Nick says, And we came back, didn't we? A couple of teenage car thieves running from the cops. Remember that state cop in Arizona? He stopped the suspicious-looking pair of crew-cut white kids in T-shirts driving a new Oldsmobile 88 with Massachusetts plates, and while he sat inside his cruiser checking to see if there was an APB for the two or if the Olds had been reported stolen, Fife, who was behind the wheel, dropped it into gear and kicked the accelerator to the floor, and they took off. And they got away with it. By the time the cop looked up, they were almost at the California line.

Fife says, After six weeks of living like teenage desperadoes, we decided that we'd made the wrong choice and came mincing back to Strafford. He remembers begging whatzizname, Mr. Collucci, their high school principal, not to hold them back a year if they made up all their homework assignments and took the quizzes and exams they'd missed.

And begging my old man not to shoot us at sunrise for stealing his car and then trying to sell it in California, Nick reminds him. Don't forget that part. And me begging him not to put me in the harsh hands of the Jesuits at St. John's Prep, which he did anyway.

Right. That's what Fife is talking about. They came back into the fold, lowered their heads and tails, and confessed to having been wrong and irresponsible and foolish and dumb. Not to mention cruel to Fife's bewildered, bereft, abandoned parents and Nick's widowed father and little sister, who had earlier been sent away to boarding school in Rhode Island so his father could screw the nanny, and who, Nick adds, was never told that her big brother stole Daddy's car and ran away to California with his best friend, Leo Fife.

Fife's and Nick's decision to light out for the territory with heads and tails held high marked the end of their innocence, Fife explains. Every decision that followed was made under a cloud of guilt, heads and tails drooped low. Ever since, whenever Fife on his own or Nick on his own has decided to change the nature of his life in any meaning-ful way, it's been the same. Dropping out of college, getting married, getting unmarried, moving far away, coming back. Getting married a second time, in Fife's case. Going back to college, in both cases. Gradu-ate school. Having kids, even. Abandoning kids. Moving to Vermont. The same.

We were like Huckleberry Finn, maybe, Nick suggests. Not so bad.

Yeah, or Jack Kerouac. But he came later. Anyhow, Fife explains, taking off in Nick's father's Oldsmobile was in both their cases totally unique. It was a true initiation. An end to innocence and the begin-ning of experience. It began a thing without at the same time ending something else that they had chosen at an earlier time in their lives.

Fife checks his watch. Jesus Christ, it's after four! I've got to split. I promised some people I'd get there for dinner. He gulps down the rest of his scotch, and his eyes sting and fill with tears. I'm sorry, man. I really am.

Aw, c'mon, stick around, Nick says. Let's tie one on for old time's sake. You can stay at my place tonight. I've got more empty rooms in that house than a goddamn hotel. Whyn't you call these Vermont friends of yours and tell them you'll make it in time for lunch tomorrow?

No, I can't, Fife says. He has to see a realtor in the morning, he explains. If he stays here, he'll have to leave at dawn. Besides, he has to pick up his suitcase at the bus station in Montpelier. The airline lost it when he connected in Washington and is sending it on.

It's time to leave, that's all. Why use my suitcase as an excuse? Fife asks himself. There's nothing important enough in his suitcase to keep him from picking it up at the bus station tomorrow. Just his clothes and shaving gear. He's not sure if he's keeping his eyes on it or it's keeping its eyes on him. Who's watching whom? Inside is the pink two-piece printed, stamped, and signed check for $23,000 drawn on Alicia's trust account. Thin and delicate, yet stiff enough to crack edgewise against a banker's desktop, sharp enough to slice a fingertip, if one is careless with one's soft caress. He likes the color, official pink, the fleshy backup to cash currency. And the fact that it's in two pieces pleases him. It's only fitting that to put such a substantial check to work, one has not only to sign it, but also to tear it in half lengthwise along a perforated edge. One keeps the torn part, the useless noncon-vertible half, like a cast-off snakeskin—For Your Personal Records. When such a check has been printed and stamped and signed in an office in a bank in Richmond, Virginia, when it has been inserted into an envelope and sealed and placed into his hands by a representative of the bank, when all those elaborate rituals have been completed before witnesses, the check cannot be replaced. Another check for the same amount with all the same stamps and signatures might have to be is-sued later on, but it can never replace the original, the one handed to him two mornings ago in the oak-paneled office of the executor of his wife's trust.

I'd like to hang out with you, Nick, Fife says, but I've got at least three more hours' drive before I can sit down and forget about the clock for a while. I'm really sorry.

Nick says he gets it. He signs for their drinks and follows Fife out of the dim, windowless bar.

Nick drives Fife quickly back to the rented Plymouth parked in Strafford in front of Feeney's Pharmacy. His crazed drive from Feeney's out to Happy Jack's terrified Fife. He drives the same way back to Strafford, but thanks probably to the scotch and the easy, nostalgic tenor of their conversation, Fife's not frightened this time. He hollers over the throaty roar of the engine, Whatever happened to Cliff Ericson? Did Harry Roberto remain a shit, and is he still boxing professionally? And do you know what became of my beloved Evelyn Rose? Is she still beautiful and smart and kind?

And Nick yells back, That goddamn Ericson, he married some chick from Medford and settled down and is running a fail press at Transitron five days a week. And, naw, Roberto's okay, he got his brains scrambled pretty bad after a couple years of losing to stiffs, and he's working for his old man's construction company now. And Nick doesn't know what happened to sweet little Evvie, except she got married a while back, he read in the paper. Married some kind of lieutenant, air force or navy, some guy from the Midwest stationed out here.

Fife figured that's how she'd end up. She's lucky she didn't end up marrying him. He's probably lucky she didn't, too, he says.

Nick screeches the Mustang to a stop in front of Feeney's and swirls it into place again behind Fife's Plymouth. For a few seconds the friends sit in silence. Nick lights a cigarette and inhales to the bottom of his lungs. He says, Well, I hope to hell you get back here after you move to Vermont. I got a couple friends here in town, of course. I know practically everybody. But nobody I can talk to. You know what I mean?

He waits in silence, but Fife says nothing. He doesn't know what Nick wants him to say. He studies his hands.

I mean, they're all nice enough guys, good for fucking around with. Hanging at Happy Jack's, watching ball games on TV. That sort of thing. But he can't sit down and talk straight with them. Like he can with Fife. Sure, I know I ain't some goddamn genius or intellectual, he says, but Jesus Christ, I can tell you things about what's happening inside my head, and you know what I'm talking about. He pauses again.

Fife says nothing and thinks, This isn't working.

Like, you know, when I'm coming on strong about how cool everything is with my old man being dead and me with all his ill-gotten gains and house and my Italian wife living in Boston, I mean, you know where that's really at, don't you? he says. He looks out the windshield and along the humped hood of his car. I mean, it's mostly true, he adds, but maybe it's not as cool as it sounds.

What do you mean?

I don't know, man. I guess I ought to see a shrink or something. It's like I'm walking straight down a dead-end street, and I'm all the time telling everyone it's a four-lane highway or something. It makes me feel crazy sometimes. You believe me? he asks, still not looking at Fife.

About it being a dead-end street?

Yeah.

I believe you. Sure, I believe you, Fife says. I'm glad you know that's what it is, a dead end. If that's what it is. Even if it makes you feel crazy sometimes.

Fife tells himself, There is no way this can be made to work, no way at all. There's no light in his response to Nick's confession. It's airless and dark.

That's the trouble, Nick says. The crazy-feeling thing, I mean. I lie about it, but I do know the truth. My fucking life has turned out to be fucking lousy. It's got so I have to get myself stoned and drunk every night just to fall asleep. Every night! I'm only twenty-seven, Leo, and I got a bad stomach already. And fucking nightmares, man. Killer nightmares. And migraines. Hives. I'm even hearing voices. When I'm not talking to myself. No shit, voices.

He pauses for a moment, as if inviting Fife to comfort him, but Fife can't think of anything to say.

Nick says, I don't know, maybe you're right about when we took off at sixteen like that. I haven't been right in the head since then. Since coming back, I mean. Maybe we should have kept going. All the way to Australia.

Fife reaches for the door. Me, either, he says. I haven't been right in the head since then, either.

I'm thinking of enlisting.

What? You want to go to Vietnam? Why?

No, I'm signing with the air force, he says. Now that he's out of college and divorced, he's draft bait. The recruiter told him they need guys who speak foreign languages, and Nick has Italian nailed. They promised after basic training to send him to Italy, not Vietnam. Aviano Air Base in northeastern Italy, they told him. It's in Friuli–Venezia Giulia in the north. Could be a way to start over, he adds. Like going to Australia, only with better food.

When do you leave for basic?

Not till the end of the summer, they told him. Nick turns and looks at Fife and asks him to call when he gets moved up to Vermont. Now that they've reconnected, they should stay connected. He says not to worry, he'll call his buddy at Avis and get Fife a break on the car rental. And anytime this summer, till he's shipped out, Fife should feel free to come down from Vermont and bring the wife and kids. He'll have two kids by then, right?

Two kids. Right.

Plenty of room at casa Dafina. Will he do that, call and come down to Strafford with the wife and kids?

I will, Nick. I promise.

Fife gets out of the car and closes the door. He leans down to say goodbye, and Nick grins up at him and says, What the hell, Leo, you coming back to Strafford like this, bringing up those memories about our early wanderings and all, what the hell, I might write a book about that little escapade. You're the only writer I know, so you'd have to check it out for me, right? I've actually thought about it a lot.

I don't think there's much of a story there, Fife says. Except maybe for you. But if you write it, sure, I'll check it out for you. He shakes his friend's hand and turns away and walks to his car.

Nick whips his red Mustang onto the street and roars past, waving at Fife as he speeds down the street, headed toward the lake, where the car turns right and disappears from sight.

And once again New England slides past, north to south, from in front of the green Plymouth to behind. The highway ripples smoothly beneath the car as it passes the last suburban thatches of pastel-colored bungalows and split-levels and the small, windowless factories where printed circuits and transistors and tiny gyroscopes—weapons for the war in Vietnam—are manufactured in buildings that look like they're wired to implode if a trespasser sets off an electronic alarm. The interstate cuts an unbroken longitudinal line from Strafford through the northern suburbs and family farms and thinning forests to the lake and mountain vacationlands of New Hampshire and Vermont. It bypasses the abandoned mill towns along the Merrimack River and slices efficiently through the pastures and woodlands and small patched-together dairy farms east of Lowell and west of Lawrence, as if the old brick cities no longer exist, as if in fact they never existed at all. Beyond the dairy farms, scrawny second-growth flatland forests of scrub oak and tulip trees, their skeletal branches lightly frosted with green buds, alternate with unplanted, unplowed fields still sopped with snowmelt.

Gradually, the light, rhythmic joggle of the tires meeting the macadam at a steady seventy-five miles an hour draws Fife's attention away from the scenery and sends it drifting back to his conversation with Nick at Happy Jack's and afterward in Nick's turbocharged Mustang in Strafford. He remembers how anxious and shamefaced Nick looked when he spoke of his present life, and how secure and relaxed he had seemed earlier, when they talked about their boyhood flight to the West. It wasn't a look of nostalgia, as if he longed to return to a less complicated time than this. Nick knows how painful and complicated those years really were for both of them. He's even less likely than Fife to idealize them.

Nick must have been responding to memories of that first flight, much as Fife himself was, and must have sensed the difference between that flight and all those that followed—to Jesuit prep school and college, to Italy and working for his father, to marriage, his return to college, and now divorce and living alone in his father's house, supported by his father's pirated treasure. And finally this last flight, enlisting in the military. He must have sensed the nature of what the difference between the first and the last implies. Maybe that's why he wants to write a book about the first. Maybe he glimpses the possibility of judgment there. Or redemption. Or the truth. Even so, writing a book might be more useful to him than joining the US Air Force. Fife has a feeling Nick will end up being shipped to Vietnam, not Italy.

He remembers Nick as he was ten years earlier. He was a gentle, complicated sixteen-year-old boy back then, who faked being tough and simple. Now it's the opposite. Nick no longer fakes his toughness and simplicity, it's who he is. Instead he fakes the gentleness and complexity, Fife decides. The sequence, too, has been reversed. When Nick was a boy, he led with his genuine feelings and confusions, and afterward, afraid that he'd be rejected or ridiculed, threw up a hard, brash mask of coarse humor and casual hedonism. Back then the mask amused Fife, but slightly frightened him—it made Nick both difficult and all too easy to understand.

He remembers the night they got drunk together in the YMCA in Amarillo, Texas—drunk for the first time in their lives—and shudders. Jesus, that was horrible. He recalls in sudden, vivid detail their riotous laughter and screaming and falling down and vomiting and the dizzy sleep and three-day hangover that followed.

They ran out of money in Amarillo and talked the director of the YMCA into renting them on credit a tiny, closetlike room with two narrow iron-frame cots. There is no other furniture. The cinder-block walls are painted sickly green, and the single small window opens onto an air shaft. Is this where they stick the winos? Fife mumbles. There isn't even a table for a goddamn Gideon Bible, he says to Nick and plops his suitcase onto the bed nearer the window.

Any port in a storm, man. We need a shower and some sleep. Then, goombah, we got to figure out how to raise some moolah, Nick says and, eyes closed, falls backward onto the second cot.

Affirming the YMCA director's faith in the wisdom of his charity, they both succeed on their first full day in Amarillo in landing jobs as dishwashers in a bustling German restaurant in the center of the city. It's the late 1950s, and there are jobs everywhere for a pair of bright, physically attractive sixteen-year-old white boys willing to work. As the result of a flipped coin, Fife gets the day shift and Nick the night, six days a week, and six days later, as Nick comes whistling into the steam-filled kitchen to begin the last day of his first week of washing dishes, Fife has already finished his. He flaps his $58-and-change paycheck under Nick's nose and says he'll pick him up after work at one a.m. and leaves.

He drives Nick's father's Olds straight to the YMCA, where he cashes his check at the manager's desk off the lobby. He pays their $10 weekly rent and goes up to their room and takes a long shower and changes into clean clothes. Later, after burgers and fries at the diner across the street from the Y, he fills the gas tank for the first time in a week and crosses through the city to the North End, driving with the windows down and the radio up, his arm draped across the chrome jamb, smoking a cigarette, feeling light and clean and white as a cloud in the warm breezy glow of a spring evening in North Texas.

Old cast-off tires, torn political posters, flapping newspapers, an abandoned bicycle frame and baby carriage, and overflowing trash barrels litter the sidewalks and doorways and front porches of low shotgun houses. Before long, he spots what he's been searching for—an elderly Black man in tattered work shirt and baggy trousers walking unsteadily along the crackled sidewalk. Fife eases the Olds over to the side of the street and paces the man for a few seconds, casting a wary eye up and down the darkening street. Few cars and fewer pedestrians in sight. Halfway down the block, wedged between a storefront church and a laundromat, is a narrow store with blacked-out windows and a small neon sign, LIQUOR, above the door.

Hey, mister! Fife calls to the man. C'mere a minute, mister.

The man approaches the car slowly, cautiously, and flashes a grin at Fife through the open window. Yes, sir, young fella. What can I do for you?

Listen here, Fife says, suddenly frightened. He's about to do something illegal. And he's never spoken to a Black person before. He checks the street and sidewalks for a cop and sees no one. The man's head is very large, and he doesn't seem as old as Fife first thought. The white of one eye is scarlet, and a half-healed finger-width cut ridges his forehead, as if he's recently taken a nasty fall or a beating. He seems unable or unwilling to stop grinning at Fife.

Listen, mister, Fife begins again, I wonder if you'll do a favor for me.

Glad to! Yes, sir, young fella, glad to do you a favor!

Fife points down the street at the liquor store. If you'll go in there and buy a jug of wine for me, I'll pay you a dollar.

Glad to! Glad to do it!

Fife waves two dollar bills in front of the man's face. What kind of wine can you get for this? I want, like, half a gallon. Or a gallon.

The man appears to be pondering the question, then brightens with the answer. Thunderbird! You want some Thunderbird, young fella?

Yeah, right, that's fine, Fife says, handing over the dollar bills.

There's another buck for you when you come back with the wine. But if you don't come back with the wine, he says, I'll come looking for you.

Oh, don't you worry none, young fella. You just sit tight, and I be right back with the wine! He limps away from the car and crosses to the liquor store. Fife waits, smoking a cigarette, clenching and unclenching the steering wheel, racing the engine as if for a quick getaway.

Suddenly the man is grinning through the passenger window, a large brown paper bag clutched against his chest. He sticks his free hand palm-up through the window.

Fife edges away from the hand. What's the matter? he says. What are you doing?

I got the Thunderbird for you, young fella. So I guess you got something for me, eh?

Let's see the wine. Give it here.

It right in the sack, the man answers. He steps back a few feet from the car and opens the sack and offers Fife a peek at the bacon-colored bottle nestled inside.

Fife takes a crumpled dollar bill from his pocket, carefully straightens it, and lays it on the seat next to him. That's yours. Put the bag down on the seat and take it.

The man places the bag onto the seat and grabs the bill as if plucking it from a fire and stuffs it deep into his trousers pocket. He's no longer grinning. He offers merely a thin, knowing smile. Fife lifts a corner of the bag and confirms that there is indeed a gallon jug of Thunderbird inside.

Anything else I can help you with, young fella? He winks his good eye and licks his lips. Know what I mean? Maybe a little company to help you drink that fine wine?

No. No, thanks. Nothing else.

Then I be seeing you. The man turns abruptly and heads toward the liquor store. Fife drops the Olds into gear, makes a U-turn, and drives it back the way he came.

He hides the jug of Thunderbird under his cot, untouched until Nick gets off work and they can crack it open and celebrate together. That's his plan. He descends the three flights of narrow stairs to the lobby and grabs a pool cue and settles into shooting pool at one of the three tables. He leans along his pool cue, banking shots into spinning arcs that end with satisfying plops into corner pockets with increasing regularity. Every fifteen minutes or so he checks his watch and racks the balls and starts the sequence over again.

A thick-bodied man in his forties, his graying brown hair cropped unevenly in a rough crew cut, sits on a crackled leatherette-covered couch. An elaborately harnessed German shepherd lies on the bare floor next to him. The man smiles blankly in Fife's direction, listening with apparent interest to the clicks and pings of the balls as they run their course across the table. Finally the man says, Are you waiting for someone? Or just bored?

Both. I'm waiting for my buddy to get off work.

Ah, yes, the man says. He pats the dog's bony gray forehead with short, rapid strokes of the hand. The man squints at a spot near the ceiling slightly to his left, as if listening and speaking to someone in an adjacent room. He's about forty, or maybe fifty, Fife guesses. An old guy. No sunglasses, but the guy must be blind.

In a soft, oddly formal voice, the man asks where Fife is from. New England?

Yeah, Massachusetts. You recognize the accent?

He says yes, he was there once several years ago. He is an Iowan himself, and he came to Amarillo after his mother died to live with his sister. His sister's husband has made it unpleasant for him, he adds, so as soon as he got a job he moved here to the YMCA. He works in a small clock factory several blocks away, he says.

No kidding? So you can like do that kind of work okay, despite being blind and all? That's impressive.

Some things one can do better by touch than sight. I acquired my skill as a child at the Iowa Braille and Sight Saving School in Vinton, Iowa.

Cool. My grandfather was a watchmaker, y'know. In Portland, Maine. Had his own shop.

Really. That's quite a coincidence. What's your name?

Leonard Fife. Leo. But my grandfather's name was Samuel Beede. You wouldn't have heard of him, though. He had a small repair shop in Portland. That was years ago. He died before I was born, even.

How old are you? the man asks, scratching his dog gently behind the ears.

Sixteen. Fife bangs a hard one the length of the table, perfectly weighted and placed. It nudges the 6 ball six inches to the right, sends it along the bank and slowly over the lip into the corner pocket. Beautiful! he shouts. He feels good. Relaxed and fearless. He hasn't felt this good in the whole ten days since he and Nick sped out of Strafford. He hasn't felt this good all year.

My name's Swenson, Paul Swenson, the man says.

Oh, glad to meet you. Fife twirls the tip of his cue slowly into the cube of blue chalk. What's the dog's name?

Ike. The leader of the pack, he says and smiles.

Fife guffaws, racks up the balls, and begins his solitary game over again.

Why are you waiting around for your friend? Are you two fellows going out with some girls tonight?

Naw. They're gonna tie one on tonight. He and his buddy plan to celebrate their first week's pay, he explains. A week ago things looked pretty bleak to them, he goes on, but tonight things look bright again, so they intend to celebrate over a jug of Thunderbird.

What's that?

Thunderbird? It's a kind of wine. I bought it off a guy. I hear it's pretty good stuff, though.

If it's what I think it is, it'll make you ill.

Naw, I got a stomach like iron. No kidding.

Well, if you'd like a decent drink, I have a bottle of scotch upstairs in my room. I was thinking of going up and having one myself before I turn in, and if you'd like to join me, I'd welcome the company. Swenson rises from the couch, and the dog comes to attention beside him. We'll have to be very quiet about it, though, he warns. We're not supposed to keep any alcoholic beverages in our rooms, you know. It's against YMCA policy.

Yeah, right. Young Men's Christian Association, Fife says and drops the stick back into the rack on the far wall.

They leave together, Fife keeping a few steps behind Swenson and on the side opposite the dog, as if their leaving together is coincidental rather than intentional, strolling stiffly past the dozing desk clerk and up the stairs. Swenson's room is on the second floor at the far end of a long, narrow corridor. It's twice the size of Fife's and Nick's room, with curtains, a carpet, a dresser and nightstand, and a comfortable chair next to a large window facing the street.

Boy, you got a swell room! You ought to see the goddamn cell they stuck me and Nick in. You wouldn't believe it! Fife says and flops into the chair.

It's comfortable, Swenson says. He drops Ike's leash and closes the door behind him. Ike walks quickly to a corner of the room and lies down and starts grooming his front paws. Swenson reaches under the bed and gropes in the darkness for a few seconds and draws out a small leather suitcase. He takes a key from his pocket and unlocks and opens the suitcase. Withdrawing a nearly full bottle of Ballantine's scotch, he holds it out at arm's length and says, Would you care to pour? There should be two glasses on top of the dresser. I'm sorry not to have any ice, he adds.

Fife takes the bottle and half-fills the glasses. He remembers seeing Alan Ladd pour whisky into two glasses that way. He can't recall the name of the film, but Alan Ladd was wearing a tuxedo, his face filled with fear and worry, and one of the glasses was for a beautiful woman whose long, dark hair half-covered one side of her face. Veronica Lake? No, that isn't right, it was Rock Hudson in *Giant* pouring Texas-sized drinks for himself and Elizabeth Taylor, pissed off because he just lost all his money to James Dean, who is about to rub salt in Rock's wounds. Fife saw the film at the Revere Drive-In with Evelyn Rose on a night so cold he had to keep the motor and the car heater running almost from the beginning to the end, and it was a really long movie. He remembers wrestling both hands easily under Evelyn's coat to the downy pink sweater and wool skirt beneath. Meeting only scattered resistance, he slides one hand under her sweater and the other under her skirt and along the inside of her thigh. He slips three fingers under her slick nylon panties. He crawls through the curls of her pubic hair, and to his astonishment, she opens her legs and practically invites him to enter. So he does. And she groans, and before he realizes what is happening, she has unzipped his fly and has released his standing cock into her hand and in less than ten seconds has brought him off, all over the front of his corduroy trousers.

Recalling all this in the passage of a few seconds, he recalls also the damp, fishy smell of his own semen in the chill air of the car and Evelyn's bewildering silence afterward, the way she turns her attention back to the film, as if nothing has happened between them, while he cannot stop listening to the pounding blood inside his ears and the rasping sounds of his corduroy trousers as he rubs them clean with his handkerchief. He wants to say something to her—maybe he should say that he loves her—but she seems intent on watching *Giant*, so he says nothing.

It happened barely six weeks ago, and yet, remembering it here, two thousand miles away in a far, flat corner of the continent surrounded by strangers in a strange land, it seems to have happened six years ago. Or decades. Or to someone else. He realizes suddenly how far from his previous life he has come in ten days, the first four days and nights spent inside Nick's father's Olds speeding south and west on Route 66, the following six days and nights living in a tiny, barren room in a YMCA and washing dishes in a German restaurant in the middle of the Texas panhandle. For the first time in his life, he has discovered that he is alone in the world, that he has always been alone and will be alone for the rest of his life. Alone and unknown. He sits in the chair, holding the glass in his hands, and his eyes fill with tears.

What are you waiting for? Swenson asks. Drink up.

Fife drinks. He who has never before tasted anything stronger than beer downs the scotch as if it's beer and he's in a hurry to leave. He gags, coughs, feels his throat and stomach rebel, and he begins to weep.

Easy, Leonard! Go easy. Swenson laughs.

Fife's coughing subsides, and he looks up to see Swenson standing next to him. It's okay, I'm all right now, he stammers. Just went down the wrong way, that's all. I'm okay now.

Of course you are, Swenson says softly. You're not used to good things, that's all, he says. He places a hand heavily onto Fife's shoulder.

Fife is facing Swenson's belt buckle. In the shape of a horseshoe, he notices. Then he sees the bulge below, and he says, I'm just a kid! Really, I'm only just turned sixteen.

Oh, no, Leonard. You're a man. I'm sure you're a man, Swenson murmurs, moving his hand from the boy's shoulder to his face, groping softly across his cheeks, nose, and brow, fluttering delicately over the flesh and bones.

Fife pulls his face away from the hand and leaps from the chair. Ike comes immediately to attention in the corner. Seeing the dog, noting its size, Fife moans, I'm just a kid! He's afraid he's going to bawl.

Swenson talks to him rapidly, quietly, in an intense monotone, No, don't worry, don't be afraid. I'm a very lonely man, is all. Don't be afraid of anything, Leonard. I'm not going to hurt you or do anything that you don't want me to do.

But Fife can hear only the tone of Leonard's voice, not the words, and it frightens him.

Again the man reaches out, and one of his hands finds Fife's shoulder, and smiling easily, gently, looking off and up to his left, as if peering through the venetian blind that covers the window behind him, he places his right hand over Fife's cock, cupping it and pressing lightly, bringing it suddenly, unwillingly, to life, until it presses back.

Shoving the man's hand away, Fife stands and takes a clumsy step forward. Look here, he says, keeping his voice as low and even as possible, trying to sound like a grown man. Look, I'm really sorry about this, but I can't do this, what you want me to do. I'm sorry, but I never have, and I just can't do it. Now, I'm going to walk out of here. If you try to stop me with that dog, or if you lay a hand on me again, I'll start yelling, and everyone in this whole goddamn building will know what you are trying to do. I'm sorry about this. And they'll know you got whisky here and you're giving it to a minor.

He checks the dog and takes another step in the direction of the door. Ike turns away from him and circles once in his spot and lies down.

Fife looks back at Swenson, assuming that the man has dismissed his dog with a gesture. Swenson stands beside him in profile now, peering at the covered window, grimly intent. Holding his erect penis in his hand, Swenson slowly masturbates, lost in darkness and solitude, locked into the small, dark closet of his body.

Fife stumbles out the door to the corridor. He runs down the stairs, crosses the empty lobby and out to the street. He circles the building to the parking lot in back and gets into the Olds and inhales deeply, filling his flushed face with the familiar, friendly, cool, dry odor of upholstery and dashboard and floor mats, tamping the image of the blind man masturbating as far back into his visual memory as he can. He can't unsee it, but he never wants to see it again.

He glances at the dashboard clock—it's almost midnight, time to pick up Nick at the restaurant. He starts the engine and lights a cigarette and pulls out into the scattered late-night traffic, thinking, It never happened, did it? Maybe he only imagined it. Maybe he misinterpreted the guy, and he wasn't really jacking off. He only glanced over at the guy, and he wasn't sure he had a hard-on, and when he brushed his hand against Fife's cock it could have been by accident since he's blind.

At the restaurant, the Würsthaus, Nick is waiting impatiently in front of the darkened door. He walks to the driver's side and holds out his hand and says he'll drive the Olds back to the Y. It's Nick's father's car they stole, not Fife's. Fife's father doesn't own a car. Ruefully, Fife passes him the key, for a second feeling like a wife picking up her husband at work.

All the way back to the Y, they talk excitedly of getting shit-faced on T-bird, as they now call their liquor. For no reason he can name, Fife reassures Nick that he didn't touch a drop of it, Nick will see, the jug is still unopened, hasn't even been cracked. Nick gently answers that it doesn't matter if he's taken a drink or two already, because he won't take long to catch up, not with the goddamn thirst he's got after eight hours in that fucking Kraut kitchen.

No, no, man, I didn't take any of it. I just shot pool all night, that and talked bullshit with some blind guy who had a seeing-eye dog and waited around for you to get off work. I figured, what the hell, we should celebrate together. Right?

Right, Nick answers. His voice is low, quiet. He's very tired. Nick is slender, almost delicate, with narrow wrists and hands and thin arms that grow heavy with fatigue long before Fife begins to feel the same weight in his thicker, more muscled arms.

So what are we celebrating? Nick asks.

I don't know. Payday, I guess. Money in our pockets, man. Getting out of this fucking town. Between us we've got almost enough to get the rest of the way to the coast, man.

Fife runs up the two flights of stairs to their room, Nick trudging slowly, wearily behind. When they enter the room, Fife locks the door and pulls the paper blind down, covering the window, while Nick sits on his narrow bed and leans back against the pillow. Fife unscrews the cap on the jug of Thunderbird and takes a swig of the rust-colored, sickly sweet liquor. He passes the jug to Nick, who does the same. They both smack their lips with evident pleasure.

Soon Fife has noticed that he takes two swigs for every one of Nick's. After about an hour of intent drinking and short bursts of idle gossip about their coworkers at the Würsthaus, Nick's head slumps back onto the pillow, and Fife realizes that he has fallen asleep. Fife holds on to the jug and paces unsteadily about the room and continues to drink. He reels from one corner of the room to the other, muttering thickly to himself. When he holds the jug up to his open mouth, he sloshes the contents of the jug across the front of his shirt and down his arm, dribbling the liquor onto the vinyl-covered floor.

Gradually, with the room spinning like a gyroscope, his peripheral vision deserts him. He peers out of tiny eyeholes cut in a stiff mask. His cheeks feel numb. He shoves his mouth and cheeks into a broad, toothy grin and feels no change in the arrangement of his flesh, as if his face has been anesthetized. Bumping hard against Nick's bed, he jostles his friend awake for a second. He grabs one of Nick's slight, bony shoulders and shakes it back and forth, mumbling, C'mon, Nick, don' fall asleep on your ol' buddy, c'mon an' have a drink of T-bird with your ol' buddy.

Nick rubs his eyes and smiles indulgently. Sure, one last slug, he says. He wipes his mouth with his sleeve and stretches out on the bed and turns his back to Fife and falls asleep again.

Fife says he has to imagine the rest, because he cannot remember it. Somewhere in the night Nick must have been wakened by a choking sound. Half drunk and fuzzy with sleep, he sits up unsteadily and peers around the room, looking for the source of the violent gagging sound. The room looks as if a drawn-out, viciously inflicted homicide has occurred. Fife's cot lies on its side against the wall, blankets and sheets tangled together on the floor. Their suitcases, which have served as both dresser and closet, are opened, emptied, left gaping, the contents scattered about the room. Clothes, toiletries, shoes, towels, and a half dozen paperback novels lie scattered about the room. And there is Nick Dafina's best friend, sixteen-year-old Leonard Fife, on his hands and knees by the door, expelling with the force of his entire body the last pool of clear, viscous liquid contained in his stomach, hurling it at the floor again and again. And then, finally, nothing. Fife's stomach is empty and dry. But still he arches his back and heaves. A puddle of orange vomit spreads slowly under the closed door into the hallway beyond.

At last Fife ceases heaving. Nick gets up from his cot and puts Fife's cot back on its legs. He lifts his friend's body like a slumped mattress into a near-standing position, turns him on his base, and lets him pitch forward onto the cot. Fife's eyes are shut, and for a few seconds of darkness, before lapsing into a white, dreamless sleep, he watches bits of fiery light shoot past in orbits around a hot silvered needle that sits at the exact center of his brain.

Fife wakes in acute pain to the cold, acidic smell of his own vomit. This he remembers and has no need to imagine it. The room foully exhales. Bit by bit he remembers most of what happened before he blacked out. He groans in confusion and shame and physical pain. His clothes and face and hands are rank with the stench of vomit and spilled liquor.

Lying on his narrow bed, Nick opens his eyes. He scans the room and recoils. Man, we are in serious trouble, he says. The YMCA guy has a thing about booze in the rooms.

We got to get the fuck outa here, Fife croaks. They're gonna kill us when they see this room. They probably already know. He swings his feet off the bed to the floor and carefully eases his body into a sitting position.

Where we gonna go? Nick says. He has shut his eyes against the disorder.

California. Anywhere.

In abject silence, they straighten the room as well as they can, squaring the second bed back on its feet and sliding it against the wall, shoving the soaked remnants of bedding and towels under it and packing their clothes and other possessions back into their suitcases. They move slowly and with great care, as if their bodies are made of cracked glass.

They grab their suitcases and steal from the room and descend the back stairs and slip out the rear exit to the parking lot. Nick drives. Fife's hands shake violently, and his arms, legs, and head droop under their own weight and throb with pain. The boys talk little and only of the routes west. They decide to stick with Route 66. Twice in an hour Nick has to pull over to the side of the road so Fife can get out and try to vomit away his dizziness, his throbbing headache, and his pummeled gut. The third time Nick slows the car, it's to park at a roadside diner. Fife sits sullenly in the car while Nick goes inside and a half hour later returns to the car, picking bits of bacon from his teeth with a toothpick. Fife glowers at him.

Nick slides into the driver's seat and says, Great pancakes, man. You know, I was thinking. When we get to the West Coast, we ought to try and sell this car. I mean, we can probably get fifteen hundred bucks for it. Maybe more.

Why? What's wrong with the car?

Nothing. It's just that, if we sell the car, we can divide the money equally. Even though it's my old man's car. But I'm okay with that. I'll split it fifty-fifty. And then we can each pick up something of our own, something the cops won't be looking for. A used Fiat, maybe. Or maybe even a used MG. That would be cool. Or use the money to get to Australia.

You won't be able to sell this fucking car, Fife grunts. It isn't yours to sell. You need the title.

Yeah. You're probably right. Nick's face drops, and he starts the engine and pulls out of the parking lot and puts the Olds back onto the highway again.

A few moments later, Nick says, What the hell, if we don't like California, and we can't sell the car, we can always turn around and head back, right? Nothing lost, except some weeks of school. My old man would be so glad to have his goddamn Olds back, he'd go easy on me. Your parents wouldn't give you any trouble if you came back, would they? They'd be so happy you came home safe and sound, they'd probably welcome you with open arms.

You're out of your fucking mind if you think I'm going back there. Not now. Not ever, Fife says. He pulls his head in like a turtle and crosses his arms over his chest and closes his eyes, as the car shoots west and south into the deserts of New Mexico, thinking, as he descends into himself, it's over. That chicken-shit bastard. Over. As soon as we get to LA, I'm taking off on my own. A loner, that's what I am anyhow. Like James Dean in *Giant*. Nick can go running back to Strafford, if he wants to. His old man can wire him the goddamn money, and he'll roll the Olds on home, and the next day he'll be back in school as if he'd never left. For Fife, nothing will ever be the same. He's gone too far now to ever go back. It's all over for him. At least back there in Strafford it is. If there's anything left for him now, it's going to have to be out in front of him. On his own. When they get to LA, staying hitched to that goddamn wuss Nick will just be lugging excess baggage, he decides. And a few moments later, Fife is asleep and dreaming.

19

FIFE SAYS TO EMMA, THIS IS MORE LIKE A BIOGRAPHY
or a bioflick than a filmed autobiography or interview or whatever the
hell it is that we're making here.

What do you mean?

From page one, we know how a biography is going to end. The subject dies. With an autobiography or interview, you can't be sure how
it'll turn out. It ends where the author or the fucking interviewer or
interviewers want it to end, not where it must.

He has said this sharply, in a hectoring tone, as if angry at his wife.
But he's not angry at Emma. He's not angry at Malcolm or any of the
others, and certainly not Renée. He's angry at his cancer. *His* cancer.
Not cancer in general. There's a saying among oncologists: Everyone
has his own cancer. As in, Everyone has his own body. No two can-
cers, no two bodies, are alike.

Emma interrupts him. What? What are you saying, Leo? I don't
understand, darling.

He answers, Fuck, shit, piss. Fuck, shit, piss. He means, I'm pissed off, this is horseshit, I'm fucked. He says, Wait a minute, I'll get it right. Nick and I, he says. In Amarillo in 1956 and Strafford in 1968. They're all tangled together, but in a coherent way. Like a double helix, he says. Then somehow the DNA that controls their relations breaks down. Mutates. The coherence disappears.

The damage his metastasizing cancerous cells are doing to his body and brain is keeping him from connecting what he sees and hears in memory to words that can be heard and understood by Emma and filmed by Malcolm and his crew. Everything is coming back to him in an irresistible rush, a tsunami of memories that he's unable to share. He knows how he must sound to Emma and Malcolm and the others. He sounds like a madman, like one of those homeless schizophrenics wandering the city, murmuring to themselves. But he is not murmuring to himself, he's talking to his wife, pointedly so, and being filmed while doing it. She hears him, and the others overhear him. The trouble is, he can't hear or overhear himself.

Why bother trying? Why not just sit here in the wheelchair in silence in the black box and watch and listen to his unfolding memories with no audience, no listener, but himself? He's nearly dead and gone, anyhow. When a man knows he is to be hanged in a fortnight, it concentrates his mind wonderfully. Who said that? Samuel Johnson? A death sentence about to be carried out concentrates one's mind, not on the sentence or the world that's about to disappear, but on itself, on one's own private, unique consciousness, the flickering light at the center of an expanded universe, a consciousness loosed on the world to do its ugly, omnivorous work, as random as a single malignant cell broken off a cluster of perfect cells that, despite having fathered and mothered a malignancy, continue to express their perfect cell-fate, as if they were not doomed.

Hanged in a fortnight, eh, Dr. Johnson? Fourteen days seems like a decade to Fife's concentrated mind. More likely he won't last forty-eight hours. Not consciously, anyhow. His heart may go on beating for a fortnight, but only if it's wired to a machine. He will be long gone by then.

As a very young child, before he was able to speak of it or knew that anyone else felt or thought the same way, Fife was aware of the contingency of his occurrence on this earth. Almost from the start, he perceived the contingency and randomness even of the earth itself, the lack of any inner necessity for its or his existence. How miraculous and irrelevant his very existence, then. The miracle and irrelevance of reality. For most of the rest of his life he ignored that miraculous irrelevancy, shunted it to the side, as if it belonged to someone else, like a stranger's vague memory of having once met him on the road.

Until now. Until he's told that his bones have been invaded by cancer cells that have spread like seeds from a tumor grown from the cells that make up his bladder. Carried by his blood, the seeds planted in his bones sprout into new blooming tumors that send their seeds on to his liver and esophagus and intestines.

First it's metastatic cancer with an unknown primary. Best guess, the bladder. Then angiogenesis. Counterattack with Cisplatin. Back up the Cisplatin with Adriamycin. Which damages the heart when combined next with a regimen of Paclitaxel. Throw in a few reinforcing doses of Mustargen, causing disabling nausea and extreme weakness and a lowered white blood cell count. The rapidly reproducing noncancerous cells cease reproducing: white blood cells, hair follicles, fingernails, toenails. A return to infancy. A return to the womb. Nature's way of cleaning house, putting out the trash.

All creation starts as a single cell of energy that explodes with a bang and becomes the universe. Cancer starts the same way: a single differentiated rogue cell breeds a tumor that metastasizes and sets to eating the body and eventually devours and displaces it. It's the same with consciousness. It starts at birth as a single erupting cell of awareness that swiftly multiplies and starts eating the world, until you become the world. That must be how it feels to be an infant human being, a newborn human baby. You are the universe. An utterly dysfunctional state that, in order to function as a self-sufficient organism, has to start differentiating itself from the world, the way one's organs one by one take on their unique shapes and functions, until cell-fate equals self-fate.

Equals self-hate? That's the cancer cell, the malignancy metastasizing.

For the first time since he was little more than an infant, just as it is about to come to an end, Fife is amazed by the miracle of his own existence. He's about to merge with whatever will exist after his death, to become a part of whatever there is without him. Everything he knows, everything he remembers, everything he did and didn't do, in a matter of days or possibly hours will disappear, as if he never existed. His work, his films, will perhaps linger after him for a few years, but soon they'll be forgotten, too. Other people's memories of him will hang around for a while, of course, for a few months, anyhow, and maybe, for Emma, even years. But not his own memories. The second his cancerous body shuts his brain down, his memories will be vaporized.

His first glimpse of the larger world beyond him, his first awareness that he was only a tiny cellular part of that world, filled him with an unsayable solitude and a terrible fear that he could instantly be absorbed by that larger world. When a child discovers that he is not his mother, and worse, his mother is not the entirety of the universe, he perceives the utter absurdity and meaninglessness of his separation from the world. This is how Fife saw himself when he first saw himself. Then for a lifetime, until now, seventy-seven years later, he hid that sight from himself.

Now that early vision of absurdity and meaninglessness has returned with awful, inescapable clarity. With it has come an irresistible longing for the endgame merger that so terrifies him, a longing for an end of consciousness of contingency and separation from the great unknown, from the allover, from the undifferentiated universe. Though it shakes him to his deepest level of feeling, at the same time he longs for it to come quickly and take him. It's the only conceivable way to end the terror.

All the years between his infancy and now, Fife has known that he is human, that all human beings are mortal, and that therefore he is mortal, too. It's only logical, right? An irrefutable syllogism. Yet until now he has been unable to apply it to himself, to Leonard Fife, to this particular human being. He has been unable to imagine a world in which Leonard Fife, this particular human being, does not exist as a separate, differentiated part, a free-floating rogue cell broken away from the perfect, coherently structured and functioning universe, sailing freely among the galaxies, somehow managing to avoid being yanked into orbit by the gravity of a star or a planet until at last he plunges into fiery dissolution. Until now. He sees himself dropping out of the darkness faster and faster toward the light. He has only hours, minutes, seconds to live—to remain separated from the light.

Beyond the terror of dying, he wants the pain to end, the awful, relentless, drugged pain caused by his cancer's insatiable appetite for his body. And yet he does not want it to stop, any more than he wants his memories to stop. The pain and his memories—regardless of how fuddled and distorted they have been made by the drugs that are supposed to wage war against his cancer and mask his pain—are the only evidence he has to prove that he has not yet died. His pain and his memories confirm his ongoing existence. He needs no one to witness his pain. No one can. But his memories cannot exist unless they are heard and overheard.

He has told Emma that he is confessing his abandonments and betrayals. That's not quite true. He's saying his memories, is all. As if on his knees at the side of his bed, he's saying his prayers to the only God that he believes in. Except that there is no God he believes in. There is only Emma. Who irritates him. Angers him, because of her inability to understand what he's saying, as if he's praying in Aramaic or some other dead language. So it's not just his cancer that he's angry at. It's Emma, too. He's angry because of her alliance with Malcolm and the others, who persist in lying to themselves and to him, despite the obvious, undeniable truth that he is dying and cannot be saved. Every night before she leaves him for her own bedroom, she touches his forehead with her cool, dry fingertips and asks him how he feels, and he says, has said it for weeks, Worse. Worse than the last time you asked.

You'll feel better in the morning, she says, making a promise that neither she nor anyone else can keep.

Only if I don't wake, he answers.

Malcolm is the same. Diana, Vincent, and Sloan, too. They want a talking corpse for their film, a career-maker for Malcolm and Diana, who haven't been able to get a film financed for six or eight years now, and a real job for the intern, Sloan, and a cinematography prize for Vincent, and lots of CBC work for all of them in the near future. They tell him how great he looks. Lying in their gummy teeth, big smiles on their faces. He knows what he looks like. Not great by a long shot. Since they last saw him in the hospital, he's lost nearly half his body mass. His gray skin hangs loosely off his bones and skull, his arms and hands are like splintered kindling, his teeth are yellowed and loose, his tongue and lips covered with a chalky paste.

Yet they keep insisting that he looks great. Diana suggests that he just needs to eat more, forgetting that he's fed through a plastic tube bypassing his disintegrated esophagus directly into his stomach.

Why bother to correct the idiots? Just agree.

Sloan, when she reattaches his mic after it's slipped off the placket of his shirt, pats him on the shoulder as if to say, Good dog, good dog, all the while holding her breath because of the odor of urine and feces clinging to his clothing and body. She is so youthful and fertile and clean, so strong and flexible! He loathes her fecundity and her beauty.

She has a perfect pain-free body, and all he has is a stinking, rotting carcass.

Vincent tells him that the camera loves him, lit from overhead by the Godox Speedlight, with nothing but darkness surrounding him. He looks like some kind of guru or ancient magician. Like Merlin. Otherworldly, he says. You're a fucking high priest, Leo.

Yeah, Fife answers. A fucking high priest officiating at his own funeral.

Stop lying to me, he says. Stop lying to yourselves. He knows the truth, and he's not afraid of it. No, that's not true. He's terrified of it. It's got him by the throat, and it's strangling him, and he's too weak to resist. Their lies don't help him resist. All the lies do is strengthen the grip of the truth on his throat and make it harder for him to breathe.

Only Renée refuses to lie to herself or to him. She knows he's a dying man who cannot be cured or saved by any measures, no matter how extreme. She knows and admits to herself and to him that, yes, she is a healthy, strong, beautiful organism, and he is all but dead, weak and hairless as a newborn baby, and ugly. Very ugly. To keep his pain only partially numbed without putting him into a coma, she methodically delivers his medicine according to schedule and prescribed dosage. To prevent microbial and bacterial infection, so that he will be killed by his cancer and not sepsis, she washes his ass and catheterized prick and the other holes in his skin. To hydrate and nourish him, she keeps the IVs filled, prolonging the agony until his lungs finally overflow with phlegm and he drowns or the effort to breathe becomes too much for his heart to handle and it stops sending blood to his brain and the few dim remaining neural lights in his cerebral cortex go out one by one, and it's over at last.

Renée is the only person left who does not lie to him or to herself. Before her, the last to stop lying were his doctors at the hospital, Schultz the oncologist and McKenna the surgeon, both men in their early forties, overachieving medical jocks, engineers who view their patients not as people to be saved but as problems to be solved, equations to be worked out, contests to be won. When it's clear that the contest cannot be won, that one side of the equal sign cannot be made to balance the other, that the problem, due to the way it was originally proposed, is unsolvable, they abandon the patient.

That's when Fife stopped hating his doctors. They lost interest completely, simply ceased coming to his room, turned him over to the administrators and the floor nurses, who from then on did what they could to make him comfortable. Which quickly became impossible. He will never be comfortable again.

Fife told Emma that he does not want to die in the hospital, please get him out of here and home, so he can die there instead. She insists that he stay in the hospital for another week, she does not think she can properly care for him herself, so he relents. One week becomes two, until it's clear even to her that the doctors have washed their hands of him. The hospital is crowded, and the administrators would like to give his bed to a patient they might be able to cure, a problem they can solve. Emma meets with them and agrees to bring her husband home. She will hire a nurse to care for him during the days, and she will care for him at night herself, changing his bedpan and catheter, washing him, making sure his IVs are refilled until the nurse arrives in the morning. She rents a hospital bed for him, moves their marital bed into her office, and turns their bedroom and home into a hospice center.

When he is transferred from hospital to home, Emma rides in the ambulance with him. I feel better today than I've felt in a month, Fife tells her as they whisk down Sherbrooke. See if they'll switch on the siren, he says. Let's make a big deal out of my escape from the hospital. Announce it to the world.

Emma leans toward the front seat and asks the driver to turn on the siren. My husband wants the entire city of Montreal to know that he's going home.

The driver grunts, Uh-uh, and says in French, We cannot do that. We cannot use the siren except when we take someone to Emergency. This is not an emergency.

Fife shouts, Of course it's an emergency! I'm a dying man, and the only thing that will keep me alive is the comfort and familiarity and peacefulness of my home! I didn't want to die in a hospital, and I damn sure don't want to die in an ambulance stuck in traffic on Sherbrooke at rush hour. So turn on the fucking siren!

The driver sighs, glances at his helper in the passenger seat, and shrugs, Why not?

The whoop-whoop-whoop of the siren first thrills Fife and then soothes him. He takes Emma's hand in his and squeezes it. The noise has pushed all the rage and fear out of his head, and in their absence, the pain goes. It's better than any drug. Wouldn't it be wonderful, he says, if we could just keep going on and on like this, stopping only to get gas and sandwiches for you and these two nice attendants, crossing the continent back and forth from one coast to the other with the siren wailing? Until finally, just before he dies, they park the ambulance and wheel him from the ambulance in a dolly and settle him under a tree, and he looks up through the newly budded branches at the sky somewhere in Nova Scotia or out in BC, and he dies there. What a way to go, eh?

You're not going to die, she says.

Oh, fuck you, Emma! Shut the siren off, he says to the driver. And the driver complies, and the ambulance is silent the rest of the way home.

Vincent says to Malcolm, Okay, we're ready.

Malcolm asks Fife if he's able to continue. He's not too tired, is he? They can take a break if he likes. They can come back tomorrow and continue then. Still got a lot of ground to cover, he says, a lot of questions to ask. Although, to be honest, you're doing all the answering without my asking any questions, he says. It's like I'm a camera is all.

What's that famous Christopher Isherwood line? I am a camera. I am a camera with its shutter open, passive, recording, not thinking, blah-blah-blah. Fife knows the line, he used to quote it in class. Someday all this will be developed, printed, fixed. Something like that.

Pure bullshit, Fife says. Another fucking lie. He doesn't think even Isherwood himself believed it.

Really? Did you believe it back then when you used to quote it to us? Malcolm asks. You getting this, Vincent? I didn't do the clapper yet. Leonard Fife interview. Montreal, April 1, 2018, he says and claps his hands in front of the camera lens.

Yeah, I'm shooting. I got it, the Isherwood bit.

Fife says, I can keep going. Until I can't anymore. You'll know when I can't, because I'll be dead. I plan to die on-camera and make you famous, Malcolm.

Don't even think that. Jesus! All right, then. So what about the Isherwood I-am-a-camera line that Fife says is bullshit? Did he believe it back then, when he was quoting it to his film students at Concordia?

No, of course not. He was trying to get the young filmmakers to stop seeing what they wanted to see, which is almost always only what they think the audience wants to see. Which Fife is sure will happen here when Malcolm and Diana sit down with all this footage and make their film from it. They'll see what they want to see, and it'll be what they think their audience wants to see.

And what is that?

Oh, Malcolm, believe me, they'll want to watch me die.

20

THIS HE REMEMBERS, AND TRIES IN VAIN TO MAKE
Emma see and hear all that he has seen and heard.

That the cut of the land has changed radically and with sudden-
ness somewhere in New Hampshire north of Franklin. But he did not
notice the change until this moment, when it's almost dark. Where
earlier the road sliced across a coastal plain, it now follows a river up-
stream, countercurrent, tracing the river north back to its icy source.
At first, in southern and central New Hampshire, the river was the
Merrimack. But the Merrimack alters course above Franklin, where
it dribbles to the east and north into rapid shallows, then bogs and
swamps, before spreading out again at its head as two large, cold lakes.

He cuts diagonally west at Plymouth and crosses the wider, deeper
Connecticut River at Orford and enters Vermont. Off to his left the
sky has gone to watery pink and orange. Funneling the broad, shad-
owed valley, the hills have been replaced by granite mountains slath-
ered with patches of old snow. Oak and elm, beech, black cherry and
tamarack trees cling to eroded, narrow-shouldered slopes and gradually give way to conifers. Hemlock, spruce and fir, white pine, jack pine,

and shaggy cedar clutch the steep sides of heaps of glacial rubble. Fife would like to live in a cabin at the top of one of those piles of stone. To hold it against the world. To become a hermit poet, like Han Shan.

Because of the wind out of Canada, the tree line here is low, four thousand feet. The crystalline wind would tear all the slag from his mind in a single season. He'd have to live in a cave like a bear, with a bear's slow, sleep-thickened thoughts to keep the wind and snow and ice from snuffing him out. To survive, he'd have to think thoughts as simple and clear as a mountain stream. That's what he wants. It's what he believes he needs.

The road swings slowly north again, and then west. The valley that shaped it for a hundred miles is closing, and from here to Quebec continues as a series of gaps and occasional high plateaus. With the sun gone, the cold has quickly descended, pressing like a gloved hand against the twisting, rapidly rising land. The eastern horizon has disappeared in darkness. The western horizon is a fading pink line scratched halfway into the sky. Below the line, he makes out the lights of scattered farmhouses. Farther to his left he can see the lights of Montpelier, the state capital, a city not much larger than a town.

Three miles east of Montpelier he turns onto a narrow two-lane road that winds north along the Winooski River. Hundred-foot pines and spruce trees loom on both sides of the river, and behind the trees, where scraps of crusted snow gleam in last light, lie the mountains, black, massive, impenetrable. His hands have grown cold. His face is cold. He can't find the heater knob and doesn't want to stop and hunt through the maze of lights, dials, switches, and levers. He can see the sky, but only ahead and above him, a cloak of deep blue shot through with stars. A crescent moon flashes through breaks in the trees. He looks for the Big Dipper, but instead he finds the Little—Ursa Minor. And there is Polaris at the end of the bent handle. It's upside down. Sign of rain? Draw a line from Polaris, you'll come to two of the stars in the Big Dipper. Or is it the other way around? You draw a line from the two end stars in the cup of Ursa Major, the Big Dipper, and you'll find Polaris. That's about all he remembers from his one undergraduate astronomy course at RPI. Naming stars places him in the universe, not to navigate his way from one place to another so much as to locate his body's exact position on the planet relative to the rest of the galaxy. He spots and names Vega in the east. And dead ahead, Cassiopeia, resting on the horizon.

A dozen miles above Montpelier he enters a wilderness of heaving shadows, broken only occasionally by the lights of farmhouses. He rounds a quick bend in the road—remembered from his and Alicia's trip north back in January—and slips through a notch in the mountains. The Winooski River gushes noisily at the side of the road, and high rocky cliffs huddle tight to his left and on the far bank of the river. He can't see the cliffs, can see only the road illuminated by the headlights of the Plymouth. He knows the cliffs are there in the deeper darkness. And the wide bend in the river, he remembers, marks the presence less than five miles away of the village of Plainfield—twenty or thirty white houses, a handful of stores, and the half dozen dormitories and classroom buildings and administration and maintenance buildings of Goddard College, where he is about to become more or less gainfully employed. Also down there in the village, the house that by tomorrow afternoon he and Alicia will own and call their permanent home.

At the fork a mile south of Plainfield, he turns right onto an unpaved road leading away from the village. A hundred yards beyond the fork, he turns left onto a narrower dirt road that crosses the Winooski on a one-lane wooden bridge, passes the sign that reads ENTERING PIERCE'S MILLS, a township without a town, a hamlet without a center, and plunges into the forest. Darting into hollows and curling slowly out and up slopes, with each new ascent expecting to see the road level out, he gains the top of the ridge that has coursed along on his right since leaving the main road near Montpelier. Then it's over the crest, with nothing revealed except a wide swath of starry, blue-black sky.

He descends a hundred yards, and suddenly he's there. He pulls the Plymouth off the road onto Stanley's rutted gravel driveway and brings the car to an abrupt, clattering stop before the open door of the barn.

The engine ticks in the sudden silence. The headlights of the Plymouth illuminate the interior of the barn. It looks strangely cold and empty, as if abandoned. Maybe they've moved, Fife thinks. Maybe since I talked to him on the phone a week ago something terrible has happened, and he's left this place for another and couldn't tell me without putting himself in danger. He flicks off the headlights and opens the car door and steps into a gust of chilled night air.

Maybe Stanley has left Gloria. Maybe he left her for another woman. Stanley and Gloria have no children. Maybe he just left her. Easy when you have no children to abandon.

He inhales deeply, grabs his briefcase, and makes for the house behind and to the left of the barn. Because of the cold and the cruel topography and the Indians, the township called Pierce's Mills and the village of Plainfield were settled later than the rest of New England. Stanley's house, built in the early 1800s, is one of the oldest structures in this part of the state. Surrounded by second- and third-growth forest, it's a typical early Cape farmhouse, an almost perfect square with a large roof run through by a thick center chimney. The living quarters are connected to the barn at the kitchen by a woodshed, and the house, shed, and barn face a narrow valley and a set of north-running glacial moraines and eskers. When Fife and Alicia were here in January, Stanley claimed that on a clear day you could see the Presidential Range in New Hampshire in the east, the Green Mountains of Vermont in the west, the Berkshires in the south, and Quebec in the north. On any other day, you can't see beyond the dirt road that loops past the house and heads into the forested valley below.

Stanley's renovations of the house have consisted of little more than simple interior decoration. It has no electricity and no plumbing, other than a dug well and a hand pump at the kitchen sink and an outhouse.

For heat there are the fireplaces, four of them, and two woodstoves, one in the kitchen and one in the large first-floor parlor that serves as Stanley's studio. In cold weather they close off the small four-square second-floor bedrooms altogether and sleep in the parlor on a mattress thrown on the floor in front of the fireplace. They live like early-nineteenth-century settlers. By choice—Stanley's choice, Fife is sure, not Gloria's.

Before he has a chance to knock, the door opens, and there he is, big as a grizzly bear, red-faced, bearded, grinning, wearing overalls and a plaid wool shirt. Stanley grabs Fife's hand in his huge mitt and pumps it up and down in happy silence, as if miming a staged greeting, then grabs Fife with both arms and envelops him in a hug, lifting his friend onto his toes before releasing him. He leads Fife gently by the hand into the living room, turns him to face the door to the kitchen. Beaming proudly, as if Fife is a newly completed painting, he shows his old friend to Gloria, who enters the living room from the kitchen, wooden spoon in hand. This is how Fife always pictures her, coming into the room from her kitchen carrying a spoon or spatula.

He's here! Stanley bellows. The man is here! We thought you must've got lost! he hollers. Fife squints against his friend's noise. After having been apart for so long, it always takes Fife an hour or two to adjust his hearing to Stanley's shout. He once asked Stanley why he was shouting. It's! How! I! Talk! was the answer.

Gloria smiles at Fife from across the room, typically saying nothing, balancing her husband's noise with willed silence, but apparently, from her one raised eyebrow and slightly upturned smile, pleased to see him again.

I sort of got waylaid, Fife says, addressing them jointly. He's rarely able to speak to Gloria alone. He either talks to Stanley or addresses the two of them as one. He has a feeling that Gloria prefers it this way. He and Stanley have been close friends since his early twenties and Stanley's early thirties in Boston, long before he was introduced to

Gloria—Meet my new one! Stanley roared, when she first moved into his Symphony Road studio with him. Fife believes that his friendship with Stanley will outlast the marriage, in the same sense that their friendship will likely outlast Stanley's ownership of this battered old house in the wilds of Vermont. Alicia has followed Fife's example. She sees her husband's bond with Stanley as the only meaningful link between the two couples, and while she says she likes Gloria well enough, even admires her stoic willingness to endure what to Alicia is an unendurable kind of existence and marriage, she treats the other woman as just one more inexplicable aspect of Stanley's chaotic life. Stanley himself she treats as a harmless, amusing remnant of her husband's early bohemian life, his fast-fading past.

Fife tried to erase his wife's fears of their coming isolation by reminding her that she will already have a friend in Gloria. Gloria? She laughed. Gloria's sweet, I know, but I doubt I'll be driving twenty miles over those roads from Plainfield just to sit around in a drafty room over a cup of coffee talking about . . . what? How miserable she is? No, thanks, hon. I'll make my friends in town, probably.

Of course, Fife says. He reminds her that though the college is small, there will be a number of interesting young women for her to befriend. Faculty wives or something. And the women professors. I'm pretty sure they'll have some female professors.

Well, I'll have two kids to keep me busy.

Sure, sure. These things take care of themselves. They always have. They didn't know anyone when they moved to Charlottesville, either.

That was Charlottesville, Virginia, a major urban center compared to Plainfield, Vermont, she reminds him. But don't worry, she'll do fine. This is what she wants, too. She wouldn't be doing it, if it weren't. We're in this together, she says and smiles at him.

He promises her that it'll work out.

Fife searches the spare simplicity of the living room, looking for a chair, finding none. The room is Stanley's private art gallery. The white-washed walls are covered with his large, black-and-white abstractions. Forget them, Stanley says, assuming Fife is checking out the paintings. We can look at pictures tomorrow in the daylight. They're not made to be seen in candlelight anyhow. C'mon into the kitchen, it's warmer there, he commands. He grabs Fife's elbow and leads him into the large kitchen, lit to an orange glow by a pair of kerosene lanterns on the countertops and a third placed at the center of the pine table. Let's get us some beers! You want something stronger? Hell of a long drive, right?

Fife nods wearily, suddenly aware that he is deeply tired, as if he's spent the last twenty-four hours holding himself in tense expectation of imminent disaster. Yes, a cold beer would be most welcome, he says. The room, hot and close from the fire blazing in the stove, smells of freshly baked bread and roasting meat. Fife and Stanley sit at opposite ends of the long table and crack open cold cans of beer and slice off hard chunks of Canadian cheddar, while Gloria goes back to work preparing supper, washing and chopping vegetables next to the hand pump at the black stone sink, stopping every few minutes to check the oven temperature and adjust the drafts on the large cookstove. Fife's clenched stomach and back muscles relax. As if it were an altogether novel feeling, he realizes that he is simply and purely grateful to be situated where he is at this moment in time.

I haven't eaten all day, he exclaims, as if surprised. Well, not since this morning in Richmond, he remembers. It seems like yesterday or a week ago. No, I had a sandwich for lunch, he murmurs, remembering the stop at Feeney's in Strafford with Nick. Losing track of time, I guess. It's been a weird couple of days.

Gloria smiles and silently goes on with her work, as if expecting him to explain. Stanley pulls open another can of beer and keeps talking. With his thick mustache and beard and tangled mat of coarse black hair, he looks like a character from a Russian novel. His face is broad, with a flattened nose and small dark eyes set wide and almost lost behind high protruding cheekbones. His face has always reminded Fife of photographs of Franz Kline, the painter, and Stanley enjoys the comparison. Kline has sat for years in his pantheon of heroes and gods as something more than a hero and only slightly less than a god. Lately Stanley has found himself struggling to include a new name among the demigods, Jasper Johns, but he doesn't quite dare. Johns confuses him. He suspects that his confusion is the result of the prejudices he inherited from his pantheon of up-to-now utterly reliable heroes and gods. They have never led him into heresy, so it doesn't seem quite right to include this new name. Not yet, anyhow. The implications are far-reaching, and he knows it, so he is proceeding with caution. If Jasper Johns is right, if his work is important, then there is a lot that is wrong in Stanley's reading of the history of art. He is therefore rereading his art history, he tells Fife. And carefully.

Art history? Fife asks, smiling. This is an old and familiar conversation for them. Why not leave art history to the art historians? There's no right and wrong when it comes to art. Stanley is a painter, a good painter. And he'll probably be an even better painter when he can forget about things like the unfolding logic of art history, Fife says, quoting Stanley back to him. That's just so much academic bullshit, he says. You've been spending too much time hanging around Goddard after class, rapping in the faculty lounge, he adds good-naturedly.

Fife is loosening up. The beer tastes wonderful to him. The sharp cheddar cheese crumbling in his mouth and the pressing heat of the kitchen and the smell of wood burning noisily in the stove and the big intense face of his old friend across the table all come together naturally, and he wonders for a second if last winter he chose well by deciding to buy a village house in Plainfield, when he might have settled on one more like this, like Stanley's, an early-nineteenth-century farmhouse rooted like an ancient oak to the side of a mountain miles from town. And then remembers Alicia telling him that under no circumstances could she imagine living in such isolation, deprived of running water and central heat and electricity. Especially with a baby and a toddler. Stanley and Gloria, they're like hippies, she said to him, playing at life in the country.

Oh, Stanley, Gloria says suddenly, not looking up from the stove and the pot that she's been slowly stirring with a gentle lift and drop of a wooden spoon. Don't forget to tell Leo about the phone call.

What call? Fife asks. Did Alicia call? Shit, I told her I'd call her when I got in.

Naw, her mother called, Stanley says. What's her name, Jessie? Around four this afternoon. She just said she wanted you to phone them as soon as you got here. No matter what time you got in. That's how she put it, he says, grinning down at his beer, turning the can slowly in his meaty hands.

I guess I better call them, then. Where's the phone?

Gloria answers, as if he's asked her. Right there on the wall.

Rising wearily from his chair, Fife crosses the kitchen and dials the number in Richmond, the same number he memorized over five years ago, when Alicia was home from college for the Christmas holidays and he was wandering the cold, windy streets of Boston, insisting over and over to himself that he'd better marry this girl now, regardless of where it might lead him. Better to deal later with guilt for a specific deed done than contend with a mumbling guilt for having been too timid, he decided, and having made the decision, he immediately turned desperate to marry her. But his desperation was policy, not impulse. In those days, he believed that all the errors and havoc in his life so far had been wrought by timidity, not reckless abandon.

Benjamin answers.

Hello, Benjamin. This is Leonard, Fife says. He asks if everything's okay. He just got in, and Stanley said Jessie called here earlier. Is everything all right there?

Benjamin's voice is unusually weak. Usually his voice is carried with the force of a man who believes his clichés and commonplaces, but now, apparently, something unexpected has happened, for he is stammering in a thin, distanced voice. No, Leo . . . everything's . . . ah, it's all right now. Don't worry. We . . . we were kind of scared for a while there . . . .

What's the matter? Has anything happened to Cornel? He'll kill them if they let anything happen to his son. His son, left in the care of grandparents and servants and a mother six months pregnant. He should have put this whole thing off until after the baby was born. Or never agreed to it in the first place, the job at Goddard, the house down in the village. Stayed in Virginia. In Richmond. Accepted his in-laws' offer to take over the family business.

No, no, no. Cornel's just fine. He's sound asleep now. No, Cornel's just fine. Yes, sir.

Well, what the hell's wrong, then?

He hears Jessie's voice. He pictures Benjamin turning slowly invisible. Hello, Leo? Is that you, Leo? It's Jessie.

Yes! What's happened?

Alicia's fine, Leo. She miscarried. This afternoon.

Miscarried? Oh, Jesus, no! Is she all right?

Yes.

The baby . . . the fetus?

It was a girl, Leo. It wasn't right, though. It was malformed, the doctor said. Dr. Gold, an excellent man. Jewish. His father was my obstetrician, actually. He happened to be on duty when she went to the emergency room.

Malformed? That's why she miscarried? I mean, she didn't fall or anything?

Oh, no. It came on very quickly. Right after lunch. She started hemorrhaging, and we called an ambulance, and by four o'clock everything was fine. Nothing to worry over, Leo. She's fine now. It's probably a blessing, since the baby was . . . well, you know. I talked to her an hour ago. She said to give you her love and tell you she's feeling fine, just tired, and for you not to worry a bit. She's saddened, of course. It's a big disappointment to all of us.

Do you think I should head on back to Richmond right away? I mean, tonight? Do you think I should wait till tomorrow? he asks, thinking, Jessie has perfect diction, especially for a southerner. Mrs. Robert E. Lee probably sounded like that. Alicia sounds like that when she's angry or excited, or when we're fucking. She loses that affected Tidewater drawl that so annoys him.

Jessie says she doesn't think it's necessary for Leo to come right back to Richmond. Everything's over and done with now. Alicia's comfortable and in excellent spirits, considering what she's been through. She'll be in the hospital only for two days, then she'll be coming home. Jessie pauses and adds that if it had to happen, it's best that it happened in Richmond, not up in Charlottesville at their place. They haven't any help, she points out, and Alicia would be hard pressed to find someone to take care of Cornel and keep house on such short notice.

Yeah, I guess that's right. Is Cornel okay?

Of course! I just told him that Mummy got sick and had to go and stay at the hospital for a few days until she gets better. He's a very secure child, Leo, she adds, as if she is the person responsible for his being so secure.

Well . . . what do you think? I mean, is it possible for me to call Alicia at the hospital?

She hasn't a phone yet. Jessie ordered one for her room, but they won't have it until tomorrow morning. Anyhow, Alicia is probably asleep now. This has been terribly exhausting for her. And traumatic. Deeply disappointing. You can imagine, she says. Even though it's only a miscarriage, Alicia still had to go through a full labor and delivery. She's very fortunate that her labors are relatively short. Jessie's lasted over forty hours.

Yes, I know. Then I shouldn't call?

She'll call you tomorrow at your friends'.

Right. I'll stay here tomorrow morning until I hear from her, he assures her.

No, Leo, she says. He should go ahead and meet with the banker and the realtor and lawyer for the closing, just as he planned. Alicia might not get the phone installed in her room till late in the day, and there's no sense in his wasting a whole day waiting around there for her to call. She'll be safely home here by the time he gets back to Richmond. Everything's under control at this end, Leo, she assures him.

He guesses she's right. He says, Thanks, Jessie. And Benjamin, too. Tell Benjamin I'm grateful. I'm grateful to both of you. I'll be running around Plainfield all tomorrow, I guess. You know, the realtor, getting a lawyer, the bank, et cetera. But I'll keep checking back here at Stanley's, in case she calls. Okay?

That sounds fine, dear, she says. He mustn't worry about a thing, he's got a lot to think about way up there in Vermont. They can take care of everything down here just fine. Just get yourself a good night's sleep, dear, she tells him.

He says goodbye, and Jessie hangs up first, leaving him to listen for a few seconds to the hundreds of miles of dead wire that lopes south along the byways and highways from Stanley Reinhart's kitchen to the beige Princess telephone on the end table next to Jessie and Benjamin's canopied bed in the big brick house in Richmond, Virginia, on the bluff overlooking the James River. Fife drops the receiver onto its hook and returns to his seat at the table.

What a fucking shame, man, Stanley says. Alicia's okay, isn't she? Gloria has ceased her stirring and stands silently next to the stove, her spoon dangling loosely from her hand.

Yeah, she's fine. He remembers her huge, taut belly as he looked down at her this morning in the gray light of the bedroom and imagines how it looks tonight with the baby gone. It will be deflated, not shrunken. It will lie in puddles, a collapsed tent. A girl. They don't have a name for her yet. They'll need one, probably. The Kennedys did. But they were Catholic. Maybe it's canon law, not civil law, that requires parents to give a name to a baby born too soon to live. He wishes he and Alicia had come up with one. A name for their dead, malformed, unborn female child. Not just any name would do. Patrick Bouvier Kennedy. Patricia? Would they need a funeral? A gravestone?

PATRICIA BOUVIER KENNEDY FIFE
MARCH 31, 1968–MARCH 31, 1968

The child never even drew breath, and now they're going to have a funeral for her? And a cemetery lot? He never thought about that, but it's true, a man needs to own a cemetery lot. It isn't enough that he own land and a house, that he own a barn for his machines and firewood. Not enough that he own a well for his water and a sewer for his waste and furniture for his comfort and a car to transport him and his family and tools to help him repair his things when they break. Garments to clothe him and his family and dishes and pots and pans with which to feed them. No, he still needs to own a small square of dirt, preferably on a hillside in a cemetery a short ways out of town where he can bury the bodies of his dead babies, the babies born too soon for him to name.

Alicia will be sleeping now. Peacefully, he hopes. And Cornel. The son who seems to him only rarely not the son of some other man, a man neither of them has met. Cornel is more like the son of women only, a male child whose closest male relative is his maternal grandfather, not his father. Fife can think of no reason for feeling this way about his son, unless it's because he is not able to regard himself as the father of any child, any living child, anywhere, by any woman. Yet he knows that he has already fathered three children. Two of them still live, his abandoned daughter somewhere in Florida with his abandoned first wife, and his son in the care of grandparents and servants in Virginia. Even so, and in spite of this knowledge, the sudden, unexpected birth of this female child and her immediate death and his actual great distance from both of those events, taken together seem for a few seconds to slice against the grain of all his layered, distressing, guilt-ridden senses of himself. He is finally a father! Father of a malformed baby girl, a child born dead and nameless and too soon. But he is nonetheless a father.

Gloria slowly sets plates on the table. The two men get up and walk into the living room. Stanley asks over his shoulder when dinner will be ready.

In about twenty minutes, Gloria answers.

Let's take a walk, he suggests to Fife.

Fife agrees, and they leave the house and walk slowly down the dirt road toward the valley in the deep, cool darkness, talking quietly as they walk of the sudden alterations of the land, how you can't learn its patterns because it has none.

They're old, man, these mountains and hills. Pre-Cambrian. The oldest mountains on the continent. Even the glaciers couldn't align them. The only way you can know this land is by memorizing it, Stanley says. Fatigue colors his voice, as if he's tried all the other ways.

21

VINCENT STOPS FIFE'S ACCOUNT. THE FUCKING CAMERA'S
heating up. It's not supposed to heat up. Sorry to interrupt this . . .
whatever-it-is, he adds, a little mournfully, as if, concentrating so intently on Fife's image in the viewfinder, he hasn't been listening to
Fife's words. Just his murmuring voice. He says, Sloan, can you bring
up the houselights?

Houselights? You mean the room lights?

C'mon, girl, you know what I mean.

She says she doesn't know where the switch is located. And please
don't call me girl.

He clucks with mild impatience and steps into the darkness and
flips on the lights himself and comes back to his camera and starts
switching out the card for a fresh one. It's midafternoon. Sheets of soft
black sound-absorbing cloth block the living room windows. The glass
is double-paned, and the walls of the old cut-stone Franciscan nun-
nery are two feet thick. No light or noise from outside gets through. It
could be midnight or dawn, it could be snowing or raining out there on

Sherbrooke or splashed with spring sunshine, and no one in the room would know. They are like the trapped crew of a lost submarine. They blink in the sudden light and look around and see only each other and Emma's and Fife's furniture pushed back against the walls, and on the walls the paintings and drawings the couple has gathered over nearly four decades of marriage.

Emma gets up and walks to the door and says she has to go to the bathroom. Anybody else? Are you guys hungry? she asks. She volunteers to send out for sandwiches.

Diana says, Yes, starving. It's almost three.

Sloan says, I'm okay for now, bathroom-wise. I could covet a sandwich, though. No meat, if you don't mind, I'm vegan. And gluten-free, if possible. Gluten's like toxic for me. Otherwise, anything is good. Maybe just some fruit instead, she adds.

Me, too, anything is good, Vincent says. And I don't care about vegan or gluten one way or the other, because I'm an omnivore. Oomm-niv-orous, he says and follows with a low self-amused ha-ha.

Malcolm says, Look, let's forget our stomachs for now and keep rolling, okay? I want to get as much of this on-camera as we can, while we can. It's way off from what we originally expected or intended, but I'm starting to see links that'll let us make a narrative out of it. We can slice, dice, and splice it all we want and cut in archival clips and bits from Leo's films and build out some continuity. You okay with another hour or so, Leo? Before we quit for the day? We can all take a break for a late lunch then.

Yes. I may not be here tomorrow.

Don't believe that, man. Jesus. Please. You'll be here tomorrow.

What do you mean, links that'll help you make a narrative? Fife asks. He thinks he's giving them a narrative ready-made. All they have to do is film and record it. Afterward, when he's silent and gone—and he could be silent and gone before tomorrow; it could happen this afternoon—Malcolm and Diana can make their own story out of his.

That's what everyone does with other people's stories anyhow. But for now this is Fife's, not theirs. It's his true story. And it's coherent, he believes, and sequential and consequential—at least in his and Emma's life it's consequential. That's all that matters.

Fife says to Emma, Go ahead, go to the bathroom. But then come right back, and we'll keep going. Forget the sandwiches, though. Malcolm's right, I have to get this told while I can still tell it.

That's all I mean, Malcolm says. We can pull it together later. With your input, of course.

Fife knows that his memory has huge holes in it, gaps and crevasses and whiteouts, but everything he does remember—or believes he remembers—is clear and sharply defined and three-dimensional and almost tangible to him, and he's trying to tell Emma all of it in a way that will make it the same for her. But it's like trying to relate the essence of a dream to someone not the dreamer. Whatever he says about the dream erases his memory of it, and all he's left with is his description of it, not the thing itself. His spoken words erase and replace the dream, until he can no longer remember it. Once he starts describing it, all he can recall of the dream are his emotions when he woke. He fears that the only thing he's managed to tell Emma so far is not the memories themselves, but only how his memories make him feel. Perhaps that's why she doesn't seem shocked by what he's revealed to her. Or angry or hurt. And why the others seem confused and impatient. Especially Malcolm.

Fife has begun to realize that he can't quite hear himself when he speaks, so he doesn't really know what they've heard. And he can barely make out what other people say to him. He hears himself clearly only when he's silent, when he is forming his thoughts and recalling his past life—his past lives. But not when he actually says something aloud to someone. He wonders if it's possible that the words that originate in his brain come out of his mouth distorted and garbled and disordered. He wonders if the chemical cocktails that for the last four months have been injected into his body to poison his cancer have instead poisoned the part of his brain that listens to him speak.

Collateral damage. Encephalopathy. The chemo has dissolved chunks of his temporal lobe like acid. Synaptic pruning in a stressed-out seventy-eight-year-old brain takes care of the rest. There's a disconnect between his hippocampus, where his long-term memory sits, and his temporal lobe, where his abilities to manage semantics in speech reside.

Confabulation, Dr. Schultz, the oncologist, called it. Was your husband a heavy drinker, an alcoholic? he asks Emma, as if Fife is not there, as if he is already dead.

She says no, he isn't alcoholic. Fife is seated in the small windowless examining room beside her and across from the doctor, and he is not dead yet. She is aware that her husband can hear her, and she answers accordingly, truthfully, but with caution. She corrects herself and tells the doctor that her husband does not believe he is alcoholic. A heavy drinker, yes. Habituated, she says, to one double martini a day. And half to a full bottle of wine with dinner, she adds. He almost never drinks during the day. He's a little OCD and counts everything. How many ounces of alcohol he consumes. How many cigarettes a day. How many pairs of socks he owns. Is that an alcoholic? Why do you ask?

By my lights it is, yes. It can be treated with thiamine. Not the alcoholism or the OCD, they can't be treated. The confabulation, though, is a symptom of Korsakoff syndrome and fairly common with advanced alcoholism. The doctor is surprised it wasn't on Fife's admission forms and questionnaires. There's a line for that, the alcohol-use line. Right next to smoking.

Couldn't it be something else? The chemo? The cancer itself?

Possibly. Everyone has his own cancer and his own response to treatment. But let's try the thiamine. Vitamin B_1.

Fife speaks up. He tells the doctor he hasn't had a drink or a cigarette in over four months. One hundred thirty-one days. And he owns fourteen pairs of socks. Two weeks' worth. The chemo seems to have wiped out his addictions, he says. Along with all his other needs and desires. What the doctor calls confabulation is just the way Fife sometimes tells stories, that's all, mixing memories and dreams and imagined details and meanings, embedding whatever drifts his way, exaggerating some elements and eliminating others, fooling with chronology, trying to make life more interesting and exciting than it would be otherwise, he says.

Dr. Schulz's interrogation must have taken place sometime before Fife escaped on a wheeled stretcher from the Palliative Care Unit at the McGill Cancer Centre, when he and Emma commandeered the ambulance and took off on their Canadian hegira with the ambulance driver and attendant. When Schultz said he was alcoholic, Fife was still able to walk on his own. He remembers using a cane to get to Schultz's interrogation room.

No, that was another time, a different, earlier interrogation. The conversation about confabulation and his drinking and vitamin B_1 took place in Fife's third-floor room at the Palliative Care Unit, and by then he was no longer able to walk, not even with a cane for a third leg or a walker for four. He couldn't leave his bed to go to the toilet without help and a wheelchair. It must have been after Malcolm and Diana came up from Toronto to visit him at the McGill Cancer Centre and pitched the idea of interviewing him for a two-hour documentary for CBC, and he refused to cooperate—until it occurred to him that he could use the filming as a way to get straight with Emma before he died.

The massive doses of vitamin B_1 don't work, but Fife tries to give Dr. Schultz and Emma the impression that it's cured him of confabulating: he simply stops trying to describe aloud anything that he remembers and keeps his past, right up to the present moment, silenced inside him. Like a dog, he yips only to feed his immediate needs. He keeps his demands simple and direct and obvious, which is all Renée and Emma want to hear from him anyhow. Until today, that is. When he can talk to Emma via a mic and a camera surrounded by darkness, with only a Speedlight illuminating his face. He's a talking head. Like something out of a Beckett play, a brain and a mouth still working atop a body that's irrelevant because it's inert and doomed.

Emma has returned from the bathroom and has taken her place on the sofa by the wall somewhere behind him. Fife watched her come through the door from the hallway and silently pass his wheelchair without acknowledging or touching him. If he turns around, he can see her, but he doesn't want to see her. He only wants to speak to her through Vincent's camera and Sloan's mic, and he can't do that if he is able to see her face at the same time. He loves her face, but when he sees it, he can only lie to it—because he wants her to love his face the same way he loves hers.

He's watched her beautiful face stay beautiful to him even as it's grown old before his eyes: the fine vertical lines that in her fifties began to appear above her thin lips and on her brow when she was tired or under stress and then became permanently etched into her pale Nova Scotia Irish skin; the slow dimming of the deep, pooled light in her large down-turned gray eyes that began a decade or so ago, after they returned from shooting *Cannibals* and learned that the Arctic light off the snow had damaged her lenses; the graying of the lustrous black hair that when she first walked into his Concordia classroom in 1978 was streaked with turquoise dye, the punk affectation of a middle-class wife and mother in her mid-twenties, preparing to abandon her husband and two children by going back to college to study film and have an affair with her professor. Since the moment he first saw her, Fife has loved looking directly at Emma. His gaze made her nervous and a little embarrassed, as if he were making a studio portrait of it, and she would look down and away and say, Please, stop staring at me.

Malcolm says, All right, people, let's get back to work. Time's a-wasting.

I don't want to be a killjoy, Malcolm, but, really, you should shut this down, Emma says. At least for today, if not completely. I've been thinking about what's happening here, and somebody's got to say it, and it might as well be me. It should be me, she adds. She's his wife, for Christ's sake, and she knows better than anyone what this is doing to her husband, and she can imagine all too easily what's going to end up on film and in public. No matter how Malcolm and Diana edit it, she doesn't think it will be good for Fife. For his reputation. He's too weak, and the meds and his . . . She hesitates to name it. His illness. They've combined to mix up his thoughts and memories. He's not himself, she says. It's not right to be filming Leo in this condition.

No, don't shut it down yet! Fife shouts. He is himself. And he knows what he's saying and why. He doesn't give a good goddamn what ends up on film or how he ends up coming off to the public. He doesn't give a shit about his reputation.

Please, Leo, let it go. This is Malcolm's and Diana's project, says Emma, and they're not interested in protecting you or your reputation. Whether you care about it or not, I do. They're only using you to make a film that will gain them a lot of attention down the road. She pauses a few seconds. Okay, I'll say it, that will make them famous after you're gone. It's fucking parasitical, she says.

Parasitical! Diana says. You can't mean that, Emma. My God!

Malcolm says, This will make Leonard Fife as big in our collective memory as Glenn Gould. It'll resurrect all his films and make us rethink what it means to be an *artiste engagé*. Believe me, Emma, Leo will come off as totally sympathetic. And heroic, even.

Renée looks over at Emma, tilts her head to the side a bit, and raises her eyebrows, silently asking if she has permission to wheel Monsieur Fife back to his bedroom.

Vincent says, Okay, ready to roll. Clap the clapper, Captain.

Douse the room lights, Sloan.

Emma says, So you're going to keep filming him, then.

Yes.

Diana says, We have to, Emma. And we're not fucking parasites. I can't believe you said that. You, a filmmaker yourself.

I said to douse the room lights, Sloan.

Then I'll have to leave the room, Emma says. I can't be part of this.

Fife shouts, No! You can't leave! Grant me my dying wish and hear me out. That's all I ask. He hears Emma's sharp intake of breath, followed by a sigh, and knows that she has sat down on the sofa. Sloan shuts off the lights.

In a low, custodial voice Malcolm says, Pick up where you left off, Leo. In Vermont, when you were visiting Stanley Reinhart, the artist. Your buddy. Maybe you can tell us a little about his influence, if any, on how you became a filmmaker. Since he was a well-known visual artist and all. And see if you can maybe stick more to the subject this time, okay?

Okay. Sure.

Malcolm claps his hands once and says, Leonard Fife interview, Montreal, April 1, 2018.

22

FIFE TELLS THEM HOW THE KEROSENE LAMPS INSIDE
the house blow light the color of old bone across the dirt road, brushing into the receding darkness the skulled shapes of a frost-tumbled stone wall at the far side of the road and a scrubby black stand of jack pine just beyond.

Fife walks at a rapid pace to keep up with Stanley. The puffy gray edges of his breath push intently out ahead of him, and he remembers that walking with Stanley takes effort. The man doesn't walk, he marches. But Fife's own body seems to him to crawl, moving slowly along somewhere behind both men. His body has stiffened and grown suddenly heavy in the cold, the weight of his arms and legs increasing as he walks. He's afraid that, despite willing himself to move, he will be dragged to a stop and left standing here in the middle of the road alone, while Stanley steps off into the darkness ahead.

Finally it's too hard to keep moving, and he gives up the effort to walk and comes to a stop and stands stock-still, like a stele or a tree. He's unable to raise a hand or lift a foot. Only his eyes move. They flick rapidly from his feet and the hard ground beneath to his inert hands and the empty, surrounding air.

Ten yards ahead and moving away fast, Stanley without looking back hollers, C'mon, Leo, I want to show you my truck!

Aw-w-w-w! Fife bawls, and his head pitches forward, as if slammed from behind by the heel of a hand. His shoulders and chest plunge ahead and down, his arms pinwheel, his legs lurch out in front of him, and suddenly he is running, flailing his arms like weighted pendulums in long arcs. In seconds he catches up to Stanley and thrashes past.

Stanley gapes after. Fife disappears around the bend ahead, his clattering footsteps quickly fading behind the wash of wind in the trees, and Stanley calls out, Leo! Hey, Leo! Wait up! I want to show you my truck!

No answer. Stanley starts to jog, rounds the bend in the road and follows it down another hundred yards to a second bend and a sharp drop where the road descends in a falling loop into the valley below. As Stanley rounds the second turn, Fife's face appears out of the darkness.

Jesus! You scared me. Are you okay, man?

Fife is panting heavily. Yeah, I'm okay. I . . . I've just been cooped up all day, I guess. First planes, then the car. I don't know. And now this terrible news from Alicia. From her parents, I mean. The perspiration on his face beads in the cold. A chill sweeps over him like a wind. He turns up the collar of his blazer and pulls the lapels together. He stuffs his fisted hands into his trouser pockets, forcing them to unclench and reach for the warmth of his thighs.

Stanley says, Yeah, that's fucked, man. I'm really sorry for you. Both of you. Is Alicia okay? She must be, I dunno, crushed.

Fife ignores the question. So what's this about a truck? he asks, breathing hard. You got rid of the VW van?

I needed a truck. I picked it up right after you were here in January. It's right behind you. So, Alicia, is she okay?

I don't think so. She really wanted this baby. She always wanted two kids.

How about you? Are you okay?

I'm . . . yeah, I'm okay. Fife turns, and in the shadows behind him he sees a deeper, darker shadow. Gradually he makes out the soft outline of a thirty-year-old black half-ton Ford pickup parked facing the road. What's your truck doing way down here, so far from the road? Fife asks.

He cut wood all day, Stanley explains, and didn't have a full load by the end of the day, so he left the truck here where he was cutting, along with his chain saw, ax, sledgehammer, and splitting tools, all laid on top of the stacked wood. At the edge of the clearing, off the road and behind the truck, birch and small maple trees lie on the ground in various stages of dismemberment, some with all their branches, some with none. He left everything down here, Stanley continues, so he can finish the job quickly in the morning and bring it all back up to the barn in one huge load.

I like thinking about it before I fall asleep and first thing when I wake up, he says. He visualizes the job when it's done, all the brush piled neatly, the woodlot cleaned up, his truck stacked to the gunwales with cut firewood, and all his tools cleaned and wiped dry and lying in a row next to him on the driver's seat, and the truck winding slowly up the road to the barn. I love this kind of work, he says. It cleans and clarifies his mind. Same with the truck. There's nothing in or on it that he can't fix with his hands and a box of tools. It's like work-porn, he says. Juices up the old work life.

There is nothing in Fife's life that even vaguely resembles this. He envies the pleasure Stanley takes from it, his truck, his tools, his labor. The truck looks like a piece of sculpture, he thinks. As if it's been placed here deliberately with great forethought by the side of the road in the exact middle of a bowl of darkness. He admires the vehicle, its functional prewar beauty, and when they are one by one pointed out to him, acknowledges with genuine appreciation Stanley's careful modifications—the black paint job, the painted wire wheels, the hard rubber steering wheel, the tiny electric fan next to the windshield that serves as a primitive defroster.

Stanley tells Fife that he spent February and March rebuilding the motor completely and alone. Taught myself how to do a valve and ring job, he says proudly.

Fife smiles at the image of his burly, bearded friend working on his truck in that unheated barn, struggling to get it ready in time to cart firewood from his woodlot in the spring, the same uncomplicated truck and woodcutting fantasy repeating itself from February to now, while his hands stiffen and fumble with frosty wrenches in freezing temperatures and midafternoon darkness. Fife pictures Gloria asking Stanley again and again to please take off an hour or two and shovel a path through the snow to the mailbox so she can get the mail without having to put her boots on and track snow through the house. Stanley keeps working on his truck. He neglects to shovel the path. He neglects everything that might interfere with his work.

They talk slowly in low, relaxed voices, like men feeding livestock in a barn. Then Fife asks Stanley, Where does this road lead?

This road? Catamount Road. Know what a catamount is?

No.

Mountain lion. Used to be all over these hills. There must've been a den up here back then. They're pretty much extinct now.

Where does Catamount Road lead?

Into the mountains. It's an old colonial-era road. It ties up eventually with an even rougher, older road that merges onto Route 82 on the way to Derby Line. It was originally a north-south Indian trail, Mohawk and Micmac, that the Brits followed in the French and Indian War, and after the Revolution the Americans used it when they tried to invade Canada.

Where does Route 82 go when it reaches Derby Line? Fife asks.

Well, then it's straight across the border into Canada. I can tell you a lot about that crossing, man. I've been advising kids at the college on avoiding the draft.

Really? That surprises Fife. He's never thought of Stanley as a political activist.

Me either. Since I never avoided the draft myself and served two years in the military, I have a little more credibility with these young guys than if I was an out-and-out pacifist. My service was back before Vietnam, of course. But with this fucking Vietnam War, like Dylan says, if you're not part of the solution, you're part of the problem, right?

Right. What do you advise them?

Go to Canada, man. I give them the handbook published by the Toronto Anti-Draft Programme, which details who to contact in the various Canadian cities and how to get landed immigrant status, how to find housing and jobs, and so on. There's a whole support network up there. But it's a big step for these kids, and they're scared of the consequences. Once you cross the border, you're starting your life over. No turning back.

Fife steps back and takes another lingering look at Stanley's truck. Then the two men turn and slowly walk back up the hill toward the house. The chill has permeated Fife's clothes, and he starts to shiver, his teeth to chatter. Nearing the bend in the road, he stops again and turns around to face downhill into the blackness of the valley and the mountains that lie beyond, and beyond the mountains, Canada.

Oh, Canada.

The sky is a wide, star-studded cowl stretched overhead from horizon to horizon. He can no longer see the truck or the road itself. He senses the presence of a deep bowl of empty space surrounded by dark, featureless mountains. The valley below falls swiftly away from where he stands on the hillside, opens out and creates an absence that he can feel, a vacuum that draws all his atoms, the cumulative mass of his body, toward it. He can hear the light sucking noise it makes. He tastes its starchy dry negation, smells its airless, magnetic spoor. If he were on a cliff, instead of a hill, he would not be able to keep himself from leaping off it.

His gaze slips away from the empty belly of space before him and slides down to a flattened clearing at the very bottom of the valley, where everything that grows or walks or lies upon the surrounding land violently tends, as if drawn by the gravitational force of the black hole of a collapsed star. Its pull draws him irresistibly toward it. He reaches out with both hands and clasps the slender trunk of a silver birch at the side of the road and holds on tight. Time passes—he can't tell if it's seconds or minutes or hours—until he has the strength to yank his gaze away from the black hole, and he imagines again the vacuum that hovers above it, filling the valley like a deep inland sea. He lets go of the birch and turns his face and body to the mountains on the farther side, exposing his frail human frame to the brutal intensity of the dark mass of the mountains. For a few seconds he suffers the comparison. He is breathing heavily, as if he's seen something unimaginably cruel. A wave of guilt washes over him. And all he's done is turn and look back at where he's been.

Stanley asks Fife if he's ready to go on.

Fife says yes, he's ready, and in silence they walk the rest of the way up to the house.

23

AS IF EMERGING FROM A DEEP SLEEP, FIFE COMES BACK around to the sound of Emma's voice. She's complaining. She's telling Malcolm that he and his crew are wearing Fife down, they're wasting what little energy he has remaining, never mind that they shouldn't be recording this in the first place. If it had been up to her, she would never have allowed them to do this, interview him on-camera.

Her voice is getting a little shrill, Fife notices.

It was only because Fife himself insisted on making the interview that she went along with it, she adds. But they've been filming him for over an hour now, and it's obvious that the effort to speak and the emotions his memories and thoughts give rise to are exhausting him.

Fife says, Wait a minute, what do you mean, over an hour?

He checks his left wrist for his watch, but it's not there. A needle and cannula case connect the vein at the back of his hand to a clear quarter-inch-thick plastic tube. Turning in his wheelchair, he traces the tube to the IV pouch dangling from a metal rack attached to the chair and remembers that Renée had to move it from his right side to his left. His body is running out of unblown veins for Renée to stab.

He says to Emma, A while ago you said it was after three p.m. We started this morning. So we've been at this for at least six or eight hours, right?

No, darling, it probably feels like it's been six or eight long hours. Understandably. But, really it's only been an hour and a half. Which is my point.

What about that business with lunch?

What business with lunch?

Malcolm says, See, that's why we need to keep shooting. With all the digressions and the disconnects, they'll have to overshoot and do a lot of cutting in order to pull together a narrative. But, sure, they can quit now, if Emma insists. They can come back tomorrow for another hour or two, no problem. But to come up with one hundred twenty minutes of usable footage, they'll have to shoot at least eight or ten hours.

But we're not likely to get that much time, Diana says. She starts to continue, then stops herself.

Fife says, Time. Yes. I need to know what time it is. And what the hell you all were talking about when you were talking about lunch.

Sloan says, It's, um, ten forty-seven, a.m.

Then why was everyone worrying about lunch? Was I hearing things?

Well, Vincent and I were talking about me being vegan and all. When Emma left to use the bathroom, I think.

That must be what you heard, Diana says.

Emma, didn't you say it was after three in the afternoon?

When?

I don't know. A little while ago. The last time Vincent had to replace the card, I guess.

No, I said I had to pee. Maybe that's what he's thinking of. What he heard, she means. See, Malcolm, she says, all his senses are scrambled. He's not just disoriented, his hearing is impaired. Because of the chemo and the pain meds, his senses are screwed up. Taste and smell and eyesight and hearing. Even touch. Have a little pity, Malcolm, and stop this now.

I can't.

What do you mean, you can't? Of course you can stop it.

CBC paid us to make this film, Diana says. It would be different if it were coming out of their own pocket, she adds, but they've been spending CBC's money.

No, it wouldn't be different, Malcolm says. It's not about the money. Even if he and Diana were paying for it themselves, emptying their bank accounts and maxing out their credit cards, he still couldn't stop this now. Or rather, he wouldn't stop it. Fife has started to open up about his past in such a detailed and painfully honest way—even if it is a little jumbled and fragmented—that Malcolm believes he has no choice but to keep following him down the rabbit hole, wherever it leads. Malcolm is starting to see that it's possible for him to make from this footage a truly original film, as artistic and deep as a Werner Herzog film. Or a Leo Fife film. This is no longer just a CBC contract job to him, he says. It's not even a chance to film an homage to a cinematic master on somebody else's dime. Although it will be all that. It's really a chance to make a fucking statement, he says.

Oh, please, Emma says. Give us a break, Malcolm.

A statement about what? Sloan asks.

Forget *about*. What I mean is, when you make a statement, it's a work of art. When you make a work of art, it's a statement. There's no *about*, Malcolm says. Essays have subjects, essays are about something. Journalism and most documentary films, they have subjects. They're about particular, nameable somethings. But poems, stories, novels, films worthy of being called art—they're simply statements. It's not that they're about nothing, it's that they're not about anything.

You sound like Leo, Emma says.

I'll take that as a compliment, thank you. Before he started shooting this morning, sure, Malcolm thought he'd be making a documentary film about Leo Fife. A film with a subject. But once Fife started talk-ing, he realized that this could be something more. A film that's a statement. The kind of thing you don't know how to make until after you've made it. That's why he won't shut it down. No more than Wer-ner Herzog would. Or Leo Fife himself.

Fife says, Like Werner Herzog? Like me? You think you're capable of making that kind of film with this kind of material, Malcolm? It's just, I was young, and then all of a sudden I was old. That's what's happened to time. I thought it was three o'clock in the afternoon and I still had plenty of time, but it's really ten forty-seven in the morning and I'm almost out of time.

You see? Malcolm says. That's the sort of thing I'm talking about. He tells Diana to write down what Fife just said, and he'll try to get him to say it on-camera. He tells Vincent to keep shooting, forget the lights, it's okay. He'll figure out in the edit how to use it.

Renée says, Monsieur Fife, I have to replace your perfusion. She steps forward and shuts off the valves at the catheter and the bottom of the nearly empty clear plastic IV bag and unclips it from the pole attached to his wheelchair. You can stay here and talk and I will go and refill it and return, she says to him. Unless you need to visit the bathroom again.

No, he doesn't need to visit the bathroom again, he says. Spare him that, please. He's not a fucking deflated tube of shrinking flesh attached to a smaller plastic tube. He's not a talking worm.

You catch that, Sloan?

Yes.

Or am I? Fife asks Renée.

Are you what?

A talking worm. *Un ver bavard.*

No, Monsieur Fife, you're not a talking worm, Renée says, and she gives a little laugh. But you do say some very strange things some-times. Strange and funny. Pinching the flattened IV bag with two fingers and her thumb, she passes in front of Fife's wheelchair and exits the living room.

I don't give a damn what the great Herzog would do, or what Leo himself would do, Emma says. There's no fucking way this will enshrine him in the eyes of the public or enhance the reputation of his films, she says. Besides, some of those little sins he's confessing are hers. Some others never really happened, not to him, anyhow. He's making most of it up. Not out of whole cloth, but he's grabbing it from whatever passes through his mind, regardless of how it got there or where it came from, and then making it his own.

She lowers her voice a notch, assuming that Fife with his impaired hearing can't quite hear her. It's mostly confabulation, anyhow, she tells Diana and Malcolm. Her psychiatrist advised her not to confront him with so-called reality. Just go along with whatever he claims is reality, because it's real to him, and it could be terrifying and angering to him if she challenged it. Like that baby girl he supposedly abandoned in Boston? That was her child, she says. Emma's, not Fife's. And it happened in Montreal. The late-term miscarriage was hers, too. Not some other wife's. And there were two kids, not one. It's Emma who did the abandoning. She's never made a secret of it. Everyone who knows Emma and Fife has known the story for years. She left her two kids when she left their father and ran off with Leo, and Leo has always felt guilty for it. Even more guilty than she. Emma believes that she never would have been as good a parent as her ex-husband was. That's all. And she was right. She claims she actually did her kids a favor by abandoning them. She was not made for motherhood. Fife never understood that. When Royale and Pedro, grown up now, come around to visit, which they do from time to time, Fife acts all guilt-ridden and apologetic, like he's the one who abandoned them. They actually think it's funny. Oh, and Emma's the one who was married twice. Not Leo. Emma is Fife's one and only wife. She puts it to Malcolm and Diana: If Fife had been married before he fled to Canada, don't they think he'd have told her long before this? Wouldn't it be public knowledge? Come on. It's probably the same with many, if not most, of the tales he's telling. If you believe his stories and film them, then anyone who sees the film will believe them, too.

Without turning around, Fife says, I can hear you, Emma. You're trying to protect me, but you're lying to protect me. No point to that anymore. I don't need to be protected anymore.

Malcolm says, It doesn't matter if I believe his stories or not. It doesn't matter if they're true or not. And I couldn't care less about what the film's viewers believe.

Jesus. What does matter to you, then?

The film.

Attaboy, Malcolm, Fife says. You're right, but only up to a point. It's the *filming* that matters, the process. Not the film, the product, what you call the statement. You have to keep your work separate from your career, Malcolm. The process gives you work. The product provides you with a career.

Renée slips back into the living room and reattaches the IV drip. She says, You should be all right to talk for another two hours, Monsieur Fife. If you feel strong enough.

He says he feels strong enough. If everything he's said to the camera so far only took an hour and a half, he'll finish in another hour or even less. And then you can unplug that thing and let me die, he says and flashes her a smile.

She returns his smile and clucks her tongue and returns to her seat alongside Emma and Diana, somewhere out of sight behind him.

Emma abruptly stands and walks to the hallway door. She turns and says to Fife that she can't participate in this any further. If he insists on letting Malcolm and Diana make their film, she won't try to stop them. But when they want to release it to the public, she won't grant broadcast permission to CBC or anyone else. She'll be his executor, don't forget.

I'm not quite dead yet, Fife says. And I haven't signed any kind of release yet. And I won't, Emma, if you'll just stay here and let me confess what you call my secret little sins. I haven't even got to the really big ones yet. Wait till you hear those! But please try to understand, Emma, if you refuse to hear my sins, you'll be sending me to my death unconfessed. Secretly repentant and self-hating, maybe, but unforgiven and unabsolved. Unshriven!

He's never been religious, except in a superficially social way, and that was only when he was a boy still trying to adapt to his parents' superficially social use for religion. He knows there's no afterlife and no soul that lives on after the body dies. He knows there's nothing for him now but total absence. Nothing, rather than something. Most people believe in heaven, but not hell. Fife believes in hell, not heaven. Hell is having lived a life without meaning. A nullity. If she won't stay and listen to his confession, he'll have spent his whole life in hell.

Malcolm says, Diana, did you have Leo sign the release before we started?

I figured I'd do it later, after we finished. There's no rush.

Haven't you been listening, for Christ's sake?

Emma says to Fife, You won't sign the release if I stay?

Yes.

Vincent says, I've been filming this whole thing, Malcolm, and Sloan's been recording it. I thought you wanted the footage, even with the houselights on. You asked me if I was getting it, remember? But if Leo won't sign the release, shouldn't we shut it down?

Everyone remains silent for a moment. Then Malcolm says, Fuck. Let's worry about the release later. Diana, hit the lights, will you?

24

STRUGGLING TO REMEMBER WHERE HE LEFT OFF, FIFE
starts slowly. I must be plainspoken and direct, he tells himself, but
not simple. He must include the details and the contexts of everything
that happened, so that his betrayals and abandonments can be fully
exposed and known and not excused. He wants to be forgiven, not
excused. To be forgiven, his sins have to be known. Sins afflict us with
guilt. Crimes just make us regretful, and Fife—who has indeed committed crimes—regrets nothing. But betrayal and abandonment? They
are sins. Thus the need to be forgiven. Shrived.

He remembers that it was a good dinner. My dinner with Stanley,
he calls it. Like that movie by Louis Malle, he says. My dinner in
Vermont with Stanley and his silent wife, Gloria. He can see the still-
bleeding roast beef, which Stanley clumsily, impatiently carves into
thick, shapeless chunks. And there is a liter of wine, which they drink
in half-filled water glasses. The wine is a concession to Fife. Stanley
ordinarily drinks beer with his meals. He must have instructed Gloria
to buy it when she made her weekly trek to Montpelier for groceries.

Or else his habits have changed since Fife's and Alicia's visit back in January.

Fife, in an awkward attempt to engage Gloria, from time to time breaks off his conversation with Stanley and compliments her on the quality of the meal. But she remains silent. Mostly, he and Stanley talk about the political situation and the US government and the president and the war in Vietnam and the coming election. Although they disagree several times as to why a particular thing happens to be true, they agree on the true things themselves. It's 1968, they are both against the war, but neither of them is eligible for the draft. They are young, narrowly educated white men and artists—although Fife stopped calling himself an artist soon after marrying Alicia and admits that he is a writer only to Alicia and her parents and his few close friends. Stanley, however, is a bona fide, publicly recognized artist.

Stanley calls for coffee to Gloria, who stands by the stove heating water so she can wash their dishes. He begins talking rapidly about old friends seen infrequently in Boston. Which reminds him of his troubles with the Boston gallery owners. And from that to the problems of trying to make it as an artist in New York when you haven't really made it yet in Boston. And so on, by similar linkings from one subject hurriedly to another.

The two men talk and drink coffee from tin mugs at the kitchen table. Fife smokes cigarettes, and Stanley occasionally gets up to pitch another stubby split log into the iron bowels of the stove, until nearly an hour has passed. When, unexpectedly, after talking at some length about the problems a Goddard College colleague has been having with his wife, a woman almost ten years younger than the friend and referred to by Stanley as that goddamn little hippie chick, Stanley lapses for a few seconds into a heavy silence. Which he breaks by saying, I guess you can tell I've been having some problems of my own, eh? Marital problems. I mean, it's probably pretty obvious.

Fife assumes that Gloria is still in the room somewhere and hopes that she hasn't heard. He looks around for her reaction. But she's not there. No, he says. As a matter of fact, everything has seemed perfectly normal to him. No different than the way things were last January when he and Alicia were here. He looks over his shoulder, half expecting to see Gloria standing in the doorway, listening to their conversation.

Don't worry. She's gone to bed.

To bed? Fife checks his watch. It's quarter past ten.

Yeah. Ah, shit, the whole thing just makes for a long story, Stanley says, and most of it's not even worth the telling. He's tried to get Gloria to see a shrink, he even agreed to see one with her, maybe try couples therapy. But it's useless. She's got an answer for that. She's got an answer for everything. She's just so far out of it that when he suggested going to a shrink, she laughed and said she couldn't possibly be better adjusted to reality than she is. The truth is, she's a goddamn masochist, Stanley says mournfully. The bind, he explains, arises from the fact that she hates him and this kind of life, and because of her masochism, as he puts it, the more she hates him and her life, the happier she becomes. She calls it an adjustment, one that can hardly be improved upon, except by his becoming increasingly hateful or their life increasingly difficult. Or both.

Fife says this sounds like Stanley's interpretation of a problem that might not have anything to do with him. But he's a little confused by Stanley's use of terms like masochism and adjustment. They aren't in Stanley's usual vocabulary.

That's true, Stanley says. She's the one who explains everything in those terms. He thought at first that she had found a lover. That's exactly how she was acting. Scornful, detached, withdrawn, very bored, yet never complaining. But it's impossible for her to have a lover out here in the sticks without his knowledge. He almost never leaves the house, except to teach his classes and counsel the draft evaders. And she never leaves the house except to pick up groceries. Nevertheless, he accused her of having a lover. She laughed in his face. He went down to Plainfield that night, he says, and laid one of his students. And that's about all he seems to be able to do now. He's fucked every one of his attractive female students at least twice, and now he's starting to fuck the unattractive ones. He knows it only makes things worse, but what can he do? She's got him in a complete bind here. He's even confessed his little nightly escapades to her. Does Fife want to know what she told him?

Yes.

She said, Good. Just don't get caught, because you'll get fired, and then you'll be so miserable you'll blame it all on yourself. This way he can still blame her, she told him, and everyone's happy—Stanley, Gloria, and the lucky students, too. But if he gets caught screwing his students, nobody will be happy. That's what she told him.

Well, what're you going to do? You can't keep going on like this.

Stanley admits that he can't. It's driving him out of his mind. The whole project, coming up here from Boston, teaching at the college, living out in the woods, the whole thing has gone sour for him. He's thinking of trying somehow to get through the summer with her, and if nothing has improved by next September, he thinks he'll try to make it in New York. He suggested this to Gloria, and she answered that as far as she's concerned, he might as well leave now. As long as he leaves her the house. She'll get along fine here alone.

Alone?

Yeah. That's where she's at now, that's how far she's gone.

Another hour has passed. Stanley's gone back to drinking beer. Fife continues to drink coffee. They talk a while longer about the crumbling of Stanley's marriage and Gloria's psyche—to Fife, difficult topics for serious conversation. He feels they're merely theorizing. As far as he can see, nothing actually contradicts what Stanley is telling him, but nothing confirms it, either. It all seemed so damned near perfect! The house, the valley, the mountains all around. The passive, adoringly silent wife. The comfortable position at the college, which gives him for the first time in his life money and social prestige and time to paint. It's just too nearly perfect. It's what Fife wants for himself and for Alicia. For his family.

What about the students you're counseling on avoiding the draft? he asks. Are you just going to abandon them? And what about me and Alicia? I took that position and we decided to move here because you were here. You and Gloria.

Ah, I'm just bullshitting myself, Stanley says. But the kids don't really need me, even though I'm the only guy on the faculty who actually was in the military and also took training on how to beat the draft or evade it by going north. We're so close to the Canadian border they can walk across. They don't need much guidance these days. The Canadians welcome them with open arms. And Trudeau refuses to extradite them back to the US. He even kicked the FBI out of Canada. And Gloria will eventually either pull out of this whatever-it-is or else she'll have a nervous breakdown. Besides, I'm not ready to face the New York painting scene yet. I'm not going anywhere anytime soon.

Stanley's short, staccato sentences begin to be punctuated by long, drawn-out yawns, and finally he admits that he is tired and will have to go to bed. He was up early and cutting wood all day, and he has to teach an eight o'clock class tomorrow. He apologizes and says that Fife will have to sleep on a cot in the living room. It will be warmer there than upstairs, with the fireplace and the heat from the kitchen stove. He confesses that since he and Gloria are no longer sleeping together, he's moved into the other upstairs bedroom, where there's only a single bed, the same bed that Fife and Alicia slept on last January. He assures Fife that he'll be more comfortable sleeping in the living room anyway. Warmer, he says.

They get up from the table slowly, and while Stanley damps down the kitchen stove for the night and builds a fire in the living room fireplace, Fife walks along each of the four walls of the long, narrow room, looking at Stanley's paintings—all of which he has seen before, he notices sadly, when he was here last time. Stanley's not been doing much painting.

In the exact center of the room, placed like a bier in the nave of a chapel, Gloria has set out a folding cot with a flannel-lined sleeping bag rolled up at its head. She must have put it there just before going up to bed. He's suddenly exhausted, emptied out. He sits down wearily on the cot and is washed by a wave of gratitude toward this slender, silent, grimly forbearing woman.

Stanley soon has the fire in the fireplace crackling. Keep a close eye on it for a while, he warns. There's no screen, and sometimes a spark will jump out.

The flames leap and dance hungrily across the kindling and chunks of dry birch logs, tearing the paper-thin bark from the logs as if with teeth. The two say good night to each other solemnly, and Stanley goes out of the room and passes through the doorway at the far corner and clumps heavily up the stairs. A moment later, Fife hears Stanley's shoes drop, one, then the other, overhead. Watching the fire, he suddenly remembers Stanley's perfect pickup truck and its load of perfectly cut and stacked firewood. He grimaces and puts the image out of his mind. That goddamn truck! Why does he hate Stanley's goddamn silly-ass truck?

The fire is burning well now. It has devoured the kindling and is beginning to eat into the meat of the logs. Fife looks around the room and realizes that Stanley has left him no more wood than what's burning at this moment. And the damped fire in the kitchen stove, he knows, is slowly turning to ash and coals and going out.

For a short while the flames continue their work, long enough to warm the chilly room, and then, as if beginning to consume themselves, dwindle. Shadows, long slender spears of darkness, dance across the walls and ceiling and mingle with the rectangular shapes of Stanley's paintings, animating the shapes. In the shifting firelight, the harsh chiaroscuro and calligraphic forms of the paintings are calmed and soothed into warm swirls. To Fife's eye, the paintings are improved in this light, and the gallerylike room itself—having lost its chill, its precise edges loosely wrapped in shadows, its emptiness filled with dancing firelight—is reassuringly attractive. But in less than an hour there will be nothing remaining in the fireplace but dully glowing coals. He decides that he had better try to sleep now, while the room is still warm.

He unrolls the sleeping bag and covers the cot with it. Sitting down, he unties and removes one shoe, and then remembers his suitcase. He forgot all about the damned thing, hasn't thought about it for hours. What was it the lost and found clerk at the airport said, that he'd send it to Montpelier on the bus?

He looks wearily down at his feet. Well. Should he drive back down to Montpelier now, tonight, so that tomorrow morning when he gets up he'll be able to start the day with the reassuring convenience of having all his possessions close at hand? No, he decides. Stupid and obsessive-compulsive to cause himself that much trouble and expense—twelve and twelve for the rental car, he remembers— just to get a small moment of anxiety-free comfort in the morning. To hell with it. He'll pick the damned thing up sometime tomorrow when it's convenient. There won't be anyone at the bus depot at this hour, anyhow. The last bus from Boston to Montpelier is probably the only bus from Boston to Montpelier. He unties his other shoe and slides it off and begins to undress.

The calm, pleasantly shifting, hazed gentleness of the room is rapidly disappearing. At the blackened floor of the fireplace, where the burnt wood has tumbled crumbling from the andirons, the flames ripple in low waves along the edges of lumps of char. The only light in the room is from the fire. Fife crawls into the sleeping bag with difficulty and with greater difficulty zips it up almost to his neck. Wrapped in the musty-smelling quilt, lying flat on his back with his hands crossed on his belly and his legs straight out and his feet dangling over the bottom edge of the cot, he closes his eyes.

But images, vague and almost transparent, and phrases, then whole sentences, trickle in, until a gabble of voices and glimpsed faces start to accumulate. He struggles to focus his mind's eye, as if it were a physical organ of sight, to see his body and where it is situated, to scrutinize it closely, from right up next to it and then from the far side of the room. He sees the long thin body inside the lumpy sleeping bag. Only the man's face is exposed to the cooling darkness of the room, that bony, grim face, mustachioed above the downward slash of a mouth, eyes jammed shut, as if by a stranger's fingertips. The skin across the brow and forehead is tautly drawn, and the net of thin lines crossing the narrow, rectangular plane seems to have been etched into it. He scans the entire length of the body, longer than the cot. Then he gazes at the cot itself—cross-legged, located in the room precisely where all the diagonals intersect, with the cot's width corresponding to its length in a numerical ratio that, to Fife, matches the proportions of the room. He watches as the paintings on the walls and the door and windows, even the fireplace, meld into the smooth planes of the wall and become thick, somber-colored stains. Except for the gurgle of dwindling flames, the room is silent. The light cast by the tiny flames suddenly flares, increased a hundredfold by candlelight, and the candles, seven tall ivory-colored candles in a wrought-iron standing candelabra at the foot of the cot, fill the room with light. Darkness rushes into far corners in rivulets and rapidly disappears, as if seeping into the floor. The room fills with blinding white light.

He hears a man's voice. Is it Malcolm's? He's speaking a language Fife has never heard before. The words aren't clear, as if he's speaking in tongues. He's excited about something, upset, scared.

Then a second voice cuts over Malcolm's, a woman's, low and calm. Fife thinks it's Renée, and she's trying to get Malcolm to be quiet and move away.

Emma says, Oh, my God! Renée, do something!

Renée says, He's fallen asleep while talking. He's very fatigued. I should take him to his bed.

Emma says, Are you sure?

Yes.

I mean, are you sure he's just sleeping?

He's waking now. I still should take him to his bed.

Fife opens his eyes. The room is in total darkness. At the bottom of the fireplace a few coals glow deep red, but there are no flames. He sits up, still wrapped like a mummy in the sleeping bag, and swings his legs off the cot and sits, feet on the floor, squarely facing the fireplace. Except for those few red, pulsating coals, there's no difference if his eyes are closed or open. He's surrounded by darkness.

Suddenly off to his right a new light enters the room, the pale-yellow spray of a flashlight beam spattering across the uncarpeted floor from the far corner. Someone is coming down the stairs. He waits silently, and as soon as whoever it is has followed the flashlight down the stairs into the room, its beam is thrown directly onto Fife, blinding him a second time.

Stanley? Fife asks, struggling to free his hands from the hug of the sleeping bag. He turns his head away, blinking off the circular red after-image, and the light moves off him and swishes back to the corner.

No. It's Gloria, comes the answer. She crosses to the side of the cot and stands next to Fife. I brought you a blanket, she says. That sleeping bag's not very warm once the fire goes out. Dropping the folded blanket onto the cot, she turns and starts to leave.

Gloria, wait a second. I was wondering, is there any more wood I can throw on the fire? I hate to bother you.

I'll get you an armload, she says, and she makes for the kitchen and the shed beyond. A minute later she returns, carrying half a dozen pieces of split hardwood. She drops the wood on the floor next to the fireplace and tosses one of the smaller logs onto the bed of coals and gets down on her hands and knees in front of the fireplace and begins to blow lightly on the fading coals.

Fife has managed to free his upper body from the sleeping bag. He leans forward with his forearms across his knees and watches Gloria breathe life back into the smoldered fire. She's wearing a man's old-fashioned maroon bathrobe, wool with pink piping on the cuffs and broad lapels and a thick belt knotted at the waist. Her faded pale-blue flannel nightgown drapes below the bottom of the robe almost to her ankles, and on her feet she wears a pair of fuzzy gray slippers. Her hair tumbles loosely across her bent shoulders and back. She usually wears her long hair in a honey-colored braid wrapped around her head, giving her the look of a shopkeeper's daughter. Now her thick hair ranges freely across her broad back, and with her hands pressed flat against the hearth and her face as close to the tiny, growing fire as possible, she looks like a shepherd's young wife from Fife's vision of the Old Testament. The flames catch on the dry bark of the new wood, crackle weakly, and cast a flickering light on Gloria's crouched form. Fife is glad that she switched off the flashlight as soon as she got down before the fire. It's better to watch her in firelight. He pats his knees, his left hand on his right knee, his right hand on his left, and pitches his tongue from inside one cheek to the inside of the other.

She stands and with her hands on her hips faces the fireplace. Well, that should keep you warm enough, she says softly, still not looking at him.

Yes, thanks. That's great. I was having trouble falling asleep. It's much easier to sleep when it's warm.

Of course, she answers curtly.

Her shift in tone catches him off guard. I hope that we, our talking . . . that Stanley and I didn't keep you from sleeping.

No. The walls are thick.

Well, good, Fife says. He leans his weight on his knees and watches the slender woman intently as she warms herself before the fire. Listen, you're probably cold too, he says. Why don't you sit and share the fire for a minute before you go back upstairs. As I recall, those bedrooms are pretty breezy.

Yes, they are. She turns around and comes and sits next to him on the cot, then returns her gaze to the fire.

Fife motions toward the stairs with his head. Is he asleep?

Dead to the world. The beer knocks him out, and he was tired, too. I couldn't wake him if I wanted to. And I don't want to, she adds.

You're . . . not getting along, the two of you, Fife says. They both stare straight ahead into the fireplace. The wood has caught and is burning well.

No. We're not.

Are you going to leave him?

Yes. Probably.

For another man? he asks.

For another life.

There is a long silence, broken only by the noise of the fire. Fife reaches around her waist with one arm, and she moves against his side, and he says, Well, here's to your new life. He looks at her thin, serious face. She is waiting for him to kiss her, so he does, once, quickly. She buries her face between his neck and shoulder, snaking both arms around him, moving softly but swiftly against his chest with her small breasts. He lets his hands respond at once and slides them over her shoulders and down across her thighs and quickly back again. Then he has her robe undone and is caressing her cool, dry skin beneath the flannel nightgown, brushing lightly over her thighs, across her belly, and up under the soft, loose cloth to her breasts. She kisses his neck and shoulder and slides her hands down his sides and, working the zipper of the sleeping bag with one hand, opens a way for the other, which she thrusts down into the warmth of his groin. She wraps her fingers around his stiffened penis and begins working her hand up and down inside the sleeping bag. His fingers probe her vainly for a few seconds; then her legs spread, and with a gentle shove, he finds a way in. She shudders. Move it, move it, she hisses into his ear, and he slides his finger back and forth, rapidly and then slowly, side to side, and then suddenly fast, then slow again. Until she gasps and squirms against his hand and comes. He feels his cock become the center of his body and feels it tighten from inside out and feels it ejaculate into her pumping hand, smearing semen in the darkness against the quilted sleeping bag.

Slowly, silently, she withdraws her hand and pulls away from his. She stands and walks out to the kitchen and returns with a paper towel. He looks up at her and smiles slightly as she passes him the paper towel, but her face is without expression. There is no sign of happiness or relief or even anxiety. He has no idea of how he himself should look, so he imitates the absence of expression he sees above him.

He cleans himself and the smeared sleeping bag with the sheet of paper towel, and when he is satisfied that there will be no stains tomorrow on the sleeping bag and his undershorts, he looks up and sees that Gloria has crossed the room to the stairs and is about to go up.

Well, good night, he says.

She says nothing and goes up the stairs. Fife crumples the paper towel into a ball. He pitches it from the cot into the fire. It bursts into flame and then goes suddenly black and crumbles into a delicate fist of ashes.

25

MALCOLM SAYS, JESUS CHRIST, THAT WAS FUCKING
scary! I thought for a minute there . . . Well. Yeah. Are you sure he's
okay?

Renée answers, No, no, he is not okay. I must take him from
you now.

Yes. I'll go with you, Emma says. Sloan has switched on the lights,
and the room is a living room again. Emma steps around Renée and
Fife and walks quickly to the hallway door and holds it open. Renée
puts her stethoscope back into her satchel and releases the brakes on
the wheelchair and rolls it toward the door.

Sloan runs after them and says, Wait a second, let me unclip
the mic!

Malcolm tells her to forget it, just use the boom.

Halfway to the door, Fife reaches down with both hands and flips
the brake handles, and the wheelchair rubs to a stop on the bare floor.
I'm not going anywhere yet, he says. I'm staying here until I finish telling my story.

No, you can't, Emma says, her voice breaking.

Malcolm tells Vincent to keep shooting, keep shooting, for Christ's sake. Leave the tripod and go hand-held.

Emma says, This is insane! Do you want to die on-camera, Leo? Is that it? Are you willing to give that to Malcolm? What a gift! she says, almost in tears now. Malcolm would love it if Fife died on-camera. It'll make Malcolm more famous than the late great Leo Fife himself.

Emma is admired for her equanimity and rational, pragmatic approach to crisis management, the perfect foil to Fife's impulsiveness. She has never accused Fife of wanting fame or glory. From the start she bought into his public image of humility and moral seriousness and selfless dedication to the art of cinema. But they've been partners in marriage and filmmaking for nearly forty years, and she's no fool for love. She saw early on that his pride sometimes overfloweth, as she puts it, and he has always brimmed with vanity and competitiveness, especially against men younger than he, men like Malcolm, his ex-student and onetime acolyte. It's for her husband's sake, not hers, that she doesn't want Malcolm to profit from Fife's death. Until now, Fife wouldn't want it either. So why is he doing this?

Please, darling, she says. Let Renée take you back to your room. I'll stay with you there, and you can tell me everything that you need me to hear.

Fife says no, he wants to finish telling about Stanley, who was the real deal, counseling American kids on how to avoid the draft. Stanley was like Ralph Dennis. Does she remember him telling her about Ralph Dennis, the guy who guided Fife through the whole resister process when he came up to Canada? The man who gave him his first camera? Ralph Dennis was another real deal.

Malcolm tells Vincent to bring the camera in and give him a tight closeup on Fife. Don't worry about the lighting, they can heighten it with the edit.

Those two men, Fife says in a trembling voice, Stanley and Ralph. They were like that damned pickup truck of Stanley's parked in the trees and loaded to the rails with perfectly cut firewood. Stanley restored that truck with his own hands. He made it beautiful. And Fife, he was like that big fucking rented Plymouth. A traveling salesman's car.

What about Nick Whatzizname, your high school buddy? Malcolm asks.

He was like that turbo-charged Mustang of his, Fife says and laughs. Yes, Nick, too, was the real deal.

What's a real deal, Leo?

Someone lovable when you're incapable of loving anyone. Someone you should have loved. His second wife, Alicia, she was the real deal. And their son, Cornel, abandoned in Richmond. And Alicia's parents, Benjamin and Jessie, them, too. And Fife's poor teenage first wife, Amy, hauled from Florida to Boston and shipped back with their baby, Heidi, to Amy's parents in Florida. Abandoned and betrayed, all of them. Even Fife's parents, they were the real deal, too, though he never realized it until this moment. All those people who, if they're not dead by now, will have rightly forgotten him or else long ago erased him from their minds. He wishes he could do the same, erase him from his mind. He wishes his life began in Canada. Maybe he's reliving his past like this so he can forget the man he was and his life can have begun in Canada.

Is Emma the real deal, Leo? Someone lovable you're incapable of loving? Someone you should have loved?

Jesus, Malcolm! Emma says. Leave me out of this! And leave him the fuck alone!

As his producer, Emma's been her husband's advocate for forty years in health and now in sickness. But she's never had to protect him before. Neither of them has had to protect anyone before. They're both the only child of cold, withdrawn parents who themselves never protected anyone. It's one of the bases for Fife's and Emma's early and long-lived attraction to each other. Back when they started sleeping

together, he liked to tell her that she was the first woman he was attracted to who didn't need him more than he needed her, and she said
the same thing back to him, that he was the first man she was attracted
to who didn't need her more than she needed him, and they both took
it as a compliment. As a sign of their maturity. As proof that they had
at last outgrown their childhood conditioning.

Fife looks directly into Vincent's camera lens and says, You want to
know if Emma, like all those others, is the real deal? For nearly forty
years, she was, yes. Until this morning, when he woke and knew down
to the bottom of his mind that he was dying and therefore he no longer
had to be afraid of dying and realized that at last he truly loves her
and desperately needs her to love him before he's dead. It's that simple.
He needs to be loved by her more than she needs to be loved by him.
Emma is still merely afraid of dying. For Fife, it's too late now to be
afraid of dying.

The feared thing itself has arrived, and its towering dark presence
has made it possible for him to need his wife's love more than she
needs his. He has not failed her the way he failed all the others. So,
no, Emma is no longer the real deal, he says to Vincent's camera. She
is the beloved, he says, and he laughs.

Renée releases the brakes of Fife's wheelchair and steps between
him and the camera, blocking its view with her body. Vincent backs
up and films her. Crossing her arms over her chest, she turns and announces to the room, I am in charge of Monsieur Fife's care. If I am
not permitted to do what is right for his care, I will have to resign.

No, please don't do that! Emma says. Please, we need you.

Renée says, I'm sorry, but he must lie down and rest now. She
shoves Vincent's camera away with the flat of her large hand and starts
to push the wheelchair toward the open door to the hallway. You must
not film me! she says. I will not be in your film.

Malcolm says, Okay, ma'am, I get it. You take him back to his
bedroom. To Sloan he whispers, Keep him miked with the boom and

follow along behind her. He glances at Vincent and nods, silently instructing him to keep shooting.

Fife has heard him, he knows what Malcolm is up to, and this time he does not resist as Renée, with Emma in the lead, pushes his wheelchair into the hallway, rolls it past the wide arched entry to the dining room, past the closed door to the lavatory, past the large open kitchen and the door to Emma's office and bedroom, with Sloan and Vincent and Malcolm trailing along behind, while Diana switches on the overhead lights, illuminating the long corridor ahead of them as they follow the wheelchair to Fife's bedroom.

Renée helps Fife into the rented hospital bed and covers his gaunt body with a thin cotton blanket. She unfastens the IV pole from the wheelchair and clips it to the metal headboard and, using the remote, raises the top half of the bed forty-five degrees. It's good for your lungs, she says, to lie at an angle like this. She goes to the windows and draws the curtains, dropping the room into deep shade. The rain is coming down hard now, turning the crusted April snowbanks below to slush. Emma adjusts her husband's pillow. Sloan holds the boom over his head, out of camera range, and Vincent is positioned at the foot of the bed, filming. Malcolm and Diana stand together behind Vincent. It's a large room, once the bishop's bedroom, and most of the nonessential furniture has been removed, but it feels crowded.

Emma says, I want them out of here, Leo.

I don't.

Then I'll have to leave.

No, don't. I want you here.

Malcolm whispers to Diana, I like this gray fading light.

Hmmm. We'll have to wait and see what it looks like.

What was it about your old American friends, Stanley and Ralph and Nick, that made them lovable? Malcolm asks Fife.

Emma picks up the straight-backed chair from the corner writing desk and carries it to the side of the bed and sits down. She takes

Fife's hand in hers. She seems to have changed her mind and decided not to leave, as if, by sitting beside him with his hand folded in hers, she can better protect him from himself than if she leaves him alone with Malcolm and his crew. She can't ask Renée to protect Fife from Malcolm and Vincent's camera and Sloan's mic. Monsieur Fife is her employer, and if he won't obey her, she'll just quit the job and walk out. Emma can't quit. She's married to Monsieur Fife, and it's clear that he is not about to make Malcolm and the others leave, and they won't go away on their own. They're like a pack of hungry wolves that has separated an old bull elk from the herd and now has him surrounded. He's wounded and tiring, but still dangerous. He hasn't signed the release yet. They just have to keep him surrounded and wait, and eventually they'll get what they want. They want him to die in front of the camera.

Fife says, The military. That's what made them lovable. The military. Stanley, who was older than Fife, got drafted into the army between Korea and Vietnam and was an MP in Germany and France. Ralph got drafted into the army in '66 and, to avoid being shipped out to Vietnam, deserted to Canada in '67. Nick Dafina enlisted in the air force in '68, and because he spoke Italian probably served his two years in Italy and got honorably discharged without having to go to Vietnam. Fife is guessing this, he's hoping it, because after the day he ran into Nick in Strafford, he never saw or heard from him again. In any case, all three of them did what Fife did not.

What did you not do, Leo?

Military service.

What did you do, Leo?

Vincent says, Shit, shit, shit. I've got to change cards again. This one's full.

Make it quick, then.

Yes, Fife says. Make it quick.

26

WHAT DID HE DO THAT THE OTHERS DID NOT DO? FIFE has never asked himself the question that way. All these years he's been asking it backward: What did he *not* do that Stanley and Ralph and Nick did? And the answer has always been the same. Military service.

Wrong question. Therefore, wrong answer.

He was a resister before there was a resistance, he tells Malcolm. His draft notice found him in Boston in December 1961, and a month later he reported for his physical. He asks Vincent if he's shooting this. Is he still miked?

Yes, we're up and running now. And you're miked on the boom.

I didn't hear the clapper, Fife says.

Malcolm claps his hands and says, Leonard Fife interview, Montreal, April 1, 2018. Card three. Is that right, Vincent? I've lost count.

Yes, three.

Fife wonders what Joan Baez would have thought of the way he handled being drafted, if he'd met her then, backstage after a performance at Club 47 in Cambridge, and she and Stanley and Stanley's roommate Bobby Zimmerman, who turned out later to be Bob Dylan, drove back to Boston in Stanley's '53 DeSoto, and the four of them went out together for beers at the Gainsborough, Stanley's favorite neighborhood bar. It would be February 1962, and snowing and not much traffic, which is lucky because the tires on Stanley's old DeSoto are bald and the car swerves, slips, and slides along Massachusetts Avenue all the way over from Cambridge to Boston. They are giddy and sharing a joint and young enough to believe they will never die.

Whoa! Wait a minute, Leo. You smoked grass with Joan Baez and Bob Dylan before he was Bob Dylan, and went out drinking with them?

Fife ignores him. He's remembering the Gainsborough, a long, dark, narrow room with a bar running the length of one wall and a dozen spindly tables and chairs scattered along the other. It's a beer-and-a-shot bar for young men and women who aren't laborers or assembly-line workers but dress as if they are, and the jukebox has a large selection of songs by folk singers like Peter, Paul and Mary and the Kingston Trio and Joan Baez. Most of its customers are artists and teachers from the School of the Museum of Fine Arts, Boston, and musicians studying or teaching at the New England Conservatory, with a mix of beatniks, bohemians, and apprentice poets and writers living in the brick tenements and row house apartments clustered between Symphony Hall and the Fens. Stanley's apartment, where Baez has been staying with Zimmerman, is on Symphony Road, a block behind the hall. Fife's place, where he lived for six months with Amy and Heidi and now lives alone, is ten blocks away, across the Fens on Peterborough. He's unsure if Zimmerman and Baez are lovers. They act more like younger brother and older sister.

Stanley slides the DeSoto into a parking space directly in front of the Gainsborough, and he and Fife and Baez and Zimmerman enter laughing and shivering from the cold and shaking petals of snow off their heads and shoulders. Zimmerman is wearing a lightweight denim jacket, tan work shirt and jeans and engineer boots, and Baez wears a Mexican poncho over the scarlet blouse and peasant skirt she wore for her performance that night at Club 47. Stanley's wearing his fleece-lined sheepskin jacket and black watch cap, and Fife has on the olive-green US Army field coat he bought a year ago at the Surplus Army-Navy over on Boylston Street, when he and Amy first got to Boston from Florida. It has become his favorite jacket, and he wears it in sunshine or rain or snow.

Except for Stanley, they are hatless, and their heads are covered in youthful luxuriant hair. Beneath his watch cap, Stanley's is a thick black pelt. Zimmerman's is an uncombed, tangled mass of curls, and Baez's is long and straight, coal-dark and shining. Fife's hair is the color of polished oak and falling over his collar to his shoulders. The four of them are healthy and handsome and sexy and smart, and three of the four are reveling in the abundance of their talent and recently received recognition. Stanley, who has been attending the School of the Museum of Fine Arts on the GI Bill, has been invited by the director of the painting division to teach two classes in the summer program after he graduates in May. Baez's second album has hit number 13 on the Billboard chart and has been nominated for a Grammy. And Zimmerman has just been signed for his first album as Bob Dylan at Columbia by the legendary producer John Hammond. Fife, who has been unable to get any of his poems published, is thinking of starting a novel based on his recently ended teenage marriage. He is not reveling in his talent and its rewards like the others. He's twenty-one years old and believes that he has ruined his life, and it doesn't matter to anyone except him.

Tonight at Club 47, Baez in the middle of each of her two sets invited Bobby to come up and sing a pair of his original songs, and everyone seemed to love the words of the songs and Bobby's focused intensity and asked for more, but he declined, and when he came back to the table, he told Stanley and Fife that he didn't want to steal any of Joannie's perfect golden light. Stanley and Fife consider themselves jazz aficionados and have less than zero interest in folk music, and in

fact until this night they have never been to Club 47. They followed
Stanley's roommate and his beautiful friend across the Charles River to
Harvard Square only because they are attracted to the beautiful friend.
They associate folk music and Club 47 with Harvard University and
view all three with the light contempt of self-alienated hipsters. Fife
thought Zimmerman sang off-key and through his nose, and Baez's
songs were nostalgic and sentimental, although he did think Baez had
a sweetly plaintive voice, and he was impressed by the imagery in Zimmerman's songs, especially "Song to Woody." The other, "Talkin' New
York," was lost on him.

Baez says she likes Fife's jacket, where'd he get it? Was he in the
military?

Army-Navy surplus store, he says. Want to try it on?

She laughs and says sure and stands and shrugs the poncho off.

Fife takes off his jacket and passes it to her. Be careful where you
wear it, he says.

She tells him to try on her poncho. One size fits all. She slips his
jacket on and twists her long hair to one side and turns the collar up.
Why should I be careful where I wear it? she asks him.

He pulls her poncho over his head and shoulders. It's heavier than
he expected, and shorter on him than on her. Too short, he thinks.
Maybe one size doesn't fit all. He admires the way she looks in his field
coat—like a sexy, world-weary war correspondent. He decides to tell
Joan Baez a story that's mostly true.

Like this one, he says to Vincent's camera. Emma has stepped away
from his bedside. She leans forward at the foot of the bed with hands
clamped to the flat metal rail and from time to time lets go of the rail
and massages her husband's feet under the cotton blanket, while Vincent, who has taken her chair, holds his camera tight on Fife's face.
After checking Fife's pulse, Renée has made a slight alteration of his
medication, increasing the morphine drip. She finishes adjusting the
IV and takes a watchful position by the window.

Late one night a week ago, Fife says to Joan and Bobby—Stanley has already heard this story and has gone to the bar to buy them a round—he was walking along Huntington Avenue on his way to the Lobster Claw. It's his, not Stanley's, favorite bar. Stanley is looking for a girlfriend, and Fife is not. He has a new girlfriend, Alicia Chapman, a Simmons College student from Richmond, Virginia. He says he prefers the Lobster Claw to the Gainsborough, because the art and music students and their teachers rarely go there. The regulars, of which he is one, are mostly workers from the neighborhood, off-duty waiters, waitresses, dishwashers, and cooks in the area restaurants and clerks in the stores along Huntington and Boylston Streets and janitors and building superintendents, many of whom live in the nearby South End. To judge from his song about Woody Guthrie, Zimmerman would dig the Lobster Claw, Fife tells him. It's a racially mixed crowd, more so than the Gainsborough, and because they serve food off a full menu, a glass of draft beer at the bar costs fifteen cents instead of twenty-five, and the jukebox is filled with modern jazz. No folk songs, he adds, and smiles, as "Where Have All the Flowers Gone" plays over his story.

When he approaches the entrance to the Lobster Claw, two white men a few years older than he come out to the sidewalk, he tells them. They are both wearing unbuttoned field coats like his, with US Army uniforms underneath. Enlisted men, noncoms. One man is short and dark and wiry, the other is taller than Fife and heavier. Clean-shaven and short-haired, they look fit and aggressive. Standing beneath the red neon lobster claw that hangs above the entry, they wobble a bit, as if slightly drunk. The short one yanks his folded side cap from his field coat pocket and squares it on his head and stares at Fife, while the other carefully cups a cigarette with one hand and uses a chrome-plated Zippo to light it. With his cigarette dangling from his lips, he puts his side cap on with two hands and joins his friend in staring hard at Fife. Their caps have a badge with three stripes attached, which Fife thinks means the men are sergeants.

Fife steps around them and reaches for the door. The short man grabs his wrist. He says, Wait a second, buddy, in a voice so high and thin that it surprises Fife.

Fife says, What's the problem?

You regular army? Does he look like regular army, Kenny? he says to his friend.

He looks like a fucking beatnik.

Where'd you get the field coat, buddy?

I bought it. Army and Navy Surplus store. It's legal. You don't have to be regular army to wear it. And I'm not your buddy, Fife says he said.

Bobby Zimmerman grins and says, Oh, wow! Bad idea, man.

Stanley has returned from the bar with four open bottles of Narragansett. You guys want glasses? he asks the others. They shake their heads no.

Renée brings Fife a glass of water and holds it to his lips, and he sips from it through a straw. In a low voice she says to him, Maybe you should take a rest from talking for a few moments.

Fife hears Malcolm as if he's calling up from the bottom of a steep staircase. He hears him ask Vincent, Where are the first two cards? The living room?

Number two's in my pocket, Vincent answers from the top of the staircase. The other's in my bag back there.

Christ, keep them together, Vincent, will you? And not in your fucking pocket. This stuff we're getting is precious and can't be reshot. Renée, can you go to the living room and bring Vincent's black canvas bag here? The bag for the cards is inside the smaller of the bags.

No. I have to stay with Monsieur Fife. I don't work for you.

Diana says she'll get it, and she leaves the bedroom, and Fife continues talking, but in a lower, weaker voice than before, and slower, in short sentences with long pauses between them.

He's not sure what he says to the camera, but he remembers tell-

ing Bobby Zimmerman and Joan Baez that those two half-drunk sergeants outside the Lobster Claw, they had a point. For a couple bucks
Fife gets to wear a coat for which the soldiers have paid a much higher
price. So he says that to the sergeants. And offers to buy them each a
beer. And they accept his offer, and the three walk through the door
into the Lobster Claw, where over several rounds the sergeants tell Fife
how they turn twenty-year-old draftees into soldiers in ten weeks of
boot camp at Fort Benning in Georgia.

Joan Baez says, That's a nice story. All's well that ends well. But I
will be careful where I wear it.

Fife doesn't tell her and Zimmerman, and hasn't told Stanley, either, that after the first round of beers, when the taller of the two
sergeants, the one named Kenny, asks him about his own draft status,
Fife lies and says he hasn't been called up yet.

So you're not twenty-one yet? the sergeant with the high voice
says. You using a phony ID, kid? he asks and winks.

Fife stays silent, and the sergeant grins. Fife doesn't tell him and
Kenny or Stanley and Fife's new folk-singing friends that it's been
barely a month since he followed the instructions in the letter from
the Boston draft board and showed up for his physical exam at the
Second Battalion Military Entrance Processing Command located
among warehouses down in the South End on Summer Street. He has
prepared for the exam by swallowing methamphetamine inhaler wicks
for three sleepless days and nights straight. He arrives at the induction
center long-haired and unshaven, gaunt and pale and jittery, with large
dark circles under his eyes. He's heard that for the physical exam the
inductees will have to strip to their undershorts and sockless shoes,
and to stand out from the crowd, he has worn a jock strap instead of
undershorts and engineer boots.

The process starts with a paper-and-pencil aptitude test, he remembers, and he tries for a high score, but makes sure that he fails the
paper-and-pencil part by writing his name and address on the wrong

lines of the cover sheet and breaking the point of his pencil several times. To correct his mistake, he asks for a fresh pencil and erases his name and address so hard he rips through the sheet and has to request another. Then he does it again. There are forty or fifty young men taking the exam with him, and he is the first to complete it. When he turns the numerically coded booklet over to the enlisted man administering the test, he tells him that he wants to get into the tank corps. He likes tanks. He makes the sound of a tank, brumm-brumm. The soldier remains expressionless.

When everyone has finished the aptitude test, a different soldier marches the group to a locker room off a large gymnasium on the second floor, where they are instructed to remove all their clothing, except for their undershorts and shoes. Some of the inductees near him stare at Fife in his jock strap and boots and shake their heads and elbow one another. He smiles benignly back.

They are told to bring their cover sheet from the aptitude test and march from the locker room to the gymnasium. Fife leaves his sheet on the bench in front of his locker, and when it's his turn to have his vision tested, he has to run back and retrieve it and go to the end of the line. He seems not to know his left eye from his right, and the wrong eye keeps getting tested, until the medic realizes what is happening and by pointing with his finger slowly shows him which eye to cover when he reads the chart.

Now he believes he did tell this story to Stanley and Zimmerman and Baez that snowy night at the Gainsborough, because he is wondering again what Joan Baez would think of him if she knew how he dealt with being drafted. He's having memory slippage again, and if he wants to tell her and Bobby about what he did when he was drafted, he has to let go of his memory of the Mariposa concert and Joan's ardent denunciation of the American draft resisters and deserters, her belief that to stop the Vietnam War they should not have run to Canada, they should have gone to jail, like her husband, David Harris.

He describes the inductees marching in the gymnasium from one medic to another. After the eye test, they line up to get their hearing tested, which Fife passes, but only after dropping the headphones on the floor three times, until the plastic cap on one earpiece breaks loose and they have to be replaced with a new pair. It's easy for him to screw up the hearing test, because no one can hear what he hears or doesn't hear through the earphones, so he says yes and no and maybe at random.

Then they are checked for hernias, which Fife makes difficult, once he gives the requisite first cough, by seeming unable to stop coughing. This is followed by what turns out to be, for Fife, the final test, the urinalysis. The medic hands him a four-ounce plastic cup and instructs him to step behind the curtain and pee in it. He does as instructed. But instead of peeing one or two ounces, he fills the cup to overflowing. He holds the cup out carefully for the medic, who glares at him and takes it between his thumb and the tip of his forefinger, holding the cup with great delicacy so as not to spill urine onto his bare hand.

A sergeant holding a manila file folder suddenly appears beside him. Leonard Fife?

Yes, sir! Leonard Fife, sir!

Come with me, Fife.

Yes, sir!

The sergeant turns and leads him across the gymnasium to a windowless door in the farthest corner of the enormous room. The sergeant knocks and enters and gestures for Fife to follow. It's a small office with an uncluttered, almost bare desk and a single straight-backed chair facing it. Behind the desk sits a trim middle-aged man with a pale-gray crew cut and a stylish dark-brown Errol Flynn mustache, smoking a pipe. He is a ranking officer—Fife's not sure how high— with three silver bars on his shoulders. A captain, maybe. The room is dimly lit by a low fluorescent desk lamp, nothing else. The tall window behind the captain is covered by a closed venetian blind.

The sergeant salutes the captain, who Fife surmises is a psychiatrist. The captain salutes slackly back, and tells Fife to sit in the chair. The sergeant says Fife's name and lays Fife's cover sheet and the manila folder on the desk and salutes again and leaves. The chair is cold against Fife's naked back and bare buttocks.

The psychiatrist opens the folder and leafs slowly through the sheaf of papers.

Your name?

Leonard Fife.

Date of birth?

Fife silently counts to fifteen, as if trying to remember his birthday. He points to his cover sheet and says, It's all there, sir.

Yes. I'm making sure this file is yours, not some other idiot's.

Thank you, sir, Fife says, and tells him his date of birth.

The psychiatrist sucks on his gurgling pipe, which seems to have gone out, and slowly reads over the results of Fife's tests, including his score on the aptitude test, Fife assumes. Suddenly the man wheels around and yanks the cord on the venetian blind and floods the room and Fife's eyes with blinding sunlight. That light is the same obliterating white light he saw in Stanley's living room gallery the night he had strange sex with Stanley's wife. It wasn't sex, it was something else. What was it? Masturbation? Certainly not lust or desire. Betrayal? Revenge? Or just fear, fear of what was going to happen next. By then he knew what would happen next. He just couldn't say it, even to himself.

Mr. Fife, the psychiatrist says, are you a homosexual?

Fife rubs his eyes with his fists for a few seconds. Finally he answers. Not really, he says.

The psychiatrist pulls a printed form from his desk drawer and scribbles on it quickly, as if writing a prescription, and passes it across to Fife. He picks up a brass Zippo lighter and relights his pipe. Fife wonders, What is it with Zippos and the military? Maybe they sell them at the PX at a discount.

The psychiatrist says, You're 4-F, Mr. Fife. Take this form and your folder and report to the sergeant who brought you here, and get your clothes and go home. You'll receive your draft card in the mail in a few days, he says.

Fife takes the printed form in his hands and reads what the psychiatrist has written: 4-F. Schizoid personality. Reject.

Stanley laughs and says, Jesus, he wishes he'd thought of trying that when he got drafted in '55. Maybe if the Korean War was still on, he would've. But the war was over by then. The army made him an MP and sent him to France, he says, so he got to see a lot of art at government expense.

Joan Baez doesn't laugh or even smile. She takes a thoughtful, ladylike sip from the bottle of Narragansett, as if she's not used to drinking from a bottle and actually would prefer a glass.

Zimmerman leans forward and tells Fife, You did the righteous thing, man. It's like the draft is the war machine's assembly line. It's a vital part of the military-industrial complex, like Eisenhower said. Everything Fife did that day fucked up the assembly line, he says. If enough guys do what Fife did, the factory that makes soldiers would grind to a halt, and the masters of war would have to find another, more expensive way to make soldiers. And if people like Fife make it too expensive to wage war, they might be forced to go into some other line of business, one where the end result isn't death and destruction.

Joan doesn't agree. The way she sees it, Fife's place in that line was filled by someone who otherwise would not have been drafted. Good for Fife, who avoids being drafted and gets to stay a civilian. But what about the poor kid standing at the cutoff point behind him? Number forty-one or whatever. He moves up one notch, and now he's stuck in the army for two years and is more likely to end up dead or killing people in some African or Asian cold war hotspot or invading Russia than looking at French paintings at government expense.

Fife, who is facing the door, sees Alicia Chapman enter the bar from the street. She is tall and slim and beautiful. She stops just inside the doorway, brushes the snow off her coat and pushes the hood back like Red Riding Hood, and scans the room, searching for Fife. Her auburn hair is as long and straight as Joan Baez's.

He must be drowning, because, as promised, his life is flashing before his eyes. So it's not just a cliché, after all.

He knows he's not literally drowning, but he is dying, and the flow of time has broken through the levees and dikes that have held back his secrets for nearly a lifetime. His mind is flooded with memories, and the overflow has captured the flotsam of his secret fears and dreams, his hopes and ambitions and fantasies, along with songs, stories in books, poems, and the movies he has loved—the rubble of his life—and unable to differentiate between them, he is telling them all.

Alicia makes her way through the crowd along the bar toward Fife and his friends, until she finally sees him. Since entering, she has not smiled, but now her face stiffens with anger.

Fife stands to greet her, and he realizes that he is wearing Joan Baez's Mexican poncho, and Baez is wearing his field coat, and that is why Alicia is angry. He has done something that he would not have done if Alicia had been present, and she knows it. He has been flirting with another woman, a particularly attractive and exotic-looking woman. Alicia doesn't know that the woman he's been flirting with is Joan Baez, the famous folk singer, but if she did, she would be even more angry than she is.

Fife says, Hey, Alicia, I thought you were gonna stay in the dorm tonight. To the others he says, She's southern and hates the snow.

Alicia says, Fuck you, Leo! Fuck you! She turns and stalks back the way she came and exits into the snowy night.

Stanley says, Woo-hoo! You've got to ditch that rich bitch, man. One of these days she'll cut your balls off.

Joan Baez asks what Fife did to piss her off.

Bob Dylan looks like he knows the answer, but he stays silent.

27

WAIT A MINUTE, WAIT, WAIT! MALCOLM SAYS, BUT FIFE can barely hear him. He sounds like he's in another room shouting through a thick wall. Something about Bob Dylan and Joan Baez. Malcolm wants to know more about Dylan and Baez.

But Fife, at the same rate as he described it, has already forgotten that night at the Gainsborough in February of '62. And Alicia's sudden appearance, the jealous college girl, his rich Virginia girlfriend—she's gone, too. The day a month before that night when he beat the draft—a blank. The night outside the Lobster Claw, when the two sergeants confronted him over his field coat—erased.

As quickly as those scenes filled his mind, they have been emptied out, washed away. As if they never happened. As if he did not remember or imagine them and did not speak about them to Emma, while Malcolm and his crew filmed and recorded him, all of it overheard and watched warily, protectively, by Renée. It's as if those scenes and events and people were present in someone else's distant past, a stranger's, or in the pages of an unread novel.

For the first time since he started telling his story, Fife wants to keep his mind empty. An empty mind almost has a taste, a moist, fruity sweetness. Until now he has been afraid of the erasure that he knew lurked behind his memories, waiting to devour them and leave behind only a blank, an absence. A nothing. But suddenly that emptiness is tempting. Soothing. Beckoning. He senses that his mind is a deserted island, dry and high above the waters that surround it, where all he has to do is lie back in the sun-dappled meadow amid the wildflowers wobbling in the soft summer breeze and wait to be rescued and carried back across the sea to his origins. To a place he has never been. He has learned all at once, as if from someone much wiser than he, an angel or a prophet or a shaman, that to return to your origins, you first have to die. You are born and fill your lungs with the earth's air, and then you are free to flee. Your entire life becomes a tale of abandonment and flight right up to the end of it, when you are finally allowed to return to where you took that first breath. To where your memories started being born.

Overhead, wide strips of gleaming white clouds flash past. There is no sound. Even the waves flopping on the shore below are silent. He watches the wind in the scudding clouds and the bobbing heads and stalks of wildflowers and the thrash of foliage and can feel the breeze brush like a smooth hand against his face, but he cannot hear it. The bright sunlight is splashed all over his mind, but no shadows, as if his island is located on the equator at exactly noon, and when he looks up at the sky, he cannot find the sun itself, the invisible source of the visible light. Which is simply there, covering everything in sight, like air.

He sits up amid the tall grasses and flowers and peers out across the glistening water and sees away out at the horizon a dark, oddly shaped speck. After a few moments the speck has grown larger, and he realizes that it's an open boat with a group of people aboard, men and women and children, and it is slowly approaching his island. It's unclear how the boat is powered; there is no mast and sail or oars that he can see or engine that he can hear. It appears to be pushed from behind by the invisible hand of some ancient god of the sea, Poseidon or Neptune.

Soon he can make out the figures on the boat, some standing unsteadily, some seated, some huddled by the gunwales as if frightened by the low waves. The boat slows in its approach, and just beyond where the waves rise and break upon the shore, it comes to a stop and rocks gently in the water, as if waiting for Fife to stand and come down from the meadow and greet its passengers and be greeted by them. Who are these people, and what do they want from him? He is afraid that they have come to take him away from his island, his emptied mind, and by raising this anxiety, they have already partially succeeded.

Standing in the bow of the boat, a young woman in Bermuda shorts and a pale-blue sleeveless top gestures with her hand for him to come forward. She is little more than a girl, nineteen or twenty years old, fresh-faced and blushing, her bobbed hair pinkish blond. She is youthfully slender, but her tanned, exposed arms and bare shoulders are muscular, a working girl's body. Yes, it is Amy, the girl he impregnated and married in Florida and abandoned in Boston. She reaches down into the hold of the boat and, smiling, lifts up an infant and holds the naked baby out to him, as if to present her to him, to give her back to the father who rejected her so long ago.

With difficulty and sudden searing pain in his back and legs, he gets up slowly, awkwardly, from where he has been sitting among the wildflowers, but he does not move toward the boat. When he looks down along the slope to the shore, he sees that the sea has risen slightly and now covers most of the low, layered rocks and the sandy, crescent-shaped inlet beaches, as if the tide has turned and has begun to rise. From his standing position he can see more clearly now who else is in the boat. He recognizes a woman seated in the bow next to Amy. It's Alicia, and she smiles and waves to him in her familiar, oddly affected, excited way, making her seem happy and relieved to see him, as if he did not abandon her but instead was taken from her, captured on a foreign field of battle, imprisoned, held incognito for half a century. She points proudly at a small boy seated beside her and, taking the boy's hand in her own, seems to encourage him to wave to Fife. Wave to your father, Cornel, show him how happy you are to see him. The boy shyly complies with his mother's wishes and waves to Fife, slowly at first, then with growing enthusiasm, as if it has dawned on him who the old man alone on the island really is.

He's unsure if they're waving hello or goodbye. Maybe it's a ghost ship, and the ghosts are inviting him to come aboard and join them. He can make out some of the other figures there now—his father and his mother, looking, as always, downcast and defeated, needing comfort from him but not daring to ask, and beside them old Mr. Varney with his hand extended toward the shore, as if he's still waiting for repayment of the cash and clothing Fife stole from his store the night he ran off to Florida. And there, standing at attention in the stern, wearing his US Air Force dress uniform, Nick Dafina raises his hand in a slow-motion military salute. A man seated next to Nick stands up unsteadily. He grabs Nick's arm and holds on to it, and Fife recognizes Ralph Dennis, who is wearing a US Army field coat like the one Fife let Joan Baez wear, except that Ralph's field coat has a peace symbol sewn onto one shoulder and a rainbow-hued dove on the other. And in the middle of the boat, brushes in hand, is Stanley, his overalls spattered with paint, looking like he just stepped from his studio, Stanley the artist. There are more, for the boat is large and crowded, and many of the faces are familiar, but not quite recognizable. He knows them all, he is sure he betrayed and abandoned them all, but can't remember when or where or how. But where is Emma? His beloved Emma. Why is she not aboard the ghost ship? It occurs to him that he is doing this, telling his story for the camera, in order to keep Emma off the ghost ship, to save her from the fate of all those who have loved him and he did not love back.

He has noticed that the tide is rising faster now, and the sea has covered the rocky shore and the inlet beaches, and still it continues to rise. His emptied mind is refilling. It was a trickle when he first saw the ghost ship in the distance and grew mildly anxious, and then, as it neared shore and he identified the passengers, it became a tidal flood. Soon, very soon, his island of mindlessness will disappear beneath the sea from which it first arose. The water has already reached his feet. His knees. His chest. And now he is afloat, his back arched and head rolled back, eyes wide open staring at the unbroken blue sunless sky, his mouth agape and gasping for air. And as the solitary old man's island of empty mind is swallowed by the rising sea of memory, he returns to that final night when he fled down the mountain from Stanley's house in Vermont and drove the big rented Plymouth sedan through the woods into the darkened valley below.

He is that Plymouth, just like Nick was his Mustang and Stanley was that damned pickup loaded with perfectly cut firewood, and once upon a time when he was a youth, Stanley was his '53 DeSoto with the bald tires slipping and sliding across Massachusetts Avenue on a winter night, and when they were boys Fife and Nick were the Olds 88 they stole from Nick's father in flight across the continent. You are who you are, and you cannot change, right? If you're a soft, gray, conventional, mass-produced, rented Plymouth sedan, you can't turn yourself into a candy-apple-red 1968 Mustang Fastback with brandy-wine interior or a 1932 Ford Model B pickup truck or a beat DeSoto that Jack Kerouac and Neal Cassady might have driven from Denver to Manhattan or a stolen Olds 88 barreling across the country from Massachusetts to Pasadena.

Or can you? Isn't that what he's been trying to accomplish by putting himself in front of Malcolm's camera with Emma in the audience? The only audience, as far as he's concerned. He's trying to become at the last possible minute a different person than he has been for his entire life. He can't atone for the person he was and forgive himself for the sins and crimes he committed without first changing who he was and is.

How does one do that? Is it even possible? An addict can't make himself into a nonaddict just by refusing to use the drug. It's why the addict has to chant one-day-at-a-time. He's still an addict.

Fife suddenly remembers the briefcase. Where is it? He left it back in Stanley's living room next to the cot by the woodstove. The bank check for the house that he and Alicia are about to purchase, the pink cashier's check made out to cash that he is supposed to deposit in a local Plainfield or Montpelier bank tomorrow, it's inside the briefcase, $23,000 drawn on Alicia's trust account at the Richmond bank. It's after midnight, and he's running in two directions, which for the first time he sees are opposite. In his fat gray Plymouth he's driving down to the bus station in Montpelier to pick up the suitcase that the airline sent by Greyhound from Logan Airport in Boston, so that tomorrow he can complete the purchase of the house in Plainfield for him and his son Cornel and Alicia, who has just miscarried their second child. He is arranging a future life for his grieving wife and their son and his wife's kindly, wealthy parents who want to pass the family business on to him. He is arranging a settled domestic life that will create a context to justify their otherwise unjustified devotion to him. And he has left behind next to the cot, where he has just committed something like adultery and a flagrant betrayal of Stanley's loyalty and friendship, the briefcase that holds the check that will make that future domestic life—family life—both possible and inescapable. And at the same moment he is running away from that check. He is in flight from a piece of pink paper.

He hears Emma tell Malcolm to stop this. She is standing at the foot of Fife's bed, but he can't raise his head high enough to see her, and he can't see Malcolm either or Vincent, who's hidden behind his camera, or Sloan, holding the boom mic somewhere above his head, or Diana in the shadows at the back of the room. Emma says it again, Malcolm, you've got to stop this now.

Midway between his face and the lens of Vincent's camera, Fife makes out the shape of Renée's large round face, hovering above him like a huge fawn-colored moon, eclipsing the camera's gaze. The pupils of her wide-open eyes are almost black, like smaller, darker moons passing across a tan planet. He tries to love Renée, and he succeeds, and he feels his chest swell with gratitude. I am loving her, he says to himself. It's something you do!

She says his name, Monsieur Fife, says it calmly in a low voice, as if trying to wake him without startling him. Monsieur Fife? It's a question this time, almost as if she's asking him who he is, or if the man lying in the bed really is the Canadian documentary filmmaker Leo Fife.

Malcolm says sharply, Renée, please, the camera! Step away, please.

Vincent says, Malcolm? You sure about this, man?

Malcolm orders him to just keep shooting, he'll tell him when to cut. He softens his voice and again asks Renée to please step away from Fife so Vincent can film him.

Diana says, Maybe we have enough, Malcolm. Maybe you should let her take care of Leo off-camera, and we can shoot the rest later. Or tomorrow.

Fife can tell from Diana's voice that she has come forward and now stands beside Malcolm. He still can't see either of them, though. Or the others. Or Emma, who he loves. He can see only Renée, whom he now also loves. He asks himself, What about Malcolm and Diana and Vincent and Sloan? Can he come to love them, too? Does he have enough time? It is character that lets us love one another? We can't simply will it. Fife wonders if a person can really change his character. It would make him into a different person. He knows one can change his personality. Actors do it with ease, the rest of us with difficulty, but it's doable. Personality can be faked, willed. Character cannot. He's trying to explain this, but no one seems to be listening, not even Emma.

Fife turns silent and tries for a moment longer to follow what his wife and his nurse and his friends are saying to one another, but he can only hear scraps of it, and after a few moments he's pulled away and back to his drive through the village of Plainfield in the dark of night, along the winding narrow road that follows the Winooski River into Montpelier. It's a thirteen-mile drive, and barely two or three cars approach and pass by, students returning late to the college from the bars of the state capital. A doe and her spotted weeks-old fawn dart across the road ahead of him, and the pair disappears into the forest.

Halfway to Montpelier, where Route 2 crosses from the east bank of the river to the west, he slows, and as the car comes off the corrugated steel bridge back onto the paved road, a black pentangular shape, an enormous bird, a great horned owl on its nighttime hunt, suddenly swoops from behind the Plymouth a few feet above the roof and hood of the car. Caught in the glare of the headlights, the bird slices the cold air with its powerful wings, once, twice, three times, and carves a wide dark arc ahead of the car and soars into the night sky.

Shaken, Fife brings the Plymouth to a stop at the side of the road. For a long moment he tries to regather his intentions, his reasons for being out here in the first place. Finally, he pulls back onto the road and resumes his journey.

In Montpelier he leaves Route 2 and recrosses the river onto Main Street. The city seems shut down and all but deserted, as if its inhabitants have packed up and moved elsewhere for the foreseeable future. He drives past three blocks of darkened redbrick storefronts and offices of lawyers, doctors, realtors, until on the right he spots in a store window an unlit neon image of the familiar profile of a running greyhound. It's not so much a bus terminal as a one-room glass-fronted smoke shop where Greyhound bus tickets are sold, a pickup and dropoff spot, and there are no lights on inside, there's no one to retrieve his suitcase for him so he can return to Stanley's house in Plainfield, and no one to sell him a ticket to anyplace else, someplace a thousand miles from here. A ticket back to Florida, or back to Amarillo, Texas, with Nick. Or to Boston again to roam the narrow streets of Back Bay. Anywhere but here.

That sort of thing doesn't happen in real life. It's only in a dream or at the end of a novel or a movie that the hero gives up and buys a bus ticket to someplace distant where he can start his life over. The bus station is always open, and there's always a bored, sleepy-eyed clerk able to put down his magazine and sell the hero a ticket. That's how a novel or a movie or a dream ends. But here, in real life, the hero, after mutually masturbating with the wife of his best friend in his best friend's home, has left in the middle of the night and driven thirteen miles on a winding country road to the Greyhound bus station to retrieve his lost luggage, and he finds the bus station closed. In real life the hero parks his rental car in front of the darkened bus station and gets out of the car. He's remembering the ominous shadow of the great horned owl crossing above him on the road. He's conjuring a literary thought in real life. He walks to the doorway and sees next to the door what looks like his suitcase. Attached to the handle is the airline luggage tag with his name written on it. In real life the hero picks up his suitcase and carries it to the car and places it like a salesman's sample case on the passenger seat and gets in and drives out of town the way he came.

No cars pass between Montpelier and Plainfield. At the center of the village, just beyond the turnoff to the college, there is a fork in the road where Route 2 continues north and the road to Stanley's house, Catamount Road, breaks off to the right. Fife signals a right-hand turn. He drives for a hundred yards or so and lets up on the gas and brings the car to a coasting stop on the left side of the road under a streetlight in front of a white two-story colonial house with twin fireplace chimneys and a wide side porch and attached two-car garage. It's the house that back in January he and Alicia contracted to buy. It was built a century ago, but has been modernized and well maintained by the previous owners. It's a New England college professor's New England village house. In the side yard a child's swing dangles from the branch of a sturdy old sugar maple tree. There is a slatted wood glider on the porch. The windows are dark and curtainless. The previous owners, with their house all but sold, have packed up and moved on to a retirement community in Columbia, South Carolina.

Fife lowers the driver's-side window and catches the wet smell of last year's fallen maple and oak leaves soaked and moldering under snowmelt. It's cold, close to freezing. Maybe below freezing. Winters are hard here, and spring arrives late. Not like Virginia. He studies the house and yard from his open window and exhales and watches his breath make a pale cloud. A glistening silver skin of frost covers the sharply angled roofs of the house and porch and garage, reflecting the sodium glow of the streetlight. It's spectral, the silent ghost of a house, not so much haunted by ghosts as emptied of its contents and abandoned and already starting to deteriorate as one season gives way to another, winter to spring to summer. By fall the white paint will be cracked and peeling, and by next winter the water pipes will freeze and burst, and a second-story window will be shattered during a windstorm by a fallen dead branch from the maple tree, and snow will drift into the upstairs rooms. Shingles will blow off the roof, and spring rains will leak into the attic and seep between the walls, and the floors and sills will start to rot. The mortar in the chimneys will crumble, and bricks will loosen and fall into the high grass and encroaching brush below. College students and neighbors will stroll past the dilapidated house and ask what happened to the family that used to live there. No one will know the answer.

Fife raises the window and puts the car in gear. Slowly, deliberately, he cuts the wheel hard to the right and makes a U-turn and drives back the way he came. At the intersection, he makes a right turn onto the highway and heads north toward Derby Line, an hour and a half away.

It will be dawn when he approaches the border. In the east, a white, newly risen sun shines dimly through the distant alders and the morning haze beyond. A few hundred yards south of the line, he pulls over and parks the Plymouth at the side of the road. He shuts off the engine and, leaving the key in the ignition, takes his suitcase from the passenger seat and walks the rest of the way to the border. The wide, flat fields on both sides of the road are streaked with remnant slubs of unmelted snow. The forested mountains and dark valleys of northern Vermont lie far behind him. In a few hours, when Stanley's wife Gloria comes downstairs to stoke the fire in the kitchen stove and prepare breakfast for her husband and their visitor, she will find in the living room the visitor's briefcase with the $23,000 bank check inside it. The visitor will have gone.

Emma calls after him, Leo! Leo, darling! She pushes Vincent away and bats at Sloan's overhead mic and shouts at Renée, Do something, Renée! Bring him back! Please bring him back. She kneels beside Fife's bed and with both her hands clasps his limp hand like the body of a small gray bird fallen from the sky and brings it to her lips. She shudders and starts to weep.

He tries to say, "Forgive me," but all he can say is, "Foregone." He feels himself being pulled as if by the crushing force of gravity into a black hole from which not even light can escape, and he wants to let it take him. But he fights its pull. He tries to stay here, standing on the borderline between one country and another, between the past and the present, between living and dying. His body feels like a dry, papery, nearly weightless shell containing just enough air to keep it from collapsing into itself. For the first time in three months, four, for the first time since the day he realized that he was sick and likely to die of it, he feels no pain or discomfort. He is not healed, but he is no longer sick. From where he stands at the borderline, he can see the white disk of the sun rising out of the mist beyond the line of alders at the horizon. When the sun has risen higher than the alders, its glow through the lingering mist flattens everything that exists and turns it perfectly white. And then he is obliterated.

28

TO FIFE, ALL THIS HAPPENED IN AN INSTANT. TO THE others, his dying agony continued for over two hours. Throughout, Vincent and Sloan, at Malcolm's insistence, filmed and recorded him, waiting through his cries and groans and incoherent utterances for his final intake of breath. Toward dusk something in his throat rattled. He gasped, and his body twitched as if to shake off a fallen leaf or feather. When at last he was silent for a long while, he closed his eyes and gasped one more time, and after several minutes did not exhale. Renée reached over Emma's bent shoulders and touched Fife's neck where the carotid artery passes to the brain. She held two fingers against the artery for thirty seconds, waiting, waiting, then withdrew her hand and crossed herself with the same fingers. "Woy, woy, woy," she sang in Creole. "I'm sorry for you, Madame Fife," she said.

Emma's face was wet with tears, but she was no longer weeping. "I'm okay," she said. "Thank you. It's a mercy he's gone. His suffering is over."

Vincent asked Malcolm in a low voice if he should cut.

Malcolm said, "Just hold on his face a few seconds longer. Once Renée gets off-screen. Renée, could you move a little to your left?"

Renée carefully finished detaching the morphine drip from Fife's body, and then she turned and yelled at Malcolm, "Obènite!" She pushed her big chest against the lens of Vincent's camera and backed him away from Fife's bed. "Vye bagay, kalanbè," she cursed. Switching to English, she said, "You have done a very bad thing, monsieur, making this movie of a dying man. A very bad thing. And you have taken pictures of me with your camera, too. I did not give permission."

"Okay, okay!" Vincent said. "I'll shut it down."

"You will all be punished for this," she said. "God will punish you."

Vincent turned to Malcolm. "That's got to be it, man. I'm done," he said and ejected the CF card from the camera. He slipped the card into his trousers pocket and looked around the room for the small nylon bag that held the others. Diana picked it off the floor beside her and passed it to him, and he took the card back out of his pocket and placed it in the bag with the two used cards and returned the bag to the floor. Then he left the bedroom.

Renée waved away Sloan's mic with the flat of her hand. "And you, Miss Sloan, you have done a bad thing, too," she said. Sloan pulled the pole back and laid it on the floor beside Diana and with eyebrows raised cast a glance at her, as if asking for permission. Her eyes were filled with tears. Diana nodded approval but said nothing.

Malcolm shook his head. "Fuck it. I'm the director, but suddenly everybody's a goddamn expert," he said. "Okay, I guess it's a wrap."

Sloan proceeded to dismantle the boom and moved on to unscrew the camera from the tripod and collapsed the tripod and began to coil the cables. No one spoke. Renée drew the light cotton blanket up and covered Fife's face and head. Emma stood beside the bed and laid her hand flat on the blanket above her husband's stilled chest. Then Vincent was back, dragging his soft black zippered bags, and began packing his and Sloan's cables and lights and equipment.

Malcolm reached out and placed a hand on Emma's shoulder. "I'm really sorry for you, Emma. Can I give you a hug?"

"What? No! Get away from me," she said and stood and faced him. "Pack up your gear and go away, all of you. I need to be alone with him," she said. "Not you, Renée. Just them."

Renée said, "I should also leave now. So that you can be with him. I will report to the agency what has happened. And also the referring hospital. You must call his doctor for the death certificate," she added. "And a funeral home, to arrange for the care of his body."

"So do you think the stuff he told us is true?" Vincent whispered to Malcolm.

"Not now, man. We can talk about that later. It doesn't really matter, does it?"

"I guess not. Pretty hard to make sense of it, anyhow."

"What matters is we got our film."

"Jesus, Malcolm," Diana said. She approached Emma and took both her hands in hers. "We'll go to the living room and put the furniture back where it was and take down the window coverings. I'm so sorry for you, Emma. I'll stay awhile to help you, if that's okay. With the doctor and the funeral home people, I mean. You shouldn't have to deal with that alone."

Emma nodded as if she understood and approved, although she did not appear to be listening.

Vincent and Sloan and Malcolm dragged the large black bags out to the hallway and hauled them back to the living room. Renée watched Malcolm pass Diana at the door and heard her say in a low voice, "I need Emma to sign the release."

"Do it now. Could be harder later on. Get one from the nurse, too."

"In a while," she said. "It's not the moment for that."

He flashed her a thin smile and moved on.

Renée excused herself and left the room. When she returned a few moments later, she was wearing a maroon cardigan sweater and hooded blue nylon rain jacket over her white uniform and carrying her leather satchel of medical supplies and instruments. Emma was alone in the bedroom, still standing beside her husband's covered body. On the floor next to the wall was the small nylon bag containing the three filled CF cards. As Renée walked past, she reached down and snatched up the bag and dropped it into the side pocket of her rain jacket.

She embraced Emma and said, "If you need me for anything, Madame Fife, call me or the agency, and I will come back to help you. My work is finished here, so I must leave now."

For a few seconds Emma rested her head on the taller woman's shoulder, then straightened and said, "Thank you. He was not easy. None of it was easy. But you were very strong and kind. I loved him, Renée, and I know he loved me. That's all that matters, isn't it?"

"Yes. That's all that matters."

Renée walked from the room and turned down the long hallway leading away from the living area and went out of the apartment. She passed the elevator door and descended the two flights of wide cast-iron stairs to the lobby and exited from the gray renovated convent to the street.

It was dark and cold and still raining, and the streets and sidewalks, lit by traffic and streetlights, glittered in the rain. Renée approached the STM bus stop shelter two blocks east at the corner of René-Lévesque and Atwater. A dark-green municipal trash bin was located on the sidewalk next to the shelter. She pulled the small nylon bag from the side pocket of her jacket and dropped it into the bin and took a seat on the bench inside the shelter to wait for the bus to Outremont.

She thought of her husband Louis, who would be arriving home in a few moments from the Musée des Beaux-Arts, where he was employed as a guard, and wondered if he would mind going out for dinner again tonight. He had been eating out on his own every night for ten days in a row while she took care of Monsieur Fife. The Fifes had not wanted to hire a night nurse, so she had been working late. But she was tired and did not want to cook Louis's dinner. Maybe they could invite their son and his new wife to join them at an Outremont restaurant, she thought, and then remembered that their son had custody this week of his two boys and would not want to leave them with a babysitter. Well, why not ask him to bring the boys to the restaurant with them? They were old enough, six and eight, to eat at a restaurant with adults. Besides, she hadn't seen her grandsons in a month, and she missed them.

Someone called her name. She looked to her left and saw that it was Malcolm, and he was rapidly approaching the bus stop. He was in his shirtsleeves and not protected against the rain. He sat down beside her, dripping wet, and Vincent, also in his shirtsleeves, arrived and stopped a few feet behind him. He carried his camera and began filming them through the falling rain. She wondered what kind of camera could film people in the dark and the rain. It must be very expensive.

Malcolm said, "You took the cards, didn't you, Renée?"

"Yes. I did."

"What did you do with them?"

She nodded in the direction of the trash bin.

Malcolm stood and left the shelter and walked to the bin and peered into the opening below the domed top. He pulled out his cell phone and switched on the flashlight app and shined it into the bin. Reaching down, he retrieved the bag with the cards and passed it over to Diana, who Renée now saw had come along behind Vincent. She wore a bright yellow rain jacket. Sloan was not there. She must have stayed behind with Madame Fife. Renée was angry at Sloan, but not as angry as she was at the others. The girl seemed basically kind, and Monsieur Fife's death had upset her.

Vincent continued to film Malcolm and Diana as they examined the CF cards and made sure they had not been damaged. Rescuing the cards would become the final scene of *Oh, Canada*, Malcolm's movie about the life and death of filmmaker Leo Fife. The film was supposed to be about something, and the life and death of Leo Fife was its ostensible subject. Not the nurse, Renée Jacques, to be sure. And not Emma Flynn, Leo Fife's widow. It was not about the life and career of the filmmaker, Leo Fife, either, although that was what the Canadian Broadcasting Company had paid for and how they promoted it. In a sense, just as Malcolm had intended, the film was without a subject. It was a self-referential portrait of a group of friends filming a man's dying. It's not what the dying man himself had wanted. But it's unclear from the film what exactly Fife did want or why he had agreed to sit for this filmed portrait in the first place.

Emma, after lengthy negotiations, did grant CBC permission to release *Oh, Canada* on Canadian television. She believed that, despite his lifetime of secrets and lies, her husband had loved her, and she had loved him, and that was all that mattered to her. *Oh, Canada* seemed to confirm his love for her, and now that her husband was dead, she saw no reason to oppose its release. She did not think it would taint his reputation, and it didn't. *Oh, Canada* was never seen in the United States, however, where neither Fife's nor Malcolm's films were known, except by cineastes, Fife being too overtly political and Malcolm too Canadian. Renée refused to grant them permission to use her image in the film, but in the end, thanks to Malcolm and Diana's skillful edit, keeping the Haitian nurse off-screen was an easy enough workaround.

At 6:15 p.m. the Outremont STM bus pulled up at the corner of René-Lévesque and Atwater. By then Malcolm and Diana and Vincent had returned to the Fifes' apartment for the rest of their gear. Renée boarded the bus alone and found an empty seat on the aisle halfway back. She wondered how she would describe Monsieur Fife's death to her husband Louis. Fife was not the first of her patients to die on her watch, and the way he died was not unusual or difficult to describe. But he was the first of her patients who had insisted on being filmed while he died. And he was the first who had talked almost to the moment of his death, despite being in great pain and heavily sedated. She understood his English well enough to follow what he said, but since he was hallucinating, most of it made no sense to her.

She would probably not try to describe the death of Leonard Fife to Louis. It was too complicated and weird and strangely upsetting. Instead, she would talk with him about having dinner tonight in a restaurant with their son and grandsons and their son's new wife. Renée did not want to think about the death of Leonard Fife.

FADE OUT

ACKNOWLEDGMENTS

THE AUTHOR WISHES TO THANK HIS LONGTIME ASSIS-tant, Nancy Wilson, for her help with research. Filmmakers Atom Egoyan and Denis Mueller were generous sources of technical information. Any factual errors, however, are the author's own.

The author also wishes to express his gratitude to his agent, Ellen Levine, and editor, Dan Halpern, for their help in carrying this book home to publication. They have both been his lifetime collaborators and coconspirators.

In loving memory of lost friends, this book is dedicated to Carl Wallman, Stan Plumly, Paul Pines, Ivan Strausz, and Bill Corbett.